KING
PERRY

EDMOND MANNING

Dreamspinner Press

Published by
Dreamspinner Press
382 NE 191st Street #88329
Miami, FL 33179-3899, USA
http://www.dreamspinnerpress.com/

King Perry
Copyright © 2012 by Edmond Manning

Cover Art by Anne Cain   annecain.art@gmail.com
Cover Design by Mara McKennen

ISBN: 978-1-61372-378-4

Printed in the United States of America
First Edition
February 2012

eBook edition available
eBook ISBN: 978-1-61372-379-1

To Queen Ann,
who recognized my kingship before I could.

I now understand why authors make great lists of acknowledgements. It's pure arrogance to stand here and shout, "I DID THIS ON MY OWN." With great humility and eyes brimming with gratitude, I would thank the following players who helped me construct Vin's world: Ann Batenburg (my first reader), Tony Ward, Rhyss DeCassilene, Joe Kieffer, Craig Ball, Audie Howe, Thomas Heald, Judy Testa, Larry Axelrod, Doug Federhart, John Mederios, Michael Seward, Tom Devine, Fredi, Josephine Myles, L.C. Chase, Ted Invictus, Joel Showalter, and my wise lady mentors from Book Architects. And the Bear Walker king, Theo Bishop. Come home, Theo.

—Edmond Manning

The events in this novel take place in 1999.

PROLOGUE

PERRY,

YOU ARE CORDIALLY INVITED ON A KING WEEKEND.

FRIDAY, THREE DAYS FROM NOW, MEET ME ON PIER 33 AT 6:00 P.M. DON'T BE LATE. IF YOU SPEND THE NEXT 40 HOURS FOLLOWING MY EVERY COMMAND—ABSOLUTELY EVERYTHING—YOUR LIFE WILL CHANGE IN SURPRISING WAYS. COME AND MEET YOUR TRUE JOY.

THIS IS NOT AN S&M THING. YOU WILL NOT BE DRUGGED. YOU WILL NOT BE ABUSED. WE MAY EAT ONION RINGS IF I'M STILL CRAVING THEM BUT HONESTLY, I DON'T CONSIDER THAT ABUSE UNLESS THEY'RE COLD. BUT YOU MUST SUBMIT ALL WEEKEND; NO SUCH THING AS A TIME-OUT. PACK A SMALL WEEKEND BAG.

REMEMBER WHO YOU WERE ALWAYS MEANT TO BE, PERRY. REMEMBER THE KING.

VIN VANBLY

P.S. WEAR SOME SEXY UNDERWEAR; YOU HAVE A GREAT ASS.

ONE

"THANK you," I say to the ponytailed caterer after she offers me wine. "Fancy party, huh?"

She smiles briefly, nodding with deference before stepping deeper into the gallery. Okay, not much reaction. She's working; let it go.

I sip the red wine, swirl it in my plastic cup, creating little maroon waves of merlot. I'm more of a beer guy, but I like doing this, wandering around this art gallery as if I'm part of this town, as if tonight is an average Tuesday night for me. I love how faraway places sometimes feel like home.

This party is groovy, a bash for lesser-name surrealists of the 1960s and '70s. Painters who understood a doorknob could wear a green sparrow's beak, and yeah, it works. With red and brown tiger stripes spilling out of a bathtub behind it, somehow it actually works.

The jagged colors, the juxtaposition of impossible realities, so similar to real life. Sometimes this world is hard for me to reconcile, its unfair sorrows and unexpected brilliance. I love that surrealists tried to paint the reality they saw, this impossible world. I dig this one with the bathtub and the sparrow beak, the *Trombone Symphony Drowns Alone*. No trombones in sight. I guess they drowned.

Looking around, I'm not the only tourist pretending to be a San Franciscan, examining art. Instead of gawking and taking photos, we work hard to pretend that we live right around the corner and popped out for a carton of milk. Maybe it's only around the Castro where we gay tourists fake our residency. We have a certain swagger we hope communicates, "I belong. I have always belonged."

This isn't exclusively the pretentious queens, oh no. It's the bears like me. The twinks. The leather daddies and the androgynous gigglers.

The white collar gays with slick briefcases and the business lesbians openly cuddling at Market and Castro, waiting for the light to change. We're so eager to slap on our labels and march behind our distinct parade banners, but inside we're fundamentally the same: we all want to belong in the Homo Homeland, to find a corner of the world where we are each uniquely celebrated.

Wandering around, twice I overhear the famous joke repeated: "How many surrealists does it take to change a light bulb? *Fish.*" Gotta love the classics.

One painter strikes me as truly unique: Richard Mangin. He's no one particularly famous, but I've read his name once or twice as an innovator. Details in his paintings hum to me, whisper things.

The largest of his three, *Siren Song*, really snags my attention. A shapeless guy plays a cello in a funky green desert, and a pumpkin patch melts into gold in the lower right corner. I recognize that Dalí reference. The purple sky includes a dozen shades of violet occasionally slashed by a crimson streak. In one corner of the sky, white dove wings fade through tarnished iron bars, wings more on our side than caged. Maybe a little cheesy symbolically, but still, it's cool. He wanted his point crystal clear. I wonder why? Then again, maybe I'm reading it wrong.

Oh.

That guy over there is watching me. I swear I have acquired a rat's twitchiness about these things.

I study *Siren Song* and simultaneously check out my watcher. He's handsome. A few years older than me. Maybe thirty-three or thirty-four? Short brown hair, a few locks carefully flopping over his forehead in one spot. Clean-shaven. He has those classic, sharp-planed features you'd see in a Sunday Sears ad, a father pretending to enjoy lawn furniture, showing off his wrinkle-free Dockers. Lawn Furniture Guy wears a charcoal gray suit that hangs off him perfectly, possibly custom tailored. Peach shirt, peach tie. That guy from *Millionaire* is doing the same color shirt and tie combo. Regis someone. Okay, this man's definitely a step or two up from Sears. Let go of first impressions.

Is he the painter? No, that guy would be in his sixties or older by now.

I drop my key ring, stealing a glance at his shoes as I bend over. Gucci, which means he has money. Is he... I dunno, a Realtor? Or... huh. I also pick up a certain unease, even from this far away. Nervous? Nah, that's not quite it.

No, not a Realtor. A Realtor would network around the expensive art, meeting potential clients. I certainly wouldn't stake out someone dressed like me. I bet I could work as a San Francisco Realtor.

Ms. Ponytailed Caterer passes near me, and I wish I could have made her smile. She's so demure, almost apologetic. In a few more months, she'll have enough experience to become more callous.

I stand before *Siren Song,* waiting for him to get over here, and puzzle at the multipurpled sky. He'd better make up his mind soon or I'll miss my ride. In the sky across from the prison bars, those must represent—

A firm voice at my side says, "You a big fan of the surrealists?"

"Not really," I say, smiling wide. "That's my initial in the sky. *V.*"

"Oh. Actually, I think those are—"

"I know, I know," I say, grinning like an idiot. "My name is Vin Vanbly, so it caught my eye. With two Vs."

Though it's awkward with my wine glass, I make two peace symbols with my fingers and then bring them together, index fingers touching, as I sometimes do when I'm being goofy with my name. People relax around me when they think I'm stupid.

His face halts its surprise as he tries hard to suppress any further reaction.

"The painting is cool," I say, turning toward him and jabbing my thumb over my shoulder for emphasis, "and I was grooving on my initials in the sky. I like the wings and bars part too. Very symbolic."

"Hi, Vin," he says, recovering quickly. "My name is Perry."

I raise my plastic cup. "Good wine."

His eyes flinch, but he says, "Yeah, it's okay."

I say, "I fix cars. I don't know a ton about surreal art, but I know what I like."

I launch a few questions about the mighty San Francisco. He answers politely at first, then a little friendlier. He's actually warming up, not being a dick. Good for you, Perry. And while I'm definitely playing blond bear, I'm not being a complete idiot, so we have a couple of nice moments together, chuckling at a comment the other makes.

Let's see what happens when the game changes.

I say, "I can totally see the cello guy as the Surrealist Manifesto's concept of absurd humor."

Perry says, "Didn't you just say you knew nothing about art?"

"I said I didn't know a ton. I read a few books."

He pauses and then says, "How many car mechanics know the Surrealist Manifesto?"

"How many car mechanics do you know?" I say, keeping my face pleasant and blank, interested to see where he takes this.

Perry extends a cautious smile, deciding whether I'm teasing or getting angry.

"None," he says at last. "Sorry. Didn't mean to be rude."

"No sweat. I read a lot. I brought six books with me on vacation. You read much?"

"Financial journals, mostly. I'm an investment banker."

His eye contact changes after this, like he's no longer searching for a way out. I believe I've been upgraded from Dumb Tourist to Person of Interest. We chat about the exciting life of an investment banker, and the also exciting life of a garage mechanic. We discover we both enjoy Thai, and he recommends a good place for panang curry in SOMA. Over slightly more friendly smiles, we find additional common ground. He owns a home e-mail account, which not everyone does. I share my AOL website address, and he says how he's been meaning to sign up.

I nod at his shoes. "Gucci."

"A mechanic who knows surrealism and fashion. Clearly I need to meet more mechanics."

"We're into show tunes too. Put a bunch of mechanics near a piano, some beer, and watch out. Gay or straight, it doesn't even matter."

He smiles. "Show tunes, huh? You also a big Madonna fan?"

A willowy man, midtwenties, appears at our side and inspects *Siren Song* closer, dragging a lock of long blond hair behind his right ear for Perry's benefit. He nods toward the painting and says, "This represents Vietnam, right?"

Perry hesitates before he speaks. "I don't think so. It's around that time, but a few years later."

Wait, what was that? What was that thing on Perry's face?

Our interloper, finding no suitable reaction, pretends to study it a moment longer, then saunters away.

"That guy was hitting on you, Perry."

He smiles and says, "I don't think so."

"Please. That whole 'isn't this Vietnam?' He didn't give a crap about the painting."

"In this town, everyone hits on everyone and nobody counts it as flirting. It's practically saying hello."

Is it possible that Perry couldn't see it?

"Check out that one," I suggest with a nod. "Mother's Day gift."

Perry says, "Arbor Day."

"Doesn't your mom like trees?"

He says, "I think she preferred her trees with less blood."

"It's sap."

Perry says, "The branches are fingers and they're bleeding down the trunk."

I exhale hard. "Thanks. Now I'm queasy."

He used the past tense when mentioning his mom. Is she dead? I should check that out.

I shoot a barrage of questions his way about absurd topics: favorite birthday presents, great vacations, San Francisco neighborhoods perfect for night walking, giving him the chance to trot out his best stories, the ones that show "this is the real me." I want to understand his connection to these three paintings. I could ask him directly, but this is more fun.

"Vin, check out that dude over there."

"*Dude?* Are you sure you're young enough to use that word?"

Perry ignores me and shares his observation, during which an idea pops into my mind, a theory about my new friend.

I point my wine cup at a painting across the room. "That one looks like onion rings smothered in cheese. I'm so fucking hungry, I'd buy it. Would it kill your city to put out some damn chips and salsa?"

He tilts his chin upward for a split second and laughs.

Got it. I know who he is; I now understand his interest in these Richard Mangin paintings. Well, it's a guess. But I make good guesses. I don't think I'll bring it up. Let's see where this goes.

"Are you Irish?" Perry says. "You're fair. Of course, you could be German."

"Maybe. Or Nordic. My birth records were spotty on a few key details, and I grew up in foster families, so I'm one of those oddballs who doesn't know his own ethnicity."

"Oh." Perry's face falls. "I didn't mean to pry."

"Don't sweat it. I'm curious myself. My guess is German, you know? Pale, big square head like a block? Who knows, though, maybe I'm a blond Russian."

"You're built like a German dude," he says, his shy smile returning. "Big chest and all. I bet you're hairy."

I guess Perry decided to go for it.

Glancing around the gallery with pretend distraction, I unbutton my top two shirt buttons, scratching my strawberry-brown curls. I'm a bear, by the gay world's definition: stocky and hairy, the only two requirements for membership. Two weeks ago, someone on AOL used the term *otter*, so maybe we're evolving into a "woodland creatures" group.

My face is fairly undistinguished, except I have a goatee. I'm not hideous and I'm not Lawn Furniture handsome, which nobody is now that Perry revealed his name. Vin, let that one go. *Perry.*

He sips his wine and shakes his head, chuckling. "I'm not usually this forward. I sucked down two vodka cranberries at an after-work party before I came here. You're terrible, by the way. You're turning this into the opening scene in a porno."

I make my voice deep and chesty. "Fuck yeah, buddy.... Oh, yeah, just like that...."

Perry snickers. "You know that your name sounds like a fake porn star name, right? I mean, *Vin Vanbly?*"

"Fuck yeah, baby," I say, slapping the imaginary ass in front of me.

Perry says, "That's why you thought that guy was hitting on me. Because *you're* hitting on me."

"Maybe. You like?"

One corner of his mouth curves upward. "Maybe. What's with the lumberjack outfit?"

"Just got back from camping in Marin County. You like to camp?"

"Sure, sure," he says, "being out in nature is great. But I assumed you dressed that way for some leather bar later."

He insists on checking my biceps to see if I chop wood, but we both recognize and appreciate the sexy excuse to be extra close, to touch in public. I have some muscle, but it doesn't show much. Well, maybe biceps show a little bulge. I can run two city blocks, but after about three blocks, I end up wheezing, hands on my knees.

Who am I kidding? When was the last time I ran two city blocks?

We talk about the movie *Fargo*, which he loved, and the Minnesota accent, which I love. He asks about winters in my adopted state, as everyone must. I explain the beauty of Minnesota's spring thaw, and he dismisses it instantly. There should be a word for an attitude between snobbish and unconscious, describing someone who doesn't realize how strongly he holds his own opinions.

I like Perry, and he's definitely sexy, but that doesn't guarantee I will find the spark I seek. I can't fuck casually, and I'm not great at small talk unless I'm hunting for that spark. But I can probe a bit longer, see if I recognize kindling for a bonfire I might try to ignite. If nothing comes of this, I will have enjoyed chatting with the handsome investment banker in a San Francisco gallery. That in itself is pretty sweet.

More people enter the gallery, and as others nudge by, the two of us jostle for position. Our chests graze together as someone squeezes behind me and we bare naughty grins. I want to believe that Perry and I are both imagining each other naked. Well, I am. The shifting crowd becomes suddenly too much for Ponytailed Caterer, who falters behind Perry, her tray of wineglasses dipping disastrously for a split second, three of them sliding to the floor right at his feet.

"Sorry," Perry says, raising his voice. "Sorry! I did that. I bumped her."

Almost no time passed before his reaction.

She shoots him a look of gratitude so quick and sly that it's gone right away. For everyone else, she wears an impassive expression, clearly bearing no ill will toward the man who, everyone believes, professionally humiliated her. Group consensus shows it wasn't her fault.

No paintings are damaged, no Pradas irrevocably stained.

People gaze at him coolly, and he nods in meek apology. She mops up the floor with napkins and then disappears into a corner to restock. He's so busy accepting silent reprimands from the art patrons that he doesn't notice her two white-aproned coworkers fixing on him with undisguised anger.

"Sorry," he says to Cute Twink, who also bears an unpleasant expression.

The commotion is over, the wine scrubbed from the scene. People turn away, gossiping about him, everyone eager for a topic besides the art. I can't help but notice Perry and I have a few extra feet of space around us, no one eager to be implicated by proximity.

Perry turns to me and says, "Well, that was embarrassing."

I wait a few seconds before speaking. "Why did you do that?"

"I stepped—"

I cut him off with my hand and say, "No you didn't." I nod to the space behind him. "Seriously. Why?"

He blushes and then lowers his voice. "I worked as a caterer when I first moved here. That was my third job, my weekend job, in addition to my day and evening jobs. In San Francisco, competition for the good catering gigs is savage." Perry adopts a sinister, serious face. "You'll never pour merlot in this town again, kid."

Compassion.

Compassion toward someone who can do nothing for him, someone who offers nothing in return. He'll never see her again, but his response came immediately. They'll never even exchange names.

The spark.

I've got to keep him talking. "Did you like catering? I bet you have some good stories."

Okay, don't get ahead of yourself, Vin. But while he talks, I can run the checklist.

Personality. He's unconsciously snobbish and spontaneously compassionate. He's got humor and humility. But damn, he's way uptight. He evolved his first impression of me, moving beyond his initial judgments. Chemistry. Fuck yeah, I'd suck his dick, and I think it's pretty mutual. Issues. He still hasn't volunteered his connection to the paintings. That's big. I've got an idea to test this. He seemed pretty happy about that Transformers birthday present, so I'm thinking he was under twelve. Need to establish timelines; I can't do the math this quickly. 70-what? Skip it; come back. Emotions. Other than a little affected, I think he's solid.

And he couldn't recognize a suitor. Why is his heart so shut down?

Who is this man, this handsome banker with a broken heart?

King him.

My own heart pounds.

King Perry.

Okay, that's it; message received. Let's fucking do this.

I wait for Perry to wind down his catering anecdote and then say, "Are you ready to get kinged?"

"Not sure," he says, and glances around the gallery with a mischievous smile. "Which painting are we talking about now?"

TWO

"SERIOUSLY, what did you mean?" he says. "Is it a painting here?"

"Never mind. Hey, what brought you to San Francisco? Why'd you move here?"

Perry stumbles conversationally, not sure what to make of my refusal to answer.

Wow, how cool is this? The hot investment banker and I are about to have a King Weekend together. Dun-da-da-dah. Bring out the capital letters.

Well, if he wants it.

I've gotten a few "fuck off, weirdo" responses to my admittedly unorthodox invitation. Nothing is in stone; assume nothing. Still, I see their faces as I talk to Perry, different kings I have known and loved. I try to imagine some of them wandering in the crowd tonight. They're giving me the thumbs-up: "Go for it. We like him." Perry's smile reminds me of Ryan. He's got some grit in him too, reminding me of Kearns. Could I see Mai Kearns and Perry as friends? Hell yes.

What would you risk to find a lost king? And what if he doesn't remember you?

Maybe word of free wine reached the happy-hour bars a block away, because our little gallery party turns into a gala, more locals and more tourists pretending to be locals. Or maybe the surrealists only come out at dusk. Perry and I flirt more openly now that we have established that Perry likes hairy guys with big chests and thick love handles. I have always held lawn furniture in the highest esteem.

If I king Perry this weekend, I won't sleep much tonight. Too much planning, too much to figure out. We'll start Friday afternoon, of course, which is only a few days away. I have to deliver the invitation right away. I sneak a few glances at *Siren Song*, not wanting to be too obvious, but I need to consider a few details and how to put together an interpretation.

Tonight is Perry's and my only opportunity to speak until Friday, so I must make the most of our time. I ask about favorite San Francisco spots and who he's taken there, trying to learn discreetly about friends, family, and locations. The slight reluctance on his face tells me I need to slow down, not fire so many specific questions. Patience. Never been one of my strong suits, which is too bad, because I like the word *patience*, the *p* is puffy like a cloud and—

Wait, is he *the one*? Is he the one I finally take to my favorite San Francisco spot? The hair on the back of my neck stands straight up as I realize that Perry is most definitely the one, *the one* I will introduce to the Human Ghost. Holy crap, it's Perry.

Wait, wait. I don't have to decide that now. But I think, perhaps, I've been waiting for many years to meet Perry.

Stay focused. Chill out. Look around.

The collective short-term memory of the shifting crowd means we're no longer art gallery pariahs. Every now and then people edge near us, and we let our body language indicate we're engaged in a private conversation, moving a foot or two to the side when necessary to appease an art connoisseur.

Let's see how he handles some forced intimacy.

"Hey, Perry, ready for an art gallery game?"

He says, "Does this involve the shovel painting or the onion rings?"

"Neither. The game's called Big Secret. We both share something big and juicy, not just 'I cheated on my '94 income taxes,' but a big ugly secret about ourselves that almost nobody knows. I'll go first."

Perry's face registers confusion, and he says, "Wait—"

I say, "See these tiny, crisscrossing marks right here by my hairline?"

I take his hand and guide his fingers to my skull, ignoring the alarm on his face and resistance in his arm.

"They're from rat bites."

He jerks his fingers away and looks at me with naked disgust.

Ow.

But I can do this. I can show Perry all my love.

"When I was twelve, I used to hide in the basement of this one foster home. The guy and his lady neighbor pretended to be married so they could get foster money from the state. His name was Billy. Shitty place to live. Billy's idea of a garbage disposal was to throw food down there for the rats to eat. I would hide from him every third Wednesday of the month, and I thought if I lay still, the rats would get tired of biting me, but honestly, it wasn't a great strategy. Twice, child and family services hospitalized me."

With one hand, I draw quotation marks in the air. "Scars."

All my love.

"I know that this makes me seem creepy, because it is creepy. It's disgusting. That's why it's one of my big secrets. This is me showing vulnerability, Perry, and if you look into my eyes right at this second, you will see I'm afraid of you thinking I am disgusting."

His face changes as he sees me, really sees.

Shit. That was harder to say than I thought.

"Your turn," I say, as if I've been waiting for him to speak and my nod is additional encouragement to break his silence. "Something big."

Perry looks around us. "Vin, I never said—"

"Go," I say, adding the slightest urgency to my suggestion. "Do it fast."

He pauses.

"C'mon, something big," I say in a commanding tone. "*Go.*"

"I don't cry," he says, the words falling out of his mouth. "I mean, I can. I broke my hand playing softball when I was twenty-eight and I—no, no, honestly, I didn't cry then. I swore a lot. That's mine. I don't cry anymore. I've even tried watching sad movies, but nothing."

"Could you ever?"

"I cried some at my mom's funeral," he says, "but that's the last I remember, ten years ago. I miss her all the time; I just don't cry. I don't know if that's normal."

I nod and take this in. Good reveal. I say, "Your mom died when you were twenty-four?"

He says, "Yeah."

"I'm sorry."

He steps back, careful to make sure he's not bumping into anyone, and he glances around to see who may have overheard. The crowd fills in the gaps around us, but nobody's eavesdropping, and the constant chatter around us muffles our conversation. Nevertheless, this uncomfortable turn of events has left a crease between us.

I say, "Relax. It's just a game to learn about each other."

He says, "No, of course."

His face and tone don't match his casual words, a surprised discomfort lingering as he thinks about what he shared with a stranger. But his expression morphs quickly into something else.

"Seriously, are those…?" His fingers move tentatively toward my skull, and I turn my head to give him free access.

He slowly traces his way along my bristly hairline as his fingers tenderly express what verbally he cannot. He pushes over the blond spikes and stops to stroke the tiny canyons in my geography. I've run my fingers over them enough to understand that only the softest touch can fully trace the grooves.

Fifteen minutes ago, this great tenderness would have been far too intimate for a first meeting in public, for how little we know each other. But we've crossed another threshold together. His repulsion is gone, replaced by sad curiosity.

"Does it hurt?"

"Now? No. Just looks funky when you notice it."

"I didn't see it until you pointed it out."

"Uh huh."

He presses harder, still in the realm of gentle, as he explores further. I hate it when anyone caresses these freakish souvenirs from a fucked-up childhood, yet I have to admit his fingertips soothe me.

"Were you scared?"

"Terrified."

"Wait, why were you hiding again?"

"I hid from Billy, the guy who owned the house. He hated the rats, even though he fed them."

I can't explain more than that. I think he's had enough creepy stories for the night.

A woman sidles up to the paintings and *oohs* in appreciation.

"People suck," Perry says slowly. "They really, *really* do."

Our new neighbor says, "Excuse me, who did this?"

"Richard Mangin," I say, louder than necessary.

Perry looks disappointed but nods. His arm falls away, and he takes a step back.

"Is that a Dalí reference?" the woman asks, a petite blonde with dangly gold bracelets way too big for her slender arms.

Perry looks annoyed.

I don't mind; I didn't want to get all chatty about me. Besides, it's showtime.

I nod and in a louder voice say, "Yeah, the shiny gold flank. For a while in the '60s and '70s, a small number of surrealists would sometimes paint a rounded, metallic sheen into their canvas, not exactly a melting clock but still a homage. It's called the Golden Curve, also referencing a physics theory regarding the underlying architecture of the cosmos. As a convention, the Golden Curve never caught on with more than a handful of painters, a whimsical tribute from Dalí devotees."

"Oh," Dangly Bracelet Woman says. "Nice."

I shoot Perry a look that says "I got this," but I don't think that's a problem; his eyes are wide.

I've been waiting for an opportunity like this. I could have created one myself, but the art gallery is crowded now, and since we're all invading each other's space by circumstance, another interruption seemed inevitable.

I step away from Perry and our new friend, maneuver to the second painting, and use a commanding tone to say, "The Golden Curve is also in Richard Mangin's medium-sized canvas. That one."

My sudden pointing grabs the attention of three or four people nearby.

Speak louder. Draw them in.

"Notice in the petals of the third sunflower you can see the Golden Curve again. The shadows from two tree branches almost form hands on a clock. And if you look below the Golden Curve in the flower stems, you can see this artist was definitely integrating Impressionism."

Perry remains stunned. I don't know if he knows this or not, but he's sure surprised I know it. I lied when I told him I didn't know much about art. He's going to be pissed about that, I bet.

I say, "He started imitating Monet and then changed his mind, painting over the blurred edges, creating something interesting and new. It doesn't quite work, but Mangin's style as a painter was evolving."

Nine people in our crowd now. Ten.

Quit counting. Pay attention.

I face Perry.

"Unfortunately the painter died young. I'm not sure, but I'm guessing mid- to late-forties. His style had not yet matured, not fully. Who knows where he might have gone. He himself might have become the next Salvador Dalí."

Perry's lips part. He looks as if he might drop his own cup of wine.

"Look at this one, his final big canvas called *Siren Song*." I wave to the painting behind me, but I never stop staring at him.

He flinches, and I know my intuition was on track.

Others draw near.

"The adult man behind the instrument is strong yet formless at the same time, more shapes and colors than a human outline. Naked potential. The painter had not met this man; he is the future. But note the face, such joy and youthful energy. I bet the only time Richard

Mangin could get his son to sit still was during cello practice. If you ran into this kid as an adult and made him laugh over a joke about onion rings, I bet you could catch a glimpse of that same smile, even if he grew up to become an uptight investment banker."

Perry's blue eyes lock on to mine in surprised threat.

Throw open the kingdom gates; it's on.

Perry gets nudged closer as more pack in, and my hunch is he can't tell what to make of me, of this show. Maybe I shouldn't have called him uptight. Gently, Vin. Let his face be your compass.

"This painter knew he was dying. *Siren Song* is an instruction manual to a man he would never meet. Richard Mangin says 'Son, it's pretty fucked out there. The sky is slashed and bleeding, but don't be alarmed. The purple is everything. Trust the violets, the lavender whirls, the eggplant streaks. Don't let anyone tell you what kind of man you should be. You are more than flesh; you are swirling light and formless energy.'"

"Yes," someone says. "I see it."

"The Golden Curve. Right there."

Murmuring ensues. Murmur murmur murm—

You're fucking talking, you moron!

I jerk my arms to mimic the contours.

"Threatening, jagged rocks crawl across the desert, yet this parched land is painted watery celery green, as if from between dead cracks emerges life itself. The painter says, 'From your desolation, my son, create yourself anew.'"

I soften my face and breathe. I speak into Perry with quiet authority. "A dying king painted this, a love letter to his young son. It's a father's final blessing. And its message is…."

The crowd remains still in anticipatory silence.

Perry's face remains locked in alarm.

"Its message is," I say, drawing out the words, "remember who you were always meant to be. *Remember the king.*"

Perry flinches and backs up, pushes his way out of the crowd in a manner that's somewhere between polite and hasty.

Crap.

Still talking, Vin.

"Notice those wings and prison bars. On one level, it's obvious, but look again."

Dammit, Perry, don't leave. I have more to say.

"You can see in the position of those prison bars that the Golden Curve is not the only physics reference. Those bars curve to represent cosine…."

Perry scissors his legs toward the giant glass doors. Seconds later, Perry Mangin disappears into the night without glancing backward. Cute Twink nods with relief.

Well, fuck.

Scrap the old plan; I've got a new one. *Siren Song* gets purchased tonight. Maybe I can help all three of these paintings get sold. I have to get Perry's attention, get him back to the gallery. While I can't force anything, I bet king energy can influence this. I can influence this. Three or four people seem awfully interested. I try to make extra eye contact with them as I wrap it up. That dude over there is hooked.

Dude?

Oh, right. Perry said that.

"… and a tribute to his son," I say and clasp my hands together. "If giving this painting as a gift, a mom or dad might retell this sad story and say, 'Like this painter, I would find a way to cross time and death just to tell you how much I loved you.'"

I pause and then dip my head. "Thank you."

A smattering of polite applause follows.

Jeez, I drove Perry out of the gallery.

A man in the crowd blurts out, "I'll take it."

Someone else—perhaps a rakish real estate agent—disagrees. Quite politely, I might add.

The first man says, "Two hundred above asking."

"Three hundred above asking."

Act surprised by what's happening, Vin. Look *surprised.*

"*Four* hundred."

"*Five* hundred."

On the plus side, Perry's bolting counts as proof enough my arrow found its mark. He doesn't need to know any more about a King Weekend; I wouldn't have explained much anyway. And I was totally right, he does have a great ass. Those corporate guys hang out at the gym.

I should get a gym membership.

"*Eight* hundred."

The bids climb higher and higher, everyone eager to see who first quits this expensive game of leapfrog. My new banker friend would undoubtedly frown on spontaneous art investments, but he's not here to stop the outcome. Folks across the room notice and cross over. Who's that lady with the scarf?

I see a few individuals, possibly savvier, considering Mangin's two remaining paintings in a new light, wondering if this is one of those ground-floor things you hear about in the art world: someone who is nobody suddenly becomes somebody.

Cute Twink looks flustered. Arms crossed and keeping his distance, he's still cool. But I'm sure he didn't think anyone would actually purchase tonight with such dramatics. An older man, casually but meticulously dressed, accepts Cute Twink's nods to let this unfold. That must be him, the gallery owner. Shame on me for not noticing Scarf Woman. She knows what she's looking at when it comes to art; she's into this.

The first bidder looks at me desperately and says, "Two thousand dollars over."

"I will pay double the asking price."

Art gallery patrons gasp because, hey, big drama. It's fun watching stuff like this: spilled wine, dramatic bidding war. All that's missing is a super-hard face slap and a big exit. Well, Perry made the big exit; check that off the list. I wonder if I could manage to get my face slapped? Probably.

At last, the bidding war is over. We have a winner!

I'm tempted to shake hands with the man who lost and compliment him on his good taste, but he shoots me a dark look. Maybe he already planned to buy this painting prior to my little show. Sorry, dude.

Crap. I'm going to have that word stuck in my head all week.

A few folks chatter and move to the other Mangin paintings, saying, "Yes. Right there. The Golden Curve."

Scarf Woman nods at the Mangin painting to the right and says, "I'll take this one."

Well, good. I knew she had taste.

I shake some hands as people compliment me and ask me what gallery I work for, and I have to explain that I'm no art dealer, I'm a Realtor from the Mission who is showing a two-bedroom condo with a ton of early afternoon light.

Someone nearby asks, "What are the cross streets?"

Shit.

Ignore that. Smile and ignore. Get out of here.

My voice sounds mournful as I hear the words pop out of my mouth. "I can't believe I don't have any business cards."

Shut the fuck up!

Business cards? What is wrong with me? I'm drunk. What if there's an actual Realtor in this crowd? Get out of here, you moron.

I think I'm drunk on Perry.

I extricate myself and take a moment or two to think things through. I step away to the glass-topped desk in back.

Our caterer friend appears in my peripheral vision; she looks forlorn, glancing toward the front door. I bet she thought Perry liked her. Well, I'm sorry about this one, Amanda, but he plays for my team. I think Perry and I are going to spend the weekend together having great sex. But much gratitude, my Queen, for bringing us together.

The gallery will call him to inform him of the two paintings purchased; I'll confirm that. I'll tell them what to say; I have to make sure they say "Mr. Mangin, your friend left you a note. He believed you might want it right away." Those exact words. How much to tip for something like that? Twenty dollars? Forty dollars? Too much might seem creepy.

I chat with the still-surprised Cute Twink, breathing a little king energy into him, congratulating him on creating an event certain to be discussed tomorrow in Castro wine bars. He jokingly asks me if I want a job, but then he says, "Seriously, was all that stuff true about the Mangin paintings?"

While he flutters around the desk creating sales bills, I take some of their squiggly-scripted stationery and dangle the pen over the blank page, waiting for the right words to emerge. While considering, I realize my decision is already made: Perry is most definitely the man I introduce to the Human Ghost; he's the one. Goose bumps rise on my arm.

In regular lettering, I write about how much I love *Siren Song* and how I wish I had the resources to purchase it myself. I suggest he may want to reprice his father's paintings, as they might be worth more than he realizes. On the second page, in block letters I write a variation of my standard invitation.

My eyes linger over the words "PACK A SMALL WEEKEND BAG."

Who am I kidding? He won't pack a weekend bag.

But he'll think about it.

Not packing one will give him the freedom to show up on the pier, convinced he's not coming with me. The weekend bag line works, a tried-and-true commitment test. Always tells me how hard to push.

I finish my business and tip forty dollars to Cute Twink, who is now Jason, Vin. Jason. Remember him. He promises to call Perry with my exact specifications. We make plans for my follow-up.

As I head toward the gallery exit, I wonder how to best reach Mr. Perry Mangin, investment banker. Will he forgive my little speech? Will he show? Maybe I've overestimated our connection. Perhaps I am not the one to reach him. I probably assume too much. I'm like that sometimes.

Don't think that way, Vin. Love this man.

Past experiences race through me, recycled motifs with new possibilities. My brain flashes to racing through an Illinois cornfield, slogging through New York sewers, and of course, dancing with kings at Burning Man. Colors whisper; names appear and then dissolve. Blue like his eyes? Chili red? Could we do something together in North Beach, like at Coit Tower? And there's always *this* neighborhood.

As I emerge into the Castro night, three or four androgynous gigglers are forced to alter their course around me, and one of them mutters, "Damn bears."

His friends laugh.

Welcome to San Francisco.

Help me, kings, guide me. Give me enough humility and grace to find Perry Mangin, the painter's son. If we're meant to spend the weekend together, please help me pull this off, figure out how to make this work. I got a hit back in the gallery. Does that king name fit with our launching point from Pier 33? Oh yes, yes it does. I do believe we have a king name, ladies and gentlemen.

Wow, that drag queen is gorgeous. As she saunters by, I can't resist saying, "You look fantastic."

She says, "I know, sugar."

Practical concerns.

I need weather reports, a few more backpacks, and a homeless shelter for Saturday. Things to buy: night vision goggles, a dozen alarm clocks, PVC piping or something similar. King Aabee is necessary this weekend, which is awesome. I love King Aabee. A giant birthday cake? Hang on, let's rework this, Mr. Vanbly. No need to race. Let the landscape rearrange itself.

It's fun to be a surrealist.

But seriously, where the hell am I going to find a duck?

THREE

ROUGHLY ten minutes before 6:00 p.m. on Friday, Perry Mangin, investment banker, strides toward me with what I must describe as vigor. I like the word *vigor*. It makes me think of an English clergyman pedaling a bike.

I try to see how Perry comes across to his clients: strong-jawed, trustworthy, kind face. He's that kind of handsome you want to trust, a regular guy who is accidentally handsome. As he draws closer, I see his kindness has been replaced by a distant menace.

Wait. That's a vicar, not vigor.

Perry's stride conveys his confidence that he's definitely not going with me, so this should only take a moment. Unless he is going with me. But no, no, he's sure he's not doing this. No weekend bag over his shoulder. And yet here he is. It's hard work to be a Lost King, requiring a lot of mental agility.

As he draws near, he slows and makes his face blank. I'm sure he wants me to know showing up meant nothing, no big deal. He reaches me and squares off. No glasses. I notice dark crescents beneath his eyes; I wonder if he slept much last night. I put my hands in the pockets of my black leather jacket.

"Hey, Perry. Chilly, huh?"

"Yeah, hi," he says, confused for a second. "Thanks for the creepy invitation, but I'm going to pass."

"Okay."

Perry frowns, his mouth open.

He seems ready for me to attack him with reasons, but I have none. If he doesn't want to play, it's cool. But nevertheless, I keep drilling him with my eyes, burrowing king energy into him.

Remember, Perry.

"I wrote—here."

He thrusts a cashier's check into my hands. It's a hefty little sum. I mean, I couldn't vacation for a month on this, but it's enough for first-class tickets somewhere, and I do like to travel.

"Thank you," I say, resuming my hard gaze. "That's quite generous."

"Yes," Perry says, and he looks confused again. "The art gallery told me that your speech prompted, you know, a bidding war."

We stand in silence, looking at each other.

He says, "I'm grateful."

He's lying.

He doesn't appear grateful. Or if not lying, withholding. Or if not withholding, confused. Or if not confused, there's definitely a question mark dangling near. Something's happening in him, because a certain energy goes with true generosity, a quiet excitement ripples over a person, making them shimmer. Actually, anything but this posture, arms limp and dangling, face hard and cautious.

Thanks, Big Bro, for teaching me to read people. I'll call Malcolm Monday night and tell him about my vacation. I will tell Malcolm about how Perry showed up to bring a total stranger a generous check because his heart was so eager to love again.

"It's very generous."

Perry nods. "One of the two buyers already paid, and the one who bought *Siren Song* is going to pay the balance this afternoon, so I'm asking you to wait two or three days—"

I rip the check in half and then in half again. Perry sputters, and when the pieces are clearly destroyed beyond scotch tape's capabilities, I dump them inside my flannel shirt pocket against my heart, never breaking eye contact.

"Okay," Perry says, the word dropping out of him like a brick. "I only brought the one check, so that was your shot, dude. That amount was more than fair."

"Dude? You're really calling me *dude*?"

"You're not getting more money from me."

I smile. "I understand. Dude."

Perry starts to sneer, but his face won't quite conform; his expression keeps melting into something else. He wants to remain angry, but it won't stick.

Perry's not going to spend the weekend with me? Fine. But if he didn't know Pier 33 launches the ferry to Alcatraz when he received my invitation, I'm sure he figured it out during the intervening days. This island is arguably the wettest, chilliest spot in San Francisco, influencing the prison's eventual closing. Perry's wearing a worn brown leather bomber jacket and two heavy shirts underneath, jeans, and thick hiking boots. He dressed for Alcatraz.

Everyone thinks California sunshine automatically equals warmth, but San Francisco is damn cold. I blame those raisin commercials. They should name themselves the Southern California raisins, or the LA Raisins, or something. It's fucking misrepresentation.

He frowns at me. Well, not frowns. But what's the word between *frown* and *confusion*?

I stare into his eyes. *Remember, my king.*

"I can't do this," he says, pleading. "I don't go out and have sex weekends with strangers. I work in a bank; I have an office. It's not big, but there's a real glass door that closes. I'm not a kinky sex guy."

"I understand. No judgments."

He says, "We could go to a winery or something instead. I know a guy who works backstage at Beach Blanket Babylon. I bet I could get us tickets for tomorrow night."

"I wish you well, Perry Mangin."

I take his right hand and turn over his meaty paw so the soft, vulnerable interior is available to me, his fingers weak and exposed. I raise his hand and lower my head to meet it, kissing the palm right by the thumb. My kiss is slow and gentle, yet Perry does not jerk away.

I release him and nod my goodbye.

I turn away to watch the Alcatraz ferry chug slowly toward our dock.

Every corner of the sky awkwardly showed up wearing the exact same thing, a moody gray dress accessorized with flat clouds. If North, South, East, and West were drag queens, this would be bad, very bad. Unfortunately our day is not foggy, which, I must admit, disappoints me. I hoped Perry would have to make his decision while mystic vapor caressed us. You can never count on the city's fog when you need it.

Still, in this gray afternoon light, Alcatraz looks downright menacing—a lonely ghost tower rising defiantly from a crumble of island boulders; a hazy, floating castle right on the ocean, one in which the dungeons were kept topside instead of hidden in caverns below. The wind bites, reddening my cheeks. I enjoy it, but then again, I like the cold. I'm a Minnesotan now.

Silently, the ferry duck-waddles back into Pier 33. Eventually the gangplank is secured, and tourists escape with vigor, happy to have earned their parole back into society.

Uh oh. That word.

From the corner of my eye, I see Perry hasn't walked away.

Funny. I imagine that Perry walked away from many things in his life: friendships, opportunities, boyfriends, fear. I don't know this is true; it's a guess on my part. But he couldn't stay at the art gallery the other night. I bet he keeps others away more than he knows. Does Perry say "I'm not putting up with this shit," and leave before he gets seriously hurt? My hunch is yes.

"Was it true?" he asks in a sharp tone. "The rat scars story? Or some bullshit to trick me?"

"It was true."

Perry zips up his jacket and looks away.

"Why did you do that? The secrets game? And why did you ask me if I... when you said, 'Are you ready to get kinged,' is this what you meant? This sex weekend?"

We both turn to watch the tourists disembark as they clomp through the chain maze toward the exit.

"I think I deserve an answer," he says, even more linear than before.

This sounds like his professional voice, the steely one used to convince his bank customers that he is trustworthy.

"Of course you deserve answers, Perry. But you're not getting any. Sometimes an invitation appears and you say *yes* or you say *no*. This is your…"

Billy.

"… your moment to decide."

Wait, where did that come from?

He huffs at my side, clearly not happy.

Billy? No, no. Random thought. Nothing more. Focus on Perry.

We watch a moment longer, listen to snatches of passing conversation as tourists brag about their photos, the hilarious "behind bars" shots that will be perfect for Christmas cards.

He doesn't look happy, watching the last stragglers saunter down the gangplank, the ones who refused to partake in the mass exodus, preferring a more relaxed departure. I study his face as he ignores me, and the irritation I see helps me breathe easier. Irritation, frustration, impatience… all good signs.

Every little bit of jangled confusion helps guide this big moment, the split second where he decides. When an engine refuses to start, you have to ask what's needed right in this second: fire, air, or fuel? I have decided this is less of a fuel issue than… no.

Vin, no.

This is vacation. Not cars. Think beautiful.

Let's just say that Perry's curious. Or hopeful. Who cares what we name the impulse that calls us to be better men?

"Perry, after the art gallery, did you cry? Maybe a little?"

"Goddamn it, Vin. You're a fucking serial killer, aren't you?"

"So you did cry."

"No, I did not."

He's lying.

Perry takes a step back and rubs his hand in his eye socket again. My guess is that he intentionally didn't wear his glasses today. He wanted to show me he is strong when he looked me in the eye. Men often think submission indicates weakness, that letting someone else take charge betrays a character deficit. But we all submit to strangers who drill into our teeth as long as we can see the parchment on their wall which reads "Dentist."

I should tell him that.

"We all submit, Perry. To the dentist, to doctors. Therapists. Hell, in a hospital, anyone who says, 'Put on this paper gown'—and seconds later, my jeans are at my ankles. I don't even know their credentials other than they happen to be wearing aqua-colored scrubs. So, you know, get over it."

His arched eyebrows suggest he doesn't much care for this direction of the conversation.

"Also, I don't kill people. I get sick to my stomach when I imagine punching someone or causing them pain. If you want a safety break this weekend, start talking about blood and broken bones and get descriptive. It will be super hard to kill you when I'm on my hands and knees barfing.

"But you should know, Mr. Mangin, I'm a whiner when it comes to vomit, which means you clean it up while I walk it off. No matter if we're in the woods or in a shopping mall, or even if there's a janitor nearby, you still have to clean it up. That's *my* safety so that you're not an asshole and make me yak all weekend for your entertainment."

"We're going into the woods?"

He said "we."

"Hypothetical. Best-case scenario, what I promised comes true and your life changes. Worst-case scenario, I'm all bullshit and we have a fun, sexy weekend together. Either way we don't talk about blood and guts, and the weekend is 100% murder free."

Perry's mouth opens.

Talk, Vin.

"But what about this? Maybe the words 'remember the king' touched something in you that requires no explanation. You want answers? A weekend agenda? Perry, no offense intended, but *fuck you.*

It doesn't work that way. Your layers of warm clothes say you came prepared to go with me. So quit your fucking games and get in line. We're going to Alcatraz."

Don't get too cocky. This is hard for him.

Perry says nothing, glumly watching the people around us pack tightly together, gearing up for boarding. He probably jumped through big mental hoops just to deliver the check, allowing himself the leeway not to decide until this second.

If he decided back in his house, he's wearing sexy underwear. But I won't get an answer on the Underwear Test for a few more hours. I failed the Weekend Bag test, so I can't be too much of an asshole.

He says, "Why are you doing this? I'm not... I never even heard of a king weekend. None of my friends heard of this."

"Perry, why are you here?"

"To bring you a check," he says with exasperation.

"You did that. Why are you still here?"

"I don't know."

I nod at him. *Remember.*

"I'm an investment banker, not a sex pervert. I'm trying to figure this out. Why did you rip up my check? Why would you think I—"

"You're calculating the returns."

"No. Not exactly."

We both chuckle.

He says, "If you would tell me more about this weekend—"

"No."

Perry looks away and says, "Tuesday, I planned to suggest we have dinner while you're in town. I was going to buy you dinner, Vin. You don't... from one conversation with a stranger, you don't set up a dominatrix weekend."

"A dominatrix is a woman. But hey, I don't have a problem with it, because I like words with the letter *x* in them. Speaking of words, do you like the word *vigor*? I do. It reminds me of the word *vicar*, one of those English reverends with wild hair who meddles in everyone's business. It's my new BBC series I'm pitching for their Tuesday nights:

The Vicar with Vigor. He rides his red bike all over the village and he gives awful advice, turning lives upside down. Blurts out people's secrets. But in the end, everyone ends up better off. Also, whenever he lectures young people about celibacy, they end up having sex almost right away."

Perry stares at my cheery delivery with alarm.

"I invited you because you took the blame for the caterer's fuck-up instantly, and I felt humbled to stand near a man so rich in compassion, so beautiful a person. That, and I think we're going to have rock star sex all weekend."

"Vin—"

"Having a single word trapped in your head is worse than having a song because you can only repeat the one word over and over. Vigor, vigor, vigor. If you emphasize the *v-i*, it's like ocean waves. *Vig-grr, vig-grr, vig-grr.*"

The line presses forward around us, catching us up in the swell.

I pull two tickets from my back pocket and hold them in front of him.

Perry scowls.

"I have a ground rule," he says, "and your answer must be the single word *yes* with nothing else after it, or I leave right now. I will not discuss the topic of my father at all this weekend. You can't bring it up. *Not fucking once.* Agreed?"

"Yes."

Perry jerks a little. "Wait, seriously?"

"Yes." I pause to mirror the solemnity in his eyes. "I will not bring up the topic of your father. I promise."

If he considered ground rules, that means he showed up ready. Or at least having given it some thought. That's good. Another tipping point in our favor.

"However, Perry, if you invite me, I get to talk about him. I get to ask anything. But you have to open the door and verbally confirm I may."

"Agreed," he says, still surprised. "But I won't bring him up. You guessed pretty well at the art gallery about me playing the cello and him dying young but—"

"I will not initiate a discussion about your father."

Perry frowns a little, another big argument cut short. I don't think I gave him the answer he hoped for. "I'm serious. I did therapy, books on tape. Saw a psychic once."

With intentional firmness, I say, "We're done with this point."

"Fine," he says, watching the Alcatraz pilgrims tentatively shuffle the chain-link maze of walkways leading up to our ferry.

I can't resist needling him. "You saw a psychic?"

"I was with friends and they dared me. But this counts as you bringing it up."

"Okay. We're done talking about your dad. Unless, of course, you initiate the conversation."

We are quiet for a moment.

"Which you can."

We advance a step or two.

"Anytime. Like, whenever."

"I'm allergic to bees," he says. "I have meds with me, but still, no tours of bee farms. And charming serial killers from the Midwest. I'm allergic to them too."

I like his tone. This is exactly the right growl I need from him right now.

"Perry, if you add onion rings to your forbidden list, swear to God, I will rip up your ticket."

"Please don't be a serial killer," he says in a joking tone. "I showed several friends your note and described your appearance. My friend knows HTML. If I go missing, he could put up a website."

"That's cool. By the way, we should trade e-mail addresses when this weekend is over. About a week ago, I installed a counter to track the number of hits to my AOL page. It's pretty cool. Some AOL pages have, like, many, many hundred hits. My page already has 118 hits, which is crazy. I don't even know 118 people."

Perry does not strike me as comforted.

In a deadpan tone, he says, "You're a World Wide Web fanatic."

"I do AOL and CompuServe, but I wouldn't say fanatic. Less CompuServe these days."

He grunts. We shuffle forward.

"Perry, if you don't have an AOL account by next year, you're going to be in the minority. If we're not all killed by Y2K in three months, AOL is going to take over the world. They're going to completely own the World Wide Web in 10 years. But we won't call it the World Wide Web anymore. We'll call it something like, the AOL. Everyone will say, 'Did you see so-and-so on AOL today?' We'll do all our socializing—"

"I don't use the World Wide Web," he says brusquely. "Just for work."

Nice to have that confirmed. I thought he seemed a little overly vague when he expressed his enthusiasm on Tuesday night. He may have lied about other things that night as well; I better be careful in my assumptions.

Since we're bumper to bumper in three lanes of people, all of us trudging forward in half steps we believe will help hurry our experience, Perry says no more but jams his hands in his jeans pockets and grumbles throat noises.

Why did Billy creep into my thoughts a few moments ago? Don't care for that.

The dock crew seems relieved to board the last shipment of cattle, playfully jeering at their coworkers trapped on the boat. I present our tickets to a college student who hands us back our stubs with undisguised boredom.

The boat itself is nothing to romanticize. Every footstep squishes on the soggy Astroturf carpeting, and a film of dirty white paint covers the boat, chipped, repainted, and chipped yet again in many places. Grasping the handrails reveals that the undersides are dotted with sticky globs of gum. The entire ferry smells stale: overcooked hot dogs, burnt popcorn, burned oil. We crowd each other politely, model prisoners all, wandering the confines of the vessel, discreetly checking out our fellow inmates.

"You want a hot dog?"

"No," he says, turning toward the center of the boat. "Is that that smell?"

"Yeah, I think so. That and burned popcorn."

"It's disgusting."

"Yeah. So, anyway, no hot dog?"

"Do I have to?"

"No. I'll let you know what's required."

Perry nods stiffly.

I leer at Perry and waggle my eyebrows a little. "I hope you get off on getting your dick sucked."

He cracks a weak smile. I don't think sex is on his mind right now.

"Would you consider *waggle* to be a real word?"

Perry does not smile. In fact, he looks seasick.

Once we launch, most everyone crowds the island-facing side of the boat, watching the famous landmark grow closer. I lead Perry to the opposite side, the open water facing the iron bridges connecting the East Bay, Golden Gate's working-class cousins. For a moment, we watch the cloudy sky in silence.

"Ever visited Alcatraz?"

He says, "No. People who live here rarely do the touristy things. No offense."

I nod. "Yeah, people are like that."

We chat about tourists, San Francisco, and places we've always meant to visit, continuing a Tuesday conversation. He remains uneasy, but he's closer to the man I met that night: not flirty-relaxed, but more relaxed than on the pier. I bet Perry can't believe he's on the boat.

The topic of his father was important, his automatic excuse for saying, "No thanks." Men often show up with a safety net. While he definitely won that battle, he somehow knows he won the battle that didn't matter, resulting in him headed toward a prison island. In terms of symbolism, not great for Team Perry.

What he does not yet realize is that I am also on Team Perry. Hell, I'm our team cheerleader.

Three seagulls fly formation alongside the boat, our winged guards. They're waiting for popcorn or bun nubs, whatever food drops into the bay, and plenty of our shipmates oblige. One college-aged woman chucks a handful of popcorn at the birds, and after swooping to avoid her attack, they dart to retrieve the bounty bobbing below. I like the idea that we're escorted, that they're taking head count. I think to make the Alcatraz experience more realistic, the people who run the island should distribute orange jumpsuits when the boat docks.

Halfway across the bay, I close the foot or two distance between us, standing close, too close perhaps. I see that Perry would rather not be this intimate in public. He backs away slightly, and I nod at him to stand still. He's good at reading physical cues; we established that on Tuesday night.

"Vin," he warns me slightly.

"Aren't you curious to see what happens if you refuse to submit? Do you suppose the challenges get harder? Even bigger public displays?"

He frowns at my cheerful tone, squints his eyes closed, and purses his lips, waiting for our first kiss. I almost laugh because his strained expression looks as if he's expecting something painful.

Instead of kissing him, I trace my thumb from his eyebrow to his jawline, stopping him from leaning closer. He opens his eyes and exhales oddly, a half breath of confused expectations.

I move close, cheek to cheek. Over his shoulder, I watch until the skyline has receded enough that the buildings no longer shrink dramatically on the horizon. The Transamerica building points its metallic finger to God, a stern demand for repentance. But who is to blame and who must repent? City or God?

The ferry coughs out a regular series of discordant grunts as we cross the final stretch of water. The engine stinks. Someone's not putting in the right oil. It shouldn't make that grinding noise either. Maybe that's the burned oil smell, not popcorn.

Focus up, Vin.

Despite our intimate proximity, I doubt Perry could hear me whisper. The boat lurches through choppy waves with resonating booms, tourists chatter with excitement, and the woman throwing popcorns squeals whenever our seagull guards reappear, ready for the next assault. Conditions aren't ideal, perhaps, but it's time to begin.

"Once there was a tribe of men," I say in a strong voice, audible to none but him, "a tribe populated entirely of kings. Odd, you may think, and wonder how any work got done in such a society with everyone making rules. But these were not those kinds of kings."

Perry nods against me.

"They required no throne rooms, no jewels, no gold crowns. They chose to king as they went about the business of living. The gardeners, the blacksmiths, even the tax collectors, were fair and just kings."

I must glance to my right every now and again to keep an eye on the approaching dock.

"In this tribe, all brothers were rightful owners of the kingdom. You might come across King Ryan the Protector or King Galen the Courier, on your way to visit The Sculptor King. They loved freely with open hearts, some lying with other kings and some seeking women as their queens. I met one such king, a queen seeker, King Malcolm the Restorer, an African giant whose powerful voice commanded love and goodness from those who had abandoned their true selves."

As the boat rocks itself into the dock, our shipmates shuffle toward the stairs, but I keep Perry standing close to me, speaking right into his ear. The boat sounds have lessened now that we're not hitting the water at high speed, so I may speak more quietly.

"The orchards were full of ripe, luscious peaches; the beer brewed amber and frothy. King Nareeb the Baker of Gifts delivered blueberry pies and fresh, buttery croissants. You could often find King Jimbo the Bruiser stomping across the countryside tracking Kalista, his beloved falcon. Life continued exceptionally well for a timeless age, more kings discovering themselves and suddenly arriving."

From the corner of my eye, I watch the front of the boat, ready to elaborate if necessary. But nope, it's time. "Yes, life was good. Until some got lost."

A horn blows.

Perry jumps.

The captain welcomes us to Alcatraz Island with the lack of cheer you'd expect from the warden and asks us not to shove our way down the gangplank.

Perry fakes a chuckle and says, "Good timing."

"Thank you. I practiced."

As we head toward the stairs to join our fellow inmates, I describe my first visit to Alcatraz, how excited I was, how cool the buildings are to explore.

"You'll love it," I assure him.

Perry offers a queasy nod. "I'm not trying to be a total dick. I just… I've never done anything this crazy, Vin. I don't know how to be right now."

"You're not being a dick. You're being nervous."

I grin big and put my hands on his shoulders as I follow him down the narrow interior stairs.

I'm happy.

I always love the moment when someone begins a journey. Perry will find a piece of himself on Alcatraz, and he'll abandon something that no longer serves him. A different man will leave this island.

Once we have officially disembarked and have more room around us, he turns to me and says under his breath, "You like to kiss?"

I say, "Definitely. For hours."

He smiles and looks away. He's trying to come around.

The island glows with green life, despite today's lack of direct sunlight. The shiny, rubbery leaves of blackberry vines, the honeysuckle draped elegantly over thick cement walls. A dozen recognizable flowers, yellow and slender, red geraniums too, survive in the under-tended gardens. The enormous gray prison still dominates the landscape, but chirpy white blooms and bold orange nasturtiums suddenly appear around corners along the winding paths to the prison entrance, cheerful surprises amid the dreary stone and sky.

I push my shoulder into his, and he's startled by this. He scrutinizes me, but when I grin his way, he pushes back some, ready to play.

"What's with the king story?" he says. "Did you make it up, or is it something I should already know?"

"You may not have heard it, but it's an old story."

"Should I be memorizing all these guys' names? I forgot most of them already."

"No worries."

"So what happened when they got lost?"

"To be continued."

"When?"

"When it's *time*. You have to wait for the story to unfold."

He frowns, nodding.

I think he's pondering this. Not my answer, which was simple enough, but the fact that this weekend will unfurl without explanation, without an agenda, and will possibly include an impossible monarchy full of legislative contradictions. It's a lot for me to interpret from a single head nod and the silence that follows, but that's what it looks like to me.

He says, "I've always meant to come to Alcatraz, especially when I first moved to San Francisco. Once a year, I think to myself, 'I should go,' but then I never make it happen."

"Today's your lucky day."

He says, "I should get a T-shirt."

"I have three. I recommend the one covered in prison bars. Always a classic."

I push him with my shoulder again, and this time, he's ready with a little resistance. When we reach the prison entrance, the guide asks if we want the audio tour and I make a puppy face at Perry, so he says with a droll inflection, "Of course we do."

The uniformed guide nods and says, "Return the sets as you leave."

Once we've crossed into the gloomy interior, Perry punches my arm. "You didn't want a sex buddy for the weekend, you wanted a tour guide. We're going to be tourists all weekend, aren't we?"

"Absolutely. Wait until you see what I have planned for the Golden Gate Bridge."

He laughs.

The audio tour always impresses me with its ability to evoke the prison's dark history, incorporating the sounds of muffled clanking doors and prisoners yelling up and down the galley. We walk when we're supposed to walk, stop and look where the narrators tell us to stop and look. I occasionally point to a thing as it's explained and shoot him a meaningful glance implying "Cool, huh?" We gawk at the bullet holes riddling the floor from a failed prison escape and share uneasy glances as a former prisoner describes the weekly regime in detail.

He pulls off his headphones to ask, "What time were cocktails?"

I remove mine. "After the oil painting classes."

We snicker at our little jokes, the same jokes every other tourist makes, but we think they're funny because right in this moment, they're uniquely ours, and suddenly every observation is hilarious compared to the hard lives whispered into our ears. While we stroll through the abandoned dining room, a thousand scraping knives and metal forks shriek in our ears as an invisible horde slops down chow.

Though we don't have great conversation while listening to the prison tales, we read each other's expressions, small gestures, and movements, gradually attuning to each other. He expresses disbelief at a few details, and I nod in agreement. It does sound horrible. I can feel Perry relax further, somehow reassured that we're compatible.

I take off my headphones and point at a bunk. "Those look comfy."

"Ugh," Perry says, pausing the narration. "I'm exhausted and even I wouldn't lie down on it."

Exhausted? Good to know.

I say, "Why? Do you believe in Alcatraz ghosts?"

"No," he says, "I believe in vermin."

His eyes flash in recognition for a split second, remembering my art gallery story, and he starts to stutter a shocked apology.

I hope my smirk indicates that it's completely okay.

I say, "Do you believe in rat ghosts?"

He reads me; I can see it on his face. He makes a significant gesture of pushing Play, and he turns away.

There are no rats on Alcatraz.

If there were, I would smell them. I can always smell them.

I have hunted for traces of rats or mice on previous visits, idly wondering which would feel worse: Billy's basement or a cell in Alcatraz. I used to think Alcatraz, because they locked the door. But I change my mind right now. Choice is always harder.

Billy used to call down that it was my choice whether to leave the basement. He would stand at the top of the stairs yelling at me, offering asylum from the dark. But I knew he wasn't alone up there, so I stayed below, never answering.

He wasn't alone.

Maybe bringing Perry to Alcatraz wasn't such a great idea. I thought I considered all the angles, thought that I could handle it. But Billy already popped up a few times today, and I can't have him in my head all weekend. I don't normally associate Billy with Alcatraz. Why today?

C'mon, Vin. Perry's making sexy, grinning faces. Pay attention.

One snippet of the audio tour always grabs me: the description of New Year's Eve. Prisoners would unite in total silence to listen for party sounds floating in from across the bay, remnants of a life they would never know again. Behind the narration, a faint piano tinkles and partygoers laugh, sending chills down my spine, every single time.

We finish the tour and dump our mechanical companions. We decide to explore the rest of the island, wandering at a casual pace and watching the waves. Perry and I exchange observations on prison life and wonder what we would miss the most. Would we break? Could we endure?

I say, "I would miss onion rings first, then lasagna, then cake, in that order. But part of it is that I like the word *cake*, so I might have to put deep-fried cheese curds ahead of cake."

He says, "Sounds gross. What's a cheese curd?"

"Little nuggets of deep-fried cheese. They're popular in Minnesota and Wisconsin, but not in Illinois, which I don't understand. The land of Chicago-style hot dogs, deep-dish pizza, and deep-fried anything, but they don't serve cheese curds? It doesn't make sense. But I bet in a Minnesota prison they serve cheese curds."

Perry is quiet for a moment but finally says, "You would have eaten one of those hot dogs on the ferry."

"Cheese was only seventy-five cents extra."

"Now *that's* gross. It's canned cheese from a dirty ferry, Vin."

"Would you eat cheese cubes on a fancy cruise ship?"

"That's different."

"Oh, please. Cheese on a boat."

"Completely different."

"*Cheese on a boat.*"

We wander the south part of the island, fondling the low-hanging leaves, admiring flowers, and watching gulls hop around on one foot. We discuss the merits of hot dogs in general and climb the steep, twisting stairs up the landscaped terrace facing the San Francisco skyline. After admiring the city from a few strategic spots, we stroll through an empty foundation, a great cement slab on the southeast side of the island, perfect for valet parking if that were remotely feasible. Or useful.

I lead us around the perimeter of the foundation, pointing out heron nests as I spot them among the rubbery honeysuckle, and we contemplate four or five enormous debris hills dotting the parking lot foundation. Entangled with giant metal rods and crumbling cement blocks, these things could pass as modern sculpture. Instead they suggest a hellish, futuristic landscape built on the ruins of a previous hellish landscape.

I have a nice little "I'll be back" moment for Perry tomorrow. It doesn't have to work out that way, that tone exactly. But let's see if this is a hit.

I say, "I heard they're thinking about making another Terminator movie."

"Never saw the first two. Were they any good?"

"*T2* was awesome, but I think they should leave well enough alone and skip the third."

He says, "Yeah, they always do that."

Okay, no Arnold Schwarzenegger lines. I guess the guy doesn't have much impact on Perry's world of finance. Chatting about movies, we wander further and descend a half dozen stone steps to a vista facing east, right to the edge of a low stone wall with a wide, flat top. Another lovely view, more bay than skyline, beautiful for different reasons.

"Join me," I suggest, crawling on the wall and dangling my feet over the edge.

Perry nods in acknowledgement of my suggestion but makes no move. He says, "See that gold dome? I actually knew a—"

"Perry." I pat the space next to me. "When I *suggest* you do something this weekend, I expect you to do it."

Perry stiffens and remembers, glancing in all directions before awkwardly hoisting himself to sit by my side. He drags his legs to dangle over the wall facing the bay. Except for the rare appearance by one or two people a good distance away, we're fairly isolated. After all, we arrived on the last tour of the day.

I say, "This reminds me of the wall in the Charlie Brown comic strip."

Perry looks around and says, "Yeah, I guess."

I say, "Who's your favorite Charlie Brown character?"

"Marcie."

"Lemme guess. Her glasses?"

"I liked how she called Peppermint Patty 'Sir' all the time." Perry smiles and says, "Don't read too much into that. Your favorite?"

"Sherman."

Perry's face scrunches. He has no clue.

"Black-haired kid, lanky, sometimes with Violet and Frieda. He didn't interact much with Charlie Brown or Linus."

"I don't even remember him."

I say, "Nobody does."

I hop down three feet to a ledge below us. "Let's go."

Perry jumps immediately, perhaps extra sensitive to suggestion after my recent rebuke.

I still haven't figured out the original purpose of the giant limestone blocks beneath the Charlie Brown wall. Perhaps they were dumped here, or, more likely, they're from an older wall. Of everyone I've asked, nobody is sure. Perhaps they're a fossilized circus train from prehistoric days.

I put my hand behind me, and when he doesn't grab it right away, I snap my fingers. His fingers find mine, and I lead him downward. Our ancient circus train winds down a couple of hundred feet toward the gravel shore, following the island's curve. After a moment, we're not visible from the Charlie Brown wall. But before we get close to the smashing waves, still a hundred feet away, I guide Perry to a patch of green earth.

I love this spot, the Hammock. Roughly the size of a small bedroom, it's plenty big enough—I'm delighted to confirm—for both of us to lie here comfortably. Two thick trees block a good portion of the ocean's easterly wind; the canopy of branches hides us from anyone above who happens to look over the railing. I drop to the grass, patting the earth next to me.

"Let's lie down."

He shivers and complies.

"Cold?"

He says, "Chilly but not bad. I'm okay."

I turn him toward the wall, blocking him from any ocean breeze, and wrap my left arm around him, holding him until he is quiet. We breathe this way for a few moments, feeling each other's warmth, listening to the breaking waves.

In a hoarse whisper, he says, "Are you going to jack me off here?"

"No thanks," I say, with an exaggerated whisper to match his.

He lies still and waits for a longer amount of time. But still, nothing happens. A significant boat whistle rings out from the other side of the island, which means either "last call for happy hour" or our ride is getting ready to chug home for the night.

"*Vin.*"

"*Yeah?*"

I love that we're whispering. With the ocean behind us, yelling at the top of our lungs would get swallowed up.

"What the fuck are we doing here?" Perry's voice is shrill but still quiet, his body rigid next to mine.

"I'll answer that. But first you have to tell me something."

"What? Why?"

"Because you do. Why did you come to the pier, Perry? The real reason."

"*We have to go.*"

He starts to rise. I push his body back down. He resists, scoots around to face me, and I can see the fear in his eyes.

"Why did you decide to come with me, Perry?"

"Vin, *c'mon.*"

"Why show up on the dock today? The reason besides handing me the check."

"I don't know. Why does this even matter right now?"

"That boat horn meant the twenty-minute warning. They tell everyone departure is fifteen minutes away, but it's actually twenty minutes."

"Vin, we have to go. What are we doing here?"

"Relax, Perry. I'll answer you after *you* answer me. There's a sexy, invisible *x* in relax, if you let it be there. Listen to the word and I'll stutter my throat, like this, reeeeelaaaaaaaa—"

"*I wanted to have sex with you*," he says, his voice getting tighter. "Jesus, you maniac, I just wanted to, I don't know. People can get sex anywhere in this city and I haven't been with a guy in over a year. I don't date anymore. It's getting to the point where I don't try. It's too much work and guys in this town are sometimes real game players, so I—"

He sinks deeper, against his will, as it now comes out easily, the thing he was fighting, a big piece of his resistance.

"After Tuesday, I thought you were a psycho, of course."

I say, "Of course."

"But I showed up to see if I'd feel that spark of chemistry or whatever. I don't feel it very often anymore. I still want to fall in love someday."

"Thank you. And did you feel that spark on the pier?"

"Yes, but trust me, it's gone now."

Perry says nothing more.

Neither do I.

Finally he says, "I drank two vodka cranberries before the art gallery. I wasn't sure if I was a little buzzed and horny Tuesday night or I actually was interested in you. I enjoyed myself, for a while at least, until you started making your big speech about my dad."

"Yeah, you had mentioned the drinks."

"By the way, that's not me bringing up the topic of my dad."

I nod and stare back at him. His eyes are so blue.

He says, "Okay, that's the answer to your question. I liked our little spark. So, what's the plan?"

I remain quiet for a moment.

"Roll over again and face the stone wall."

He complies. This may go easier if he can't see my face right now.

With a buzz in my throat, I say, "You liiiiiiiike me."

Perry's chest tenses. "You asshole, I answered—"

"What we're doing here, Perry, is resting."

"*Vin.*"

"Perry."

I no longer hide my full voice, preferring to employ the purr of my authority. I snuggle down into him so that my warm breath is right in his ear, my hand on his stomach. I can feel his heartbeat this way.

"We're spending the night on Alcatraz. So relax. Take a deep breath."

I push on his stomach through his jacket, forcing a small exhale. He inhales with exaggeration, if only to pacify me.

"Okay, I'm breathing. So. The real reason?"

"We're spending the night on Alcatraz."

He pauses and listens to the words, which are gone already, smashed against the rocks by strong ocean waves.

"You were kidding. We can't do that."

"We can. Because we are. Relax your body. Reeelaaaaaaaaax."

"It's illegal," he says, his voice sharp.

"And dangerous," I add, nibbling his ear.

I massage the front of his throat with the tips of my fingers and kiss the side of his head.

He says, "Dude, you never said—"

"First off, you gotta stop with the word *dude*. And secondly, have you ever done anything so significantly outrageous, so beautiful and insane, that on days when your life feels dull, these shining moments leap out? Do you have an answer to the question 'Did I live? Did I touch the world?'"

Forgive the archer, Perry, and let this golden tip pierce you.

"Do you have those sparkling days? Do you have Diamond Days, Perry?"

I breathe my love into him, stroking his throat. Perry's major muscles remain tense, but other parts of him have already begun an unconscious surrender.

I wrap my arms tightly around him.

"Patronizing jerk," he says, his tone surprisingly soft for words so strong. "I've—"

"Have you ever made love in the shadow of a haunted prison?"

Breathe, Vin. Elongate.

I whisper, "*Under the stars....*"

His body trembles, and a spasm travels through him. An influx of king energy can do this, exhaust you when you're not ready for it. Something in him lets go. All that tension I stirred up in him floods out, dragging more of his resistance out to sea.

"The stars," I say, using a husky tone, "shimmering, blinking, silently skidding in and out of existence, shone down upon them, basking the kings in every region, revealing secrets to those who dared to stare at the midnight sky."

The sky is a darker gray, but it's nowhere near nightfall.

Nap time.

Perry says, "We can't."

"You have no idea what you're capable of. Inside you lives a flavor of giftedness that I already see and you cannot. It's coming for you, Perry, make no mistake. On the pier a while ago, back when I suggested this weekend might all be bullshit? I lied. It's not bullshit. You're going to get *kinged*."

The words cannot possibly be comforting, only further confirmation that I am delusional. But he does relax somehow, takes another deeper breath, and maybe he's winding up to argue more, but all that fresh ocean air has the impact of swallowing a whole box of Tic-Tacs, and he gasps for another breath, and this one is even deeper.

Each minute submission opens the next door, the next step down, down, down. Time to go into the cave.

"The kings loved the cool fragrance of inky night, a darkness so much like when you close your eyes. Try it now, Perry. Close your eyes and see the pinpricks of light, almost like stars."

"No," he whispers.

I growl against him to quiet him.

"Perry, in a few minutes the second boat siren will announce the ten-minute departure, which they tell everybody is the five-minute departure. Jogging, it will take us four minutes to reach the dock. I've timed it. For now, I'll coax you into this relaxed state, like a guided meditation, and when the next boat horn blows, we'll sit up and discuss it and still have enough time to make the ferry. Okay, buddy? I want you to make this decision relaxed, not stressed. I only need a few minutes."

Before he can argue more, I continue.

"Back in the kingdom, they made love under the stars all the time," I say, using my thick voice, the one that sometimes gets quieter when the man is not expecting it, and he finds himself straining to catch the words.

"The kings celebrated their bodies with relish, the chunky kings and the oddly thin. Those with small dicks and those with long beards. They laughed at themselves naked, laughed with joy to live in their physical bodies and be at such peace. Thick-necked muscle studs kissed their nerdy boyfriends under the stars, men loving each other until each one radiated light. The Night Walker hiked the rugged hills of North Carolina, inhaling the humid scent of decaying green."

His shoulders droop. Tense as Perry is, he also hasn't slept.

"King Augustus the Zephyr would glide through German forests, practicing silence, listening for the stories told by leaves brushing together. Can you hear them, Perry, the leaves brushing together, whispering their tales?"

A thousand leaves in the enormous tree above us participate in my deception, rubbing their veiny little hands against their neighbors. I feel his heartbeat slow, and I take deep breaths, guiding his breath to match mine. Soon our chests rise and fall together.

"The Butterfly King fluttered near his favorite Manhattan bakery, his face pointed skyward, breathing the warm scent of night-baked sourdough, catching occasional wafts of sweet, sugary frosting. He grows a butterfly army in New York, powerful, savvy men taking back their city, street by street. Such is their love for each other and the Butterfly King...."

He sags.

I repeat certain lines for emphasis and Perry falls further. Softer and slower. Softer. *Slower*. My hand strokes his neck, diffusing love into Perry, and my repetitive breathing slows while I rock him into a gentle slumber. All my love, Perry.

My new friend surrenders to unconsciousness, the reward for his latest submission.

More time passes. No boat siren.

I love it when things work out in my favor. I must write the captain a thank-you card.

Sleep well, Perry Mangin.

When you wake, great trials await us.

FOUR

PERRY still sleeps in our green bedroom when I return from my errand, and I wrap myself around him, easing in slowly so as to not wake him. As my arm touches his chest and grows heavier against him by small degrees, I think about snow falling, soft, delicate flakes, gradually making their presence known. I must be careful, very careful.

Snowflakes... snowflakes....

Our bodies touch in a more meaningful way, and it won't take long before I stop withholding the true weight of my arm, the presence of my hips.

While I'm settling in, I have a few minutes to think about Billy. I have to work this out of my system. I can't think about him while I'm kinging Perry. And I don't hate him anymore. I'm over....

No, Vin, don't lie.

I hate him, but in smaller measure. Some days I almost don't hate him. I try not to spend time wondering about Billy's life, just extend some general empathy his way. But then I hear his drunken slur in my head, his wet, slippery words calling me, daring me to come up.

You tired of those rats yet?

He thought I wouldn't recognize the dare behind his words, or hear the scraping metal chair legs on the linoleum floor, his Wednesday night poker buddies deliberately quieter while Billy held the basement door open.

Billy's invitation was soiled. I hate that word, the greasy way it rolls around your mouth. *Sssssooooooooiled.*

Not a great time to dwell on that shit. Think beautiful, Vin.

A few word games later and I can actually enjoy the darkening sky, the slow thudding fall of a darker gray. The day part of "today" is officially over.

Gray light slips away, the curtain drawn, and Perry in my arms.

He's so warm.

I have to tell him to….

HE SAYS, "Night. It's *fucking night*."

Huh?

Sleep is good but wake up fast; Perry is freaking out. No more distractions. *Wake up!*

I say, "Don't yell. I'm awake. Hang on."

Perry's entire body tenses, every muscle at once. "Fuck!"

I'm ready. I'm awake now.

He says, "It's night. *It's night.* I don't fucking believe this."

"Don't worry, Perry, I've seen this happen, night following a few hours after day. It only lasts until just before morning and then it goes away."

"You tricked me to sleep," he says, a shrillness rising in him. "I was going to leave."

He pushes himself up on his right side.

I say, "I prefer coaxed. But I like words with the letter *x* in them. Tricked has a *k* sound. *K*, in some ways, is the arch nemesis of *x*, which is awkward at Christmas because they actually have relatives in common."

"Holy shit." Perry bounces to his knees and then his feet, ready to run with nowhere to go. "I could get fired for this. Of course I'll be fired. Oh God, that's a given."

"Relax," I say, sitting up and offering a hand to him. "You gotta relax, Perry. Trust me on this."

He says, "Prison time is on the table. This is a *federal crime*."

"True. But it's only a federal crime if we are caught. Otherwise, it's an adventure."

"Pretty sure it's still a crime."

His tone is icy.

A section of San Francisco's skyline provides a fairly constant glow to our surroundings, allowing me to read the big emotions on Perry's face: fear, anger, and panic, all fighting for dominance.

In a hushed tone he says, *"We're going to prison."*

I say, "How convenient. We're already here."

I'm tempted to explain that he doesn't need to whisper, nobody could hear us over the ocean's roar. Perhaps emphasizing our isolation may not comfort him much right now. I'll keep that little detail quiet.

"C'mon back down here and snuggle."

He refuses to take my offered hand, so I leave it dangling in the air. Instead, he chooses to pace around our small green bedroom, my straight arm following him like a magnetic needle.

"Take my hand, Perry. It's going to be okay."

"Way to go, Vin Vanbly, if that is your real name. You have successfully freaked me out within a few hours of our hanging out together. I am officially freaked out, you psycho. I wasn't kidding when I said I told friends. And what was that crazy shit about the letter *k* at Christmas?"

Probably not a good time to tell him that my real name isn't Vin Vanbly.

He looks at me and says, "Bloody finger stumps and hacked-open stomachs with intestines spilling—"

Oh, God.

"Stop it!" I put up my hands over my ears and curl up. "Seriously, please stop. You're not in any danger, Perry. But stop."

He does stop, but he glares at me from a safe distance. He says, "I'm not dying out here tonight."

Picture cherry crepes and warm pasta, and yummy bacon. I love bacon.

Come back. Talk him down.

"Perry, you wouldn't have fallen asleep unless you felt safe with me. You felt safe with me because of how much fun we had this afternoon wandering around Alcatraz. That was real. If I were a serial killer, I would have tied you up or done something to you while you were sleeping, not fallen asleep next to you. At the very least gagged you, because, yes, blood and guts is too much for me. There's a gun-carrying night guard casing the island right now, and if you get completely afraid, scream your ass off and he'll hear you. Before you do that, however, lie down and talk to me."

Throughout my speech he softens, not completely, but he hesitates only a moment before taking my raised hand. Nevertheless, I feel resistance as he returns to the ground.

"He has a gun? Serious?"

"Lie here with me and breathe for a moment. This is one of those suggestions that's more of a command, Perry. You agreed to submit all weekend, so c'mon."

"Vin, this stupid weekend ends tomorrow as soon as we dock. Assuming we're not shot dead by the trained professional."

"Awww," I say, letting the words trail off into a throaty grumble.

I need to discover how badly freaked out he is. I massage his neck and spine with one hand and rub the back of his head with the other, using short, soft strokes. Through his leather jacket and heavy shirts, I can feel he's tight, of course, but his body tells me that he's not completely overtaken by fear. He's more angry than afraid.

Actually, he should lose the coat.

"Take off your coat so I can work your back muscles."

He kneels and yanks it off, using jagged movements to communicate his feelings.

I think we're okay.

I work his upper shoulders for a few moments and feel some of the tension actually leave, which is nice. I massage his shoulders with intention, putting my love into him, letting him feel something else for a split second, something other than fear.

"Holy fuck," he says, and this time there's a hint of excitement, just a hint. "Who spends the night on Alcatraz?"

"I do," I say in an injured tone. "Roll onto your side so I can work your chest and stomach muscles."

"You've done this before?" he says with surprise.

"Massage? Sure."

I like being dense with him. Teases his irritation to the surface.

"*Slept here.*"

"Yeah." I wrap my arm around his chest and note his heartbeats. "Let's snuggle. I'll rub your tummy."

"Wait," Perry says.

His body stiffens briefly against mine but then melts in smaller degrees.

He says, "You've slept here before tonight?"

"The night I met you, I only intended to duck into the art gallery for a few minutes before catching the last ferry to Alcatraz. But you were so sexy in your peach shirt and peach tie, I stayed. I thought you looked like a lawn furniture model. In my head, I called you Lawn Furniture Guy."

He says nothing.

"I missed the last ferry on Tuesday. But I had my sleeping bag in the rental, so I slept in Duboce Triangle. It's a good park."

"Oh my God," Perry says.

"I could afford a hotel, but I like camping."

"You, you camp here," Perry says. He laughs at normal volume but immediately covers his mouth.

"Sometimes. C'mon, man. Don't make me ask again. It's snuggle time."

We lie in the cold, dark grass, and Perry asks whether I've ever been caught, if the guard patrols down here, what time the first boat comes in the morning, and other questions that he thinks are relevant.

"Hold all questions, please," I say in my best Disney voice, "until the Alcatraz tour comes to a complete stop."

I may have to repeat that line a lot this weekend, depending on how many questions he asks. Best to set up a standard reply now so he stops pushing.

He grouses more about how he was deceived, and encourages me to think of a plan to get us both off the island. He falls silent because he undoubtedly realizes leaving before morning is impossible unless we depart by police boat; I think he'd prefer transportation with fewer flashing lights.

I stroke his hair, strum his chest, and occasionally kiss his shoulders and neck, more gestures of affection than any serious intention, feeling his body torque itself into grudging acceptance. Once his heartbeat returns to normal, we're ready.

"Let's go, pardner," I say in my best cowboy delivery, shaking him as if to wake him up. "Rise and shine, little doggie."

I stand and stretch.

"Where?"

"We have to follow the night guard for a few laps, get to know his patterns."

"We can't do that," he says.

"We must. How else are we going to know how to avoid him?"

Perry refuses to stand up with me but sits up and watches me as I touch my toes and perform the stretches I sometimes watch joggers do. I bet the implication of strenuous activity does not please him. I should start jogging. I should lose some weight.

He says, "No."

"Yes. We can do this. Trust me. Get up."

He won't.

I cross to a rock and dig behind it, coming back with a plastic bag containing a few black items, one of which I toss toward him, a few feet away.

"Get up, Perry. We're leaving."

He crawls over and picks it up.

"Dude, I am not wearing a ski mask."

"You'll thank me in an hour when your neck and face are toasty warm. I brought you a black sweatshirt if you don't want to wear your jacket. I wasn't sure how warm you'd dress. Why don't you lose that bomber jacket and try on the sweatshirt. It's a hoodie."

"If you kill me tonight, Vin, with my dying breath I'm going to scream out your name as loud as possible." Perry's teeth chatter, and he's trying to joke, but this isn't funny to him. "I'll make sure the guard hears your full name, Vin. Swear to God."

I offer him the gloves but do not move toward him. He'll have to stand to take them.

"Perry, the story about the kings? Making love under the stars and all that? Several plot twists are coming, including an adventure in exotic Turkey, but no murder sprees. It's not that type of story. So take a deep breath and relaaaaaaaaaax."

"Good," he says, grimacing and standing to snatch the black gloves. "Good. Let's think of the non-murdering kings who trick people to sleep on Alcatraz."

"Coax. *Coax* people to sleep."

Using the ambient sky light, we creep back up our limestone blocks, back to the Charlie Brown wall. There, I teach him hand signals for move forward, hang back, and stay perfectly still. Once I have sufficiently terrified him, we're ready.

"We've got to get close enough to see his moves, but we have to stay out of his flashlight beam."

"You said he carries a gun?"

"Yeah, that's the bad news."

Perry whispers, "What's the good news?"

I pause. "I read recently that eggs aren't bad for you anymore. There's, like, new research."

"That's not even remotely funny," Perry says. "This is me not laughing, Vin."

"It's hard to tell with you in a ski mask. You might have thought it was hilarious."

"Trust me. Not laughing."

"If Peppermint Patty had said it, Marci would have replied 'Hilarious, Sir.'"

I can't be sure, but perhaps he's glaring at me. Maybe. It really is hard to tell.

We hop the wall easily, both of us fairly quiet, and I give Perry a few pointers on how to run in silence: keep your toes pointed up, watch the ground every few feet but glance up regularly to keep your balance. We practice running from debris pile to debris pile, and I give him a few pointers on not scuffing his heels against the ground and how to always be aware of where his shadow lands. We peer around after every sprint, and eventually, during one of our practice runs, we spot the guard's flashlight beam, still far from us but definitely headed in our direction.

I say, "From this point out, try not to think of my name. That way you won't be tempted to yell it out if you trip or something. Think of my name as *X*."

"Quit talking," he says, hissing at me. "He's coming."

"Fine, you can be *X* if you want. My Alcatraz name will be Alaska."

I give him the signal for "forward to the left," and he hisses, "*I don't remember that one*."

"I'm pointing to the left."

"It's dark out here."

"It's not *that* dark."

"*Quit talking, Vin.*"

"*Alaska*. I'm going by *Alaska* now. Think about your Alcatraz name and let me know."

Perry nods hard, I'm sure just to get me to shut up. The nameless night guard is still nowhere near close.

The city's glow casts incredible shadows all around us. If I thought these fifteen-foot heaps of scrap metal looked like hellish science fiction a few hours ago, the genre has switched now to horror: the steel girder legs jutting askew at all the wrong angles resembling a malicious, deformed creature seething in slumbering rage until its grotesque awakening.

I whisper, "Don't these look like alien monsters right now?"

He does not answer me, but stares at me from his ski mask.

Well, I think they look alien.

We hide well, and when the night guard arrives in the cement foundation, we watch his flashlight sweep in lazy circles. He wanders around a few debris piles, mostly ignoring the entire area, and eventually heads toward the Charlie Brown wall.

"Have you thought of your Alcatraz name?"

Perry refuses to answer me. He crouches with his hands over his ears as if to block the sound of our imminent capture.

The guard ambles back toward the stairs, and soon we hear him clomping down the southern steps, beginning his return trip across the island.

"Let's go."

I have to pry his hands off his ears before I can get him to follow.

Alcatraz is a fairly big island, but it's less big when two people are carefully avoiding the third person while simultaneously chasing him. A few times during the next hour of our stealthy chase, Perry panics. I have to remind him to breathe occasionally, and once, when I worry he's going to explode, I give him a math problem. "If I bought a 10K CD at 4.2% for a five-year return—"

At this, he pushes me away, but the distraction serves its purpose; he cools down for a few more minutes. We chase the guard for another segment of the island, beyond the main prison gates, as he sweeps the northern buildings.

During another moment of panic, Perry stands up straight, intending to turn himself in.

"I can't do this, Vin," he says at a normal volume.

Luckily the guard faces the opposite direction and Perry's words are lost in the strong wind.

I pull him down and quickly pull up his ski mask, then mine. I kiss him hard, kiss strength into him. My goatee rubs against his chin, and I massage the tight tendons on either side of his skull. I stroke behind his ears with my thumbs in gentle circles to calm him, soothe him, while sucking the air out of him.

We break from the kiss, and he gulps in heavy breaths.

"That was nice," he says and takes a few more breaths. "We're stalking a guy with a gun, but at least you're a good kisser."

"Maybe that's the good news, better than eggs. Though I do like eggs."

I grin against his face so he feels the contours of my smile and kiss him again, softer this time.

"You're a good kisser," he says again and knocks his head gently against mine. "But you're killing me. I'm not built for this. I'm an *inv*—"

"Investment banker. Yeah, I know. Be here. Be here with me. I've done this many nights, and I always spend two hours chasing the guard to see how he patrols the island, where he looks and where he doesn't. I know what I'm doing."

I lean in and pull him against my chest.

So far tonight, I've heard "I'm an investment banker" three times already. Sure, numbers dance for Perry. I know they do, because he calculated and whispered to me our respective ages after prison sentences of fifteen, twenty, and thirty-five years. The numbers dance is cool. But he has soaped and showered himself thoroughly with that job title for so many mornings, over so many years, that he smells nothing more.

Perry breathes after our kiss and looks into my eyes. I can tell that the worst is over and he can continue again.

He checks his watch. Good reminder.

"I'll take your watch for now, and your wallet and keys. I'll let you know when it's morning. Trust me. You got a cellular telephone? Really? I figured an investment banker would. My pockets have padding in them, and I don't want you to lose stuff tonight."

"I won't lose my wallet."

"Trust me on this one," I say, chuckling. "I once spent the entire night hunting down my car keys after I dropped them. It's not how you want to spend your night."

Perry makes grumbling noises but hands everything over.

Wow, that went easier than expected. Push it.

"Spare change? Yeah, that too."

I could have asked for this stuff earlier, but I want him to hand everything over while distracted. I need every subtle advantage I can muster for what's to come. That worked nicely. I have to remember to....

No. No reviewing or thinking too far ahead while in the weekend. One of the four pillars of kinging: be here, Vin. Be in this moment, right now.

I guide us from landmark to landmark, ancillary buildings, quietly discussing which shadows offer the best protection. I encourage Perry to watch the guard's beam to learn how wide he swings the light, how closely he looks behind corners, and we survey our immediate surroundings to determine obvious spots where the guard might direct his attention if looking for unwanted guests. I point out good hiding places in case we get separated and plan a rendezvous spot. Perry is not crazy about hearing this, and truthfully, there's no chance we will be separated. I wouldn't do that to him. But I'm okay if he's afraid of that possibility for a while.

"Do you like the word *ancillary*?"

"Vin," he says, threatening me.

"*Alaska*. You have to use my Alcatraz name. What's yours?"

"I don't know."

"Well, come up with one or else I'll have to yell out your name."

He says, "Nevada."

"You're copying my state theme? Lame."

"Still not laughing under this."

"Nevada, you have to learn to relax. You're way too tense."

We skirt the security guard twice and tour almost completely around the island, ending only about 500 yards north from where we first made our initial disappearance over the Charlie Brown wall. All that separates us is the bird sanctuary.

I guide him toward the stone stairs outside the sanctuary gate and we descend, lower and lower, until we find ourselves standing in an abandoned building structure. We're far enough below the night guard's walking path that his beam won't reach us even if he directs it our way. I consider this space to be my Roman safe house. A cement foundation littered with stray twigs supports two stone walls but no actual roof. Each wall boasts enormous floor-to-ceiling rough-carved windows.

It feels Roman to me: austere, commanding, with a legacy of violence. Caesar might have told his troops to make camp here on the eve of battle. I could imagine fires in the corner, square shadows jerking, rectangular ghosts and maybe a flogging over there. Geez, Vin, don't think about Roman brutality. I almost barfed when Perry talked about spilling intestines....

No. Stop.

Talk about something.

"Don't you think this place could use some big curtains? Over those windows? Something that would ripple in the wind, like maybe thick, velvety maroon. Big ferns in the corner over there and a bust of Caesar on a column. Nothing excessive, but it's a boxy space, so maybe something—"

"What are you talking about?" Perry asks, mouth frowning through his ski mask. "Why would you hang curtains?"

"I'm decorating. It's what we, as a people, consider when confronted with unfinished space like this."

Perry is silent for a moment. Then he says, "You were freaking me out with all those words-that-start-with-*x* stuff. Now this."

"No, no, the word doesn't have to start with an *x*; I like words with *x* in them, or sound funny in some way. *Boxy* has an *x*."

"Could you not be that way while I'm freaking out to death, please? Seriously."

"Sure. Let's sit."

I move to sit behind Perry and position him so we can watch for the guard's light. I hold him and massage his neck to help him relax.

"I'm sorry I freaked you out with the word stuff. That was me being goofy to get you to calm down."

Perry leans back into me, a gesture that indicates he is more relaxed with me than his brain realizes. His body reveals that he's not worried about me being a serial killer; he just dislikes feeling fear.

After a few minutes, Perry says, "The few times this week I actually considered your weekend thing, I worried about you talking the whole time about spark plugs and changing out engines. I thought we wouldn't have anything in common." He pauses. "Clearly, I worried about the wrong shit."

"I try not to talk about cars while I'm on vacation. I think about cars way too much. But not while I'm on vacation."

Perry grunts and says nothing.

"I'm glad you're here," I say softly. "I will always remember this vacation with you."

He says nothing, but he chuckles into his chest, some joke he does not share, relaxes a measure further, and then pushes back. I think he's trying, for this moment, to appreciate this.

When we see the guard's beam flash in our direction, Perry's arms tense, but I rock him and we watch in silence. Soon the guard turns around and heads back north, which means it's time to ascend. We stretch out our arms and legs.

I kiss Perry again, this time with more sexual intensity, because while this might be scary, we really are attracted to each other, and during our seated rocking, his fear shifted so that more of his personality is present.

I make the hand signal for "go forward," though it's completely unnecessary. We climb a dozen steps until I signal a stop and leave the stone staircase. With the moon glowing behind clouds, the hillside remains dark. No problem; I did not hide my tools far. But the rock they're under is big enough I have to put a little muscle into moving it.

I return to our stair a moment later and without words indicate he should take them.

"What are these for? Metal file and—what is this exactly?"

"It's a combo screwdriver and wrench. It's a custom made, specifically designed for oil pans on tricked-out Subarus, not the standard engine. I know a guy. He crafted this for me."

"It bends funny."

"You carry them."

"Why?"

"Perry, just do it."

He takes the two tools without further argument.

"One in each back pocket. Don't want them to click together and make sound. How tight are those jeans on your ass?"

"Tight enough."

"So they won't fall out?"

"No."

"I'll have to check, Nevada."

I grope his ass, checking the firmness of each muscular cheek. "Yeah, I'd say the jeans are tight."

He chuckles. "Wow, that was classy. And subtle."

"You do work on your ass at the gym, right? Some machine for glutes?"

Perry scoffs.

"Is that a yes?"

Perry says, "Yes."

"Awesome. Your ass is amazing. Let's go."

As we climb the stone stairs, I'd like to ask Perry if he thinks the phrase *stone stairs* sounds like a right angle, but I'm going to respect his wishes and talk less about my word quirks. For now, at least.

Climbing these stairs reminds me of ascending from Billy's basement after the kitchen light had been extinguished—the crack under the door turning black at last. Or daylight broke through. Poker night ended for another month.

I don't know why it took me so long to learn that I could crouch midway up the stairs and kick the rats down when they climbed up to find me. I guess I wasn't a bright kid. Of course, if Billy had opened the basement door one of those exact moments, he would have seen me huddled, ripe for the picking. Always a risk to hide right there, but after an hour or two, he would stop daring me to come up.

Stop it.

What's with all the Billy stuff? Is it because I told Perry my big secret about the rat bites? Is that why he keeps coming up? Billy has no place here, no place on a King Weekend. It's my turn to banish him to the basement of my thoughts; I'm upstairs now. But for some reason, it doesn't seem to work; Billy's still at the top of the stairs.

Go. Away.

Stone stairs, stone stairs, stone stairs.

We pass a tangled mess of chain-link fence, stomping over complicated shadows, and continue to sneak upward, climbing the remaining distance. Perry huffs, and I do too, because I could stand to lose some extra pounds. But I've done these stone stairs enough times to pace myself and know when to pause and breathe.

We reach the top and pass through a ruined archway, emerging into a spot we visited earlier this afternoon.

"Recognize this place?"

"Their back patio," Perry says, peering around.

I frown. "Back patio?"

"I can't think of the word. It's the, the exercise yard."

"There you go."

The prison yard stretches into a big rectangle with four giant rows of cement bleachers facing San Francisco, inviting convicts to sit and watch life across the bay. The absence of any amenities suggests an intention to taunt men with "Here's what you're missing."

I scurry across the moonlit space to the slim shadow at the base of an enormous wall, and Perry follows. A black wrought iron staircase attaches to the exterior prison wall. Although solid and secure, the structure feels so exposed and so steep, you can't help but feel the whole thing is precarious and rickety. Now, there's a good word: *rickety*. Shadows cast through the latticework create an intricate spider web on the wall below. We leap up each step until we arrive at the impossible door barring our entrance to Alcatraz. We make no discernable sound, or rather, we have the ocean to thank for masking the noises we do make.

At the top, I feel him twitch next to me, his head darting from side to side, so while I fiddle with the mechanism on the lock, using small tools and wire from inside my jacket, I ask him to recalculate my release age after a twenty-five-year sentence, give or take six years for being a model prisoner. He's freaking out; I need to keep him occupied while I'm busy.

"Do you think they'd let me work at the prison library?" I say. "I could make book recommendations to other prisoners based on what crimes they committed."

"Vin," he says, trying to play along, but his voice betrays terror.

"Thieves would appreciate poetry, and murderers get nonfiction, biographies, I would think. Biographies of famous British people, mostly. The Tudor kings or something."

A moment later, the door swings open with surprising silence, the bank vault opened at last. Good. A red glow spills out, its source nothing more sinister than an exit sign bolted to the ceiling, yet somehow it still pulses impending doom.

In the moonlight, I see Perry's eyes, a snapshot of Halloween horror because while maybe his brain has accepted that he's here on the island, he hadn't anticipated we'd actually go in the prison.

I say, "I oiled the door Monday night. It's more work than you would think being the Human Ghost."

From within his ski mask, Perry shakes his head from side to side, like a kid refusing vegetables.

I step inside and reach my hand back to him. Already, red light devours half of my body.

He says, "No."

"Cross this threshold, my king. We can do this."

He looks at me, and I think at this second his brain tenders its resignation, collapsing under stress. With no remaining faculty for resisting, he takes my hand and allows me to pull him inside and push the door closed. The mechanism clicks locked.

Bathed in the red light, I kiss him deeply, spooling a different light into him, one that he needs, all my love, to survive this next challenge. Perry breathes sharply, but he's trying to soften his rapid breathing, so we kiss more naturally after a moment, lips and mask fabric creating an interesting friction. Soon I feel a warm pressure in his lips that suggests he's at last feeling this, maybe even enjoying it.

I grip the back of his head and kiss him so hard that we're both statues. After a half minute, I break it off and he whispers, "Damn."

I tug his hand. He nods with a sexy confidence.

"Take off your ski mask," I say.

He complies, and we tuck them into our back pockets.

He takes my hand, and unless I'm mistaken, something inside him digs this, despite the fear. We're two adventurers, disobedient school kids who have abandoned the tour. We tread with silent footsteps up and down the sullen galleys, occasionally reminding each other of the security guard's schedule. I check his watch a few times to make him feel safer. We have lots of time.

While we could speak at normal volume, we keep conversation to a minimum. As much as I would like to point out the lack of rats, I do not, because sometimes pointing out the absence of a thing draws more attention. I lead us to the furthest east galley, the one facing San Francisco, where strong moonlight filters through chain-link windows and hits the floors with crisp, institutional lines.

Oh. Moon's out.

"Look. Moon's out."

He nods.

As we trudge slowly forward, it's easy to pretend that we're walking down Death Row.

Perry shudders.

Even without living occupants, each cell radiates invisible, angry life. I almost dread looking inside them, afraid of encountering the furious gaze of someone not yet paroled. The last few cells along this galley are unusual because their doors are solid iron, where the worst of the worst were sent, the ones who could not stop ripping apart humanity, though they were mostly tearing through themselves.

These rooms are sensory deprivation tanks, steel walls offering no glimmer of light. On the audio tour, one former convict reported that while in the Hole, he kept himself sane by ripping a button from his uniform and throwing it into the invisible night, spending hour after hour on his hands and knees finding it. He played this game over and over, and somehow he lived through his darkness. The solid doors remain bolted open so vacationing older brothers can't traumatize their younger siblings. I lead him to the doorway of one in particular and instantly feel his resistance.

He says, "Alcatraz is closed."

I arch my eyebrows at him, not getting his meaning.

Perry puts the palm of his hand to his eye socket, and a silent guffaw animates him. "That was stupid."

I scratch my goatee. "True, we're stretching visiting hours. Trust me, Perry, this will be an experience you never forget. And by that, I mean you will live far beyond this weekend to remember it, barring unforeseen San Francisco bus accidents and future earthquakes. King's honor."

Though his face expresses doubt, he squeezes my hand, giving me a slight nod, and a shock of his brown hair nods over his forehead too, in that sexy, clean-cut way. I'm here with Clark Kent, which is super hot. Sure, Superman boasts muscles and he flies, but I always wanted to fuck that nerdy reporter from *The Daily Planet*.

"I need the two tools."

He hands them over, and I work quickly to loosen the bolt. By day it appears firmly attached to the floor, like its neighbors, and it is. The nearby floor joints are another matter. I remember the night I rigged this. God, what a fucking night. Work, work, work, night guard! Scurry and hide. Work, work, work, night guard! Scurry and hide. But I had to know what it was like to play the button game.

When I finish this task, I take his hand in mine, and we cross over into the darkest dark, joined only by our slight physical contact. From the inside, I swing the door closed, extinguishing the moon's ghostly presence.

I will not separate from him, not for a single second. We're in a land between worlds now, this one and the next. If our connection snaps, if the tether is broken, the damage could be irreparable.

I turn my front to his and wrap my arms around him, his ragged breaths in my ear, his heart pounding against my chest. I turn us a half turn. With my knee, I nudge him back a half step, communicating my demands through caterpillar touch. With me guiding our movements, we take tiny, black footsteps over the abyss.

We inch slowly toward what I believe is the middle of the cell. I drop my arms to his waist and ease him against my chest. The complete absence of sound mirrors the lack of visual data. We huddle together, suspended by a midnight rope over an inky sea. The floor is gone; walls cease to exist.

We are nothing.

I lean in to kiss him, my breath informing him of my intent, so he leans the remaining quarter inch to meet me. With small shifts, I turn us clockwise, slow movements, junior high dance steps, our silent lips pressing softly and retreating. Only a hint of warm breath between us indicates when we're apart.

"It was bound to happen, and eventually it did. A few kings started wondering what lay outside the ancestral kingdom."

My voice shocks us both, a barely audible whisper, a butterfly flitting against his warm neck. In the absence of light, words become a living trail of undulating vowels and shiny, bronze consonants, a twisting coil of physical matter. When I rub his cock through his jeans, Perry gasps against my neck. The mere inhalation of breath is a tangible sound in this mausoleum.

"Various explorer types, such as King Wesley the Wonderer and Diego the Tourist King may have been first to leave. Of course, DuRay the Best Friend King might have been eager to meet those beyond the kingdom. Or perhaps King Mai the Curious withdrew first. You couldn't stop him. He was one of those Midwestern, corn-fed boys. A bubba."

We kiss. Perry's okay with this part, the soft, luxurious kissing, each one a tiny breath of life.

I lean in, pushing him slightly backward again. We have made two full rotations, if I am oriented correctly, which means that in minuscule movements, I guide us toward a wall neither of us sees, aiming us right next to the cell door.

I think. I hope.

I practiced this ten or eleven times, turning myself slowly, testing how many steps it would take, counting how many were necessary to find the correct wall. I have to get us into position for the next part.

"They left the kingdom, one after another. They weren't in hiding, these kings, or worried about protecting their borders. They were never in danger of attack because the tribe could only be found by other kings. Their very natures meant exploring was inevitable. Of course they left the kingdom. This was not the problem."

Perry shifts back another step, and his forehead presses against mine.

"Their explorations of new worlds inspired greater courage, and wild tales were told of their exploits, but some lost touch with those qualities that made them kings. They forgot that they served a higher mission, lived in devotion to a kingdom where all men were necessary and equally blessed. Many became lost."

Perry exhales in surprise as he touches the wall behind him. I continue sliding him slowly along the wall, a foot or two to the right, and he follows my every subtle nudging with impressive sensitivity.

I stroke his chest with my left-hand fingertips, graze his collarbone and neck as I trace his body. With my right hand, I trace the wall, searching for—ah, there, the seam of the door. Thank God. I would have been lost myself if I hadn't found it.

You tired of those rats yet?

No. Concentrate.

"Every king mattered: the one who made toast well, and the king who awarded college scholarships. King Derrick the Aged, a man so ancient he could not walk to his own front door, was equal in importance to King Tyrol, the man who ran the largest city. The loss of any man was devastating, because what would the kingdom do without its one true king?"

"Wait," Perry says as the words tease him, stroke him, as their small hands and spinning vowels caress him, tingle his skin.

No, Perry, no stopping now.

"Quite a few got lost, the Accounting King, the Turnip King and the King Who Loved Turtles. Kings who once maintained the golden orchards now worked at McDonald's. More and more men disappeared, showing up in the terrible land of the Lost Kings. This is what the remaining kings called them, the Lost Kings or the Lost Ones. Men who forgot their gold, vanishing into a world that looked much like our own."

Perry inhales deeply and pushes his chest into mine. My hands slide over his body to cup his ass, and the sensation surprises him, surprises his whole body.

"The kings sent scouts. Search parties. The Oil Change King and the King Who Was Gruff. But these men did not return. Once in a while a king might return with a newly found brother; arms around each other's shoulders, they passed through the eastern gates, grinning fantastically under those ancient marble arches. But many never came back. Whenever a king left the tribe in search of lost brethren, the remaining kings met him at dawn on the grassy fields at the kingdom's southern gates."

Perry is probably already hallucinating; it doesn't take long in here. Maybe he envisions kings on horseback, the sunbeams on fresh, dewy grass. I wonder if he recognizes any faces among the kings.

"The southern gates had been crafted into existence by metalworking kings, twisted gold, fashioned into tangled vines and flat, broad leaves reflecting every gleam of sunlight. Intertwining the gold, flowed brown copper vines, alive with barbaric intention. As the dawn re-painted the black grass to spring green and the gold metal leaves began to shine, two questions were always asked of the departing brother. The first was this: 'What would you risk to find a lost king?' Each king answered with what he was willing to sacrifice, and it was always worth more than anyone knew."

I imagine a peach, its ripe juices trickling down my throat, as I say, "The second question asked was, 'What if you find a lost king and he does not remember you?'"

Perry says, "Oh."

His sound disappears, swallowed by darkness.

I feel his whole body twist slightly away and then melt deeper into me. His eyelids vibrate furiously against my neck. He surrenders to the story, the golden sparks drawing him in, calling to him. His heart beats slower. Coming home can do that.

"That is to say, what would you do if you found the King Who Fixed Toys? Or stumbled on the Lavender King in some corporation's mail room?"

The words waft as autumn leaves in a Vermont forest toward the invisible floor, pooling at our feet.

He sags.

I unzip his jeans. This normally inaudible noise now drums like wooden blocks clattering together. Perry winces; I feel it against my body.

"When King Andrew, the Singer of Souls, was asked 'what if he doesn't remember you,' he shouted as his horse galloped away, 'I will show him my love. I will show him all my love.' Andrew himself was so beloved that many adopted this as the standard answer to the second question."

He moans, and in his vocalization I swear I see a pale apricot mist, fading, fading away.

"All my love," I say, softer than sound, using the smallest amount of air that I can possibly use. I trace my lower lip up his neck, over his chin, and eventually curve his lips into mine.

Perry rests his head on my shoulder, exhausted and somehow defeated. Wait, why does that word come to me now, *defeated*? Why do I sense sadness? It's sad, sometimes, when friends leave to go somewhere exciting, to see them ride out to embrace their destiny and yet yours seems elusive.

Why is Perry sad?

My fingers trace his face muscles, not disturbing their tensions but listening to them, feeling the mild acceptance that replaced his fear. I kiss the side of his neck, and instead of shivering, he rubs my head with his, nuzzling me in horse-like recognition.

I lick his neck with tiny cat-tongue strokes, rubbing his cock with my thumbnail, and he shifts, moans. I see a blue surge of electricity when I stroke his cock through his underwear. The clatter of his jeans hitting the floor sounds like yelling.

I kiss him again, fold his body into me. Without light to confirm our boundaries, we have no outlines; we are no longer distinct physical creatures, merely a mass of sensations and quivering skin. The only way to confirm that we are human is to keep grasping and caressing the planes of each other's flesh.

When I lower myself to his cock, breathe on it, he arches his body, his hands trace my back, my shoulders, my head. I feel heat from his prick, feel it radiating in this dark, cold cell. It jerks, it vibrates. I see it without seeing it, a fascinating sensation I indulge by breathing warmth onto it and feeling his fattening cock bob near my mouth. When I lick the plump head, his breath jumps raggedly, spinning into wispy silence, darkness erasing the sound.

In a swift motion, I suck down his dick and instantly feel his breath on my back. He has collapsed forward, it seems, but I do not feel his weight. I sense the rusty maroon color of each breath, more Vermont leaves pooling on my back.

I bet Perry's father would approve of this surreal experience.

I suck Perry slowly and think of the painting *Siren Song*. I hope that each long stroke feels like white silky wings, fluttering against his hard prison dick. I will use this fat stub of iron cock to free him. Maybe that imagery from that painting prophesized this moment, and I'm an agent for his father.

Yeesh. I don't want to think about Perry's father right now.

Refocus.

Perry's cock lengthens, gaining a heft that increases my enthusiasm. The damn thing keeps getting fatter. Each trip down his shaft makes him twitch and bend as I feel him fold around me. I see lemon-lime zigzagging of his jerking breaths.

I suck his cock to the root, and he clasps my head with both hands, his arms vibrating. I bet he'd scream if he dared to create sound, but he teeters silently between worlds, the pleasure of tension and sweet agony of impending release.

I stop at this moment. I open my mouth around his cock and let it lie on my quivering tongue. I feel his heartbeat pulse through his wrist as I breathe heavily around his cock.

When it's measurably softer, I begin again.

I suck him differently now, using long, powerful strokes as I infuse my love. I love this man. I worship this man. He responds, his touch deepens, his body greets the new rhythm I have created, and he meets my deep strokes with long, eager thrusts because we're a surprisingly good match.

I wonder if he sees what I'm seeing. How much of our reality is shared without light to unite us?

I see powerful sparks, orange and pink, traveling from my mouth to his cock. If he's anything like men I have loved, his cock acts as a megaphone to the rest of his body, so I yell my love through it, pink and orange love, sparking through him, reminding him, enticing him, increasing his ability to handle more, to give more, to want more. I take him so deep and with such fervor that our bodies merge into silky black liquid, working in mostly silent harmony toward an invisible explosion.

My hands snake up Perry's torso, feeling his body writhe at my touch, stretching and folding with a sexual glow, each of his lingering hisses attuned with some unheard song. Tonight may be too much for him, this midnight sex in Alcatraz, but as long as we're here, we're going to make this a big one, an orgasm that reminds us how lucky we are to be men.

Far away, a metal door clangs open and Perry's body clenches, almost enough to make him come.

I rise immediately and clasp a hand over Perry's mouth, which, sure enough, has opened to scream.

His chest heaves rapidly, and I grab his soaked, drooling cock to distract him.

I say, "Be quiet."

Despite their soft tenor, I'm sure my words sound like yelling, as if I'm deliberately trying to draw the night guard's attention.

"I have to open the door. Stay here. Nod if you understand."

My fingers feel the nod.

I relinquish my hand on his cock but keep one hand on his chest until I push the door half-open.

No sound.

I should hope not. Had to file down that bottom right side with a metal sander for three nights back in 1991. Or was that '90?

The sudden appearance of ghost light on the cell floor almost blinds us; I can see Perry's eyes clamp shut. But there's light again, so I can release him; we're back from the abyss.

I whisper, "He's not in our row so we have a minute or two. Keep quiet, Perry, and we'll get through this."

I don't have time to fix the door, just enough to open it all the way and press the bolt into the floor, make it appear close to normal. The odds are slim that he notices anything. He's the guard, Vin, he is the night guard. I'm only gone for a few seconds to prop the door and then return to Perry's side.

The footsteps move somewhere inside the prison, and Perry pants with terror, his body vibrating against the back wall. I maneuver him forward so I can stand behind him and pull him into me. I pull his naked ass against my jeans and clamp my hand over his Adam's apple, loosening my fingers so he can breathe.

I turn his head and pull him back to me, kissing him deeply, grabbing his nuts with my free hand, feeling his body jump at my touch. He would protest this course of action, the insanity of it, but arguing requires words, and he can't afford an argument right now, not with me stealing his every breath.

Breathe, Perry. Let the air become you, and then leave you. Forgive each breath because although it abandons you, every single time, it also brings you life. A man who cannot forgive the air has no chance of living.

My insistent kissing forces Perry to take large, gulping breaths. These gulps make no noise, but I feel his chest heaving, his heart pounding. His jeans remain bunched around his ankles.

I coil my spit-soaked hand around his balls, tugging downwards, forcing his still mostly hard cock to bounce. It doesn't take much to get his dick back to battle-ready status—a few wet bounces and my tongue down his throat.

The footsteps draw closer, perhaps down our galley row.

I feel my saliva ooze between my fingers as I stroke his wet dick.

Perry clenches.

The guard's boots strike casually, I'm sure, but each stride sounds like iron boxes slamming the floor. I pull away from his lips. If Perry screams, so be it.

He breathes in unison with me.

The loud footsteps draw closer.

I stroke his hard cock and use my other hand to tweak his left nipple with some extra pressure. Perry's body throbs, head to toe, with power, with life, with fear. He can't maintain this much longer. He's going to have to release something; he can't keep straddling the middle. Will he scream out his mouth, surrendering to fear? Or scream out his fat cock, his instrument of love?

The Alcatraz guard walks directly in front of our cell.

I suspend my jacking, squeezing hard instead, keeping the damn thing quivering and bloated.

Time to use those wings, Perry.

The retreating footsteps are only a few feet beyond us when, vibrating his inner ear, I whisper my demand, "Come."

Perry squirts, strong and fertile. I don't see it, of course, but I squeeze so hard that each pulse blasts through my grip before it reaches air. Everything goes out his cock: sound, light, intention, everything. I'm no longer worried about Perry making noise; I don't think he's capable at this moment. The only proof of his release is a wet splat that wouldn't normally be heard, but right now, I swear it echoes as it hits the floor.

The fact that his mouth isn't screaming doesn't mean the rest of his body keeps quiet. His head spasms hard, bouncing against my collarbone, which I should watch out for. Can't let him knock either of us unconscious. Both of his hands clamp my arm, working me like a jackhammer as he continues to shoot.

From your desolation, my son, create yourself anew.

I'd say Perry just did that.

He inhales, which sounds loud but isn't.

I push my head against his, use mine to slow his thrashing.

Perry comes back down the mountain. He slumps backward, and I catch him in my arms, hold his torso as he heaves the big breaths, coming back, coming down. He can't completely relax and let go, because he must also remain silent, so the compromise means spurting a few extra times, tension and release, tension and release. I can feel more of him drip over my knuckles.

Wow, that worked well.

A few minutes later, another door clangs open and shut. Perry whimpers, daring to make sound. The nameless guard should roam outside for another fifty-five minutes, checking smaller buildings and walking the winding trails. Now would be a good time to leave.

Easing myself out from behind, I turn and face him, allowing him to lean back against the wall. He wheezes as I pull him close to me.

"Prison break. You in?"

He makes no reply, but his head nods against my shoulder.

I am so fucking happy right now because I finally get to say those words. I have always dreamed of bringing a man I love to Alcatraz as part of his King Weekend. Tonight, that dream is realized. Poor Perry. His nightmare is a years-long fantasy of mine. He is my Alcatraz King!

Focus up. I need to hear his voice to make sure he has returned.

"Dude," I say, adding a sense of urgency. "Escape from Alcatraz. You in?"

Now that I've teased him for using the word *dude*, I should start using it. That ought to drive him a little nuts.

"Yes," he says, the word sounding crumbly. "Yes, please."

"This might go easier if you pull up your jeans."

I give him space and soon I hear the distinctive jingling of a belt buckle. Every prisoner in Alcatraz knows that sound. Perry takes my hand, and I navigate us around the door. When we reach the moonlit galley, we rub our sore eyes in irritation and appreciation.

I kiss him deeply, and he kisses back. Perry's so excited by what happened that right now he can't be angry. It's like a magician who rips up your twenty-dollar bill, but the trick is so cool you say, "Wow, do it again."

Does Perry know what happened just now? Does he understand? Probably not yet.

I take a few moments to fix the flooring so that no one else will see which piece I've altered. Tomorrow's tourists may tug at this door bolt hard as they want. It won't budge.

I'm so fucking happy; I will always love this amazing night.

Perry wobbles around me while I work, occasionally walking down the galley but staying close. He's a dog off leash, eager to race away but somehow reluctant to stray. I look up once to find him grinning at me, that same shit-eating grin I used on him at the art gallery on Tuesday.

God, he's handsome, smiling like that. I lunge to kiss him, and he responds with equal intensity.

He wanders behind me, a human helium balloon tethered by my right hand. I walk him to the exterior door that leads to the yard. Perry follows willingly, still drunk.

"Nevada, stop. Let's put on our ski masks."

There's no reason; we won't encounter the guard for a while. I just think it would be more exciting to escape from Alcatraz wearing ski masks.

I get out the tools to fix the exterior door and pause to study him.

In his ski mask, he nods.

It only takes a moment to make this work right again. I should change out those screws, though, get some new ones and blacken them up. Next trip.

I nod at Perry when I finish, and we join hands. It's fucking hilarious to do this without words. Where's Sean Connery when you need him?

My heart soaring, I lead Perry down the metal staircase with its spider web shadows. Speaking right now seems pointless because the ocean shrieks at the top of its lungs. I'm not sure the ocean has lungs. But each individual wave must have its own unique name, and each wave insists on introducing itself at once. The sound is deafening.

Obviously, we're still adjusting.

Perry and I hold hands as we sprint across the moonlit prison yard and descend the stone stairs, lower and lower, further and further, stone stairs, stone stairs, stone stairs, until 106 steps later we reach the Roman safe house.

Perry moves with catlike energy. The ocean regains its normal cacophony, a word I frequently use in association with an ocean. *Cacophony.* Good word. I wonder how soon I can talk to him about word stuff without freaking him out? Better give it a while.

We stand, breathing heavily amid the Roman ruins, and I take his other hand, pulling us together. In the moonlight, Perry stares at me through his ski mask.

Looking into his eyes, I can see that he has touched the fire.

FIVE

WE SIT to catch our breath and discuss our strategy for returning to the camp. We sit as we sat before, me leaning against a wall, him leaning against me. We keep an eye toward the path above, waiting for the night guard. We need to know his exact position before striking out.

Perry says, "Can't we spend the night here?"

"Our alarm clock is in the original camp."

He nods.

A moment later, he says in a flat voice, "So I'm not getting killed on Alcatraz?"

"No, Sir, you are not. You are getting fucked, however, when we get back to camp."

Perry leans back into me. "I think I might actually like that, you pervert. You perverted me in there."

I wrap my arms around his chest and squeeze. "Didn't take much."

I feel his body unclench everywhere, even his legs.

"I can't believe you. That guy was five feet away. He was *right* there."

We recount our crazy sex game in the isolation cell, relishing the minute details, explaining what we each saw, what we experienced. Perry actually chuckles a few times.

He says, "I thought I was going to die."

"But you didn't."

"No, no, I meant, it *felt* like I would scream."

"But you *didn't*."

He turns around and we kiss tenderly, with a new appreciation for each other's courage.

When we break and pull back a few inches, a beam of light above catches our eye.

Perry says, "He's back."

His tone isn't panicked; he sounds as if he's announcing our bus has arrived.

We stand and put on our ski masks. I love this night.

"Why does the security guard turn around right there?"

"That's the bird sanctuary for night herons. He turns around at the gate. We passed it on the way down here."

"It's too bad we can't go through," Perry muses. "It's a straight shot. We could get back in about ten minutes."

"There is a cement path right through the middle. And the gate's easy to climb."

"You're kidding," he says, blowing out the words with exhaustion. "Well, shit, Vin. Let's do that."

"Nope. We take the long route home. It's one of the Alcatraz rules: can't fuck with the birds."

"So, federal laws—"

"Some rules should not be broken. The birds don't get disturbed, even if it means we get caught tonight."

Perry snorts and paces away, gazing at a slim corner of the San Francisco skyline.

I give him a minute to sulk before I say, "C'mere."

I jog across the Roman safe house to one of the empty cement window frames, reach beyond it, and from the rocky ground below, drag up first one, then a second backpack. I hand the smaller one to Perry and keep the one with the frame for myself. He accepts it instantly, without surprise.

I could have hidden these Wednesday night in the Hammock, but where's the fun in that? Tonight, we are adventurers.

He says, "Is that a sleeping bag attached?"

"Yup."

"Won't we need two sleeping bags?"

I shoot him a grin. "Nope."

When we reach the bird sanctuary, he looks longingly in that direction, but only for a moment. Huh. I expected more of a fight than that. I point to where the guard's beam of light is moving further away, and he nods when he sees it. I give him the "move forward" hand symbol, and he nods again.

After the guard is a safe distance away, I say, "Boy, I wish I ate one of those hot dogs on the boat."

Perry ignores me, crouching.

I don't really get why he's crouching, but I join him down there.

Our trip back across the island feels different. Perry is now my partner, even giving me the "be perfectly still" gesture once. He no longer complains about the sweaty ski mask, and more importantly, he stopped explaining in hushed tones how if *he* were a night guard on an allegedly deserted island, he would probably adopt a "shoot first and ask questions later" mentality. Forty minutes later, after the guard passes our latest hiding spot and heads back toward the prison, we now have a full hour to ourselves on the south side of the island. We brazenly claim the main path and climb the southern stairs in a relaxed way, as we did many hours ago, holding hands and making small talk.

I wonder if Perry snores. I'm not going to ask; first dates can be so awkward.

Fuck it.

"Hey, do you snore? I hate to ask, because I know how awkward it is to bring up on a first date."

Perry spit-laughs a gob of drool. "You're unbelievable."

"So, yes?"

"No, I do not snore."

"You look like a snorer."

When we arrive on the top stair, I take off my ski mask and stop him, turning us both toward the magnificent San Francisco skyline. I need to see his face. He pulls off his ski mask and stares.

Unconsciously, Perry stands up straight. If there's a single moment I hope he remembers from the weekend, it's this one, facing San Francisco, a victory moment.

San Francisco does not disappoint. Twinkling blue and orange lights beckon, deceptively near. My hair stands on end, imagining this island's former denizens listening for New Year's Eve parties across the bay. I hear nothing but wind. He points out a few landmarks, and I nod in recognition.

Staring at this spectacular skyline feels akin to standing in front of a favorite bakery after hours, delighting in pastries you can see but can't touch. I'm really fucking hungry.

I say, "I'm hungry. Let's go make camp."

Perry says, "Should have gotten a ferry dog."

We kiss.

BACK in the Hammock, I let Perry crawl in first. I know several lovely Alcatraz spots for camping, each with its subtle advantages. I prefer the Hammock, because the ocean is so close yet can't touch us. I always pretend I'm Robinson Crusoe, my third night away from civilization, accepting my new reality. Another advantage: we can use San Francisco's marina as our nightlight, no flashlights needed.

I assign him the chore of unrolling the sleeping bag while I unpack some necessities.

"Get naked. And get in the bag."

He smirks and asks, "Ski mask on or off?"

"Your choice. But hang on, hang on. I'd like to see you do a crime-spree striptease for me, Perry."

He chucks his ski mask at me.

"I'm serious. Take off your clothes in a sexy stripper way."

He grins until he sees I'm not kidding, and my suggestion isn't really a suggestion.

"C'mon."

I make myself comfortable on my knees. "Make it sexy, baby."

Perry starts to object, but my stupid smile informs him that arguing is pointless. I've been told I can be stubborn. He first untugs his two shirts, and it's less sexy than efficient, but he half laughs and tries to swing his hips.

"C'mon. Put some X-ratedness into this."

Perry communicates his annoyance with a deliberate look and tries to add a dance, but the movement is more "feet on hot coals." He stops and frowns my way.

He says, "C'mon."

"Okay, switch gears. Turn around. Face the ocean."

He does.

I move to stand behind him, put my hands on his stomach.

I say into his ear, "Pretend we've been dating for a year and just returned from our one-year anniversary dinner."

"Wearing ski masks?"

"Maybe. We went to our favorite Thai restaurant, ordered panang curry, and we drank an expensive Prosecco, which I know you like."

He is still. "I do like Prosecco. How did you—"

I say, "Shhhhhhhh."

I sway him gently, letting him feel me, wrapping my arms around his chest, and kissing his neck a few times.

"We both confessed our desire to live together, and soon. We are in love. Take off your clothes like that night instead."

He does not move in my arms, makes no attempt to start undressing.

I think the striptease might have been easier.

I wrap my whole body around him, letting him feel the presence of me at first, that warmth, then pressing my lips to his neck, more subtle pressure than actual kiss. "I don't like how you leave the seat up all the time, and also your—"

"I never leave the seat up."

"Okay, I always leave the seat up, and you're going to have to get used to that if we live together. Plus, babe, you eat grapefruit in an irritating way."

He reaches for his top shirt buttons, and his movements are slow, thoughtful. It's not particularly sexy.

I say his name quietly into his ear, more elongated croaking than actual pronunciation.

When he reaches his last button, he turns to face me. His face stays almost blank, a curious flicker of something which makes me examine him closer.

In a low voice, I say, "Happy anniversary, babe."

He flinches but pushes his hips against me, rubbing against me. His open palms explore my chest, and his fingers finally rest against my top shirt button, beginning to unbutton me.

I put my arms around his lower back, tracing either side of his spine with my thumbs. I sway us a little bit, pretending our favorite song sings from a nearby stereo. I wonder what that song might be.

Even though my shirt is completely unbuttoned, he leaves his arms on my chest, a barrier between us. Creating a scene in which he wants to find himself, a loving relationship, has thrown him off balance again, another forced intimacy that he can't ignore but can't fully embrace. He wants the anniversary night. He does. But he couldn't possibly let himself feel that kind of love with me. I am nothing but a weekend boyfriend and already not a very good one.

He pushes my shirt back over my shoulders, until it can drop no further without me unlocking my hands behind his back. He moves with me, his lips brushing mine in an intentional soft dragging that only lovers have permission to perform.

I say, "Do you imagine us having a favorite song?"

His face changes as I ask this, a shadow of fear passing across him. Too real. Too much. I may have pushed a little too far.

He says, "It's cold. Do we really have to do this?"

Pull back, you moron.

"No, that's enough. I don't need the whole striptease; I wanted to see your face soft and beautiful after stuck in a ski mask for so long. You got there right away."

He nods and looks away. "Okay."

Relief? Disappointment?

"Get naked and hop in the sleeping bag. Leave on your undershirt if you think you might be chilly, but that blanket I pulled out is for wrapping the parts of us that stick out. My hunch is that two naked bodies in the sleeping bag will keep us warm enough."

I kiss his forehead and return to my unpacking.

As he drops his jeans, I finally see his underwear: plain boxer briefs. Damn. I failed The Underwear Test. He was closer to not coming than I realized. Factor that in, Vin.

He turns to face the ocean as he kicks off his briefs, and I finally get to see his butt. Perry's trim, so his ass is, by its own nature, nicely curved. It's not a hard muscle butt, but beautiful in its gentle slope. Thick globes, so perfectly cut on the underside, and oooh—dimples. Love those dimples.

He crawls into the sleeping bag, wriggling around until he's comfortable.

Still clothed, I hand him a crystal flute.

"Champagne?"

His eyebrows arch in surprise, but he nods.

I rest the bottle against his back inside the sleeping bag, which makes him shiver. I uncork the bottle with a muffled pop and fill his flute, then mine, with frothy golden liquid. We toast silently.

Perry looks surprised. "This is good."

"Yeah. I got it at the Schramsberg winery tour on Monday."

Perry looks at me and says, "You really are a tourist."

"Absolutely."

As I sip, Perry faces the visible bit of skyline, holding the flute up to his eye and letting the champagne bubbles distort the city. I do the same and think about Armistead Maupin's theory that San Francisco is the lost Atlantis.

I offer him a small plastic container. "Cracker? They're rosemary flavored and they're yummy with fresh artichoke and roasted garlic, which is in this container. Here."

Perry takes a cracker, tentatively it seems. I shouldn't read much into that gesture, but I try to read everything. Is he feeling shy with me? What's happening in him right now?

We munch our crackers and some grapes I produce, a meager supper but filling enough. I supply fresh mint leaves to cleanse the palate and produce a chocolate orange for desert. I lie next to him outside the sleeping bag, still dressed, with my arm wrapped around him. Facing the ocean, I feed him a chocolate slice as we discuss San Francisco, how he enjoys living here, how different from where he grew up in Arizona. Would he return to the desert someday? Maybe. Perry is noncommittal.

The ocean lulls us into a slow thudding groove, the same waves disappearing and reappearing over and over and over.

Vig-grr, vig-grr....

Crap, not that again.

"Listen to this. Do you think the words *stone stairs* sound like a right angle? Say it a couple times and you'll see what I mean: stone stairs, stone stairs, stone—"

"Don't scare me with your crazy word shit."

"First of all, I didn't mention this at all while we were climbing the stone stairs, respecting your request, and secondly, in case you hadn't noticed, you're not afraid anymore. We're in the same danger as when you woke up from the nap, and you don't even care."

He is quiet for a moment.

He says, "I feel like we should be telling ghost stories."

I kiss his warm neck. "Tonight is for romance. Ghost stories tomorrow."

"Well then, how about how you know where to sleep on this island, how to unlock the doors and stuff."

"Same ghost story. I have good answers to those questions, but not tonight. Tomorrow over breakfast. I brought yummy croissants from Tartine's. I call dibs on the chocolate one. Or half dibs. I'd share."

Perry pushes back to bump my chest, which signifies his acceptance of the situation and also lets me know he'd rather have answers right now.

"I can't believe this," he says, staring toward the slice of available skyline. "I had sex in Alcatraz. This is the craziest fucking night of my life."

"It's only Friday."

"Yeah, I know. I assume tomorrow we're swimming out to Shark Island in hamburger swim suits."

"I love it. Porterhouse flippers for our feet."

We speculate for a while longer on tomorrow's potential adventures, enjoying the champagne and chocolate orange, and then Perry twists around to kiss me. His enthusiasm surprises me. I worry for a second that I have created an adrenaline junkie, but I doubt it—those are rare. I assume his enthusiasm relates to the brilliant moon, the stunning skyline, the champagne, or the thrill of running down those stairs during our escape. Or the big cum shot. This night intoxicates me too, which is why I return his kiss with vigor.

Dammit.

At least it's not Billy.

A few minutes later, the kisses become something wet and hungry, and we mutually reach the unspoken conclusion that snack time is definitely over. I take off my leather jacket and toss it in the grass behind us. My unbuttoned flannel shirt goes next. Perry works my belt, then unbuttons my jeans and unzips.

I appreciate his eager assistance.

I strip my T-shirt up over my head, and in our dim lighting, I see in Perry a renewed lust. He was attracted to me in the art gallery, then, I bet, repulsed by my speech. Ever since then, on the pier, in the prison, I've been pushing him away and drawing him closer and somehow, shirt off, and my own boxer-briefs visible, that flicker of attraction explodes into a wall of flame, and everything about him—fingers, eyes, hungry smile—all send the same message: he's fucking ready.

But I won't let him strip my underwear. I grab my hardening dick and trace a finger through the wet precum stain near my head.

"Suck the fabric," I command quietly, and he does it.

I bend my knees forward, and he gets the message to follow me to the ground. My jeans are still only halfway down, bunched around my calves.

He breathes heavily, groaning and twisting his lower half in the sleeping bag, humping the earth as he sucks and licks, moaning occasionally as my cock gets harder and thicker.

I back off and stand up, and he groans, then chuckles.

I start unlacing my boots.

He says, "You really camp here, don't you? This night is… it's no big deal."

"I have never brought anyone to Alcatraz; I've been waiting for years for just the right man. After our amazing night here together, I'll probably never bring anyone else. I'd say it's a big deal."

He nods, more pleased by this answer than he thinks he lets on.

With my jeans and underwear kicked to the side, I bring my dick wet with precum right to his lips, and Perry opens his mouth to say, I believe, "Damn."

I wreck his pronunciation by pushing inside him, and he gives up the word instantly.

Right away, we find the right groove, the suck groove, and I begin to speak.

"The kings gathered to greet the dawn in the ancestral fields, to let that gold wash over and through them. Each king wore a glorious shirt, beautiful raiment. Chilling blues so vivid you involuntarily gulped because seeing that color felt like gulping cold water. Pumpkin browns that smelled like Thanksgiving. Finch yellows, chili reds almost hot to the touch, every imaginable color and style. Some shirts were simple, beautiful because they were hand sewn with intention by a beloved.

"The kings' only census came in greeting the dawn. Kings checked in from all over the world, the Vietnamese kings, old Swedish fishmonger kings, young Nigerians who raced to greet the dawn with laughing enthusiasm. Their joy was matched only by those from

Australia who swaggered toward the desert sunrise with a subtle and confident thrill."

Perry makes no acknowledgement that he hears this, he's so passionate in his cocksucking. I pull his head off my dick and dangle it in front of him, slick and juicy under bright California moonlight.

"Repeat it back to me."

He does a less-than-adequate job, so I slap my cock head against his cheek and nose and then place my cock on his lips. My grip on his skull makes it clear he may go no further. I repeat the passage much the same way, this time adding and subtracting a detail, changing the colors of a few shirts but keeping it mostly the same, all while I rub my dick over his lips. He moans, and it fucking turns me on.

"Repeat it back to me."

He does better the second time around—not much better, but he remembers the kings gathering at dawn and repeats back a few of the colors.

"Suck on my cock. Suck down the story at the same time. Find the rhythm."

He nods.

I plow my wet dick into his throat, and he groans in relief. I repeat the first few sentences again, the way they greet the dawn, adding a white shirt so stark you involuntarily squint. I guide his cocksucking efforts, fucking into him on the best words.

"Attendance at dawn revealed how many kings got lost on their way to find their missing brothers. The loss of a single man devastated all, because how would the kingdom survive without its one true king? They could never be complete without every man recovered."

He gulps, and his closed eyelids flex.

"Quite a few got lost: the Accounting King, The Forgiver King, and The King Who Loved Turtles. Kings who maintained the golden orchards now worked at—"

Perry spits out my cock.

"You already said that part with the King Who Loves Turtles."

"Did I?"

"Back in Alcatraz."

"Did I?" I pretend to reflect where I left off. Were you listening, Perry? Did you hear what I actually said? "Hey, I have an idea. Why don't I tell the story, Perry, and you suck my dick?"

Perry chortles and then resumes.

God, his mouth feels warm. I do not fully comprehend why getting your cock sucked feels so amazing. Sure, sensitive nerve endings and all that biology. But the thrill of another man's warmth, his throat engulfing your dick. I love the power exchange: you worship this part of me, and I will make myself hard and worthy of your loving attention. Fuck!

Don't get too distracted.

"The Lost Kings united around common grievances, and their grievances were many. They raged about politics, injustices done to them in strip mall parking lots. They grieved about their pensions, their backyards, their sons, their husbands, their wives, their boyfriends, and late fees for movie rentals. One of their mightiest ongoing grievances was with their king brothers. They resented their so-called interference."

Damn, he's good at this. I gotta slow down here.

I pull my dick out of Perry's mouth and turn his head to my face.

"'We are not kings,' the Lost Kings insisted. 'If you consider us lost, then you must think yourselves better than us, oh high and mighty Found Kings.'"

"It's a good story," he says. "But how could the Found Kings be called 'found' if they hadn't gotten lost at some point?"

"Yes, an excellent point," I say with an academic tone. "By the way, *suck my dick*. Good. Give me that throat, buddy."

He wolfs down my cock.

Wow. That's good. I feel my cock head enveloped and squeezed. Concentrate, Vin.

"Had every king become lost and then later found? How did the tribe of Found Kings emerge if not from the Lost Ones? But these questions are not tonight's story. Suffice it to say, the Lost Kings named the Found Kings in jeering disrespect, and the kings accepted this mantle, hoping to soften their brothers. Why don't you repeat it back to me."

He tries. Sometimes I interrupt him with my hard, wet dick, pushing into his mouth while he's speaking, and then I complain that I don't understand what he's saying, insisting he back up and repeat details while I dangle my drooling cock before him. Perry laughs once or twice, and I snicker, thinking this hilarious.

"This is a disturbing fetish, Vin," he says, coming up for air. "Why can't you be into bondage like everyone else?"

"Oh, please. Story sex isn't a fetish; it's not even a thing."

"Fetish," Perry says.

I nod to his left. "Push over that rock."

"More secret tools?"

"Yes. Under that rock are tools we need for tonight, and if you flip over that rock, our entire evening changes. Do you trust me?"

Perry glances over at the stereo-speaker-sized rock not far from us. He says, "That one?"

"Yes, and hurry up. My nuts are getting cold without you sucking my cock. Decide right now if you're gonna stop being a punk and start doing exactly what I tell you to do. Decide fast."

He inches forward to get more leverage. He says, "Boy, you're crabby during sex."

"You'll know when I'm crabby."

He tips the rock, toppling it easily.

Well, *toppling* isn't the right word. It falls over with a boring thud, really. *Toppling* sounds like it jumped from a tall building and landed gracefully on its *g*.

"Am I seeing something besides condoms?"

"Lube. Under the condoms."

"Oh, well, quite a letdown. You made it sound like some big thing."

"It was. You trust me now. Pick a condom."

He doesn't have much reaction to my pronouncement, which is fine. I merely wanted to point out that his trust has shifted.

"How much sex are we having tonight, Vin? It's like a pharmacy aisle under there," he says.

"I wanted you to have options."

Ribbed on the inside or out? Colored, glow-in-the-dark, clear, or micro thin? Years of negotiating safe sex has given us all too much to talk about.

I guide his jaw to my softening cock and fuck him with it a few times, strokes that make him sit up and suck down harder, because I think he likes sucking dick, this strong man. My hunch is he really likes to submit, but of course, one of the challenges with being a strong man is that it's hard to submit.

"Suck it like that, Pear. Yeah," I say in a voice with some gravel to it.

Fuck, that's good!

I inhale that cold ocean air, and I love its raw power, so crushing and yet tender. I feel safe knowing elemental forces are demolishing nearby rocks, inspiring my primal energy. We re-enact this power relationship as he sucks my dick like the greedy land and I ready myself to flood him in waves.

But stop. Stop real quick. We can't crash here. As I urge his throat off the base of my dick, I emerge wet and strong, a quivering board out of his mouth.

Fuck, yeah. I love that wet marbles feeling, my nut juice churning from another man's skill.

The bottle is within reach, so I fill Perry's flute and mine. "Pick one."

He hands me a green square, organic lamb's sheath. Almost like raw.

"Good choice."

As I unwrap it, I squeeze into the sleeping bag behind him, pushing him to face San Francisco. I drag my wet cock down his back, across the flank of his thigh, reminding him how wet and sticky it felt a moment ago in his warm mouth.

"You've got a great dick, Vin."

"Thanks."

Lying behind him, I bring my arm around his chest, my cock pushing hard between his ass cheeks, which seem awfully defenseless right now, pillowy soft and warm. Perry squirms against me.

"Hand me the lube."

His fingers find mine over his shoulder, and the transfer of this one-time packet is easily completed.

I kiss his neck and strum his stomach as I initiate an agonizingly slow rhythm, rubbing my dick against the crack of his ass. I squeeze out lube to make my strokes wetter. I knew he worked out in a gym... this ass is perfect. I could stay this way awhile, a delicious agony all its own.

"The Lost Kings kept their own census, tracked in spreadsheets with pie charts. They cared little for who lived among them but hated that some would suddenly depart, living the remainder of their lives as Found Kings. They did not want to 'lose' to the Found Kings, even if they didn't realize what battle they were fighting."

His thick chest is relaxed as I squeeze and release his pecs.

"Repeat it all back to me."

He tries.

Actually, he performs much better than the last time, remembering more details, how the Lost Kings are grouped by grievances and not geography, how the Found Kings were named, and more.

"We're not going to fuck until I get this right, are we?"

"Nope."

"Fetish," he says.

We sip champagne, and Perry works to pass this odd oral exam, slurring his words as if drunk, writhing as I slowly drag the base of my champagne flute across his skin. He may believe the champagne got him buzzed, but I'm not convinced; the bottle remains half-full. Perry hums and floats, responding to my every leisurely thrust up through his crevice, my breath down his spine. The chilly ocean breeze surprises us occasionally, bringing unidentifiable smells dressed in spectacular mist. You'd think it would revive us. Instead, we purr together in a delicious, slow dance, testing the seams of our sleeping bag, draining us with soft exertion.

After his latest effort, I say, "Pretty good. Now try again."

He snarks out a sharp breath through his nose, a snort, and then I hear it: the resistance. "Vigilance!" cries Perry's brain. "I must remain in charge." I don't care how much he memorizes. I just want to tease out the opposition, get it naked before us.

He says, "If you gave me all this in writing before the weekend, we could have sex without homework."

I say, "If you had looked me up on AOL, as I hinted at twice in the art gallery, you could have read all this on my home page. Most guys I king already know the back story by the time I show up. Vacation guys are tougher that way."

Perry snickers and says, "I knew this was a cult."

"The Lost and Founds," I say.

We are quiet together, letting those lingering words bind us.

"Repeat it back to me again, Perry, what you know so far."

He begins anew.

I sometimes share how the Lost Kings come close to remembering through sex, and how sex is easily mistaken for the true intimacy of kingship. I don't think sex is one of Perry's big struggles, so I reaffirm my decision not to bring that up. I don't usually pursue men who I suspect have big sexual issues because I'm afraid of messing them up worse. I suppose I could king a guy without sex, but I'm horny and on vacation, and my way involves fucking.

Nevertheless, I must stay cautious while I'm acting like an arrogant prick because I've never been trained to do this. Any licensed therapist could get jail time for the shit I'm attempting, but who would sue a vacationing mechanic for his kinky camping trip? I suppose therapy has its place. I tried it myself for a while, but not once did we ever wear ski masks. So, what's the point?

Help me, kings. Remind me to stay humbly attentive to the man I'm bossing around all weekend.

"Nice," I say as he speaks the tale's latest stopping point.

I clink his champagne glass and take a generous gulp.

Perry groans, sweaty and panting, because for the last few minutes I have been pressing against him with quiet insistence, almost inside him.

According to his brain, he's been tricked to sleep, locked up in the Hole, and sexually taunted. All while avoiding a gun-toting guard paid to hunt down trespassers on an allegedly haunted prison island.

If this weren't enough excitement for the evening, he now must pass a multipart oral exam and might end up sexually manipulated until sunup, which could come soon or not, because I stole his watch and he has no concept of time.

His body collapses as I sip from my flute, watching him sink further into the sleeping bag, dragged closer and closer into an intoxicated slumber.

Time to slip on the royal robe and lube him up. The lube is slick in my fingers, slippery on my dick. The condom rolls over my head easily.

I'm proud of him. He submitted many times tonight, dozens of times, each one a slightly higher hurdle, trusting me further, then further.

"Where was I? Oh, right. The disgruntled Lost Kings."

I nudge closer, and my cock head feels ready to breach him.

He gasps.

"The Lost Kings felt confused about the disappearances from their ranks, angry about those who defected to the Found Kings. They couldn't stop it, though they tried. Men kept getting found. Who can say what makes a Lost King get found? Becoming a parent, overcoming addiction, or maybe forgiving himself. Even something as simple as hearing the right song on a certain day might cause a man to remember his higher self and then choose to become that king."

Need another few seconds. Push in the lube, right around that sweaty crease.

Perry groans.

"Some theorize that when a man sits on the same marble bench as Death, the experience may help him remember the king within."

Good. Fully covered and slathered.

"Because every man has a king inside him."

I nudge forward, and with a sloppy, wet thrust, I'm in, inching forward, approaching balls deep inside Perry Mangin, investment banker, and his fleshy, warm butt pushes back to greet me.

Ohhhhh, fuuuck.

We lie still, quivering in silence, staring at the black ocean and the San Francisco skyline. He collapses further, sinks deeper. You cannot deny a moment like this, so we remain in perfect, pulsating silence, both of us aware of the incredible sensations happening to both of us.

I kiss him on the neck and say, "All men are kings."

Perry surrenders; a wisp of sound emerges from his mouth, a firefly-sized gasp.

I move my hips, not full fucking but definitely slow rocking.

"Communication from the Lost Kings came as a discontented ramble often without any discernable meaning. If any message were sent directly, an anonymous voice rang out, and then fell back among his skulking brothers, nobody wanting to stand out."

I shift gears so that my slow, measured strokes only partially fill him up. His butt keeps urging my passage deeper.

"But in their own sullen way, they issued a demand."

According to the moon, it's almost time to get quiet. Tomorrow's a big day.

"They demanded that a Found King come to them, a prisoner of sorts, for ten years. Why that particular demand? Who knows? Men reach that brittle, demanding place all on their own, but it's faster to travel in groups."

I stop fucking, and Perry drifts for a moment before nudging back.

The bay wind is cold, but we are our own campfire.

"Hey." His words slur as he speaks. "What about the demand?"

Good. He really was listening.

I reward him with a couple of slow sideways push-ups, letting him feel every inch of me inside him, and his entire body arches back.

I grip the back of his neck, squeezing and relaxing my fingers repeatedly. I time my fuck strokes to match this rhythm so that he feels the deep lovemaking up and down his entire spine.

"The Found Kings debated the request. They considered the question within their deepest chambers and in open markets, on garden benches, and in sunrise circles. Men discussed it over checkers. One found king baked his famous cherry crepes to draw men into conversation, because baking was his gift and he loved with all his love."

"I like cherry crepes," Perry says, more asleep than awake.

"Before they could reach a decision—"

I stop.

"No," Perry says softly. "Talk."

I say, "Do you hear the security guard?"

His body tenses, but I keep fucking him quietly. We hear only the ocean and each other. Who could possibly hear a guard's footsteps thirty feet above us? Not me. I just want Perry to struggle on this plane a few minutes longer.

To his credit, the changes in his body are fairly subtle: he still pushes back to meet my thrusts and does so with some good attention. Yet his softness changes slightly, his muscles perhaps coursing with a dash of leftover adrenaline.

I say, "Sorry. I thought I heard boots."

I don't know how much actual time elapses while we fuck, listening to each other and the night sounds. The moon drifts through more sky, I know that. After a while, I feel Perry glide back into putty mode, and I roll him on his stomach for some deep dicking. Roughly ten minutes of punching his prostate knocks him senseless again.

I put him back on his side.

"Where was I? Oh yes, the demand."

Perry rolls his head drunkenly.

My hand grazes his cock to make sure it's hard, quivering. It is.

"King Samiir argued passionately that nobody should answer the demand. He remembered his time among the Lost Kings and nurtured a strong aversion to any one man responding. Tanak, the Wall Street King, argued that it wouldn't achieve anything. Others disagreed, suggesting that if the Lost Ones welcomed a Found King among them, they might soften and remember."

I speak quieter, and Perry's head pushes back so my voice is closer to his ear.

"If several key kings had been present for the debates, such as the King of Compromises or the Opera King, things might have played out differently. Those two and a dozen others possessed astonishing gifts which might have uncovered a way to honor the Lost Kings' demand. But they lived among the lost, waiting for the spark of life to remind them who they were always meant to be."

"Very ironic," Perry says, his voice fading.

"Found Kings love paradox. Lost Kings love irony, the shadow of paradox."

Perry grunts, and his words come out all dreamy as he says, "I'm not a lost king."

"The Found—"

Gross. Did I just swallow a bug? Ish.

I clear my throat with as little scratching as I can. Ignore it. Don't ruin this.

"The Found Kings puzzled over this knot of a problem, how to respect their lost brothers' request and show them love without losing a Found King for ten years. If that king forgot *his* kingship, the Lost Ones' next complaint might be 'You never sent us a Found King.' In the middle of the debates, an eighteen-year-old man stepped forth, King Aabee. He said, 'I will go. Send me!'"

I speak the last sentence louder, cheerful.

Perry half chuckles at my tone.

"The kings were astounded because they had not yet considered actually sending a Found King. That remained only one, rather smallish, possibility."

I fuck him with an even, sawing pace. Perry totters once again between fully asleep and sensually aware. The champagne's impact is probably gone, but he seems drunker than ever, more relaxed.

"King Aabee was Somali, tall and slender with coal black skin. He always wore long-sleeve white shirts sewn by his sisters, with silvery stitching that swam like tiny fishes down his arms' length. He walked among them this day, arms stretching high above his head, his long fingers held to the sky. The older kings shook their heads in gratitude, because one of the youngest adult kings was schooling them in compassion and service.

"King Aabee repeated, 'I will go. Send me!'"

Perry makes a noise in this throat, but I can't tell what he intended: a word, a groan? He is quiet immediately. Maybe he's responding to my long, slow strokes.

"With growing alarm, the Found Kings realized King Aabee wasn't quite volunteering; he had already decided. 'No, Aabee,' they pleaded. 'You do not understand. Ten years is a long time among the Lost Ones; you are likely to get lost yourself. We cannot lose our most promising king, the true leader of our people.' But Aabee met these arguments with a wide smile and kissed each brother under his thumb, an expression among them of deep honor, known as the king's kiss."

Perry's chest tightens, and I wonder if something resonates in him with how I kissed him on the pier, how I greeted his decision to not come with me. Almost immediately, his body sinks again, continues its blissful rhythm.

"The day King Aabee planned to leave the ancestral homelands, every king gathered at the southern gates, many to plead with him one last time. 'Do not ruin your life. You need not go.' Aabee greeted each brother's concern with the king's kiss, filling each man with grief and love."

Perry is losing consciousness, about to ride out of the kingdom himself. I need to keep him awake for a few minutes longer. I fuck him deeper and harder.

"Oh," Perry says. "King Aabee."

"Yes. The parting banquet they prepared for King Aabee dazzled both sight and smell, a not-too-subtle attempt to dissuade him from this journey. The foods were his favorites, which meant delicacies he had never tasted, for best of all, he loved trying new things. Wise kings made passionate arguments. A German king named Detlof tried to distract Aabee with a game of chess. King Detlof was wily that way."

"Det...," Perry says.

He's not long for this world. Better speed up the pace.

I whisper into his ear, "When they finally accepted they could not stop him, they asked, 'What would you risk to find a lost king?' 'My youth!' cried King Aabee."

Softer, Vin. Softer.

"And what will you do if he does not remember you? As King Aabee rode from the kingdom, galloping away, aw-a-a-a-ay Perry, he called out to them, 'I will show him my love. I will show him all my love.'"

He moans.

"*Remember the king,*" I say, the words more air than sound. "That's what they shouted to Aabee as he began his ten-year, self-imposed exile among the Lost Ones."

Once again, I whisper, "Remember the king."

Perry gallops into darkness himself as I continue to push rhythmically in and out of his exhausted butt. Neither of us is going to get off at this point, but I might fall asleep inside him.

I repeat the phrase a while longer, alternating which ear I speak into, massaging his neck with my fingertips. I hold Perry tight and whisper all my love, until sleep, the gentle prison we all know nightly, summons me at last.

SIX

I JERK awake suddenly, rattling Perry.

He's warm. Perry's *warm*. We're in the same position as when I fell asleep. How long ago? Could I see the faintest hint of light when I fell asleep? The sun now gleams above the horizon. Damn. I was hoping for fog.

Perry's tone is sharp when he says, "Oh crap."

The ocean wind whipping us probably reminds him we're not in a hotel room or his cozy one-bedroom apartment. The wind shifted direction at some point, hits us harder now. Yikes, that's chilly. I snuggle deeper into him and kiss his shoulder to let him know I'm awake.

"It's day," he says.

Perry breathes heavily and relaxes, pushing back against me in a friendly hello. I note these changes within the span of a few seconds, briefly wondering whether my jerking awake woke him or we both woke at the same time.

"Hey," says a voice near our feet. "Wake up."

I feel a soft jolt against my foot, presumably for the second time.

"Wake up, you two."

Perry's body jerks to instant full alert.

"All right, all right." My voice is thick with sleep. "Jeez, man, we're having a tender moment."

I already can't remember what I dreamt about. Sugar packets were involved. I don't drink coffee. I don't even use sugar packets. Maybe the word *sugar*?

Raising myself on one elbow, I see Perry's defense strategy is to pretend to remain asleep with his eyes open wide in terror. If Perry could run, he would. Of course, there's nowhere to go unless you're Jesus and can scuttle across the nearby waves.

"Morning, cutie," I murmur into his ear.

Our human alarm clock says, "Howie says you brought me three boxes. Why didn't you leave them the other night?"

I say, "I wanted one for myself but didn't want to open the box without you. Seemed disrespectful."

He says, "You've done that before."

"Yeah, but it's disrespectful. This time, I thought I'd ask you first. Did you bring me any empty knapsacks?"

"Yeah. Two."

"Good." I make sure the word communicates a soft rebuke.

He knows why.

"Oh my God," Perry says with a groan. "Is this a drug deal?"

I use a cheery voice to say, "Maybe. Define drugs."

Jerome grumbles an unintelligible response. I hear him unzip the backpack on my frame and rifle through its contents.

The sound catches Perry's attention, and he maneuvers himself to sitting. If he's to be arrested for drug trafficking, I think he wants to see which drugs.

Jerome pulls one free of the cardboard box, turns, and offers it to Perry.

"Nut Roll?" he says, wiggling it, as if this makes it more enticing.

When Perry doesn't respond in any fashion, he tosses it to Perry and it lands with a soft thud on the sleeping bag.

"Nut Roll?" he asks me, drawing out another.

"Thank you," I say, sitting up and rubbing my eyes, "I would love a Nut Roll. See? Wasn't that polite?"

Jerome shoots me something between bored and exasperated and tosses another one onto the sleeping bag.

Wait. Why was I thinking about sugar packets a moment ago?

When Perry speaks, his words are slow. "These are candy bars."

Jerome says, "Technically, it's not candy. They're Nut Rolls. You can only buy them in the Midwest."

I say, "Jerome grew up outside Milwaukee."

Perry stares up at a light-skinned black man, midfifties, peeling back a wrapper. And while Jerome hasn't seemed especially friendly thus far, he looks affable enough eating those first few bites.

Jerome looks older to me than the last time I saw him. It's funny how when you only see someone once in a while, you notice the subtle changes, the extra gray hairs on the side of his head, the lingering wrinkles. It's been at least nine months. No, wait, I was here in March. Seven months.

"How do you know HG?" Jerome says, chewing.

Perry says, "HG."

The initials hang there, a statement of sorts.

"We call him the Human Ghost," Jerome says with a nod toward me. "We don't know his real name. We prefer not to know it, actually. Or yours. Don't tell me your name. Or his. Are you a lawyer?"

Perry says, "Excuse me?"

"You look like you'd be a lawyer. You have lawyer face."

I say, "He's an investment banker. His Alcatraz name is Nevada."

Jerome ignores me. "Well, Nevada, how do you know HG?"

"I don't," Perry says, shifting against me. "We met on Tuesday. I know almost nothing about him, actually."

I say, "This is our first date, Jerome. We're weekend boyfriends."

"Well, that's weird," Jerome says, biting off another inch of Nut Roll. He nods at the champagne bottle behind my head. "You guys couldn't get drunk and screw in a hotel?"

I say, "It was a special night. I've never brought anyone to Alcatraz."

"No, no," he says. "I'm busting your chops, Ghostie. You're cool."

"Thanks, man. Seriously."

"Just don't make it a habit. It's too much work. Howie and Steve helped me sweep the island last night since there wasn't going to be any ten-minute boat warning. The three of us spent the whole time bitching about you on the walkie-talkies, about how much of a pain in the ass you are. Still, we drew straws over who got to patrol last night, because all three of us wanted to see what was up. We're meeting for breakfast when I get off, because they want to know the score. So can I tell them about your investment banker?"

"Sure."

"What'd you guys do last night?"

"Ran around the island. Spied on you."

"Go inside?"

"Yeah. You patrolled nearby once."

"Did you show him your cell?"

"No time. We were on a schedule."

"Huh," Jerome says. "Well, you did good. I never saw you two. When you coming back?"

"As soon as I get more vacation time, I guess. Probably February or March when I need a break from winter. Sorry we didn't get to hang out this trip."

Jerome grunts. "I put some letters in your knapsack. I brought you a picture."

"Your grandkids? It's about time."

I pull myself up and reach hard toward the knapsack.

He says, "Don't get up if you're naked. I don't need to see that shit."

Jerome tosses the backpack to me and I extricate the photo he enclosed.

"They're cute." I make sure my voice expresses hesitation. "Of course, as a child, I was cuter than either of these two. They're okay, though. Big smiles."

"Don't talk shit, Ghost. Anyone can see you were an ugly baby. Those kids are perfect. Jamie can read whole sentences already; he's a prodigy. Also, don't get a big head, but you were right about that sound. I had it checked out."

"I *told* you."

"I know, HG. And I'm saying you were right." Jerome picks up the knapsack full of Nut Rolls. "Don't be a dick."

"Okay, okay. Thanks for waking us."

I edge further out of the sleeping bag to shake his hand goodbye.

He says, "Next time you see them, you have to give Howie and Steve shit. After we drew straws and I won, they wanted to change it up and have all three of us patrol last night. Hunt you down, scare the crap out of you with guns drawn and everything. I reminded them how adamant you were about the regular patrolling. I didn't change anything."

"Thank you for that. I really appreciate it."

Jerome says, "First boat's in fifteen minutes. My book recommendations are in my letter."

"Cool. Did you read—"

"I read it. Didn't like it. Explained why in my letter. Gave it to Howie, and that fucker liked it, which we then debated for a week. I showed him my book review part of the letter, and he mostly scribbled the word *wrong* all over my margins."

"That's your fault. You give a letter to Howie, you know he's going to do something like that. Remember the potato chip letter?"

Jerome chuckles.

We shake hands again, and he turns, strolls up the circus train of limestone blocks. After setting the knapsack on the Charlie Brown wall, he disappears over it. The knapsack disappears next.

Perry watches this departure with surprise, relief, and more surprise. Not only were we never in danger of capture, but apparently when breaking federal law on this prison island, the guards offer candy bars to the offenders.

I ease myself back down and watch him, eager to see where he takes this.

I say, "How did you sleep, babe?"

Perry climbs out of the sleeping bag and looks to the ocean. Then back up at the island.

"I brought orange juice, sparkling water, or Diet Coke. But if you want the Diet Coke, there's no ice. It's been chilled by ocean sand, so it should be cold. It's buried about twenty-five feet from here."

He doesn't answer me, just stares.

Sitting up, I reach for our other knapsack from last night, unpacking a few Tupperware containers with pastries, fresh fruit, silver forks, cloth napkins. Perry remains quiet while I make a table from the backpack frame and prepare our continental breakfast.

"I got us a pear for breakfast in honor of you. Try to pronounce the word *pear* like the shape of a pear. Like this: peeeeeaaar. Try it. Or do you already do this with your own name? You make the *y* the stem on the pear, and twist it off. Like this. Peeeeaaaarrrry."

I flip my head.

He gazes at me with no discernible reaction.

Amid this babble, I watch him closely, trying to ferret out his emotional state. I don't care whether he's angry or relieved; any feeling is fine. I want to know where he's at, but he's more guarded than I would like.

"Peeeeeerry," I repeat, my jaw drawing an outline to match my pronunciation.

"We were never in danger."

I remain silent until he looks me in the eye. "I told you, Perry, that I would not endanger you this weekend."

"But you were willing to let me *think* we were in danger, run me terrified around a prison island all night."

"Sure. That's different."

"Okay," he says slowly.

He's not okay with this, not one bit, but he's still trying to absorb it. I'm not sure how big or small this explosion will go. Although his face now shows he's rankled, the good still outweighs the bad: I'm not a serial killer and we're not going to prison. Well, other than to have sex.

"Why'd we spend the night hiding?"

I pause, again making sure we have eye contact. "Were you insane with terror last night?"

"Yes. A couple times."

"Did you cave in to that fear?"

"Almost."

"Yes or no question: did you get crushed by your own fear?"

"I felt—"

"Yes or no."

Perry is silent.

"Jerome walked right by us. Did you scream?"

"No."

"No. You did not."

Despite teetering on anger, his face shows surprised sorrow as his lips curve slightly downward. I'm not sure what's going on in his head or heart, but I can see a slight shift.

"You blasted your nuts out. Afterwards in the Roman safe house, you told me that when you came you swore you could see that jizz splatter as neon green."

Perry stares hard at me, searching for answers.

"Do you love last night even more right now? If you don't want to give me the satisfaction of an answer, fine. But forget being mad at me for a split second and don't lie to yourself. A trained professional knew we were hiding on the island, and he never caught us. You spent the night on Alcatraz, spying on a man *with a gun*, and even though he would not have killed us or turned us in, you didn't know that. Your courage last night was real."

He says, "I stood up that one time."

"Pear, you could have given us away three dozen times, but you didn't. You kept it together. An armed professional knew we were here and never saw us."

His face wears a hard-to-describe expression, something like angry surprise. I love the in-between looks, irritated wonder, humbled judgment, and the half regret. The words we have for describing someone's appearance are limited to the obvious compass directions:

happy, sad, mad, and afraid. It's hard to categorize the half expressions, the ones which reside in between. But this morning, I'm calling Perry mad by sadwest.

He remains quiet while his expression sinks in.

"Want the juice?"

"I'll have the Diet Coke."

"I'll go get it. You okay for a minute?"

He nods.

I want him to have a little space, so this is good. Not much space, but enough to process this. I wander to the beach, push over the turkey-sized stone, and dig up his can of Diet Coke. Cold enough.

I think Joy sleeps in strange places. We're always looking for her in shiny, happy, fun times, assuming that Joy prefers her twin brother, Pleasure, when she often hangs out with her somewhat stoic big sister, Strength. Joy is not always easy to recognize, dirt-smudged and sweating, brambles in her hair. I want to believe she sometimes wears a ski mask.

I return to find him sitting naked on the sleeping bag with an uncertain expression on his face, another one I can't quite name.

"I had sex in Alcatraz," he says. "At night."

"Yeah."

"In the Hole, and then fucked in a... a...."

"Grassy island hammock," I suggest, "which I call the Hammock."

I hand him the soda, and he pops it open.

"You made me memorize a fairy tale or you wouldn't have sex with me."

"Yeah," I say, wriggling my eyebrows.

He nods at me, confirming events, and then takes a sip. He looks at the city skyline.

Perry does not love the cost of this adventure, but his investor brain is going to run the numbers. The brain always insists on being the last committee member to cave. The brain likes to make speeches that usually begin with a familiar opening: "Ladies and gentlemen, I have been wronged."

At last he says, "Tell me about Jerome."

"No."

"No?" His voice is sharp.

"Ask me again after breakfast, and try a different tone."

Perry looks surprised by my refusal, but perhaps he's equally surprised by my lack of anger. Sure, he deserves an explanation. But I want him to hear me, and he's not ready to listen yet. Something in his inflection says he wants to command me as I have commanded him. That's not a helpful attitude for Saturday's events.

I finish setting up and offer him pastries from our meager buffet. We both put on last night's shirts so we're not completely naked.

After a few silent minutes munching his breakfast treats, Perry makes a few halting jokes about waking up on a beach with no hair care products. A moment or two later, he volunteers a story about where he buys fresh fruit on Saturday mornings in his neighborhood. He's coming around.

I say, "You like living there?"

"I'd rather live in Russian Hill. But it's too expensive for a single man to buy anything."

"Yeah, that's a beautiful neighborhood. Lots of stairs, though. But Lower Haight is nice, right by Duboce Park. There's that yummy breakfast place that just opened last year."

Perry cocks his head. "Can I ask you a question about the rat bites?"

"Sure."

Dammit.

"Why didn't you fight them off or something?"

"I did, eventually. But for a while I thought if I didn't do anything to them, they'd leave me alone."

Perry says nothing to this.

I say, "Does it freak you out, the rat bite story?"

"Don't flatter yourself. I have enough to worry about without fixating on your childhood scars. But that's about the only thing I know about you. And you're a mechanic, I guess. If that's true."

"It's true."

"You don't talk much about yourself, Vin."

I wait for a few seconds in silence. "I need a gratuitous horn blowing from the approaching boat to get me out of this conversation."

He half chuckles, but he watches me.

"Perry, this weekend is about you. Not me. I wouldn't… I don't talk much about me on a King Weekend, nor do I answer many questions about the weekend itself. Save yourself some time and don't bother asking. I'm not trying to hide, but I would rather stay focused on having fun with you. Stay in the moment."

He half nods. Half resists.

"I train myself to think a certain way. All last night, I was like, 'It's the security guard, it's the nameless security guard.' I've been thinking that way about the Alcatraz guards for years, even after we became friends. It's how I do this. When I recall their names or how well I know them, I get sloppy."

The mournful horn signals the first tour boat's arrival, and we both laugh.

I say, "A little late, but thank you."

I imagine the popcorn-snarfing seagulls escorting another batch of Alcatraz tourists down the gangplank.

Perry leans over and kisses me, a slow wet kiss that says he still wants to play.

"Nice," I say, licking my lips. "A much better wake-up than Jerome kicking our feet."

This is good.

He lets me feed him a slice of pear, a test to see how our intimacy weathered the latest turn of events.

"Will you please tell me why they call you the Human Ghost?"

"First let's pack up. Then ghost stories."

It doesn't take long for either of us to dress. Once the sleeping bag attaches to the frame and our shoes are tied, we lie facing the ocean on raised elbows, me behind him. Perry's face lights up when I produce a small container of raspberries on the earth in front of him; he likes raspberries. I devour my Nut Roll in a few bites. I forget how good these things are.

He rolls over to face me. If Perry has softened further toward me, I will make this a kissing story.

Kissing is such a surreal way to interact. You press your squishiest part to his and read the connection in a dozen ways: the level of affection, the warmth of feeling, the need to dominate, the ability to explore, and various shades of hesitancy. All that communication from such a slender little strip of flesh.

I kiss him, slow, wet kisses, to reacquaint his lips and mine. I want these drawn-out kisses to communicate "I am here with you. This is still our island. Even as the prison repopulates for the day, I am still on an island alone with you."

He says, "My breath feels like oysters. I don't suppose you brought a toothbrush."

"Two. Let's wait until the ferry back to San Francisco. But you taste fine."

I chew his bottom lip and pull back slowly, stretching his lip in my grasp. With my right hand, I massage his jawline, an erotic spot uncovered last night. He purrs when my fingers trace him, his entire clothed body pressing into mine, and we kiss with long, sensual strokes for a few minutes before I finally release him.

"Is there a kissing king?" he says.

"Not yet."

We kiss again, deep, parted tangles that reveal Perry's attempt to be okay with all this. I still feel resistance, though the fact that he's making out with me suggests he's working through his feeling manipulated. Definitely no need for kissing lessons with Perry.

In the middle of a particularly luscious kiss, I pull away as if nothing significant is happening.

"I started camping on Alcatraz just after I turned twenty-two."

"And you're thirty-one."

"Yes. Jerome and I met by mistake during my second year. Jerome twisted his ankle outside and decided to keep it elevated until morning. I'd been hiding in a second tier cell and assumed that he left the prison by some door I did not know about. I eventually fell asleep."

He nods.

"The next morning, I woke up early. After listening for random noise and hearing none, I walked out of my room. I yawned big, groaned. Stretched out. I put my arms over the railing, looking around and waking up. A minute later, Jerome hobbled around the corner. He had heard noise where there should have been none. To say that we were both fairly surprised is an understatement."

Perry chuckles.

"He limped to the front door to trap me inside, and then he called it in. Once I saw he couldn't actually chase me, I quickly gathered my things but didn't feel all that threatened. The first ferry brought three extra security guards and a boatload of tourists. Apparently, they didn't let the first group inside for thirty minutes. Nobody knew I had spent the previous year creating ways in and out of the prison, rigging doors and whatnot. I would never spend the night inside Alcatraz with only one exit. I have four entrances and exits, including one very dangerous way that I prefer not to use."

"They've never been discovered?"

"I used to have five ways. Three years ago, an engineer on vacation noticed one of the exterior door's hinges were slightly different from other exterior doors. He reported it. Of course, it didn't take long for the staff to figure out that the door hinges had been deliberately refitted and scuffed to look aged. But the night guards revealed nothing when told to 'keep an eye out' because by then, we were buds."

"I take it nobody caught you when you were twenty-two?"

"No. For years, I wore an Alcatraz T-shirt the mornings after a sleepover. That particular morning, they searched the prison but could not find any suspicious guest. All day, they scanned tickets trying to find me. But everyone who reboarded the ferry owned the appropriate ticket. I left around noon."

"What about your ticket?"

"I always buy tickets for several days in a row and keep them with me. Plus, when I left that morning, I held hands with this cool rebel chick from Indiana. I told her I needed cover, and she thought it would be fun. They were looking for a lone guy. Which reminds me."

I extricate myself and drag my knapsack over, finding today's tickets in a side pocket and ripping them in half. "Take this."

Perry does as he is asked, shaking his head. "Why bother?"

"Jerome won't turn us in. But if somebody observant notices that we weren't on the first boat, they might. Jerome would be forced to arrest us, because I couldn't let him lose his job. Actually, right now we're in more danger than we were last night."

He looks at me with renewed alarm.

Good. Tease out more resistance.

"Odds are slim anything will happen, but I always wait for the second boat. I don't want to put any of the guys in an awkward position."

"How did you get to be friends with them?"

"That took years. The morning Jerome and I met, they found my second floor cell where I'd wiped the dust from every surface in the room. I left behind my sleeping bag because I couldn't risk being the only guy on Alcatraz carrying camping equipment. When Jerome hobbled to the front door to lock me in, I wrote a note that said 'SORRY. DIDN'T MEAN TO SCARE YOU THIS MORNING.'"

"You're polite to some people."

"It's true. I *am* polite."

He says, "To *some* people."

"I'm going to ignore that," I say in a hurt voice. "Years later, I learned that in an emergency staff meeting that week, Jerome described me. Another guard, someone who no longer works here, reported that earlier that year he had come across a midnight figure, same general description, staring at the San Francisco skyline. But the figure seemed to vanish as the guard drew near. He never mentioned this to anyone because he wasn't sure what he saw. Maybe a ghost?"

I pause and say, "With that other guard, I didn't just 'disappear'. I backed into the shadows and then ran my ass off, heart pounding against my ribs for like two hours. I spent the night hiding in the big rocks on the north shore, right by the water, freezing to death. I was sloppy that first year."

"And they called you the Human Ghost. And now you're all buddy-buddy with these guys."

"The nickname didn't come until later. For the next few years they regularly compared observations. One night, Howie noticed three smashed beer bottles, and then later that same night, the broken glass had been cleaned up. A year later, I watched another guard discover my secret campsite. By then they had started hunting for me, looking in spots not normally on patrol. I was forced to abandon my chocolate croissants and yet another sleeping bag. They were seriously pissing me off."

"How long did this go on?"

"Few years. When I was twenty-six, they made contact."

I kiss him, and although he responds, his lips betray he is distracted.

Perry's eyes are open when we separate. "We have San Francisco urban legends, you know. Friend of a friend claims to have spent the night out here, wandering around. It's always bullshit."

I nod and lean in. He opens his lips in anticipation, but instead of kissing him, I speak into his open mouth. *"Perry, you're the urban legend."*

His entire body jolts.

We kiss with more passion for a moment, until he pulls away.

"Why Alcatraz?"

I feel as though I'm betraying a big secret, though the secret is mine to share. Don't stop now.

I take a deep breath.

"When I was twenty-one, my older brother adopted me. We adopted each other, actually. Malcolm was forty-one and already had a brother who died in prison, so I now had two older brothers. I wanted to understand him better, the one who died. I tried to find a prison where I could spend a week or two locked up, to sleep every night in a cage. I could have gotten myself arrested, I suppose, but by the time I turned twenty-two, I was trying to turn myself around, become someone better."

Perry touches my face.

"I came to the only prison I could think of that still had vacancy."

That wasn't so bad. I feel okay.

"How did they catch you? How long have you been bringing Nut Rolls?"

"Those first few years, they compared notes, kept a log. They were angry; they felt it was a fuck-you to their profession, and to them personally. But they also liked to guess about it and eventually joked about it. They developed theories about me, and they started calling me the Human Ghost.

"I never disturbed the bird sanctuary, as far as they could tell, and they appreciated that. They had set up little traps to see if I took shortcuts. While they never caught me or could predict my next arrival, they came to accept that some nights they were simply not alone on the island."

Perry looks at me carefully.

Why did I fear telling him? Did I suppose he would laugh? When I told him about the rat bites in the art gallery, his face transformed right away from disgust to sorrow. Of course he would respond to my ghost story with compassion. I may not be good at many things, but I am very good at finding kings.

"The guards eventually agreed that if any of them ever felt the Human Ghost was on the island during a patrol, they would offer him a beer. Sit down and, no hassles, find out the score. Promise no arrest, no retribution. They kept a six pack of beer in the employee fridge for that purpose.

"One night while I chased him, Jerome knew something was different. He kept yelling, '*I know you're here tonight. Come out and have a beer with me.*' Throughout the night, he would spontaneously yell out stuff like '*No arrests. We just want to talk to you.*'"

Perry says, "No way."

"Scared the shit out of me. Half the night he walked around yelling at the wind. The other guards always tease Jerome that he 'got that vibe' half the time he patrolled, but honestly, he is a legend for making this impossible contact."

Perry shivers.

I suggest, "Let's sit up. People are on the island. In case someone gets the idea to take a look over the stone wall, we don't want to appear as though we've been here long. We're well hidden, but still."

"Last night, did you know it was Jerome?"

"After our first encounter, yeah. But I always think of him as 'the guard' to keep me attentive. Also, it's more fun that way."

"You already explained that."

"Yeah, I'm deliberately repeating it. I'm telling you that it's pointless to ask me about the next part of the weekend because I try not to think about it until we're ready for it."

"Fine. But that's fucked up, by the way."

"You're probably right."

He smiles anyway.

We kiss.

"The night Jerome called out to me, I could hear his invitation, but I didn't trust him. He repeated his offer from several spots on the island, leaving unopened beer cans on different benches. While he patrolled inside, I left a note under one can which began, 'I INTEND NO DISRESPECT TO THE PRISON OR STAFF'. The rest of my letter, written while I chased him that night, suggested leaving future correspondence under a specified rock in a plastic baggie and that it might take half a year before my next reply, depending on the price of airline tickets."

Perry makes a sound, more huff than laugh.

"For the next three years, we became Alcatraz pen pals, leaving notes for each other under that rock. I vacationed here more frequently, just to pick up my mail. We joked back and forth. I asked them to change my sheets; they left a pair of handcuffs under the rock and teased me to turn myself in. They would dare me to step out and say hello some night. In return, I offered critiques of their patrol style and asked them for book recommendations. Once, in that second tier cell I liked to use, they left me a pillow with two mints on it. They were trying to make me laugh, make some noise."

Perry smiles, but not quite the happy smile. This one is softer, more of an "I hear you." It hurts a little, this smile.

"Two years ago, Howie found a six pack of cold beer on a bench. He sat down and opened a can. After he sipped more than half its contents, I emerged from the bushes. Now we have an understanding. A full beer can on the Charlie Brown wall means 'I'm on the island tonight.'"

"I didn't see any beer."

"You were napping when I put it out. Plus, Wednesday I told Howie that I'd definitely come Friday night, possibly with a guest. I gave him written instructions and asked whoever worked last night to wake us in the Hammock. I also mentioned that if Jerome didn't bring back an empty knapsack, I'd chuck his damn Nut Rolls into the ocean."

Perry squints at me, creating something between a frown and a question.

"I shouldn't have to buy a new knapsack each time. He's got like four of them now."

When we kiss, Perry puts more energy in it.

He says, "I'm getting hard."

I get to my knees. "Save that boner for later. We should go sit on the Charlie Brown wall."

"Boner? Are you twelve?"

We stand, shake ourselves out, the ocean roaring at our side. I feel the wet mist as if for the first time this morning, though it sprayed us all night. I think the ocean approves of gushing displays of erotic affection.

He groans as he stretches and says, "My legs are sore. Actually, a lot of me is sore."

"All that crouching."

He smiles. "Really? Is that why my ass is sore?"

We kiss again, standing close and fingers intertwined, morning lovers preparing to depart for work. Perry bumps his forehead into mine and leans in, our heads touching, our breath mingling.

After a long minute or two of breathing each other, I pry us apart. I pick up our remaining gear. We survey the space and remove any final traces of our presence. I collect the unused condoms. Holding hands, we climb the limestone blocks that have become our front sidewalk. I peek over the top of the wall and seeing no one nearby, scramble up. I offer Perry my hand and he takes it, looks around as I did, and then edges himself next to me, facing the bay.

We sit. We stare.

Our Alcatraz trip is over.

I do not enjoy admitting an awkward truth, that the Alcatraz guards are the closest thing I have to actual friends. Maybe Perry understands. Maybe he sees more of the Human Ghost than I suspect.

He says in a low voice, "I don't think anybody saw us."

Say it, Vin. Tell him the rest.

"During our pen pal stage, I wrote about my two older brothers, and specifically a few details about the one who died in prison. Last year, Jerome felt I deserved some acknowledgement, so in my upstairs cell, next to the sink, he used a pen knife to scratch out in capital letters, 'THANK YOU, LITTLE BROTHER'. When I saw the words on my next trip, I bawled my eyes out. My adopted brother may not have scratched out the words himself, but the message felt as though it came from him."

He squeezes my hand. After a pause, he says, "This is weirder than anything from the audio tour, Vin."

Another horn signals the second boat's arrival. It must be seven thirty. We should make it to breakfast by nine. We're good on time.

We watch the sky, the sea, and the city, our legs dangling as they dangled yesterday afternoon. I try to think Charlie Brown-like thoughts, to get to that Charlie Brown space in my head, where life's disappointments still feel fresh and not quite so expected. I do wonder how Sherman grew up.

Perry doesn't say much. I suppose he's drinking in the previous night, the chase, the story of the Human Ghost. He unwraps his Nut

Roll and takes a few meager bites but stops. I don't think he's impressed. Maybe it's just a Midwestern thing.

I shouldn't have eaten mine right away. Damn you, Jerome. Why do I only crave them when I'm away from Minnesota?

"May I have a bite of your candy bar?" I say, closer to whining than I intended.

"Technically," Perry says, handing it to me, "it's not a candy bar."

I am forgiven.

SEVEN

ONCE we dock and clomp down the soggy Astroturfed walkways, Perry announces in a quiet breath that he wants to stop by his place and shower.

"Later. Breakfast first."

"We ate breakfast." He speaks his quiet words into my ear, perhaps still shocked that we have somehow escaped Alcatraz without retribution.

"Continental breakfast doesn't count. I need eggs. Bacon."

He says nothing.

"Plus, we skipped dinner last night, so we earned a second breakfast today. I think we both agree that we should have gotten those hot dogs, but I thought once you found out we were spending the night, you might vomit, so I didn't press the issue."

Perry says nothing.

I think we reached the end of the hot dog joke. Somehow, it doesn't fly today. Yesterday was yesterday.

Perry glances around us to see who might have overheard my casual tone. Once we're free of the tightly packed crowd, he lingers a foot behind me, following as he did last night on the island.

As we pass the last of the Alcatraz employees and cross onto familiar city sidewalks, I swear Perry shudders with relief; the spell is broken. We have returned from a foreign land, an altered space of rock and earth, wasted lives and lonely deaths. We braved the night on a mystery island that he had forgotten to notice anymore, this jaded San Franciscan.

We return to concrete and metal, honking cars and blaring car radios. Irritated locals jog past us down the wide sidewalk, dodging clumsy, slow-moving tourists. I hear the distant sea lions bray on Fisherman's Wharf.

I took a king to Alcatraz.

I'll get excited about that later. In the meantime, I have to remain on guard against over-romanticizing it. Even though it meant the world to me, Perry doesn't have to feel the same way. No Billy shit today, either. I worked that out of me last night. I'm good now.

At my insistence, we hop a crowded streetcar, the heavily populated F train. I am eager for a sardine-like trolley car experience, and we get that, including a forty-something woman who overapplied her favorite perfume. Wow, that shit is strong.

Perry's grumbling suggests he is not pleased. "We could have taken a cab. Or any other line to the Embarca—"

He stops when he sees my moronic grin.

After a few pointless questions about our breakfast destination, what happens after that, Perry watches me from the corner of his eye. As the trolley lurches forward, I pretend to stumble off balance, driving my hips into his. He smiles with a funny shyness as if this somehow revealed our sex life to our fellow bus mates. As we bounce along downtown, bumping into each other repeatedly, Perry angles his head next to mine and says quietly, "How long did you fuck me?"

"Don't know. I fell asleep."

Perry face sparks into annoyance. "I haven't had many guys actually fall asleep while having sex with me."

The streetcar screeches, so when I speak in a normal tone right into his ear, it's audible only to him. "That's too bad. I felt lucky to fall asleep inside such an amazing man. The experience was completely beautiful and full of love."

Perry pulls back, cautious and surprised, checking to see if I'm mocking him.

I'm not.

His eyes gradually soften, melting in recognition, until he finally sees me again, both of us silently acknowledging his deeper trust. I cannot know his thoughts, but I see the subtle shift as the tension in his face relaxes.

He puts his head on my shoulder—an extremely public gesture—and I understand that this affection means something. It was not his brain's idea to cuddle me this way. Some other power stirs now. Still, I wouldn't claim surprise if Perry's brain is seeking reasons to ditch me.

Breakfast could be that reason.

I hope he likes bacon.

HALF an hour later, as we wander up Polk Street, Perry does not mask his disappointment.

The Tenderloin neighborhood boasts transgender hookers and slow-driving johns, an army of teenage junkies, and a few generations of immigrants who have gone ahead and given up on the American dream. Of course, the Tenderloin also boasts great bookstores and awesome noodle shops. Dirty-windowed bakeries hide killer bungeoppang pastries next to tarot card parlors with dusty curtains, secrets of the future totally worth exploring.

But in the Tenderloin, you step over more sidewalk urine than in other parts of San Francisco. Or step around someone actually pissing. The artist who painted this part of town mixed grime into the colors, experimenting with a filmy veneer that does not quite work in the final composition. Still, the Tenderloin is Alcatraz on parole, which is why I feel at home here.

He says, "I know better areas for breakfast. You should let me take you to this place called the Front Porch in Upper Haight. Southern gravy hash browns, Vin. You'd like them."

"I do like hash browns."

"They're fantastic."

I rub my belly. "But if I'm eating at the Front Porch, I get their cheese grits."

I catch exasperated surprise in his reaction before he rubs his eye socket with the palm of his hand. He shouldn't be surprised; it's a popular restaurant.

We maneuver around discarded takeout Styrofoam, various chunky sidewalk splatters, and sure enough, fresh, steaming pee. Perry skillfully avoids panhandlers, waving them aside as he presses me for more details on my Alcatraz nights. Suddenly, we arrive at the breakfast spot I selected.

He doesn't seem to mind at first, showing no strong divergence from his general disdain until we continue right past the kitchen-side entrance and head down the long line of waiting patrons. This place is also popular for Saturday morning breakfast.

"Where are we going? Vin? No, Vin. *No.*"

I lead us around the block's corner and he sputters; I keep walking until we reach the end of the line and I make myself part of it.

He says, "We're going to *volunteer* here, right? I mean, we're going to do this king thing and serve homeless people breakfast or something, right? C'mon."

I grin and say, "We're lucky. It's Scrambled Egg Saturday, which only happens twice a month."

St. Anne's is one of those stubborn parishes that refuse to give up on the Tenderloin and its forgotten inhabitants. Their worship space smells like the Vietnamese restaurant below. Someone must have obtained permission to convert this small adjoining parking lot into a makeshift cafeteria, for a few hours at least. Wednesdays they serve dinner off card tables in Hemlock Alley. I still can't believe they serve dinner out of an alley named *Hemlock.*

"Get this. On Wednesday nights, this parish serves free dinner off a cardboard table in Hemlock alley. Would you feel nervous eating soup from Hemlock Alley?"

He looks away. "I avoid eating soup out of most alleys, Vin."

"Yeah," I say.

I hoped for rain this morning, some delicious drizzle from gray, deflated clouds, but the morning is sunny and clear. You can never count on San Francisco weather.

He turns back to me and says, "We can't do this."

"Sure we can."

"It's disrespectful," he says, his voice quivering, an anger vibration with a hint of distress. His face suggests that disrespecting our fellow diners is not his primary concern.

"I have money," he whispers.

I cup my hand and whisper back, "So do I."

"It's humiliating."

"Yeah," I say with a sigh, "I know."

"We…," he pleads and then stops.

There's simply no arguing with my moronic grin. You can't fight it.

"We meet the dress code, Perry; we're appropriately scruffy. Look, those two are dressed better than us. So is that woman too. And them. Don't sweat it; we won't stand out."

Young couples in long coats hold hands and inch forward in quiet conversation, and two young women near us fix their makeup, using each other as mirrors. True, some do mutter loudly, mostly to themselves, but who doesn't some mornings?

"You will survive this," I say, softly nudging into him and staying there, letting him feel my warmth. I caress the side of his face with the backs of my fingers. "You survived Alcatraz."

He huffs and jerks his head away.

"I know why you're doing this," Perry says, watching a woman stagger into line behind us.

I clap my arm around his shoulders, turning him to face front as the line moves forward, an undulating centipede.

He says, "We're going to learn how to be nice to homeless people. How they're just like you and me."

"Yeah, you're probably right."

"You have to understand," Perry says, attempting a casual tone, "when you actually live in San Francisco, it's different. To outsiders, we seem harsh and cold. But it's not easy, you know, with so many of them, continual demanding—money, money, money—and then they swear at you if you don't give something. Sometimes they follow and harass you."

I say nothing but watch his face while he watches mine.

He says, "I'll give money to someone sometime, and we end up having a nice connection for a second. But I'd end up broke if I gave money to every person who asked me."

"What's your limit to give on a daily basis?"

"I don't know. I don't have one. I'm saying that it's not about the money; it's how many there are of them, how often they ask. Even stopping to say no to every single one is impossible."

"Sounds overwhelming."

"Yeah," he says. "It doesn't mean I hate humanity, or I don't have love in my heart. Actually, it makes me sad."

"I get that."

Perry looks at me skeptically. He starts to explain it another way, but I haven't disagreed with him, so he pauses and his mouth snaps shut.

He says, "You didn't give money to every homeless person we passed this morning."

I nod. "True."

He's quiet for a moment.

He tries a different approach. "I'm an invest—"

"Do investment bankers eat scrambled eggs?" My voice drips sweetness.

"What if a bank colleague or a client passes us, Vin? What the hell am I supposed to say?"

"How about this: I always eat breakfast here after a night of wild sex on Alcatraz."

Perry draws a sharp breath. "Don't talk so damn loud, Vin."

We peer around, but nobody pays us attention except for the gray-haired woman behind us who seems extremely interested in our conversation. Perhaps she's just interested in any conversation. I would talk to her if I weren't busy managing Perry.

I take his hand, and although I feel reluctance at first, he lets me hold it.

We advance.

He says, "I picked up two sticks last night, sharp ones, while you weren't looking."

I say nothing.

He says, "I decided to gouge out your eyes if you tried to kill me."

"I bet you wish you had those sticks right now."

He turns an almost wistful smile to me, still uncomfortable, but he squeezes my hand.

He says, "I'm sorry. I don't know why I told you that."

"You're pissed at me, and it's easier to tell me about the sticks than say 'I'm angry'."

Perry says nothing.

"Do you have a favorite letter in the alphabet, Pear?"

He does not answer.

Tenderloin residents bustle past us, going about their Saturday morning errands. I notice that whenever a pedestrian pays too much attention to our lineup, Perry turns his back. I start wishing good morning to everyone who passes us. After a few of these salutations, I turn him to face them.

"Vin," he says with a hint of warning.

"Good morning," I call cheerfully to a couple of college-age men.

"Hey," says one in surprise.

Perry nods at them, another minute surrender.

At least I'm not thinking about Billy today. Or *vigor*.

Twenty minutes later, we reach the parking lot food tables.

"I'll do this," he says, "but honestly, don't expect me to go hugging every homeless person I meet because we ate breakfast here. On Monday, twenty people will ask me for money on my way to work, and I won't have time to ask them all their names."

"Noted. No love fest."

The woman behind us, Filipino I'm guessing, has listened carefully to our entire conversation and now chimes in, "I hate them too. They smell terrible."

When it's our turn, we present our Styrofoam trays and are rewarded with two ice cream scoops of watery eggs, breakfast potatoes adorned with greasy onions, a piece of toast lightly skinned with red jam, and a substance performing a remarkable impression of bacon.

Perry holds his tray cautiously, as if the food might attack him. "I'm not eating the bacon."

I say, "Okay, you betcha."

"I hated *Fargo*," Perry says.

"Tuesday you said you liked it."

He says, "Tuesday, I was flirting."

Okay, no *Fargo* references. I don't know if he actually hates it or he's expressing his discontent another way, but either way, message received. He's pissed.

Two rows of folding tables, the ugly brown ones you might see in a high school cafeteria, stretch the length of the parking lot. I guide us toward a space already claimed by six people, but I spy room for the two of us somewhere in the middle. I motion for him to sit opposite me.

They make room on our arrival, a few with reluctant grumbles. Our Filipino friend was on to something regarding smell. I will admit that it's hard to focus on breakfast when new odors, largely unidentifiable, make themselves known each time one of our neighbors shifts position.

He says, "This place isn't helping the new attitude."

"Compute returns in your head. Think of securities margin trading and the percentages at which the bank sells point margins."

Perry scowls. "That doesn't even make any sense."

"He's an investment banker," I explain to the man next to me.

"Hey, Banker," the man says without looking up.

"Vin. Be cool."

"But outside you were so *proud*."

Perry looks at me, a sullen pleading. In turn, I drop my gaze pointedly to his bacon.

He picks up one floppy end of the almost-bacon and puts it in his mouth.

"Good man," I say with a wink. "I knew investment brokers ate breakfast."

"Banker," he says.

Seeing my suppressed smile, he shakes his head and chews. Breakfast has gone easier than I expected; we have successfully navigated another rocky passage.

"This tastes like shoe."

"Versace or Jimmy Choo?" asks the woman to Perry's left.

She uses this unanswered question as the opportunity to introduce herself as Francine and then launches into politics. She has decided to vote Republican because she is *sick of all the fucking shit going on.* After Francine's short rant, which draws the attention of three nearby tables, we say hello to another neighbor, who politely explains she's not in the mood for conversation this morning. One man leaves our table.

Perry looks at me and holds up his finger to an invisible maître d'. He mimes the words, "Check, please."

He grins at me, the first authentic cheer I have seen since we got in line. He also settles in, swallowing his scrambled eggs and forking the potato chunks. Now that he's no longer fighting breakfast, I lean across to him. Francine leans in closer too.

"Hey, Francine," I say, motioning her to lean closer. I stand and meet her halfway across the table. "For ten bucks, let me talk to my buddy in private."

She says, "For twenty, I'll leave."

"Stay," I say and slip her a ten.

She takes the money, peers around coolly, and resumes digging in her egg mound, perhaps searching for something. I see that her fingers are red and scabbed over near the nails. She must gnaw them.

"She's going to use it for drugs," Perry says and doesn't bother to lower his voice. "She's high right now."

"Maybe so," I say, considering this and taking a bite of toast.

"You suck at arguing."

"You're probably right."

"It's not as much fun as you think, Vin, trying to have a normal conversation with you. You smile and grin a lot, but you're an asshole too."

"You're probably right."

He looks at me with exasperation.

I peer into the distance. "I wonder what King Aabee did when he lived among the Lost Kings and Queens. Would he give them money or recognize it as foolishness, given how they would spend it?"

Perry's body jerks to a new alertness. Good. He won't make eye contact or admit he's interested, but his body betrays him.

"Did you forget about King Aabee? His courageous quest? Perhaps you would be so kind as to tell me what you remember."

Perry reddens at first, but he repeats details back and does awfully well: the Found Kings meeting at dawn, kings out exploring, then forgetting, King Aabee living among the Lost Kings for ten years. Big party with his favorite foods. King Aabee saying, "All my love," and then the Found Kings yelling some things.

"Remember the king," I say, right into his eyes, and his body responds, a jolt of electricity passing through him, visible to anyone watching. Surprise flickers across his face, leaving him in a slight daze, and I would bet money that at this moment he remembers getting fucked on Alcatraz.

I jab my plastic fork at him. "That's what they yelled as King Aabee rode away."

Perry makes a few furtive eye gestures, to see who hears, who listens. He made that face at the art gallery after Big Secret.

"Aabee lived among the Lost Kings, cleaning sewers, parking cars, filing useless reports for bureaucracies. He might fold industrial laundry one month and collect recycled cans the next. No job was beneath him. At first, the Lost Kings celebrated their victory in acquiring 'a Found', and lorded their power over him. But within six or seven months, they forgot who he was or why he had come. They hated him instinctively, but for reasons they could not articulate, so they blamed his skin color or his long slender fingers. They hated his white shirts with the silver stitching, and they hated his agreeable smile because unconsciously, it reminded them he walked among them by his choice. King Aabee could have returned to the Found Kings at any time, but he agreed to stay for ten years, so he kept his word, longing for home the entire time."

"Well, that seems rather pointless," Perry says, turning to Francine.

She says, "Don't involve me, unless for another ten dollars...."

I say, "Don't take his side, Francine, or you have to give back that money."

She zips her lips, turning the key with her fingers.

Perry crosses his arms. "Way to go; you bribed a Republican. Like that was any big chore."

"Hey, there are Republican Found Kings," I say, hardening my features. I stab my fork at him again. "But this isn't about politics. It's personal."

Perry dismisses my intensity with a wave of his fork and stabs more eggs.

"That imitation bacon was gross, by the way. I still taste it."

"So," I continue, chomping my fake bacon for emphasis, "the Lost Kings steered clear of him when they could, and gave him shitty assignments when they could not. Some say it is challenging to live among the Lost Ones if you do not think like they do."

Perry glances around the parking lot cafeteria. It's completely full.

"He didn't forget anything?"

"No. He remembered his kingship, his joys, and his love. Of course, he had help from this luscious French woman with remarkable sensuality. Her cherry-tipped breasts hung pendulously, thick, swollen—"

"Okay," Perry says, leaning across the table and lowering his voice. "Spare me the sex details because I remember how descriptive you were about the kings who made love under the stars. Ease up while I'm trying to swallow these greasy potatoes."

"But there's this great part where they're sixty-nineing. With his slender fingers, he would massage her tight—"

"*C'mon.*" His eyes blaze. "Seriously, Vin."

"Okay, okay."

That went well. I adopt a meek expression and continue.

"Sometimes Aabee would help a Lost King remember himself, and more than one man, in fact, returned to the Found Kings, crossing joyfully at dawn through the eastern gates. That man would announce, 'King Aabee sent me.' The Found Kings rejoiced because their one true king had remembered himself and come home. During the homecoming celebration, they would also beg for any news regarding Aabee. Details were slim and sometimes months, even years, passed with no updates. The newly returned kings couldn't describe him well; they heard him more than they had seen him.

"Aabee's gift, you see, was playing the flute—well, a flute-like instrument from his native Somalia. Hard to describe the actual sound, though. Sometimes it produced more whistle and colored air than actual music, but some described it as four people humming the same tune in perfect harmony. But technically, it wasn't a flute."

I liked Perry's and my little Nut Roll joke from this morning, and it won't hurt to have our personal mojo bring alive King Aabee's tale. This might be quite nice, especially since I struck out on *Fargo* references. C'mon. How could you not like Marge Gunderson?

Perry puts down his fork.

"I suggest you finish your eggs."

"For the record, I'm not twelve, Vin."

"You would not believe the greasy, filthy sex between King Aabee and the cherry-nippled French—"

"I'm eating," Perry says, stabbing with vehemence. "Just stop."

We exchange snarky glances, trying not to smile at each other. I lick my lips at him and mouth the words, "I sucked your cock last night."

He chokes on the eggs, laughing a little, and I waggle my eyebrows, horn dog that I am. I like the word *waggle* better than *wiggle*. I think *waggle* sounds more like a dog. It suits me.

"Everyone experienced the sound created by Aabee's flute differently. One king said that when Aabee played, he heard mint. Others argued that Aabee's music was more of a sensation, the feeling of cold dew plinking off a pine branch onto your bare arm. Others heard shell-crusted mermaids singing the old songs. Nobody could agree."

Perry scrapes the plate with his fork, making sure I can see him pick up every last bit.

"The Lost Kings couldn't understand the strange music. Why did it pour out of the sewers? Why did it sound like the tickle of your feet in warm sand or a song your mother used to sing? Back in the kingdom, he was known as King Aabee, the Strange Musician."

"That doesn't sound flattering."

"Au contraire. Strange is an essential quality among the Found Kings. Have you heard of the Bear Walker? When the kings grow too serious, too wrapped up in some conflict, King Richard the Bear Walker stands up and lumbers across the room like a giant grizzly, swinging his arms and snapping his jaws. Every Found King follows his lead, walking and roaring like bears."

He smiles. "That's cute."

"*Cute?* Everyone realizes the Bear Walker is the single most important king; he changes everything when he stomps across the room. Bear walking softens hard feelings when people are angry and looking for a way to show it, and when nobody can accomplish a damn thing, bear walking hardens soft resolve. Acting that way is sometimes the only way to find your bearings. The Bear Walker is the one true king of the kingdom, the only hope."

"Yeah, how is that possible exactly? Everyone being the one true king?"

"Did you get my *bearings* pun in there?"

"Hilarious. I take it you're not going to answer my question."

I say, "You gonna finish that toast?"

He says, "I'd rather not."

Francine eyes the toast and me, eager to see what happens next.

"Sure about that?" I ask, picking it up and biting off a corner. "I'm not entirely sure when we get our next meal. Might be quite a while."

Perry's snatches it from my hand, pushing it into his mouth.

The dryness makes him wince.

"This is disgusting," he says, deliberately chewing with his mouth open. "I can't tell whether it's an actual berry flavor or it's just the flavor of red."

"What a coincidence. People said King Aabee's flute-like instrument sounded exactly like the flavor of red. Some gay kings insisted that his music sounded like cocksucking."

Francine begins muttering under her breath, ending with some choice phrases about gays that can no longer be considered "under her breath."

"Faggots," she says as she leaves the table. "Goddamn faggots."

Perry folds his fingers and puts his chin on top. "I warned you about those sexually graphic descriptions. Now you've alienated our only breakfast friend, a homophobic Republican on crack."

"The Lost Kings could not understand how Aabee held joyful songs inside him. He owned very little, no car, and never had much money. He lived in a crappy apartment, and for the first few years could not afford picture frames to hang photos of his beloved family."

"He needed an investment banker," Perry says and raises the last of his orange juice in salute.

"Yes, someone who specialized in the Pan-Asian market, for some of the best kings came from that part of the world."

Perry laughs.

I study him for a moment. We have both finished eating.

"Ready to go?"

He says, "Definitely."

"Okay. Let's leave. Like bears."

Before he can do anything but open his mouth, I growl and raise myself from the table, arms over my head, fingers twisted into giant claws. I thrash my head around in slow motion and roar.

Many look away. The overtly curious gaze coolly in my direction. They don't really give a fuck what's happening, but if a free show comes with breakfast, so be it.

I'm sure Perry thought breakfast could not get worse. But his face says I proved him wrong: it's worse. He silently begs me, but he already knows that pleading is pointless. I snarl loudly, but in neutral, waiting for him, until he stands and half growls. It's more of a moan. His hands hang above his head like mine, yet Perry appears to dangle from a clothesline, looking sick to his stomach.

Maybe it's the bacon.

Perry gives this latest challenge some effort, mimicking me some, but street theater is probably not one of his hobbies. I snarl and snap my teeth at him, and he tries to respond but it comes out more as a dental chair groan.

We stagger from the table.

"Get over here," I say in bear growl.

He quickly trots around the table to join me. Experience says that humiliation finds safety in close proximity. Roaring and attacking the air, we lug ourselves down the long high school table rows toward the center where the serving tables stand. Behind me, I drag the backpack frame and sleeping bag like a deer carcass.

Whenever I hear his roar taper off or sense he gives less than his best, I face him and fake an attack, forcing him to amp up his bear energy, so he quickly learns that to keep moving steadily toward the exit and keep me at bay, he must keep on floundering in the loudest and most dramatic behavior that he can muster.

"Bears," says a woman whose face I can't see. "Wait. One bear and one zombie bear."

A few feet later, one woman leans out to say, "Get clean. You can do it."

Perry stops and says, "I'm not—"

I outroar his explanation.

I catch some whispered laughter, more critiques of our performance, as we cross the makeshift cafeteria. Perry shuffles behind me. He's getting better, improving in small ways, swiping his bear arms with more energy. There's still a line edging out the entrance and onto the city sidewalk.

Shit, it's Billy! No, no it's not. It can't be. *Can't be.*

I roar louder, with some fear mixed in this time.

That guy looked exactly like Billy. What the fuck is going on?

Later, Vin. *Later.*

When we reach the serving tables, those waiting for food deliberately ignore us. They almost seem to protect the volunteer servers, but it's more likely they're huddling tighter to prevent us from cutting. I motion to Perry, and we shamble toward the last server, a raven-haired woman wearing a simple gold necklace. She dispenses toast.

Forget that guy who looked like Billy. *Forget him.*

In my best growl, I say, "We're bears."

She says, "Bears don't automatically get seconds. We're cooking more bacon, but I can't promise anything."

I roar at the top of my lungs, face to the sky, but she laughs. "Don't sass us, Mr. Bear."

I nod and drop a few crumpled twenties in front of her serving dish. "This is for feeding the bears."

"You sure you don't need this?"

I shake my head while bear muttering.

"Thank you," she says and takes the money. "You take care, Mr. Bear. You too, Bear Number Two."

Perry's clothesline claws still dangle above his head, and he doesn't respond to her, except to nod.

Donning the backpack frame and sleeping bag, I turn and stagger toward the street entrance; Perry does as well. When I bellow louder and stomp bigger, so does Perry, in imitation of my every move. I suddenly turn on him and swipe the air a few times, roaring in his face.

He jumps back, saying "Oh, hey," and then he swipes back, but with hesitation.

Right as we reach the front entrance, I say, "C'mon. The biggest one yet."

Watching each other, we both inhale deeply. I pretend that I'm going to do it with him, and even exhale big, but nothing comes out of my throat.

Perry thunders triumphantly, more explosive than I had anticipated.

He finishes in surprise, and the whole cafeteria stares at him.

Perry gapes at his audience.

We all watch each other in silence.

I snarl at them, baring my teeth, as I put a hand on his upper back and maneuver him toward the exit.

When we emerge into the city, Perry improves his bear walk for two or three feet, until I take his hand and turn him to me.

I kiss his lips, my thumb on his jawline. His lips are warm, and through my chest, I feel his heart pound faster than normal. When we finish, I put a few fingers on the back of his skull and tip him into me, our foreheads touching.

Perry says, "I tried to be a bear, Vin. I did try."

"Best. Bear. Ever."

He shrugs, a smallish lifting of his shoulders, actually. But standing in each other's space, we feel each gesture magnified, and I understand what this small gesture says about his vulnerability.

My goatee scratches the square of skin right in front of his ear, and I say, "King Richard the Bear Walker would have been proud of you."

His body tenses, and his face immediately follows suit; I feel his cheek contract—as if tears almost form, but promptly flee back to their place of origin. He unclenches immediately. I don't know if he noticed the Bear Walker shares the same name as his father. Maybe not. Something tells me he got the message anyway. I would guess Perry's brain is exhausted: so much wasted worry last night, confusion and misfiring, all the weekend's tension accruing interest. It's getting hard to tell whether Perry is being led by his head or heart.

I take his hand. "C'mon."

We're off again.

EIGHT

I CAN'T believe I saw a guy who looked exactly like Billy. Why does he keep showing up? I can't think about this right now. Later. I will give it some thought when there's a break.

Two blocks away, I steer us into a side alley. Puddles of bubbling liquid we trudge through might be stale beer or greasy dishwater runoff, dumped from any number of nearby restaurants. Up the alley, there's no mistaking the chunky liquid spray over there, but we're far enough away that we can't smell it. Near us, an older woman with frizzy black and gray hair has settled into a painted black door frame and sleeps through the midmorning light, undisturbed by the buses honking, pedestrians chattering, and every random crash or clang enveloping us. Halfway up the alley, I point to a white van parked ten feet away.

"We're gonna take this."

Perry stops. "No way. We're not stealing a van."

As he protests, I pull a keychain from a side pocket of the backpack. When I click it, the van's headlights flick on and off and it chirps.

After a few seconds, he exhales. "This is yours?"

"Rental."

Perry looks at me with amusement. "My first reaction was, 'How did Vin get the keys to that van he's going to steal?' What does that say about you, Vin?"

"Oh, please. You spent the night on Alcatraz too. Now you're an ex-con."

We both snicker and shove each other loosely, just fucking around.

"Did you do that intentionally? Act like we were gonna steal it?"

"Sorta."

"Asshole," he says, laughing.

I think he's delighted to call me an asshole. And what the hell? I deserve it.

We meet at the back of the van and lean in for a slow kiss.

I push him away. "You smell like bacon."

He says, "I'm fairly confident my breath smells *nothing* like bacon."

I open the back doors to stow the Alcatraz gear. Thick tarps cover half the back, concealing lumpy piles.

"What's under those?"

I shake my head as if I'm baffled.

"You're not going to answer that, are you?"

"Nope."

"I can't believe you're so secretive about all this."

I slam the doors closed and say, "I can't believe you're still asking me questions after I told you *twice* that I wouldn't tell you anything."

I head to the driver's side and climb in.

He hops in his side and says, "You are a total control freak."

"You're probably right."

"You can stop saying that; I get it."

"You're probably right."

"Hey, did King Aabee's flute ever sound like an investment banker's blood vessels bursting in his skull?" he asks. "Did his flute ever make that sound?"

"Technically, it wasn't a flute."

"I ate a bacon-shaped piece of shoe for you, Vin. You can answer a question or two without ruining your precious weekend."

"You're probably right."

"God, you're irritating."

"You're definitely right."

As I ease the van onto Polk Street, Perry relaxes again, sensing a reprieve. He's figuring out that sometimes we're in king story mode and perhaps other times it's just us, two buddies hanging out, learning bits and pieces of each other's lives.

He's wrong, of course; we're never out of king story mode, for I am always putting my love into him, listening, shaping the details of our weekend based on his responses, preparing him for the next hurdle and filling him up, stacking the deck in our favor. We are going to win this.

I chatter about my favorite parts of San Francisco, things I have eaten that tasted worse than the bacon, while plying him with subtle questions. I can't alter any of the big stuff this weekend, but I may tailor King Aabee's story to make sure it fits better. Perry is a foodie and asks me questions about San Francisco restaurants, places we both may have eaten.

We drive only a few minutes when I ask Perry to look sharp for street parking. It's not easy finding a spot for this big van. At the end of a long street, Perry spots Alcatraz, and he barks out a sharp laugh.

A moment later, he says, "I keep thinking about how we ran across that prison yard holding hands. That was cool."

Perry says this almost with sadness.

He reaches across the seat and takes my hand.

A lump comes to my throat. *My Alcatraz King.*

Checking the dashboard clock, I see that we have plenty of time. In fact, I pretend to miss a parking spot he points out, because we're ahead of schedule. I drive around the block, and when we return, the parking spot is gone. Good.

We finally park two blocks away from our next destination, so we have a little time to window shop on our way to the nondescript bakery. I announce to the baker that we're here to pick up a cake and give him my last name. It's a big cake, one of those massive sheet cakes with plywood underneath to keep it from crumpling under its own weight. I imagine it's the kind you get for a high school graduation party. I've never been to a high school graduation party, so really, I have no basis for that comparison. But if I had graduated high school, I would have celebrated with a cake this big.

Through the rectangular plastic lid, I delight in the finished product, thrilled by its kitschy perfection: blue frosting swirls of a gushy waterfall cascade down a green-frosted island, dumping into a sugary blue ocean. Our Hawaiian-themed cake sports plastic hula girls and plastic men with ukuleles. Perfect.

Across the frosted ocean, thick green letters shout "HAPPY 10TH BIRTHDAY." The second line reads "MARIE N. GRYPN."

"Is that Irish?" Perry asks.

"Korean," says the lady shopkeeper, punching the register buttons without making eye contact. "Grypn is common Korean name."

Her husband says something to her in Cantonese, and she responds to him in a few sharp words. She looks at us without smiling and presents me the total due.

Perry puzzles over the frosting while they count out my change and asks, "Who is this for?"

I say, "I'll explain in the van."

Our cake mistress inclines her head slightly to let us know we are done here. She speaks again to her husband, and he replies. I like their sharp tones with each other. He brushes something invisible off her shirt sleeve and she slaps his hand away, which makes him smile, and he looks me in the eye for a split second.

They hold the front door wide open, guide us halfway down the block because they worry our van is far away. They argue more in Chinese, and I love listening to their banter though I don't understand a word.

Her husband interrupts their conversation, pointing to warn us, "Sidewalk pee! Sidewalk pee!"

His wife shakes her head and walks back into the shop, continuing the conversation until the closing door cuts her off.

I feel hilarious, because this scene is comedy gold, like that 1980s San Francisco movie with Goldie Hawn where an enormous plate glass window is constantly threatened in an extended car chase scene. All around us, San Franciscans have to maneuver around our cake dance, and I chirp out apologies each time.

"So sorry," I say, using a stiff British accent.

"Quit it," Perry says with a big smile. "I'm not kidding, Vin. Don't make me laugh and drop this."

"Sworry. I'm sworry."

He laughs, so I have to continue.

"Apologies, mate," I offer to the next person. "G'day. Cheers."

"It's not even a good accent," Perry says, trying to hide his mirth.

"Your turn. Apologize with an accent. Any accent."

He apologizes in Spanish twice, and I switch to a Monty Python approach.

Once we gingerly deposit the cake into the back of the van, I grope under the tarps, never lifting them. Perry watches, amused and then pleased when my hands emerge with bungee cords. We fuss over the cake, secure it, hop in the front, and buckle up.

I explain that our destination is St. Anne's homeless shelter.

I say, "When I stopped by to find out about their Saturday breakfast hours, they were discussing a birthday party for this girl, Marie. They had already decided on a Hawaiian theme. She's particular about her name, I guess, because there's another homeless girl also named Marie, so she tells everyone she's 'Marie N'. Every Saturday afternoon, they offer computer training or something, and her mom goes. Marie N. has been advertising her upcoming birthday, so today, they're going to have a party. Didn't you see the "Happy Birthday" signs near the serving tables?"

He says, "No. I dunno, maybe."

"They hadn't taped them up; they were just sitting on the table. Didn't you see the green and pink plastic leis curled up into balls? A bunch of them."

"I was preoccupied. Why didn't you tell the serving ladies that we were coming back?"

I shoot him a smile. "It's a surprise. I like surprises."

"That so?" He pulls out his sunglasses from an inside coat pocket. "Hadn't noticed."

As we wind our way back through the streets toward St. Anne's, Perry softens even further to the whole breakfast affair, his bacon jokes freer, and he offers a few comments regarding Francine and other tablemates.

"I hope I spelled her last name right," I say, worried. "I usually print neatly, but I smeared the ink on the note I took. It could be wrong; the last name looks to me like it's missing a vowel."

We work out a plan of investigating the girl's name before she sees the cake and fixing the icing with a knife if necessary. Perry suggests, worst-case scenario, that we scrape her last name off the cake. After all, the part that matters is the "MARIE N."

Miracle of miracles, the alley parking spot we vacated a while ago remains available, so we ease right back in. I guess it's not that surprising in a grubby alley sporting dried vomit stains. Maybe it's not such a desirable parking spot.

I meet Perry in the back, where he opens the van doors and we pick sides.

"Don't go apologizing to people on the street," he warns me. "All your accents end up sounding messy British."

"You get that end out first, and I'll slam the door shut with my foot. I can kick it closed."

Perry looks at me quizzically but doesn't contradict me.

We ease the cake out, tossing a few admonishments back and forth like "Gently" and "Careful."

I ask, "Got it now? Got your arms under it?"

It's heavy and bulky, and Perry looks from me to the van door. He says, "We could set it on the bumper while you—"

I say, "Relax, I got it."

I kick the door closed with my foot and it slams shut. But the door bounces back open because I have slammed the wrong one first. Its impact propels my body away from the van, my arms falling low. Perry pushes the cake toward me, and I throw my arms up high to counterbalance, but it's too high, and by the time my other foot gets to the ground, the cake is already upside down, hurtling toward the pavement. We watch its disastrous final seconds in slow motion, unable to prevent the inevitable.

The impact doesn't sound like you'd think it would: a crinkling instead of a squish, the plastic lid crunching against blacktop like a plastic bumper in a car accident.

I hate the way they make cars now, plastic and—*goddamn it you moron, focus up! This is it!*

Perry's arms fling straight out, straight toward the ground where the cake splats, as if pointing out the disaster with a flourish. Electricity almost flies out his fingertips, he's so instantly furious.

I wait for a second to see if he makes eye contact with me, but he does not. He cannot. Instead he focuses his attention on the cake wreck.

When we cautiously turn it upright, our worst fears are confirmed: Hawaii exploded, leaving smears of green and blue earth everywhere. Ocean frosting spurted free during the explosion, neon blue splatting over the uneven pavement into a puddle of dirty water.

"Crap," I say, looking for survivors within the crumpled dome. "It's ruined."

His voice shakes as he says, "I told you."

"Yeah, you did. You did tell me."

He takes a few deep breaths as we stare at the island catastrophe.

He says, "We've got to go get another cake."

"Perry, they won't have time to remake this cake."

"Another cake. Smaller. They can print her name on another one. It doesn't have to be this one."

"Perry, there isn't time. We have to go."

"Why?"

"The next thing we're doing has a specific start time; we have to arrive on time."

He says, "I don't care. We'll make time. We'll go to a bakery that's closer. I'll pay for it."

I extract the plastic dome to see how much is salvageable. A chocolate earthquake split the island into five large chunks, ruining any hope of a unified land mass. Every ukulele player clearly choked on green frosting and drowned. It's demolished.

His voice shakes as he says again, "I'll pay for it."

"It was a surprise. She won't miss it because she never knew it was coming."

"No. We have to make time, Vin."

I wonder if he's surprised by his own rigidity on this point.

I try to sound humble. "We have to go, Perry."

He stands and at last looks into my eyes. The menace I see makes me realize I could get punched. This could become a face-punching situation, right now. If that is the case, I must give him full access. I owe him that.

"I should have listened to you, Perry."

After a few extra seconds and shallow breaths, Perry turns and walks away.

"I'm going home," he says over his shoulder.

"Wait."

He spins around suddenly. "*There's enough fucking time.* We get a cheap fucking cake and have someone squirt her name on it with some pink icing, Vin. There's enough time for that."

When I make no reply, he twists away.

"*Perry, wait.*"

He flips me off and then reaches the mouth of the alley, disappearing around a grime-colored building.

I look down to see my own hands shaking. This is it.

I broke him.

I've only got a minute to put the cake in the dumpster and set up for his return. Perry's yelling woke the sleeping doorway woman, and as soon as she sees me heading toward the dumpster, she protests in loud incoherent sentences. Soon the ruined paradise sits in her lap, and although I apologize for Hawaii's destruction yet again, she doesn't seem to mind.

"My name is Vin. What's yours?"

"Lisa," she says, licking frosting off her fingers.

"Happy 10th birthday, Lisa. Wait, you're not diabetic, are you? No? No, okay. Happy birthday."

He'll come back. He has to.

PERRY strides back into view, plowing toward me again with determination, just like yesterday on Pier 33. With vigor.

Dammit, let the word shit go! Get serious; this is big.

When he draws closer, his entire body reflects rage: trembling hands, the borderline hate in his eyes, his inflexible posture. The flicker of fire I saw in him on Alcatraz now blazes dangerously.

I stand near the front right wheel well, the passenger door wide open. While I'm feeling fairly confident I can influence him enough to stay, my heart beats faster to see him so ferocious. Don't get cocky, Vin. Show respect to this king as we navigate the third checkpoint.

"No, Vin. I'm not getting in. Gimme my stuff."

"Car keys and wallet are on the dashboard. Your change is in the billfold. You gave me thirty-seven cents last night on Alcatraz."

Perry, of course, must climb in the van to retrieve these items. But he remains in the alley, watching me cagily.

He says, "We should make time to get another cake."

I frown. "Weren't you embarrassed to be seen with these people an hour ago? Remember the bacon? How they smelled? Now you're upset because one of them isn't going to get a giant Hawaiian cake?"

"It's a *kid.*"

"True. A homeless kid who wasn't expecting a cake and doesn't know what she's not getting."

He fumes without words.

I step cautiously the few feet until I stand directly before him. My face is soft and sad. I want him to see someone besides the cake dropper, the Vin he befriended, the man weaving a story about King Aabee.

"I dropped the cake. I was seriously a dickhead not to listen to you because you called it right away. I'm sorry I fucked this up. It's my fault."

He stares hard, his eyes merciless, but he lets me put one hand on his shoulder. Even through his thick jacket, I feel his body tense, as if my very touch is abhorrent.

It hurts a little that he hates me.

"Forgive me, Perry."

I wonder sometimes why we don't have more words to express forgiveness. The words we use are so trite, so limited. How do you describe that first melting of a friend's face after a vicious fight, the moment when you suddenly know that eventually, you will survive this. I have experienced the forgiveness of prison guards who let their anger melt into curiosity. The body expresses forgiveness before the brain agrees. Where are the words for those shifts that later evolve into full forgiveness?

Though Perry offers no hint of a smile, I sense a softening, one with no real name.

"Back in the kingdom, everyone knows that forgiveness won't fit inside a single word; it is, in fact, a castle. Constructed of the bluest ocean rocks, the Forgiveness Castle blasts into the sky as if towers leapt that high naturally. Its turrets are frequently shrouded in clouds, which means on a crisp blue day, it's hard to make out the shimmering palace walls. The entire courtyard and massive interior sparkle, which is surprising because many who visit this fortress drag in their dirtiest laundry, their filthiest hurts that they could never share, and then they spill everything. Forgiveness sends them home with clean linen."

His breath is quick, so I slow my words, coaxing him to follow my pace.

"The Forgiveness Castle remains open all day and all night, and the best thing is that there are so many entrances, usually found where you'd never think to look: behind potted plants, in crayon drawings, and on old birthday cards. I have it on good authority that one entrance is through a tree fort. Many of the Forgiveness Castle's entry points remain secret, which is why you hunt around, press the blue walls gently, and wait. Sometimes saying the most obvious words, 'I'm sorry', opens a hidden door right where there seemed no possibility."

He looks away.

"You're welcome to visit this castle to wait for a friend, to sit in one of its orange and yellow gardens, or to find your own reflection in the polished blue rock and whisper, 'Please. Come home.'"

I put my right hand in the middle of Perry's chest and imagine deep blue granite. Through my hand, I feel his heart pounding. His chest vibrates.

"Forgive me, Perry."

He allows his eyes to find mine, and I meet his cold stare with humility, but I also can see that there is once again room behind his eyes.

"No," he says. "But if you're so goddamn sure we're going to be late for your next big event, we had better get going."

"Thank you."

Perry nods stiffly. It appears that Alcatraz counts for something.

I dare not press this advantage, so I head to my side in silence. As he climbs into the van, I use an apologetic tone to say, "The show starts exactly at noon. We have to leave now to get there on time. We're cutting it close."

Silence weighs awkwardly between us again.

I am sorry.

Sure, I dropped the cake intentionally, but I hate working him over this way. Perry's a good man, and I must continue to knock the stuffing out of him. Two hours from now, he might fondly remember this incident as back when the weekend was going swimmingly.

Swimmingly. Good word.

With meekness, I say, "I'd love to go back for another cake, but we can't be late for the ducks."

NINE

PERRY remains silent as I drive the van toward the financial district. Feeling the need to offer more conciliation, I explain our next destination. I'm not bringing up the beauty of the word *conciliation*. I think I better let that one slide.

I say, "There's a string of hotels across the south: Atlanta, Dallas, and North Carolina. They're super fancy, and their gimmick is that they all have a family of ducks that live in the lobby fountain. Every day, at exactly the same time, they pipe in this John Philip Sousa march and the ducks parade from the fountain to a nearby elevator. It's supposed to be adorable."

He says, "Yeah. Heard about it."

Other than a small clicking in the van's engine and the city's late-morning noise, we ride in silence. Even with Perry seething next to me, this Saturday suggests good cheer. Irregular-sized chunks of blue squeeze between skyscrapers, like puzzle pieces that happen to fit perfectly. We breathe in the late morning, the sun invisible to those of us trapped in cars but nevertheless creating a strong presence on every flat reflective surface. Sure, there's angry honking on every block, but couldn't the sound represent warm-up notes for a citywide vehicular orchestra?

And hey, Perry got into the van. That's reason enough for cheer.

Nothing is assured on a King Weekend. He could have walked off his anger, forcing me to chase him down. But he came back; we passed the third checkpoint. This silence is healthy, meditative almost. I breathe and think of my hands, invite them to stop shaking.

Relax, Vin, *relax*.

KING PERRY | 147

Ten minutes later, I creep to a stop under an opulent covered entryway, Corinthian columns creating a white marble forest. A trio of white-gloved valets argue amongst themselves. One approaches to take my keys.

The valet says, "Sir, could you wait one moment, please?"

"Sure thing."

I almost say, "You betcha," but remember that Perry hated *Fargo*. Gotta let that go. *Fargo* makes me think of King Mai and wonder what's happening on the farm today. No. Stay focused.

We sit and wait.

"This chain isn't performing well financially," Perry says at last. "Their San Francisco location was a big investment, and first and second quarters were far below expectations. They could close this site before Q4."

"Is this big news on Wall Street?"

"Yeah," he says, uncertainly.

I watch him and wait.

He continues with a quick blush, "People in the bank are talking because they want to see the duck parade before the hotel closes." He tries to chuckle, but it won't quite start naturally. "It's the women, mostly."

I say, "You'll have something to report on Monday morning, then."

He nods.

Slim conversation, but it's a start.

Our valet apologizes profusely when he returns for my keys. I cross to Perry's side of the van, and though he can't smile at me, he looks at me to confirm our destination. We head into the hotel.

The enormous gilded lobby is already crowded, camera flashes blinding me as soon as I enter. I don't understand how the ducks can survive this dizzying attention, let alone ignore it, but they paddle around the giant marble fountain as if it were a forest pond. Despite the masses of people, the lobby remains quieter than you might expect, more reverence than I would have expected. Even children darting along the fountain's perimeter whisper their excitement; their hushed exclamations are swallowed by the thick crimson carpeting. Velvet ropes mark off the ducks' exit route.

Plenty of hotel staff mingle discreetly, and I immediately note two men, plainclothes guards, whose sole responsibility is to make sure people don't fuck with the ducks. Both have earpieces, and black cords snake into their casual shirt collars. I like to study crowds to see who's in charge and who is positioned to influence the group dynamic. I always find a few folks like me, carefully studying others. We sometimes spot each other and nod in recognition.

Despite the opulent chandeliers and ornate, plush furniture, most people are dressed like Perry and me, or less weathered versions of us. The more expensively dressed patrons enter and head straight to the elevators. That's not true, Vin, you big snob. Those people over there are staying and they're dressed well. Those people too. He's wearing Armani and looks mightily entertained by the duck party. Don't be a classist dick.

A woman in a black dress brings an older couple orange juice in champagne flutes, which must mean mimosas. For some reason, this makes me think of waffles. I could go for a waffle.

"*Waffle* is a funny word," I suggest.

He says, "You have word issues."

Perry tries to say this in a casual tone, but I think that's a little fake-it-till-you-make-it attempt to get us through this rough patch. Still, I appreciate the effort.

I lean into him and say, "Waffle."

Several overeager tourists lean in too far, causing the webbed clan to quack in scolding tones and paddle away. Each time, the security guys bristle to attention, ready to intervene if some invisible boundary is crossed. Cameras continue to twinkle right up until the appointed minute, when suddenly, a jolly march bursts through a bunch of cleverly disguised speakers, music blaring from behind ficus trees and enormous bird-of-paradise flower arrangements. Hundreds of starbursts explode around me, destroying my vision until I must stare at my shoes to regain a sense of balance. This feels like a king's coronation.

Oh, that works. Maybe they're all here for Perry.

The ducks assemble. Well, two ducks and a half dozen ducklings. The ducklings are fuzzy, preteens of the duck world. The constant cooing from everyone around us only underscores Perry's subtle grumpiness. He's not impressed. Not at first.

But it's hard not to appreciate the hilarity as they waddle up the custom ramp that allows them to cluster on the fountain edge, bumping into and barking at each other, though we cannot hear them over the grand march. It's easy to invent their conversation watching their bills snap open and closed. When they are confident in their number, they all *fwump* to the ground, several young ones tipping over, then righting themselves with recovered dignity and scurrying down the red carpet after their siblings. I catch Perry chuckling once in spite of himself.

I point out different ones to Perry as we follow their wobbly trajectory. In an unscripted moment, one duckling waddles so far from his family it appears he might take the stairs instead of their private elevator, but he turns and runs crazily to rejoin them, prompting a small glow of appreciative laughter. Perry and I share a grin, which is good for our tenuous bond. The ducks march, cameras flash, and soon it's over in a thundering musical climax. The chaperoned ducks disappear into the elevator, the doors ping closed, and everyone claps, immensely satisfied.

The echo of the exhausting march rings in my ears, and the visual buzz from so many blinking cameras diminishes except over by the Duck Elevator, where people wait to pose, pretending to push the Up button.

"This is why we didn't have time to get a cake?" Perry says, looking away. "Can we go back and do it now?"

"I'm sorry, but we have to get ready for the next part."

He turns away, and we watch the audience dissolve. Tourists flow toward the gloved, grinning bellhops who hold open the enormous doors, and I remember yesterday's slow shuffle toward the Alcatraz ferry. People thank the bellhops profusely, as if they were personally responsible for the duck show, and the bellhops accept this praise with grace and wide smiles as if they were, in fact, personally responsible.

I wait until Perry finally faces me, and then I glance up, over to the second-level balcony on the left side. Then I glance over to the right. I make sure that my face looks puzzled, and hopefully he sees worry, which right at this moment, I don't have to fake. Perry follows my eyes without really recognizing it.

I announce, "Let's go."

He follows my long strides as I head to the bay of gold-trimmed elevators, accented by lush palms reflected in floor-to-ceiling mirrors. I love the tangerine birds-of-paradise perched everywhere around us. They have such unapologetic profiles, daring to boast angular spikes in a world which honors flowers for their softness, their ability to play well with others. "Fuck you," they seem to say, "we're beautiful."

"Vin," he says, catching up.

He doesn't say anything more when I step inside and press the button for the 26th floor, but his reflection in the closing elevator door can't hide his surprise.

We ascend in silence.

I take his hand.

He squeezes back, more of a formal acknowledgement that he realizes I'm here than an affectionate gesture.

On the 26th floor, we step into a pomegranate hallway. The textured ruby wallpaper implies a richness you can nearly taste. A person-sized vase, gleaming gold, sprouts pure white lilies and more of my pals, a snow-white bird-of-paradise with a yellow-tipped crown. The marble-topped table shines our blurry outline, and I see no luggage dings on the two most likely corners. Everything here seems virgin.

We move slowly down the hallway, holding hands. Good, good. He's coming back.

Though he keeps pace with me, I still feel Perry hesitate, as if we have no right to be here. He ran himself ragged across Alcatraz last night breaking federal law, but today he squirms slightly while wandering, quite legally, through a fancy hotel.

Interesting.

This matches my previous observations and wonderings that Perry didn't grow up with a lot of money. Maybe he's fond of it now, but I bet it wasn't always readily available. I'd like that confirmed verbally. This afternoon, perhaps.

All week I have wondered why Perry wants to sell his father's paintings. The money, of course. But why now? I bet he inherited his father's paintings after his mom's death, which means he owned the paintings since twenty-four. Why hasn't he tried to sell them? They're not on display; I never saw any of his father's paintings hanging in his apartment.

When I produce a plastic keycard from my back pocket, I feel Perry jerk in surprise.

I swing the door open to reveal silvery-white curtains bloated with breeze, framing San Francisco's glorious downtown and a sparkling slice of the east bay. I love that the windows open in this hotel; what a treat in a skyscraper. A puffy comforter is the cream cheese frosting on the four-poster bed, which is thick with chubby, colored pillows. A complimentary bottle of champagne attempts seduction in the center. In our adjoining study, an intricately carved writing desk, a polished armoire, and a muted lemon-colored divan finish out the large pieces of furniture. Perry leaves me to wander through the room, exploring surfaces with his fingertips. He stops at the glass-topped bar and lifts a crystal decanter.

"We slept in the dirt last night and you had rented this room?"

"Kinda."

"Kind of?" His voice is empty, not angry, not amused, almost as if he is clarifying my response.

He crosses to the window to peer beyond the sailboat sail.

Uh oh. Time to move this along. "Hey buddy, strip down. It's shower time. You want anything from the bar? Something to drink?"

"No."

We shuck our clothes efficiently, not like lovers but more like guys at the gym, which is still kind of sexy. I study his body with new appreciation, loving the curves of his ass in daylight now that I can see him fully. He sees me watching him and mugs at me, apparently reading my mind, and he's right; I'm thinking about sex. And hopefully, now he is. We had some pretty great sex last night, and I want him to remember that.

After I'm naked and my cock semihard, I head to the minibar and open some grapefruit juice. I walk it over to him.

"Thanks," he says, and his face opens.

Perry likes grapefruit juice. He just didn't know that I knew that.

Standing before him, I squeeze his shoulder muscles with slow grips, massaging him while he twists off the lid and takes a big gulp. I run the back of my fingers down the front of his chest, grazing his nipples, and he shudders involuntarily.

"Hey," he says.

"I have to take care of something," I say. "Why don't you start us a hot shower, and I'll join you in a minute."

He agrees with an expression that's both guarded and tentatively friendly and then strolls naked through the bathroom door.

Oh man, I love his ass. I like the way each petulant globe droops, the sloping curves shifting with each step.

From the armoire, I gather and lay out the clothes I have purchased for him. Expensive jeans and a few warm shirts. I hope he wears the hunter green one. I carefully display the sexy underwear I chose for him. These royal-blue briefs are gonna look great clutching that sexy butt.

I love that I got to shop for underwear in the Castro. I grooved to club music in a gayboy shop, making myself dizzy with lust thinking about making love to an incredible man. I'm no different from anyone else: I want to fit in within the Homo Homeland. For a while this week, I wasn't the Human Ghost, but someone falling in love and shopping for his new boyfriend. Sometime on Sunday, I have to tell Perry about that moment, explain how wonderful I felt anticipating spending time with him.

After making two brief phone calls, I grab a condom from the bag I have packed for him, rip it open, and then hurry off to the bathroom.

I hear Perry under the shower spray, cleaning off the morning, last night, the stains he's accumulated thus far. When I enter the bathroom, hot mist engulfs me. The mirrors offer no reflection, only trapped clouds. At last, San Francisco's fabled fog. A half dozen fluffy towels suggest the management doesn't mind if you shower all day. The marble-top counter is trimmed with gold along its edges, and with that thin golden line tracing the bathroom's interior, I feel we're trapped in a cloud cage, a paradox of form and no form.

I slide open the shower door and ease in behind him.

"Hi."

"Hey," he says, more easily. "You gotta get wet."

I say, "Okay. I want you to wash me down."

At first, his hands on me are polite, distant. But a slippery, soapy experience must inevitably diffuse boundaries, and soon my chest foams with his lather and his arms slip behind me. As soon as our chests touch, we kiss directly under the spray. I clamp his neck like I did last night, and he groans, his senses filling in the blanks for what he doesn't actively remember.

I massage his upper shoulders and pull him into my chest, making small rumbling sounds so that my chest vibrates against him. He leans in against me, and I let my strong hands knead down either side of his spine, finding and addressing his tension, helping him relax further. Our movements resemble our dance in the cell last night, and I hope this shower reminds him of that intimacy. I drag my bristly cheek along his bristly face, morning stubble jousting, until our lips are aligned and we kiss sloppily, tasting each other in this new environment, clean and fresh, sparking our unique chemistry to the surface again.

He's getting hard.

"Check it out," he says. "Ginger peach soap."

He hands me the bar and I lather my hands, letting my gaze burrow into him with a bit of what-I'm-gonna-do-to-you intention, which, who knows, may or may not be sexy. I hope it's coming across as sexy and not menacing. He smiles bashfully, which suggests he gets me and he's not against where we're heading. As my fingertips work his neck in small circles, he closes his eyes and tilts his head back enough to let the water pound his forehead.

I figured a hot shower might help us find each other again, and our few minutes of mostly quiet naked time accomplished just that.

"I really am sorry about the cake, Perry."

He opens his eyes, and I see no anger.

"Me too," he says. "I'm sorry I reacted the way I did. It just struck me as—"

"Don't apologize," I say, caressing the sides of his neck with my soapy hands. "Never apologize for compassion."

His face clenches instantly; his neck muscles seize. Again, he looks surprised, a deep well of feeling over nothing that should remotely matter to him. No actual tears surface, but the wet look in his eyes is unmistakable.

Perry kisses me in surprise, and our rift heals more. I explore his tan chest, tweaking his nipples, but there's not much reaction, as I discovered last night. I stroke the inside of his left thigh with the bar of soap, and he moans.

"The first breakfast was great," he says, during a break from the kissing. "I always drink a Diet Coke first thing in the morning."

"Whaaaa?" I exclaim and pull back. "You don't like bacon?"

"I love *bacon*," he says.

I pretend I am insulted. "That substance had many properties in common with bacon."

"Except taste."

We make a few turns, ala junior high dance moves, kissing, hands gliding over our bodies. He likes my fuzzy chest, and I give him free access. I do like having my nipples tweaked and sucked, and with my hand on his skull, I guide him there, offering encouragement in a throaty tone. Soon, our passionate kissing grows stronger, and I slow-fuck my tongue into his mouth; he grips me back with renewed eagerness. Our cocks nudge each other, getting thicker, jostling like commuters on the Muni.

I have to tell him about Friday on the Muni. I have to remember to tell him that.

"Dammit," he says when we come up for air. "You sure know what you're doing with sex, Mr. Vanbly."

My hands massage his butt cheeks in soapy circles, and he feeds me his moan. My index finger massages the deep cleft between them, and Perry writhes in my arms. While kissing deeply, I slow-turn him under the heat and spray, our cloud cage, and lean him forward against the shower door.

Hot fog curls around him.

"Uh oh," he says as I nudge his legs further apart. "This is when you usually start telling the king story."

"Yes."

"And I end up sexually manipulated. I see how this works, man."

"Yes," I say, sliding my goatee across his shoulder. "I'm trying to figure out where to pick it up exactly, because I had this whole big thing planned out for when King Aabee came back to the kingdom, after the ten years passed. But it went with the cake—a celebration and all."

Perry tenses. We stand in silence for a few seconds, my cock rubbing up and down his crack. Now that he has forgiven me for dropping the cake, I don't want him to forget about what happened.

Why do my King Weekends so often involve cake? Cake. I love cake. I want someone to make me one of those big three-tiered wedding cakes with pink frosting roses right in my living room, so over the course of a weekend I could eat a rose off the cake whenever I got up to go to the fridge. No special occasion, just cake. *Cake.* It's fun to say. Oops, Perry is waiting.

"He was twenty-eight now, King Aabee," I say, grinding my hard dick against him.

Wait, did my cock just get harder thinking about frosting roses?

"King Aabee returned to the Found Kings, and they threw him a crazy party, but I'll skip over that part. That went with the cake. Anyway, he came home, still remembering his kingship. Aabee's hair now sported premature gray, and perhaps he bore a few extra wrinkles on his midnight face, souvenirs from his time with the Lost Ones."

I reach around Perry and massage his cock with my free hand, pressing harder against him with my lower stomach. I wrap my free arm around his chest and pull us together, holding his back to my chest, my chin on his shoulder, my goatee tracing small circles.

He moans and after its whispery conclusion says, "I dunno if I can handle more, Vin. Last night was pretty intense."

I grab the ginger peach soap and let my left fingertips toy with the hairs on his slight treasure trail, trailing further down to reach his nuts with my soapy grasp. It doesn't take long to create a wet lather, protected from the full spray by the arch of his back.

"The Strange Musician played his flute-like instrument at the homecoming jubilation, and the usual good-natured arguments commenced over the exact sound. An angel choir. Cricket hymns. One king said, 'I think it sounds chartreuse.'"

Perry arches back against my cock, and he uses those gym-trained ass muscles to grip my dick. While his brain may not think he's ready, his body says, "Let's give it a shot."

The unwrapped condom remains in the soap dish, but I'm not sure I'm going to fuck him, now that we're here. Fucking is not always the goal.

"King Aabee spent his first years back among the Found Kings resolving engineering problems in the sewers. He had gained much experience, you see, and whenever a problem came up, King Aabee said, 'I will go. Send me!'"

Perry chuckles.

"Many kings encouraged him to rest, to take it easy after his time among the Lost Ones. But then King Thaddeus the Barn Cleaner asked if any king would assist him and King Aabee said...."

I nudge him with my cock, right at his sore, puckered hole. I clear my throat so he understands that this is his cue to say the punch line. Perry laughs and pushes back under the spray.

"I will go. Send me," Perry says.

I feel him relax, ready himself for the inevitable assault. I press hard against the wrinkled flesh, remembering the beautiful warmth I experienced last night.

He groans.

The heat, the spray, the sensation of my hard cock against his swollen butthole—it's too much distraction, and Perry surrenders to our gilded cloud cage. He is mine.

I withdraw the pressure and allow my cock to glide up his ass, wedged deep in the cleft. He twists, releasing the tension of anticipation, and a shudder ripples through him, the disappointment of a near miss. He wants me inside.

Yes, this is definitely better as a close-to-fucking. This will ratchet him higher, tighten his coils.

I use a softer, raunchier tone to say, "Invitations piled up, *thick eight-inch stacks…*"

Perry moans.

"…while he worked the sewers, invitations that begged Aabee to lecture at universities, meet admirers for lunch, and join friends who wished to treat him to sailboat cruises through the Greek Isles. But he was too busy.

"Over the next three or four years, King Aabee acquired a reputation for volunteering for tasks that others found daunting: sitting with the dying, waiting in hospitals for test results, and clearing storm gutters with good cheer."

I steal soapy lather from his cock and apply it to my own, creating a foamy glide between us. And while the water washes most of the suds down his thighs, I squeeze him tight, trapping enough bubbles to make our rubbings slippery.

I position myself to kiss his hole with the head of my dick and he responds with a slight stiffening when I do this, but instead of entering him, I guide my cock to stroke his taint, pushing against his balls. He squirms.

"Yes," he says in an elongated hiss, escaping like steam.

"Whenever a new communication came from the Lost Kings, someone would inevitably suggest, 'We need Aabee on this. Check the sewers.'"

Perry laughs and says, "This sounds great, this life of his. The Sewer King."

My cock stops stroking the vulnerable underside leading to his nut sack, and he tries to return us to the groove by thrusting back and forth, but when he feels me not responding, he stops and waits patiently.

"Did you have more you wanted to say?" I ask politely.

"No, Extreme Dominatrix," he says, gurgling as he lets water fill his throat.

"Now, that name could work," I say as I begin to saw against him again. "Two *x*'s. Did you just say that to suck up?"

He says, "You're probably right."

I laugh.

He says, "You're not going to fuck me, are you?"

"You're not enjoying this?"

"It's driving me crazy."

"Good."

He turns his head in a way that suggests to me he wants to be kissed, so I lean in close and he leans back, forcing my dick against him. I lurch hard, and if I were fucking him this would be a balls-deep stroke, and his body jolts in surprise as I squash him against the shower door.

This forces our kiss to work harder, to fight to keep each other's mouths together while I hump his lower half and push him away. His appetite for me grows strong. My appetite for him has never diminished, not since Tuesday.

I love him.

We break our embrace, leaving each other gasping.

Take a deep breath, Vin.

"After a while, the Found Kings recognized the sounds from his flute more than the sight of King Aabee. Yet nobody could agree on what they heard. Some heard the scent of May lilacs; others said it tasted like ginger. One king said, 'It's my grandmother's voice, singing in Swedish.'"

Perry's body ripples in harmony with my patter and our delicious lovemaking, grace and ease purring through him.

I kiss him on the neck and slowly withdraw my cock, my dribbled precum washing down his cleft. I let my dick rest against his beautiful ass cheek, hard and eager. I would so love to finish this.

"You're kidding me," Perry says over his shoulder. "You're quitting right now?"

I hug him from behind, and though he may not want our sex to end, I think he finally recognizes that I'm in charge, and with a certain new level of acceptance, he lets himself be held, allowing his head to fall back on my shoulder.

We rock this way for a moment, neither of us wanting to end our reconciliation shower. It feels good to be in love again. Well, Perry may not use that exact word, but I feel it growing in him.

"I have to go downstairs and check on something. Everything you need is on the bed. Fresh clothes, shaving cream and razor, grooming stuff. Q-tips. There's a gym bag to pack up everything, including your clothes from yesterday. We won't come back here."

I finish rinsing off. Best to depart quickly before questions begin.

"I might jack off when you leave," he says, trying for a threatening tone.

I'm happy to have fun with Perry again.

I hop out and snatch a cloud towel from the stack.

"I don't think you will. If you spurt your load, well then, you'll never find out the next chapter of King Aabee. When you're ready, meet me in the lobby. Make sure it's within forty to forty-five minutes, okay? There's a window of opportunity for our next gig."

He says, "Okay. I won't be that long."

"I bought this really sexy underwear in the Castro on Thursday for you. I spent thirty minutes picking it out because I couldn't decide which color would look best against your ass. Seriously, I had a shopping boner for like twenty minutes just thinking about you."

"Uh, thanks," he says, laughing under the spray. "Boner boy."

His lusty grin is sincere. He likes that I thought about him this week.

He says, "But if the clothes don't fit, let's swing by my place. It won't take long."

I ignore his comment.

We're not going to his place, not for anything, but I don't want to argue the point. I have worked far too hard to separate him from his San Francisco routines to let him visit a place where he feels comfortable.

I dress quickly in clean clothes and stick my head into the cloud cage as he's washing his hair. "See you downstairs."

"I'll hurry."

"Don't hurry. Just don't dawdle."

I like the word *dawdle*. Dawdle, dawdle. I also like leaving him with somewhat contradictory instructions.

Waiting near the elevator, I decide this isn't the inside of a pomegranate any longer, but a luxurious tongue designed for sensual pleasure. I should have licked his balls for a while. It's my own fault; I told them what time to meet me here.

Soon, a white-gloved young man appears from the elevator, pushing a cart draped in white linen. A silver-domed platter sits on top.

"Hi there, I'm from 2625. I ordered this food. I'd like to place this card."

"Absolutely, sir," he says with deference, a professional cousin of the ponytailed waitress from the art gallery. He lifts the dome, and I place the card strategically.

I crumple a few bills into his hand, and he smiles his gratitude. He has too much professionalism to check the denominations. With a nod, he heads toward our room pushing the cart.

"If he asks, tell him that Mr. Vanbly ordered this for his guest."

He nods, pleased. "Thank you, Mr. Vanbly."

I stand out of sight, but not too far away. I hear the soft rapping on the door and the lilted announcement, "Room service."

I hear Perry say with surprise, "We didn't order room service."

"This has already been paid for, sir," he says politely, looking at me for reassurance, "ordered by Mr. Vanbly for his guest."

The door opens, permitting the young man's entrance.

As soon as the white-gloved gentleman removes the shiny dome, Perry will see a meal identical to what we ate at St. Anne's: scrambled eggs, bacon, toast, fried potatoes, and orange juice. I bribed the cook to include onions with the fried potatoes. I wanted an exact match. He will find strawberry jam in a silver dish with a tiny silver spoon and, in the center of the arrangement, a card that reads: ENJOY YOUR LUNCH, BEAR WALKER.

TEN

PERRY crosses the lobby in his new jeans and the hunter-green shirt under his leather bomber jacket. His gaze assesses the lobby, the guests, and the décor. With the duck parade concluded, the lobby resumes its primary function as a way station for high-paying guests. Perry moves with long, confident strides, hunting leisurely for me. Perry is a classy guy; he belongs in a place like this even if he's nervous around money. I, however, dress like a delivery guy: jeans and a fresh red T-shirt with my lumberjack overshirt and my crusty black leather jacket. I love this jacket. Perry nods when he spies me engaged with a middle-aged couple and their bored preteen son.

"Hey," I say as he draws near. "What vineyard tours do you recommend?"

Perry's face blanks out. He nods at the man and woman, and they nod back. "Uh, I've heard the Beringer one is cool, I guess."

"These folks only have time for one or two. They want to see something special."

When this husband and wife chatted me up a few minutes ago, they thought I might be a tour bus driver. That's when people notice me—when they need directions. Their poor kid does not appear happy. They missed the duck parade by an hour, and despite his parents' promise to return tomorrow, he refuses to forgive.

Perry says, "Maybe the concierge can help."

"True," I say. "How about the Schramsberg tour? It's underground, in spooky carved-out caves with tons of cobwebs everywhere."

The kid perks up.

"The tasting is done in a crypt like you'd see in a horror movie, lit only by long taper candles. They say it's haunted."

The kid's eyes dart from mom to dad, trying to register their reaction. I'm not steering them wrong; it's a good tour.

"Creepy?" says the mother.

"Elegant," I say under my breath, nodding slightly toward her son.

She inclines her head to indicate she gets it. She says, "Haunted, huh? I dunno. I don't want to scare Danny."

"I won't be afraid," he says. "I promise."

She nods and looks back at me. "How dark do you go red?"

I say, "I like pinot noirs and shiraz, but after a certain price point, $35 or so, I can't say much. I'm not well versed in merlots. Those heavier red wines put me to sleep. How about you?"

I see Perry is quietly impressed with my cache of wine knowledge. I'm definitely more of a beer guy, but discussing wine in California is as essential as bitching about October rains or Muni stations you hate; you have to be ready to contribute to the conversation.

We finish with enthusiastic handshakes, and once we're alone, Perry says, "The jeans are great; so are the shirts. Thank you."

"No problem," I say, looking up.

"How did you guess my jeans size?"

"Huh," I say, making sure I seem distracted. "I need you to do something. A favor."

I don't want to answer his questions yet, how I know that he likes Diet Coke for breakfast, that he prefers grapefruit juice, which colors and fashions he wears.

He says, "Okay."

"Get the van. Throw your gym bag in the back. Tell the valet we were in 2625. Will you do that?"

Perry says with cautious surprise, "Yeah. Where are we going?"

I hand him my valet ticket and some cash for the tip. With free access to the back of the van, he could cheat and peek under the tarps.

But I don't think he will. He has decided to trust me, though I am an Alcatraz fugitive and the Destroyer of Cakes.

A few minutes from now, when we're reunited, I'll check the tarps. I arranged them in such a way that it will be obvious to me if they have been moved. He won't be in trouble if he looks; I just need to know how much he trusts me.

I glance once again at the opposite sides of the second-level promenade and squint until I see his gaze follow mine. "Meet me at the loading dock behind the hotel. You'll have to go around the block to get at it from the correct side. Back up into the alley."

"Okay," Perry says, clearly not thrilled with these instructions.

I look him in the eye and say, "Don't drive crazy, but don't dawdle."

If I weren't so focused right now, I'd ask him if he likes *dawdle*. *W* comes across as relaxed as far as consonants go and, depending on his neighboring letters, outright lazy. But this is no time for lazy *w*, time to get to Work.

"Got everything with you?"

"Yeah."

"Ten minutes."

"Ten minutes," Perry says without much of a smile.

"Hey," I say sharply, and his eyes jerk right to mine. I step in closer. "Making love with you in the shower was amazing."

He nods and unclenches. "Yeah, I liked it too."

I nod, my business concluded, and stride away.

See, Perry, I can be vigorous too.

IN LESS than fifteen minutes, Perry revs the rental van engine behind the hotel.

I lurch awkwardly across the cement loading dock with what appears to be a large black box, and I set it down carefully outside the van. I yank open one door, then the other. Perry hears my hurried movements back there, and I ignore his "What are you doing?"

After loading my cumbersome package, I shut the van doors carefully and quickly, creating as little noise as possible. I race to the passenger side and hop in.

I have to suppress a desire to grin at him; he didn't disturb the tarps. He trusts me.

"Drive. Go. *Now.*"

"Crap." Perry puts his foot on the gas, and we zoom down the alley. "What the fuck did you do? What was that metal scraping in the back?"

We emerge at the street, and Perry hits the brakes a little forcefully, causing us to jerk. I strap on my seatbelt. The box in back makes a noise.

I say, "Make a right turn. Careful of that woman with the bag."

"Did you steal something? A chandelier?"

"Not a chandelier."

"You stole something," he says. "You goddamn stole something. You are a fucking ex-con, aren't you? All that Alcatraz bullshit; I bet you can't handle the outside world. You're a fucking criminal."

"Turn here. Go two blocks and then get in the left lane. Two blocks."

I'm getting ready to take the wheel if he freaks out any further.

"*Holy crap, it's alive.* I hear it back there! *You fucking psycho!* You—"

He interrupts himself and listens; he calms instantly.

"It's quacking."

"Yeah. Turn up here. Left lane. C'mon, switch lanes, Perry. Focus up. You're driving."

He turns on his left blinker.

For a few extra seconds, we are silent.

He says, "You stole one of those ducks."

I squirm for a moment in my seat and turn to him. "I'm not really a fan of the word *stole*. Could you use another word? Maybe something with an *x*?"

ELEVEN

"THE show ducks from the lobby," Perry says, seething. "You stole one."

I remain quiet.

"Famous ducks. You stole a *famous* duck."

"Honestly, I don't think it's that famous," I suggest meekly.

When he snaps his head toward me, I adopt an earnest expression. "I don't think people actually, you know, know his *name*."

Perry grips the wheel tighter, displaying a level of stress I did not see even on Alcatraz. This is new. His eyes dart around the street, regularly checking the rearview mirror for signs of chase. Though he did nothing wrong, I'm glad to see he feels responsible. He rubs his eye socket with vigor, a word I can't seem to let go of this weekend.

Perry's right. I do have word issues.

San Francisco's streets feel particularly jammed at this moment with swerving cars and trucks too big for these narrow lanes. Saturday people threaten to spill into traffic and occasionally do, trusting that everyone will watch out because they're pedestrians. The closeness of the city presses upon us in this moment, brave souls standing in the street, waiting for a break in traffic. Even the crisscrossing power lines threaten us, suggesting we've got nowhere to run, not even up. We're doomed.

"Take a left on Divisadero when we get there."

He obeys, but we ride in angry silence. Well, near silence, broken only by chattering from the back of the van. The duck sounds happy; he's on an adventure.

"He was sad," I say and make puppy dog eyes. "Didn't you see him marching? He kept trying to go rogue, but all his duck brothers and sisters kept pushing him back."

Perry slouches back into the driver's seat. "They all walked that way. Seriously, why do you fuck with me like this? Why are you— what are you going to do with it?"

"Wuv it?"

Perry shakes his head. "No way. I'm not doing community service because of your warped sense of humor. I had started to get into this—"

"By the way, he's a duckling. I stole a duck*ling*."

"I don't actually give a shit that it's a minor, Vin. I'm not taking a misdemeanor or paying a fine. You're on your own for this one, pardner." He adds an ironic flip to the last word.

"I know," I say, keeping my voice soft. "It's all on me. All legal and financial consequences."

I'm glad to hear that despite this latest outrage, he still refers to me as "pardner." Sure, he means it sarcastically, but our strained connection remains intact. We have weathered the awful cake-dropping incident, which tightened our bond instead of weakening it, steeling him for this greater abuse of his trust and good will.

"There could be jail time," he says. "If the hotel presses charges, I bet there's jail time."

While he fumes, I steal a few glances.

His icy blue eyes, tense jaw, the rigid arm muscles—yes, everything sizzles off him, broadcasting his fury. I would guess he's asking himself why these things keep happening to him, when all he wanted was a fun weekend. Why is the world never just easy?

We're both quiet for a moment, and it's the good quiet, where softness keeps leaking in. I believe our new friend likes the back of the van.

Now that we're out of the financial district, zipping along Divisadero on rolling hills, Perry unclenches a tad, perhaps because we're further away from his work environment. Maybe the roller coaster hills have a therapeutic impact on drivers here, an unconscious reminder to breathe deeper, go slower, because the next hill's a big one. I might be able to touch him soon without his jerking away.

When I decide we're close enough to our destination, I break my silence. "Pear, I'm sorry I dragged you into this. The first night I stayed there, I found the duck room by accident while wandering around. They live in these cages, super-deluxe, floor-to-ceiling cages."

"Was the room locked?"

"A little bit, yes. But they're *cages*. I realized that together, you and I might free that little guy, make a bigger world for him. Even a deluxe cage is still a cage. "

"You can't do that, Vin. He's domesticated. He'll die out in nature."

"He's young. It's not too late for him to go wild. The ducks have to perform every day, and they never get a day off. It's literally the Hotel California for that little guy, Perry. He can never leave."

"You're going to get caught," he says, a note of sadness coloring his scolding.

"Am I? Did you get the impression that I often got caught on Alcatraz?"

"This is different."

"We're going to free the little guy. He's going to have a whole big world to explore instead of a straight line from the lobby to the third floor. His wild duck nature will kick in and he'll be fine. He'll have an awesome life."

Perry grunts. He hasn't forgiven me, but his anger grows softer. "You're unbelievable. Possibly the worst weekend—"

"It's cool," I say, moving my warm hand to the back of his neck, feeling the tense muscles radiate heat. "It's all on me. My responsibility. They would never let him fly in that hotel. Don't you think a duck ought to fly?"

Perry responds to my massage almost involuntarily, his breath beginning as an angry exhale but ending with an inaudible trickle. I bet my touch reminds him of getting fucked last night as he drifted to sleep. My fingers move in small circles, coaxing, pleading, reminding him that I am sometimes not a dick, and I can love him. I add pressure and heat against the tight cords in his neck as Perry resists me and yet is unable to resist at the same time.

Your first ducknapping is never easy.

"Take this exit."

I thought a sensory memory might be useful this weekend, to relax him instantly, so I programmed one as we fucked. The erogenous zones can be linked so that rubbing a man's neck makes his balls tingle and his butt throb, and he licks his lips but doesn't consciously recognize why. I spent a good deal of our Alcatraz lovemaking creating this trigger, even if he wasn't fully conscious for half of it. Sensory memory is fun.

I squeeze and release his neck like a rubber ball, and he shudders out a wave of irritation, one that shakes his shoulders and sends a long shiver the length of his back.

He might not blow up.

Who am I kidding?

This is it.

"Pull over here. We're going to park right there: overflow parking."

"No, Vin. Not off the Golden Gate Bridge. He'll hit the water and splatter. Or the wind—"

"Okay, fine. The duck stays in the van. We both need some time to chill out for a few minutes, to think this through. Park right there. Good. I brought us a change of clothes, so get to the back."

"It's a parking lot. We can't change here."

"Just our shirts. Go."

Perry slams the door, but he meets me behind the van where I reach under one of my tarps and pull out a tie-dye Iowa Hawkeyes T-shirt and an orange sun visor. I extract a camera with a neck strap, and after I've fussed with his visor, I hand it to him.

"The visor is too over the top."

"Not here, Perry. We'll blend in. Put it on."

I plunge my hands under the tarps again, ignoring his protests. I pull out a fresh white T-shirt and a John Deere cap with that yellow-stitched stag forever leaping across the green. I wouldn't want Perry to half strip in the parking lot alone. What he does, I do; we are a team. The king who gifted me this John Deere cap predicted I might need it one day, and apparently, that day is today. Thank you, mighty King of Curiosity. Please send us both your great love. Send us A Curious Army.

After we change clothes, I make Perry serve as my lookout, a job he does not relish, while I remove the heavy cover from the duck cage to make sure our little friend has enough food and water. The duckling makes extra noise at this new freedom, running back and forth, checking out his changed surroundings, greeting us loudly whenever he gets close to our side of the box.

Perry glances around, but nobody's near enough to hear.

I'd love to joke with Perry over our duck's jerky scrambles, but Perry may not find this as cute as I do. The little guy twice runs to his dunking tank corner and throws his head underwater. His playground is spacious. Fitting, after all. He is a minor celebrity, as Perry pointed out. I'm glad I got the big cage.

I say, "Let's go."

"We can't leave him here. He'll die."

"I cracked the windows. He's got enough food and water for a while."

"He'll cook in the sun."

"It's not warm enough for that, and we won't stay long."

"People will hear him," Perry says, adopting a new air of calm, something that I suspect he uses with difficult bank customers. "Vin, this is not the place to hide a stolen duck. Think about this."

This is not good, this slight detachment. I'm losing him.

"I need a few minutes," I say, pleading. "Give me that, please, Perry, and let me think about this here. I need you. We'll see the pretty bridge and chill out. I'll come up with something. *Please.*"

When I see from his rage that my earnestness has bought me a few more reluctant minutes, I lead us from the van, following the trickle of tourists toward our common destination. He walks ahead of me by a step or two, and once or twice turns around to make a suggestion.

But I nudge him forward and say, "Quiet. Not here."

A moment later he says, "We could put him in a cab, and pay the cabbie to take him back to the hotel for us. Anonymously, Vin. Nobody would know."

"I thought of that," I say, hesitating. "But a cabbie could take our money and then make more if he sells our duck to a pet store. We've got to keep calm. Let's not talk about it for a minute, let me think."

"We'll go to my bank. I can get out $300. They can't—"

"Perry—"

"Vin, I didn't sign up for this. Alcatraz was bad enough."

We head through a curved tunnel, under the 101, as we cross toward the tourist plaza. Other pilgrims join us, a few feet behind or ahead, chattering with excitement, so we keep our voices low.

"I thought you loved Alcatraz."

"It turned out okay," he says. "But I'm not built that way. I may live in California, but we're not all into tarot cards and bear walking in public. I can't do this crazy shit."

"You can't eat here, you can't walk like a bear, you can't spend the night on Alcatraz. But you did those things. I saw you. And by the way, yesterday on the pier you told me that you once got a tarot card reading, so don't tell me you can't do shit you have already done."

"I saw a psychic."

"Fine, psychic."

Before he protests further, I put my hand up. "Gimme a minute."

As we pass the gift shop, the trickle of tourists becomes a steady stream, flowing into two giant plateaus overlooking the bay, the delta at our human river's end. Abruptly, I take his left hand with my right so that our fingers intertwine. He tries to jerk away, but I keep my grip steady.

I say, "This is San Francisco. We'll blend in more. I've got a plan, I think."

"Oh my God," he says, shaking his head.

"It's okay. I've gotten out of situations like this before. Give me two minutes, Perry."

As we near the top tier observation deck, photo headquarters of the western world, the energy around us intensifies. Move three feet in any direction and you ruin someone's picture. All around us I hear conversations spoken in languages I cannot understand, and to my ignorant ears, every conversation expresses the same ideas: Beauty. Elation. Astonishment.

Our neighbors negotiate friendly introductions with each other, smiling and nodding, like guests at a big wedding who don't know each other's names, but know that as of right now, we're all related somehow.

Conversations in English demand eavesdropping.

"You're from Raleigh? I had an uncle who lived there for many years."

"Would you take our picture?"

"Enjoy your vacation. It was nice chatting with you."

"Yes, we saw that yesterday. But have you been to…?"

Perry and I stop.

The Golden Gate Bridge appears, fully formed, as if it leapt out from behind a curtain. My jaw drops, as always. The first time I saw it, I felt so completely overwhelmed by the raw power of this functional art, so drunk on its qualities that eluded conscious description, I only managed to pull together a single coherent thought: *Oh. Engineers. Got it.*

Sure, it's big, it's orange, and it connects San Francisco to the coast. That's one level. But no words go as high as this bridge, no words adequate to explain the joy this thing inspires. Nothing captures the sweeping majesty of the cables, the sheer improbability that a thing like this could exist except outside of fantasy. You might also stare at the Golden Gate and think, *Oh. Poets. Got it.*

But appreciating this majesty takes a certain quality—wonder—which is hard to hold, wriggly as a baby duck. Wonder is always difficult until you forgive whoever destroyed your love of surprises.

"Pretty," he says without emotion.

There may as well be a fucking unicorn prancing in the foreground.

"Don't you think there ought to be a unicorn prancing around out here? Seriously, this is a sci-fi book cover of an alien—"

He turns to face me. "Vin, I can't do this."

"I know," I say, tracing the side of his face with my index finger. "I know, Perry."

They always hate remembering.

"Hey," I call over to a thirty-something couple who have finished taking each other's photos. "Would you take our picture?"

I grab the camera strap around his neck and lead him to them, re-asking, not giving Perry a chance to speak. I extricate the camera from his sun visor and hand it over.

"That sure would be great. Thank you." I make the necessary small talk and clasp my arm strongly around Perry's shoulder. "It's all set. Just press right… yeah, right there."

"Smile," the woman says to us.

Perry smiles, but it's weak.

They are polite, these tourists, and so they make sure we're both really ready and click the button. The photo taken, I thank them and they wander off. I walk up to two grungy, black-clothed teenage boys and ask them the same question.

They look at me warily.

"Would you mind? Big help if you did."

One of them shrugs in mild alarm. I see him shoot a look to his friend, perhaps wondering, "Why is this old man asking me?" Nevertheless, he slowly wraps his black-painted nails around the camera while he trades secret looks with his friend.

This time, I put my arm around Perry's waist so it's clear we're not just buddies. Perry's body tenses. I jab a thumb at Perry's tie-dye shirt and say loudly, "You guys know that Iowa is Hawkeye country, right?"

The boys say nothing, trying hard not to laugh.

"Say *sleeeeeeaze*," says the one, and his friend can stand it no more, hawking razor-sharp laughs and then staggering away. I thank the picture-taker before he sulks off to join his friend.

"Vin," Perry says, gripping my forearm, but I resist him, stepping up to a family of five, the kids happily trailing the wake of their parents.

"Bill-lee!"

I hear the name shoot right past my ear.

What the fuck?

My voice wavers as I say, "Would you take our photo?"

She said *Billy*. It's just a name; don't freak out over nothing. Smile, goddamn it.

I put my arm around Perry, but this time my heart isn't in it. Did she say *Billy* or was that *Willie*? I already don't remember, can't tell. Does it even matter?

Snap.

I didn't even smile for that one. *Focus the fuck up, you moron.*

What the fuck is with all this Billy shit? I don't have time for this. That guy at St. Anne's who looked like Billy, then that woman now calling out that name. Coincidences. But I am leery of coincidences. They start to feel like something more, bigger plans, greater connections. But this isn't a good time.

"How is this helping?" Perry says. "Seriously."

"Oh, it's helping."

Why the hell did I say that? Talk, you fucking moron!

"Perry, soon they'll notice the duck's missing. We should get proof that we spent the afternoon here."

That works. That *really* works. Okay, this isn't a disaster. Keep going with this.

I say, "My camera has that feature where it prints the time and date right on the photos. If someone bothered to write down my license plates and follows up, we'll have photographic proof we spent the afternoon here. Who steals a duck and then takes pictures at the Golden Gate Bridge?"

He refuses to meet my eyes.

"We can get them developed at one of those 24-hour photo places."

Thank you, kings, for that inspiration. Stay humble, and quit thinking about Billy. Don't fuck this up.

"Plus, I rarely use my real identity when I check in to hotels. I have all kinds of fake ID. They don't even know who I am."

"Oh my God," he says.

"God also owns various fake IDs," I say, turning to someone new. "Take our picture?"

She agrees, and I hand her the camera.

Snap.

Every photograph taken helps bring him to the roiling point. My few disastrous attempts at making blueberry jam gave me a powerful insight for kinging: how to keep a substance roiling, the state after boiling, the simmering, bubbling, seething place where angry little bubbles continuously explode. That's Perry right now, roiling. We reached boiling last night on Alcatraz, and he spent all morning roiling. Considering how the jam experiment ended, perhaps I should drop the roiling concept. I didn't know jam could explode.

I subject him to this ritual about five more times, in various states of affection. My tongue is never down his throat, but still, I make it obvious we're a couple. Photo-takers ask where we're from and if we're enjoying the city. I tell people that I'm from the Midwest and Perry lives here. I explain I'm visiting my boyfriend, sometimes curling my hand into his, noting his passive acceptance of my affection. Two helpful couples highly recommend Alcatraz.

"It might be too late to get tickets for the next week," says one older gentleman with his wife. "But you should try anyway. You *have* to do the audio tour."

Perry half grunts and half chuckles; he can't help himself.

I shake both of their hands. "Awesome advice. Thank you."

Perry remains angry and bewildered, especially considering we have barely moved ten feet in the entire time we've been here. He seems both surprised and uninterested in the chatty conversations I initiate about cheap San Francisco hotels and how Iowa has changed over the years. A University of Iowa graduate chats up Perry until he discovers Perry has no connection with the Hawkeyes, not even as a long-distance fan. Minus Perry, we all chat happily, words attempting to express how lucky we feel to stand here on such a resplendent day. It's bright but chilly; the sun beams madly on California's famous Gateway to Marin County.

After our latest helpers walk away, I say, "It's resplendent today. I just thought of that word, and it fits, right? I like it because it's luxurious to say the word *resplendent*. Say it. *Resplendent*."

Perry shoots me a glare, but he's not actually bothered by my word shit. Instead of tensing him, his shoulders shift down; his next photographed smile is slightly more authentic than the previous ones. It's as if he can't figure out how to react. He's not exactly exuberant, but he's opted for something like glum tolerance, another expression caught in between.

Besides, who can easily exude exuberance?

"I know a resplendent way out of this," I say during our next break. "I've given it some thought, and luckily, King Aabee dealt with something similar."

His eyes flash back to rage. "You're joking. Now?"

Roiling very much achieved.

"I can't," Perry says. "I tried, but this is too much."

I take his hands, gaze softly into his fury.

He's right. It's too much. Perry has been under constant assault: every unanswered question on Pier 33, every minute on Alcatraz, from cake dropping and fake bacon to demanding his wallet. I insisted he memorize a fairy tale while sexually exhausting him. I keep requiring forgiveness for each new affront, and he keeps forgiving. But it's never enough! The sky is bleeding, crimson slashes against an otherwise purple day.

This moment is everything, the real fulcrum of the weekend.

If Perry stays, the scales tip toward his kingship within the next half hour. If not, he remains lost. But right now, nothing is clear, other than it hurts, it always hurts. Why does this shitty world work this way?

Yet I believe the dam blocking his stunted heart might crumble at last, the expected, thunder-splitting boom sounding instead like the soft click of a 35mm camera. We're that close to the edge.

Don't quit, Perry. Don't walk away this time. Stay and love.

I shake my head. "Dude, you won't believe the predicament that King Aabee found himself in."

Perry steps backward, pulls his hands free.

"Stay, my king," I say, breathing more endurance into him, my sparkling orange and pink love. "Stay for this. Stay and love."

His empty stare accuses me, more articulate than words.

I step closer, feeling my love for Perry spark off me as I open my heart to him. Feel me, Perry, loving you with all my love.

I flash to King Mai, whose crown I'm wearing as I say, "Find your curiosity."

Perry says, "No."

Even that single word betrays hurt. But if he is to survive tonight, Perry's capacity to love needs to get bigger. Stronger. This is the moment where he grows something special.

"Diego, the Tourist King, found himself in trouble, and before any other king could volunteer to assist, King Aabee cried out, 'I will go. Send me!'"

I lean in and move my hand to the back of his neck, strumming small circles with my thumb. His skin feels hot to my touch, pulsating and simmering.

"King Diego managed to get himself locked up in a Turkish prison, which surprised no one as he was always offending someone. Diego asked the questions locals did not ask. He either tried too hard to fit in, or he didn't try hard enough. But he didn't mind being a tourist. It was once considered an honorable profession."

Perry says nothing.

I hug myself around him, engulfing him. One good push would separate us easily, but this isn't about physically trapping him; it's about tipping the scales. Everywhere around us I hear clicking and sputtering at the famous landmark. Not by accident I chose a dazzling bridge as the backdrop for the weekend's Fulcrum Moment. I need every bit of symbolism and power available.

Huskily, I speak into his ear. "To become a tourist assumes a certain vulnerability, to wear the wrong shoes and not know the right times for meals. To drive too slow, alert for photographable moments, because you're awestruck that beauty exists in the world and, amazingly enough, we all happened to find it on the same damn day. To be a tourist is to be filled with wonder."

Despite the chattering sea of people around us, Perry's and my world is completely still. Perry permits me to curl him into my arms, but his posture stays rigid, his breathing shallow. Perry and I might push the boundary of "overly affectionate" to those around us, but nobody shies away. Looking over his shoulder, I see a few folks cast uncomfortable glances our way, but they're in San Francisco and, I would guess, trying to be okay with it.

"To boast *wonder* takes great courage. Being left speechless with joy is not for the weak. We forget to be surprised at everyday miracles, like toast springing up, the mesmerizing blue in the sky, or even simple friendships. To touch and remember this delicate sense of wonder, we travel. We deliberately let ourselves become tourists to welcome in this unique delight. Wouldn't you like to be *filled with joy, Perry?*"

I cannot see his face, but I can feel his breath as his irritation melts into something else. Perry's head tilts forward a few inches, resting the tip of his forehead on my bicep.

It's done.

With a slight exhale that he will never remember, it's over. Perry's going to win.

I bet someone will photograph us as proof they were in the city of gays. Boy, that would be cool, to know in a few years we will live in a shoebox under someone's bed, maybe a scrapbook. Someone may see this photo years from now and say, "Remember the gays at the Golden Gate Bridge?"

I speak directly into his ear. "Those kings who displayed the great gift of vulnerability were the envy of all other kings. Every time those men made their hearts softer, they became the most powerful kings around. But when the King of Hope keeps his shades drawn, refusing to answer emails, the kingdom mourns. Why bother going out? What's the point?"

Perry breathes slower, breathing me. I feel his chest rise against mine—one of the most intimate expressions of invisible trust, to trust someone with your very breath—and against all his better judgment, something changes. Perry resists the urge to quit this painful game of giving his heart.

I embrace him tighter, our loose hug gradually intensifying as I continue to vibrate sound right into him.

"One of the most missed kings when he became lost was the Forgiver King. Because to give your heart as Aabee did when he was eighteen, well, that was beautiful. But to forgive...."

I linger over the word.

"When you forgive, you give your heart to wonder and love after it has already been broken. Twice. Three times. More. This is a vulnerability prized above all others."

His head sinks further.

A flock of waddling tourists surrounds us, quacking to each other, photographing the unbelievable girders before us. I wonder if Perry noticed I dressed him up with a duck's bill?

"Some say the lack of forgiveness is what keeps the Lost Kings lost. If only that particular king could be found, he would help awaken his brothers by forgiving their memory, their flaws, their awful burdens. If the Forgiver King were to be restored, there might be hope for the world. Every man knows that he is their one true king. When he was lost, the kingdom was devastated."

Perry waits for me to continue, but I stay quiet, letting the words bob around us.

He finally says, "Does this Forgiving King have a name?"

I think he intends to sound sarcastic, but the words come out all wrong, and instead sound half-interested.

"His name," I say, kissing the space in front of his ear, hesitating a moment longer, "is lost. When a king becomes lost, few remember the actual name of the man, as if a curse affects the entire kingdom's memories. So, everyone awaits the day when the Forgiver King comes strolling through the eastern gates at dawn, suddenly remembered."

My lips touch below his jaw, a presence more than kiss. I rock Perry tenderly, and he responds, letting me sway us. He arches his back because when you forgive, the body says, "Thank God."

He says, "I can't believe I'm listening to this."

I kiss him briefly on the lips, and without hesitation he kisses back.

I say, "Now you understand the importance of Aabee's mission to help King Diego with the Turkish authorities. The Tourist King could jar free bleary memories, soften certainty about the known world, and introduce the quality of wonder. King Diego made the world seem new again."

Perry looks at me uneasily and then leans in.

This kiss is deeper, with more passion, but it's not lust. It's something else, a commitment. This is the kiss he could not have given me yesterday on the pier, sealing his agreement to spend the weekend together. When we break, Perry's eyes remain sad.

He says, "How much time did King Aabee waste in Turkey?"

"Two years."

Perry nods. "King Aabee is a tool. He deserves to spend two years trying to get his client out of prison. And he's a lawyer now? He's got a cocksucking flute that sounds like mint, and now a law degree?"

"All kings are lawyers," I say, trying to sound offended. "Lawyering is the highest profession among the Found Kings." I frown at him and pull back. "Perhaps you do not understand the concept of lawyers."

Perry's eyes bounce away, right to the Golden Gate Bridge, and when they come back to me, I see grim curiosity. "Yeah, go for it. I'd like to hear this lawyer thing, seeing as how I'll soon require the services of one."

"Fairy tales always describe how a king's power comes from mountainous piles of gold locked up in a dungeon. Guarded by a dragon, right? A Found King's gold is mountainous indeed, but understanding that gold often requires lawyering.

"A king is as likely to dump his gold in the garbage as take too large a share, both equally done without malice. A king brother might say, 'Let me make an observation about how your gold works and why it is trapped.' Together, they free it. Sometimes it takes a lawyer to help you slay your dragons."

Perry's mood shifts again; he is relaxed but still surly. "That's convenient for whatever plot twist you need."

"Totally. I can whip out a courtroom trial at any second."

He laughs and pulls me close to him again, close enough to kiss. And he wants to kiss. He's still angry and confused, sure. But when forgiveness leads, the brain can't quite figure out how to catch up.

Perry taps his head against mine. "If you're talking about protecting gold, maybe all the kings are investment bankers."

"Maybe."

Oooh, I like it. Would that work?

He lifts his lips to mine. I am loved by this man.

"King Aabee argued passionately on Diego's behalf, helping his jailers understand the mighty gold Diego offered while also repairing relationships with the local officials. The two kings returned to the kingdom one morning at dawn, arms around each other's waists. All the Found Kings screamed in jubilation, for their one true king had returned."

Perry's smile remains guarded. "Who? King Aabee or the Tourist King?"

"Yes, exactly."

"That's bullshit."

"You're probably right."

"Got it. No more questions, yer honor."

He smiles, suddenly, a shy one. It's one thing to forgive, and it's another to show that forgiveness, to stroll with confidence through the blue castle.

"Wait." I jump back and clap both hands to the top of my head. "What's today? What's today's date?"

He crosses his arm and says, "Why?"

"Is today October 16?"

"Yeah."

"October 16?" I say, louder than normal. "Are you sure?"

"You are not going to believe this!" I shake him by the shoulders, trying to force his excitement. "It's King Diego's birthday *today*. You're sure it's the sixteenth? Today?"

He regards me coolly and says, "I admire your dedication, Vin. It's mentally ill, but still, impressive."

I pound my fist into the air, then jab a couple fake karate moves. I do my win-the-daily-lottery dance. People are not thrilled about my over-the-top elation; no, they're frightened. Okay, startled. Perry looks at me from behind his hands, concealing both his humiliation and the fact that he's also trying not to laugh. He's definitely still embarrassed. But he forgives. Once you start, it's hard to stop.

I yell, "*You're not going to believe this.*"

He wipes his eyes and glances again toward the bridge. "This time, I have decided not to be surprised."

"You and I are in the perfect tourist spot to celebrate King Diego's birthday."

Perry says, "Uh huh. So what's the dance? I assume it's a funny dance."

"No dancing." I hand him the camera and speak into him. "We take pictures. Fifty pictures of us in front of the Golden Gate Bridge."

Perry takes the camera, mugging slight aversion. He'll do anything for the rest of our time together.

"There's no vodka involved in this birthday celebration, is there? I see your expression says no. Didn't think so. But I have two things."

"Shoot. That was a camera pun by the way."

He leans in to speak quieter. "First, we make sure it hasn't knocked over the water dish or something. Make sure there's enough air in the van."

"Okay. Right away."

"Second," he says, pushing me away, "I'm only agreeing to be photographed in this hideous shirt in honor of King Diego's birthday."

"What? We look *great*."

"No self-respecting gay man would wear tie-dye and a sun visor."

"We are *studly*."

"We are tools. What the hell is with that 'Iowa is Buckeyes' territory' crap?"

"Hawkeyes."

"Whatever."

Perry raises the camera and snaps my photo.

I say, "That one doesn't count."

"Fine," Perry says. "I'm going to need a picture of you for the restraining order I'm filing on Monday."

As we stroll toward the van, I snicker a few times and he notices.

"It's not funny, Vin."

"C'mon, Perry. We stole a duck together. It's pretty funny."

He refuses to make eye contact, but I think it's because he's also smiling and doesn't want me to see.

The duck is fine.

Perry calls him Mr. Quackers, so now he has a name.

TWELVE

THINGS are on track. This is good.

But it's not an accident that I keep seeing Billy and hearing that name. It's because I told Perry that secret of mine, that's how this started. You damn kings gotta give me some room to breathe. I mean, I know sometimes my own shit comes up when I work with another man's deepest betrayals, but distract me with Billy shit next week when I am lonely for Perry. Hit me with this then. I'll be miserable anyway.

In front of the blue gift store, he says, "We're going in here."

This is a statement, not a question, and I snap to attention. The smile on his face seems friendly, but I catch a hardness in his eyes. He's letting me know that I will now submit to him. He submitted to me in all things, beyond what is reasonable, and he will continue to do so. But he wants to know if I myself can surrender. We're in a "gentlemen's rules" moment to see what happens if he puts his foot down on this one unimportant thing.

He says, "I'm buying each of us a snow globe of San Francisco. Since we're tourists, right? My latest theory is that you work for an animals' rights activist smuggling ring. You're not a garage mechanic, I bet. You don't even talk like a garage mechanic."

"You'd be surprised how often I hear that. I don't know what everyone thinks we're supposed to talk like. Monosyllabic, I guess. But go ahead and ask me a question about cars."

"What's a carburetor?"

"1886."

Perry frowns.

"Carburetor patent date, filed by Karl Benz, later of Mercedes Benz. He's got an interesting life story. Invented the carburetor and also wrote a little poetry on the side. Or did you want to talk about where and how our friend, the gentle carburetor, works on foreign or domestic cars, at least in those older models that still require aerated gasoline?"

"So, you're really a mechanic?"

"Yes."

"You're on vacation from Minnesota?"

"Yes."

"And you're leaving town tomorrow, and I'm not getting chopped up in a box somewhere?"

"Yes on leaving town, and gross. Don't say shit like that. It's very vivid inside me, Perry."

"Yeah, I figured that out."

Perry watches me carefully for a moment before saying, "Are you going to let me buy us both a snow globe of San Francisco?"

"Yes."

Perry nods and opens the blue and gold door.

Inside, I fret about timing because we're still on a schedule, and I hope this side purchase doesn't take terribly long. But I must relax because this is one of those open parts of the day, and we can always skip the next part, I guess. Hate to miss out on pineapple, but whatever. Mice and men, Vin. Mice and men. I could talk about King Aabee's California life over dinner instead. Clock on the wall confirms I have scheduled another hour and a half for us to be here. Good lord, plenty of time.

Relaaaaaaaaaax. Stay in the moment.

Perry seems intent on browsing only snow globes. He picks up the two biggest ones, and I follow him to the counter. He hands me mine while they box up the first one. Damn, it's heavy.

San Francisco has been taken hostage and encased in thick glass. The city includes a mini-Transamerica building, a few little distinctive buildings from the skyline, and a couple of painted ladies: the famous seven sisters. An imitation Golden Gate looms behind everything, the approximate size of a single bolt taken from the real thing. And there's Alcatraz, watching over San Francisco's shoulder. I shake it and watch the impossible snow resettle itself. I do believe that the snow globe will go down in history as humanity's greatest invention. Cheesy as these things are, we somehow managed to capture the quality of wonder.

"Let me buy them, Perry."

He turns to me with a snarky grin. "*You* paid for our lodgings last night *and* breakfast in the Tenderloin this morning, Vin. Really, you must allow *me*."

We snicker.

I say, "It's beautiful. Thank—"

"No, no," he says, pointedly. "Thank *you*."

His smile turns into laughter.

We stroll toward the plaza clutching our plastic bags with our boxed balls, oversized purses almost, and I dig this even better, the two of us navigating the photo-taking expedition dragging these two bowling balls everywhere.

Balls. Ha.

"Hey, Perry, will you hold our balls for a minute?"

"I've been waiting for a balls joke since inside. You're losing your edge."

"Pear, in all seriousness, this is an amazing souvenir and I will always cherish it because it reminds me of you. It's perfect, actually. But as of right now, ball jokes are fair game for the rest of the weekend."

"I would expect no less."

Once we get back to the cement plateau, Perry asks, "How does this photograph thing work?"

"You have to ask fifty people to take our photograph together. I have a second roll of film."

"You, me, and the bridge?"

"Yeah, but if you want to ask someone to join us, I have no objection. You're the creative director of this photo shoot."

He takes the camera from me and fiddles with its operation, verifying that he knows how to work it.

He says, "For the record, if the police show up, I'm willing to photograph your arrest, ducknapper."

"Duckling," I say. "I wonder if Mr. Quackers wants his photo taken in front of the Golden Gate Bridge."

Perry shoots me a look.

"Too soon for duck jokes?"

He walks away.

He asks the first couple he sees, dressed in pastel greens, lemon, and beige, if they will take our photo, and although they present thin, terse smiles revealing mild reluctance, they agree. Who says no to such an innocuous request? Afterward, they hand the camera back to Perry as if it is slathered in spit.

Perry thanks them. He turns and mugs to me. "Forty-nine more to go."

"Yeah, fifty. Or maybe sixty. You never know."

"Won't that put us behind for the four o'clock bank robbery?"

"Your ass is super hot," I say loudly, causing him to jump, "but it's not bank robber hot."

He grumbles and turns away. "Sir, would you mind? Would you take our—thank you, yeah, that would be great."

After we cuddle up together, Perry says, "When do we meet the King of Vodka?"

Snap.

That tiny little click comes from either my camera or another band twangs free around his imprisoned heart.

Around photo seventeen, it sinks in. Drinking in all this effervescent friendliness immediately after I broke his heart yet again, changes something in Perry. The comments and the expressions on people's faces start to wear him down.

"No, of course we don't mind."

"Absolutely, I'd be delighted."

"Would you mind taking ours next?"

"Move closer together now, and *big* smile."

Almost against his will, Perry's smile keeps getting wider, more pleased.

Perry asks a straw-hatted woman in her midseventies, fussing with things in her purse. Our camera chatter reveals she's from Illinois, road-tripping with her widow friends, grouped nearby fussing in *their* purses.

After she takes our photo, she says, "Aren't you a cute couple. I wouldn't think you'd go for bears, dear."

"I don't," Perry says, surprised. "Not normally. But he's got this weird, sexy vibe. After a while you let go and enjoy it, like Old Spice."

I huff and say, "I'm going to take that as a compliment."

"Definitely," she says, handing Perry the camera and squeezing my arm.

Perry chuckles after she departs. "How the hell does she know about bears?"

I say, "Gimme."

I take the camera before he can say anything else and aim for his smirk.

Snap.

It's beginning for you, Perry.

Several people refuse, including a woman who calls herself "butterfingers," and her friend who vehemently agrees. They faux-bicker for us, and we enjoy the show. Two folks ignore us and walk away. But not many refuse; we all came to be tourists, after all.

A few clicks later we meet two best friends vacationing together, a gay man and straight woman, both in their midforties. They have been friends for twenty-one years and know now that if neither of them ever marries, they will always have the devoted love of this lifelong friendship. They decided to take an anniversary trip to celebrate their love, the flavor that it is.

We trade anecdotes with them, discuss favorite restaurants, and they tease each other like a married couple, making Perry and me laugh at their overly familiar commentary. Perry confides in them that we're on a first date of sorts, and they ask all kinds of wonderful, prying questions.

I can't resist saying, "Last night, I found out he snores."

"He's a criminal," Perry says. "One of us is lying. And here's a clue: I don't snore."

"You definitely snore."

As we start making our goodbyes, Perry asks, "How about a picture of the four of us?"

A few minutes later, Perry approaches a family with three kids, two of them shy and one madly dancing brother, clearly the youngest. After the parents help us out, Perry asks each kid their name, but only the dancer answers directly.

He shouts at us, "NICHOLAS."

Photo twenty-four.

After they leave, I say, "I bet Nicholas would like Mr. Quackers."

I turn away as if heading back to the van.

"Way too soon," Perry says, grabbing my shoulder. "I thought you picked that up after your first joke."

After photo thirty-two, two Chinese men finally approach us. I noticed them a few minutes ago, but I did not wish to embarrass them, so I pretended I did not. With a nod, I invite them to speak, and in hushed words, they do. They noticed us having our photo taken, over and over, and thought we might be international tourists, like them. We discover that for the last half hour they have been looking for someone to approach. They really want a photo together in front of the Golden Gate Bridge; it's important to them. But they do not want to make someone uncomfortable, nor do they wish to be judged.

"Would you take our photos, please?" asks the first man, with nervous pride.

His partner says, "We know it is more open here, but we are still careful."

Of course we agree, and I fiddle with their camera lens, testing the light and such, delaying so that Perry has time to talk to them.

"Smile."

They won't stand too close or put their arms around each other, but in the series of photos I take, you can see joy in their eyes. It's definitely joy.

The task accomplished, we follow them, and they follow us, wandering down the nearby walkways, scattered with vibrant yellow flowers and shiny green bushes, everyone admiring the magnificent, sparkling bay this glorious day in Eden. We ask questions about living in China. We try to answer their questions about living in the United States.

Zhong and Jian are shy again when they announce their departure. But they are eager to experience the towering redwoods in Marin County. They really want to kiss in the forest. Big secret kiss.

"Maybe more than kiss," Zhong says, scandalizing Jian.

They laugh together, blushing beautifully, and tip their heads toward us.

Perry stares at the departing figures with wet eyes.

Yup. Fifty photographs ought to be enough.

"Perry, check out that couple over there. Behind those three girls. What do you see?"

"What am I looking for?"

"No. Tell me what you *see*."

I continue to ask this before each new photograph, and he eventually starts reading people better. Not that you can ever know someone's life story by the way they wander around on vacation, but tourists repeatedly choose to make themselves vulnerable, so some of their tells are more obvious.

"Let's ask them," he says, pointing to two heavily pierced men wearing Harley Davidson shirts. "Hey, dudes."

Somewhere around forty, I suggest that he find the ones who need it.

"Need what?" Perry asks.

I shake my head. "Just look around. Who *needs* it?"

We talk about the possibilities, mostly Perry asking questions and me refusing to answer. If he would give up and look, he would realize he already knows. After a whopper of a candidate wanders into view, I put my hand over his mouth from behind and rock him in my arms, giving him a chance to look around.

My hand muffles the sound when he says, "Her."

I say, "Good choice."

A stout woman patrols the second plateau, not far from us. She's probably late thirties, with frosted-golden locks, a beautiful tangle of curly hair falling over her dark brown shoulders. Purple sundress. She slings three small backpacks over her right shoulder, packs that I bet her kids promised, promised, *promised* to carry themselves. She and her husband do their best to corral four eager children. The kids race to the chain-link fence to stare at the Golden Gate Bridge, pushing each other to get a better view, and I watch a young dancer named NICHOLAS run over to meet them. Her weary expression suggests they've been this hyper all day.

We watch.

I say, "How are we going to put King Diego energy into her?"

Perry says, "Have we been doing that?"

"Follow me."

We take a few steps toward her; then I stop him with a hand on his chest and say, "Did you love your mom?"

"Yes, I loved her," he says, surprised.

"So there was never a time in your life where you were ungrateful, or a dick to her or anything?"

His open face creases in hurt, and I see I hit a nerve. Good.

"Go with this."

He says, "Wait—"

I stride away, closing the distance, forcing him to scurry after me.

"Hi, will you take our photo?"

Tired Mom looks at me with bored anger, like I'm another kid demanding her attention and she has enough of those.

"I'm busy," she says.

"*Please.* I bet you'd take a great photograph."

This earns me a glimmer of real irritation, but I can do awesome puppy dog eyes. Please, Tired Mom, give us a chance.

I say, "I saw your kids so energetic and happy, and it made me think you'd take a great photograph, because you look like a good mom."

She turns to her husband. "Tim. Watch Devon. I'm taking some damn tourist photos." She turns back to me and says sharply, "No offense."

"None taken!" I quack happily.

Perry's smile isn't quite authentic because irritating her wasn't part of his plan, and I have once again made him complicit in another crime—this time, bothering a woman on vacation.

She snaps the photo and thrusts the camera back to me. Her expression isn't as angry anymore, the experience already over.

"My friend Perry just told me about how the Golden Gate Bridge reminds him of his mom."

Perry's eyes open wider, a subtle change not lost on her. "Yeah. My mom."

She listens attentively now; she recognizes a setup.

Without breaking eye contact with her, I say, "Big secret."

"She was strong," Perry says, the words popping out. "Real strong."

He looks at Tired Mom with anguish and says, "My dad died young, and it wasn't easy for her. We were broke from medical bills. I—I was horrible those first two years after he died. Even though I apologized over and over after I grew up, to this day I regret how I treated her."

His voice cracks during the last part. I don't think he's going to cry, but the raw emotion coming from this revelation may have been unexpected.

He says, "She died about ten years ago. I would give anything to have those two years back. *Anything* to hear her voice."

She looks at him carefully. The world can surprise you sometimes.

"She understood," Tired Mom says, her voice quiet. "She's a mom."

She turns and walks back toward her family. One of the younger girls launches herself right into Tired Mom's leg, pushing them both off center.

"My mom," Perry says and turns to me, eyes wide.

I pull him into my chest and hold him. I think he's taking a moment to see his mother in a new light. Perhaps she was a tourist as well, lost in a city where she never expected to find herself.

I don't know much about his mom, just scraps I've been able to glean without his realizing. Tuesday at the art gallery, he didn't associate that finger tree painting with Mother's Day, my first volley checking out his mother issues. During Big Secret, he confirmed how much he missed her. I thought he might be able to see an inspiring bridge and relate it to something remarkable in her. But I don't want him too emotional right now; we're not ready for that.

Using a gentle tone, I say, "That one didn't count because, technically, I asked her. You still have nine more photos to take, pardner."

Instead of protesting, his chin traces mine until he kisses me.

Our lips meet soft and subtle, the right amount of mutual pressure. Though surrounded, I feel invisible, enjoying a private moment at our own private monument.

We break apart, and I turn him around, wrapping my arms around his midsection, my chin on his shoulder, seeking her. Not far away, I spot her husband retrieving their son from NICHOLAS's family.

There she is. I nudge his head with mine toward her and say, "Check out Tired Mom."

The woman stands a stone's throw away. One child strains in her left hand while two more argue over who's in the next photo with mama. Tired Mom considers the Golden Gate Bridge.

She looks different.

Maybe it's an unexpected break. Hell, maybe she started chewing a piece of mint gum. Or, maybe she remembers a piece of her queenship, what it means to truly be strong. And now that I'm thinking of it, constantly run over. You might look at the Golden Gate Bridge and think: *Oh. Moms. Got it.*

When driving back from Sausalito, I love that first glimpse of the deep orange towers striking the rolling, lush hills, legs battered by the white-crested surf. Only a surrealist painter could juxtapose shapeless foam against steel pylons that will outlast all of us, man's rare architectural improvement to a gorgeous landscape. On those days when shadow and mist rule the earth, I love driving across, straining to see the high-reaching cables, invisible while I'm directly underneath. Golden Gate's power remains even when masked by magician's fog, hidden only by our limited ability to recognize strength.

I whisper into Perry's ear, "King Diego is not to be underestimated."

We nuzzle for a moment longer, staring at the bridge, the sky, the everything.

He shivers and says, "It's cold out here."

"It's *always* cold in San Francisco. At least in Minnesota we get to wear coats. You guys always pretend like this isn't cold."

He turns his head and searches the immediate area, another three dozen people replacing the three dozen who were here a while ago. He takes the camera from me and says, "Hold our balls."

Perry picks out an older man nearby who looks angry. "Sir, would you mind taking our photo?"

AFTER fifty-four photos, we return to Mr. Quackers. At Perry's suggestion, we decide to journey to the middle of the bridge and back. We trade our tourist costumes for our warmer gear. Feels good to wear my coat. We store our snow globes carefully, and I insist on using the cake straps to secure them in the back. No rolling around. I also want Perry to see the straps and remember the cake. That was part of our day too.

"You're not wearing your sun visor?" I ask with mock incredulity.

"I look like an idiot, Vin."

We hold hands as we stride toward the center, both of us basking in the glow. Too soon it seems, we're right at the bridge's midpoint, gazing in every direction at the fog castle kingdom. From this height, the bay remains motionless, yet every wave forms and disbands faster than instantly. The white-capped water peaks look like frosting curls, and the ocean becomes a giant sheet cake, congratulating us for participating in a perfect Saturday. Or maybe it's for King Diego's birthday. Trees on the steep hills in Marin County balance their precarious position with a relaxed California attitude. Even the lapis lazuli sky belongs to San Francisco. Small islands dot the bay, lush with ripe trees and sad histories.

"Ever walked to the center?"

"No," he says and zips up his coat. "I always said I would, though. Ever since I moved here, I've been meaning to. I figured that as long as we're celebrating King Diego's birthday, we should."

We bask.

"Oh crap," Perry says, peering toward Alcatraz, "I see I left my ski mask in the Hammock. Tell Jerome we're coming back."

"I assume you'll want to keep your ski mask as a souvenir."

"Of course. Assuming we don't need it for this afternoon's crime spree. Even though I'm not bank-robber hot."

"Don't feel bad. You're still hot."

He looks more relaxed than I have ever seen him.

I say, "Very hot."

We kiss.

"It's fucking cold out here," he says, pushing me away.

We laugh and push each other. I point out cloud shapes, inventing raunchy sexual positions where he insists there are none.

"It's too bad you wouldn't let me elaborate on King Aabee's sex life this morning, because that one cloud formation looks like—"

He pushes my forehead with the palm of his hand.

A few times we're asked to take photos and we gladly comply, with Perry almost always asking for reciprocation. Good thing we brought our camera.

When we come upon Zhong and Jian, Perry collapses into them as if they are old college friends and he's ecstatic for the overdue reunion. Although clearly baffled by this intense familiarity, they offer little resistance, for this is America, after all, and today is a day for adventure. Turns out that once they zoomed across the Golden Gate, they themselves could not resist the allure of walking to the middle. We get a few photos of all four of us together from some nearby tourist.

I suggest that if they are interested, Perry can recommend good restaurants. While Perry names a few places, I stand behind him and write against his shoulder. I always carry index cards with me for occasions like this. I like coincidences. Well, usually. The Billy stuff, I could do without.

After additional photos taken by both couples, we part again, and we all seem more giddy after our latest exchange. We wave our retreating goodbyes as we back away. Perry puts his hand in the middle of my back, enough pressure to let me know he's there. I can imagine we're on the front steps of our Victorian in Russian Hill, wishing dinner guests goodnight. When our new friends retreat, we both recognize our time in the middle is over and start retracing our steps to the van.

"Back to the story," he says. "How did King Aabee get King Diego out of trouble? Or can you not tell me that until we're skydiving?"

"I can tell you now."

Perry stops and fakes panic. "Forget I said skydiving."

I laugh. "Don't worry."

He makes an exaggerated sigh, and we resume walking.

"Skydiving's more of a Sunday morning thing."

He pushes my shoulder with his, and we test each other's strength.

"The funny thing was that King Diego had not actually committed a crime. He merely offended some local officials."

"Uh-huh. I'm not surprised; these kings of yours aren't super bright. What did he *not* do? What was the charge?"

"Ducknapping."

Perry stops.

"Technically, duck*ling*napping. King Diego rented a duck and stored it at an expensive hotel that already owned ducks."

I love his face right now.

"When he ran out of the hotel, everyone was like, 'Hey, you can't take that duck!' And King Diego was like, 'Ha, ha, I totally stole your duck! No, just kidding, I rented it.' He offered proof from his van, but they were like, 'No way, man, we're totally mad. You are *so* arrested.' Which was a shame, because he really did rent it. The receipt and contract were in the glove box. Most people didn't even know you could rent ducks."

He rubs his eye socket with the heel of his hand and then scrubs his whole face with his fingers.

I say, "Culturally, ducknapping in Turkey was taboo."

When he peels away his finger mask, he looks both furious and ready to laugh. It's an odd expression. I'm sure he hadn't forgotten about the stolen duck and that he feels a huge relief at not being a wanted criminal. But dammit, I did it to him again.

"Very, *very* taboo."

I doubt he yet realizes that there was never a girl named Marie. No birthday party.

"I fucking knew it," he says, eyes suddenly blazing with clarity. "I knew it."

I cock my head for effect. "Did you?"

"I thought it once or twice. I thought, yeah, this is probably from a pet store or something and—*you fucker*. But you're actually crazy enough. Oh, man."

Perry decides to laugh. He says, "You motherfucker. You didn't steal that duck from the hotel."

"Here's the thing…."

I pause and seem to consider my options.

"It's like this…."

I pause again.

"What you must take into account is…."

He punches my chest a few times somewhere between playful and, well, punching, perhaps hoping to pound out some truth. He gives up and pulls me into a big hug.

"Duck stealer," he says into my ear. "Is that your king name? King Vin the Duck Stealer?"

This forgiveness feels more like joy.

"Duck*ling*, by the way."

He pushes me gruffly with his chest while pulling my waist closer, using newfound energy that might knock us over.

"*Quuaack,*" I cry in protest.

He roughs me up a little more.

"*Quaaaaaaaaaaaaaaaaaaaaaaack.*"

He laughs into my chest, and I laugh too, rocking back and forth on the Golden Gate Bridge like a couple of struggling grizzlies.

It's good to be a bear and not take yourself so damn seriously.

THIRTEEN

BACK in the overflow parking, I fret over our timetable but decide our jaunt to the middle impacts nothing significant, just a little less time at the next location. No afternoon nap for Perry. I wonder how soon I can work a joke about "fowl play" into the conversation. Ugh. No, I'm gonna keep that one to myself. At least I'm not....

Oh crap.

"I have the word *vigor* in my head again. I keep envisioning an English reverend on a rickety bicycle. He's clean shaven, but his scruffy hair points out in three different directions."

"Don't scare the duck with that shit. I'm sure Mr. Quackers has enough emotional trauma after spending the week with you."

"You want this?" I offer the second finished film canister in the palm of my hand.

Perry takes it without making eye contact and unzips the duffel bag with yesterday's clothes. He takes the first canister from his jeans and packs it in as well.

I say, "Check it out. Feel our big balls under the tarp."

"Classy," he says.

"Touch it through the tarp. It's like, tarp scrotum."

"I stand by my description."

"Seriously, touch my tarp scrotum."

"Yes, Master," he says with a smirk and rubs our crinkly snow globes.

Not much later, we sail across the Golden Gate Bridge.

Mr. Quackers's travel cage rests on Perry's lap because he didn't want our little guy riding around alone in back. The wire cage blocks the view of, well, everything, which inspires entirely new Alcatraz jokes. Mr. Quackers takes the curvy California highway turns with a wobble, as he skitters toward one side of the cage, stopping a duck step or two just before the wire walls. He looks like he might be drunk.

I could be drunk, I'm so happy right now.

I say, "Keep your eyes open for unicorns. I'd hate to smash into one while distracted by the ocean down there."

Gross.

"On it," Perry says, grinning. "Where to? More federal crimes or faux-crimes? Should we pick up a matching ski mask for Mr. Quackers?"

"No, smartass. I need to do a favor for a buddy of mine."

"A buddy?"

"You know how friends are when they find out you're going to California for vacation."

Perry says, "Riiiiiiiiiiiight."

"If I drove into a unicorn and hit it like a deer, what are the odds the horn would go through the windshield?"

What is wrong with me? Ease up on the unicorn wrecks, Vin. Thankfully, Perry ignores my latest diversion. Sometimes, I think I invent shit deliberately to distract me, some self-destructive tendency to undermine the kinging.

He says, "Would this friend of yours happen to be a king?"

"Funny you should say that. He is."

"I wonder if any of this afternoon's kings will have food."

"Didn't you eat the lunch at the hotel?"

"I couldn't eat it," he says, surprised. "I tried."

As we head into another curve, I take his hand, hoping to pull him back from whatever crosses his face right now: shame, embarrassment, some odd combination of the two.

"That wasn't a dig, Perry. Seriously, how hungry are you?"

He says, "I'm okay. I was just, you know, making with a funny."

I nod as the majestic Pacific Ocean comes into view.

"I mean," he begins and then stops.

The ocean will do that.

It's hard to drive and chat with the most glorious thing you've ever seen looming around every curve.

He says, "I mean, at some point, to eat. Would be good. Wow. I always forget how this is amazing."

I say, "Yeah. Beauty is surprising."

The easy kindling goes first: a stunning ocean, a famous bridge, a mom who reminds him of his own. But today he tossed a few new logs into the fire, befriending men on their honeymoon and asking children their names. Though he protested how breakfast at a homeless shelter would not change him, he later found he could not eat the same food off a silver platter.

Perry's heart has been quietly expanding. Slender strips of violet love appear every day to remind us of this subtle fact: true, the sky is bleeding, but don't be alarmed. The purple is everything.

We head down the Pacific Highway, everything around us suggesting gingerbread homes, hills ripe for castles, and trees ready for enchantment. We chatter as I drive through the hills, the magnificent twisting roads, draped in green California canopy. Every now and then, Perry says, "Hey, Mr. Quackers, check out the view."

WITHIN a short time, we coast through a small town, one of those touristy coastline communities. The town's center reveals cafés all specializing in fish tacos, three surf shops, and a general store where teenagers from everywhere lounge on the front steps, achieving a globally accepted expression of indifference. A converted ranch home sells crystals and New Age healing books, and a block later, a three-foot mystical eye promises tarot readings revealing your true destiny. It would be easy to snicker at this town and say, "Only in California."

But it's more fun to forgive this tourist trap, and say, "Only in California!" Taco-chomping surfers chat up pale Midwesterners, explaining their love of riding waves, while at a neighboring table, a woman reads about healing others with chakras. Even the bored teenagers shoot each other furtive looks of acceptance, trying to figure out how to establish common ground.

I could live here.

Perry says, "When I first moved to San Francisco, I rented a car one weekend and drove up and down the coast. Late Sunday afternoon, I got to the same town we're in right now and realized I had no gas. The needle slipped way under the E. I noticed it off and on throughout the afternoon but remembered this town, so I didn't worry."

"Hey, quick interruption. Want to get food while we're here? Fish tacos?"

"I'm good for now," he says. "I'll wait until whatever you got planned. You *do* have something planned?"

"Of course. Anyway, out of gas."

"Right. I pulled over at this surf shop coming up on the left, right there, and asked for the nearest gas station. This older man, this surfer dude in his midfifties or so, told me that the closest was 'fourteen miles in that direction'. He just pointed, you know? And then he said, 'Fourteen miles in that direction, too.'"

I nod. I've cut it close, not quite as close as that, but close enough to cause concern.

Perry watches Mr. Quackers attack a piece of lettuce.

"How could they not have a gas station here? At first, I thought he was kidding. I stayed in his shop fuming because I had nowhere to go. I'd be stranded either way. I guess because I wouldn't leave, he finally broke down and told me of a gas pump five miles away. He said, 'You make three left turns around the lagoon to get there.' When I asked him the town name and street names, he got irritated and repeated his directions. He wouldn't say any more. I didn't have a choice, so I started driving."

Perry shakes his head and laughs. It looks good on him.

"I followed his directions, but at the same time my knuckles were pure white from gripping the steering wheel so hard. Why didn't he tell me about this town first? That was suspicious. And I couldn't believe that there were unnamed back roads this close to San Francisco; prior to moving here, California meant big cities and traffic. But I followed his directions, taking the left turns around this lagoon."

The shadowed patterns of tree leaves brush our faces. Coming up on our far left, I can make out the lagoon in question.

"Everything over there looked like rural Ohio where my grandparents lived. Rickety wooden fences, overgrown scrub trees, and homemade pottery for sale on a card table near the road. I thought for sure surfer dude set me up. Maybe he also owned a tow truck business or something; who knows? Just as my car started sputtering, I crest this one hill and suddenly coast into an artist colony town with a Shell station."

"Bolinas," I say and nod in recognition.

He says, "Okay, so you know about this?"

"I know they rip out the highway signs, anything that points toward their town."

"Exactly. I coasted into the station after completely thinking this guy fucked me over, sent me on a goose chase. But the surfer didn't lie. After I gassed up, I drove around. Cute town."

"You had faith in Bolinas."

He smiles and says, "I did."

I say, "A lot of people do."

A secret artist colony that granted Perry emergency access? I like it.

We pass the signless lagoon road, the first left, and Perry points a silent finger. I nod in a conspirator's appreciation as we chug further down Highway One. No time to visit Bolinas today, but my brain races, reworking a few details in King Aabee's next appearance. I can work with this.

Perry looks out the window as the Pacific coast flutters into view again. A thousand sparkles disappear as soon as we notice them, which should disappoint us tremendously, but they're immediately replaced by a thousand more. Holy shit, I love the ocean.

A happy silence later, punctuated only to point out some beautiful vista, an amazing tree, or to interpret vanity license plates, I pull over at the overlook area I know so well.

Magnificent overlooks dot the entire Pacific coastline, all unbelievable knockouts in this never-ending beauty contest. Driving up the coast, you might encounter the same tourists every few miles as everyone piles out of their car once more, fretting and excited because it can't be *that* impressive again, like it was a mile back there. Surely not here as well? Then the fine spray tickles your face, an authentic ocean kiss, and you realize, yes, it's that breathtaking.

This particular overlook ranks a hideous 9.6 on the 10-point beauty scale, meaning it's stunning, but the spot comes right after a steep curve, so I imagine most folks see the intimidating parking lot at cliff's edge and decide to stop at the next one. Two other cars dared to park here, so the danger obviously does not dissuade everyone.

"We're here," I announce, "at the overlooked overlook."

"Are we letting Mr. Quackers go here?"

"Nope. He goes back to his home after the weekend. Now that I don't have to pretend I'm worried about the noise he makes, we'll open the windows a good amount. Meet me in back for another costume change."

Perry expresses his lack of surprise and maneuvers himself and the cage out of the front seat. Mr. Quackers had grown docile in the past twenty minutes after finding his sea legs. Now he faces the ocean almost sleepy, eyes shut against the crushing wind and his fuzzy yellow feathers ruffling hard. He appears trapped in a wind tunnel.

After settling Mr. Quackers into a comfortable spot, Perry asks if he might adjust the tarps to create a dark corner around the cage, in case Mr. Quackers wants to nap. We discuss it, and after testing with both the doors closed, we decide the van will be dark enough as is.

"By the way, Pear, do I get any credit for using 'overlooked overlook?' Did you hear me say that when we pulled up? Six *o*'s in those two words?"

"Dude, you're scaring the duck."

"You're still trying to pull off 'dude'?"

He says, "It's friendly. It's Californian."

I say, "My, my. Look who has word issues."

I plunge both arms under a tarp, make a big show of feeling my way around until I gradually pull free two pairs of hip-high rubber waders with reinforced rubber soles.

I fish out a green sweatshirt and suggest he wears the tie-dye shirt under the sweatshirt because both are probably going to get wet. The tarps reveal another small backpack I have packed for this occasion.

Perry watches as the latest one emerges and says, "How many of these did you bring?"

"Please save your questions until the end of the tour."

He says, "I don't want to get these new jeans wet. They fit great. I mean, really great. How did you know my exact size?"

I reach under the tarp and pull out another pair, same size, same brand. Perry laughs and surrenders. We don our hip waders, and Perry walks around in circles, testing them out, getting used to their strange heaviness, adjusting his suspenders for a better fit. Boy, if he were still wearing that sun visor, he'd look more like a duck than ever.

"You want your visor?"

"Nah," he says.

"You sure? Sun's bright."

In a dry tone, he says, "I'll risk it."

After assuring Mr. Quackers of his personal safety during our absence, we head toward the cliff, discovering the first of many thick wooden beams wedged into the rock wall, a steep slope descending right into the beach. I'm glad the overlooked overlook doesn't get the same attention as its neighbors; it's a California secret right out in the open. We clomp down, stopping at a platform midway.

"Hang on," I say, "camera moment."

Like every other tourist, we gawk and photograph the most magnificent alien creature ever witnessed, the Pacific Ocean. Instead of a body of water, I behold a twitching leviathan, slumbering on its side. This all-encompassing monster, Ocean, defies explanation. How can a thing hold all the colors at once? Every shade of midnight blue and saffron teal bob away, gradations of black and green in combinations I have never experienced. How can glittering orange and yellow crest each wave's tips before cheerfully drowning? Ocean lies motionless on its side while every surface inch shivers with the ecstasy of life.

I shiver.

After we photograph ourselves, heads touching, with the ocean behind us, we continue our rubbery clomping downward.

Perry squeezes my hand, happy with the inner recognition that somehow this all fits; it's even—crazily enough—safe. He trusts me. The shift in his demeanor is obvious: his goofy cheer, willingness to play with Mr. Quackers, and lack of resistance strapping on hip waders. Exhausted, dark crescents under his blue eyes betray this surrender did not come easy, but he did it. He gave all his love.

We joke and invent king names as we pounce into the sand at the base of the stairs and tramp over toward pure cobalt. I wrap my arms around him from behind and kiss his neck, waddling us toward the creature.

Two other couples wander with us here today, both pairs stepping cautiously toward the water, then jumping back as the waves rush to greet them, probably hoping to photograph the delicate grace and rock-smashing majesty in each wave. Grace and majesty are two difficult tourist destinations to capture on film, but it's always fun to try. We snap a few photos ourselves.

Perry looks ridiculous trotting toward one couple in his big waders, a spaceman running across the moon. A moment later, Perry grasps their camera.

As I approach, I hear him say, "Say *lobster*."

They ask questions about our hip waders, and warn us about going too deep; the undertow is always stronger than you'd expect. I assure them we will use caution. Although Perry does not know what lies ahead, he agrees with complete confidence.

"We're fine," he says, "but thank you."

Perry and I continue down the shore. Hundreds of footprints in the sand precede us. I wonder where all these people are today.

"It's a funny coincidence, your out-of-gas story from earlier, because this favor is for King Bolinas."

Perry says, "Of course it is. Are you just making this up spontaneously?"

I lead him along the beach, hand in hand, our tall waders leaving deep, distorted craters in the wet sand until they are erased. We have a slight advantage over the other couples in that we don't mind if the water rushes over our ankles. The sun shines hard on the oceanic monster before us, and she wriggles in appreciation for the light of day.

"King Bolinas is the Starfish King. He scours the beaches every day rescuing washed-up starfish. In ancient days, he addressed the entire kingdom, pleading, 'Help me save the prickly and defenseless. Do not be fooled by their external spine, their roughness. They are creatures of soft beauty who need our love to get back into the ocean.'"

Perry says, "Is this the story where the moral is 'you can't save every starfish, but at least you can save this one'? I bet they sold prints of that back in that woo-woo gift store."

"Yeah it is, and you're probably right about the crystal shop."

"Sorry. Didn't mean to come across quite so cynical."

"No, you're right. I didn't mean *probably* in that shut-up way. I bet they sell macramé scrolls of that story too. But King Bolinas felt that starfish were the ocean's homeless and returning them felt like serving them breakfast."

I study his face but see no discernible reaction.

"Many kings had volunteered to help Bolinas, promises were made, and some kept their word. But others were waylaid by death or married into a family with four stepchildren, finding themselves short on free time. Unanticipated quests came up that could not be avoided, life responsibilities, and of course, some kings who had vowed assistance got lost, forgetting their promises."

Nothing registered on Perry's face when I mentioned kings "waylaid by death."

Good.

He hasn't given permission to me to discuss his father. Not yet.

"After many years of broken promises, King Bolinas's frustration exceeded his legendary patience and he wept for the lack of support. Word went out quickly: our one true king is in crisis. As the Found Kings gathered around him, all his brothers, he explained that he had calculated ten years' worth of broken promises, and he begged a man to repay the great debt."

"Uh oh," Perry says, "Trouble in the big house. I thought these guys never got frazzled or fought or anything. Isn't this supposed to be a utopia?"

"Nope. They argued. Got pissed off. Remember, dragons sometimes guard a king's gold. Thus, lawyers."

He adds, "Who are also investment bankers."

"Yes, thank you for that."

Crap. I'm no longer confident about including investment bankers. Will this come back to bite me later tonight? Maybe.

Too late. Go.

"Who else but an investment banker could polish the gold? When a Found King argues his grief, he doesn't argue to win, but for greater love, richer compassion. King Bolinas calculated this ten-year request not as outraged entitlement, but from his deep sorrow and sense of abandonment. He wanted to love freely again, to lose his jadedness. He pleaded with the Found Ones to set the scales right and free him. It hurts to live with a broken promise."

We stop.

I have marched us the full length of this private little beach, right to a cliff wall jutting further into the blue. A dark crevice appears in the impassable rock now that we're standing next to it, tall and wide enough to enter without ducking your head.

I clear my throat. "This is the cave of horrors. We're going in."

He says, "We can't go in there."

"Why not?"

"Because it's a dark cave in a fucking cliff. Plus, you just called it the cave of horrors."

I release his hand and take a few steps toward the cave. I turn back, extending him my fingers. He'll come. He surrendered on the Golden Gate Bridge.

He puts his hands on his hips and says, "There could be bats."

"Possibly."

Perry scowls and starts to sputter another argument.

I say, "Faith in Bolinas."

He looks at me and his face softens.

Perry turns to scrutinize the ocean horizon, to let me know he's not crazy about this, but reaches out to take my hand. Once again, I am forgiven. He's getting good at that.

The entrance hollows wide enough for us to enter side by side, the interior always reminding me of Marshall, Will, and Holly on a routine expedition.

"Did you ever watch *Land of the Lost*? It started out 'Marshall, Will, and Holly, on a—"

"Yeah, this is like one of those sets."

I detect no trace of grumpiness; he's over it already. "What do you mean 'sets'? That shit was real."

Before we even lose the light from our entrance, light washes in from the way out. Suddenly, we stand in blazing sunlight a few feet further down the beach. This latest private beach area remains mostly deserted because who would walk into a dark cave in the side of a cliff? That's messed up.

He says, "Really? Cave of horrors?"

I say, "I have a low tolerance for horror."

His exhale expresses everything he needs to say: that I am an idiot, and he should have known better, and of course, of course, of course. It's a lot of communication for a single wordless breath, but we know each other now. We don't need as many words.

Footprints reveal others tread this way, but only a dozen or two as opposed to the horde tromping through the overlooked overlook, which, come to think of it, may not be as overlooked as I assume. Maybe I come on off days. Huh.

Perry drops my hand and jogs into our private beach. This is the payoff for forgiveness, going somewhere completely new.

Twenty feet of sandy beach quickly transitions to another forty yards of treacherous tidal pools, more slippery rocks than sand. A few dozen feet out, on the rocky side of our cove, SUV-sized rocks stand around, bored, their backs pounded by the ocean. These are the teenagers of the rock world, not nearly as ancient as their grandparent pebbles nor as young as the infant cliffs. These teens have lived; they've seen a few things. They hump shoreward at a glacial pace, but nobody informed them that to reach the promised beach, they must allow themselves to be destroyed. But being destroyed is not always as awful as it seems.

After drinking it in, Perry returns to me beaming.

"King Bolinas wanted ten years from a single king?"

"Yes."

I offer my hand, and he takes it.

"Doing what?"

"Picking up starfish and placing them back into the ocean."

"I'll tell this next part of the story," Perry says, checking me with his hip. "The kings discussed this, but then a man with a cocksucking flute cried out, 'I'll go. Send me! Even though I have no fucking clue what you need for the next ten years, sign me up.'"

"Close," I say, squeezing his hand as we stroll down the beach, looking for starfish.

Perry says, "I'm sure King Aabee regretted it wasn't sewer work."

I chuckle.

He says, "It's a good thing that King Bolinas didn't want ten years of fisting. Aabee may find himself on the hurtin' edge of volunteering."

I'm a little shocked. Perry hasn't spoken explicitly to me, despite my own graphic descriptions. Not even when I pointed out a daisy chain of cocksucking clouds and encouraged him to find a few sexual shapes. But then again, many San Franciscans believe it's a distinguishing characteristic that they can toss the word *fisting* into normal conversation and act cool with it because, hey, fisting happens. Even if they're uncomfortable with this particular sexual expression, that San Francisco sensibility says, "play along." And then one day, they don't mind the presence of the offending word, and suddenly their hearts are more open, like an intention they made come true.

I say, "I'm fairly confident The Fisting King won't make an appearance in this story."

"Thank God. Check that off my worry list."

Perry points to a purple starfish lurking in shallow water. Tomorrow or the next day, the creature will cease to live, nothing more than a cool exoskeleton, but right now, it's alive. We wade in a few feet, fingers zinging across wet rock surfaces as we attempt to find sea legs against slippery stone below. He picks it up.

"Hold it for a moment," I say.

To my finger pads, the starfish feels like I would expect: rock, cement-stubbly and grainy. The rocks around us feel like I'd expect a starfish: smooth and silky. We stroke the starfish together, reading its life in Braille.

Before I can protest, he flings it.

Oh. Damn.

There it goes, spinning, sailing through the air until it slashes a wave and becomes a surfer.

He says, "This is the favor for your friend, right?"

"Yes. I promised some beach time. I have faith in Bolinas."

He turns to me, and his smile disappears.

"I'm trying, Vin. It's not easy for me, doing this stuff. But I'm really trying."

I jump the remaining two feet to Perry and kiss him deeply. Our kiss is forceful, the kind you might experience standing in the surf while an ocean leers from ten feet away. Our mouths now fit together perfectly, because although we have spent less than twenty-four hours together, we know each other more than those hours suggest. We escaped from prison together. He showed me his rage, and then we made love in the shower. I forced him into a life of crime, and yet he stayed. Hell, we own matching snow globes.

After a minute or two, we break, panting and grinning. Perry leans in for more, but instead I hug him and start speaking right into his ear.

"Gravely, the Found Kings discussed King Bolinas's ten-year request. Only the kingdom's finest investment bankers could determine how much of Bolinas's grief represented tarnished gold and how much was shadow dragon. Their goal was not to argue down the ten-year request: they sought to uncover the deeper grievance those years embodied, and simultaneously create a smaller debt for Bolinas to forgive."

I pull back to see Perry's sad smile.

"Every king realized that more important than the number of years was that King Bolinas felt slighted. How could the kingdom function if its one true king felt unloved? Everything on land and sea ground to a halt as the kingdom debated how to restore faith in Bolinas."

I take his hand and we continue our stroll, looking for dying starfish. I ponder all the times I lost faith in Bolinas, lost faith in someone because I decided their grievance was trivial. I refused to recognize what it represented, the buried gold unable to shine.

Perry clears his throat after I have been silent for a moment or two. "And?"

"After being so well heard, so well loved, King Bolinas cheerfully concluded that six years was enough. As you predicted, our friend King Aabee volunteered first. Some kings argued that he should let someone else carry this burden, but most everyone understood that when he said, 'I will go. Send me!' Aabee was unstoppable."

"No offense, Vin, but he is a tool. Great story, but he's wasting his whole life."

Another starfish appears in shallow water, this one an orange-colored guy. Or girl. Or both, since they're ambisexual.

I nod to Perry, and he fishes it out of the water. "Should we name it?"

"Chuck," Perry says quickly, and then catches himself with an intake of breath. "Ex-boyfriend."

I say, "There's an old belief that every starfish cast ashore enraged the ocean with some slight and cannot reenter without the ocean's forgiveness. If the ocean will not forgive, then someone else must."

"Yeah?" Perry says, walking away from me. "Well, I forgive you, Chuck."

He jerks but does not acknowledge his twitch to me. Whatever zipped through his body disappears; Perry's already wading away from some slippery memory, careful to walk steady. Wish I knew more about Chuck. Let go, Vin. That twitch revealed enough.

He winds up—

"*Wait.* Instead of throwing Chuck, let's wade out deeper and find him a good rock. If you pitch him, Chuck's gonna ride back to shore on the next wave."

We wander deeper into the tidal pools, evaluating the oceanfront real estate. If motionless, the water would lap our knees, but the ceaseless waves occasionally leap high enough to lick our inner thighs, so we leap in surprise, yelping and whooping.

After a big one, I yell, "Bad touch! Bad touch!"

Perry laughs and also starts yelling "bad touch" whenever the water licks his balls.

"Yo, Pear. I've got this great two-bedroom condo on this rock, plenty of light."

Perry disagrees. "No view. Keep looking."

"Do you think I could sell real estate in San Francisco?"

He says, "You'd get fired the minute you refused to show anything in Dolores Park because you don't like the letter *d*. Plus, Chuck was thinking of some place with less light, more rock underside. Something wet but with a view. And good neighbors."

"We have plenty of places like that over here in The Mission."

"I thought you wanted to be a Realtor for Russian Hill."

"Too many stairs. And for the record, I have no problem with the letter *d*. Mostly, I don't like *k*, and I'm not overly fond of capital *M*."

He says archly, "As a Mangin, fuck you."

The obsidian black rocks fascinate me, overrun with miniature mussels, razor sharp edges on their chatty, wide-open mouths. These little clams gossip like millions of high schoolers, daring each other to jump. I bet they say to each other, "Those kids on the other rock don't get pounded nearly as hard as we do."

"No, not that one," Perry says, snubbing my next suggestion. "Chuck should face the ocean."

We find starfish fixed to the undersides of ocean boulders everywhere around us, point out various colors to each other. Orange, neon orange, red, neon red, purple, neon purple. Very few appear splayed in traditional star form, mostly slumping and legs curling, as if exhausted by the ocean's assault.

I say, "Did you know starfish see out the ends of their arms? They have five eyes."

"Gross. Gross. Here's fine." Perry deposits our orange friend against a slippery stone surface. "That's disgusting. Is that even true?"

"Sure. I read a book about starfish. They don't have eyeballs that blink or anything, they're more ocular light sensors, mostly able to experience light and dark."

He says, "I hope you realize I have no trust for anything you say. I mean, this five-eye thing could be true or there's a five-eyed king coming up next."

We stick around for a moment while our starfish friend gets a good grip. When neither of us can tug him free, Perry and I bid Chuck good day.

We splash each other in Chuck's front yard, stand and face the smaller waves a few times. We're not deep, and yet dry sand looks twenty-five feet away. I would describe this as another liminal space between one reality and another.

Perry moves deeper into the water, just a few more feet west, and stretches his arms wide.

I try to warn him, "You're going to—"

But it's already over: the wave soaks him up to his waist.

Perry howls with laughter and jumps around helplessly because his rubber waders are now completely full. It's hard to glimpse the investment banker in this moment, the man who says to strangers, "Trust me with your money," and they do.

He yells, "Bad touch! Bad touch!"

Perry fumbles to the shore, and water spills out the wader tops. He jogs to dry sand and falls on his back, lifting his legs up to empty the waders, which of course, soaks the top half of Perry's body, leaving him sputtering for air.

Ha, ha! Ri-dikulous!

God, that was hilarious, a Charlie Chaplin move. I'm sure he did that intentionally, putting on a show for me. He drags himself out of the sand and rejoins me, more soaked and more sandy than when he left. I should warn him about moving quickly over slippery rocks, but not this second. I don't want to kill the happy buzz he created. We resume our patrol holding hands and accomplish two more starfish relocations to ocean-view condos.

I'm thirsty. Fresh papaya and pineapple sounds delicious right now. My stomach grumbling says it's time to advance the story.

I squeeze his hand and say, "Look around. I doubt that King Aabee would describe his time here as wasting six years."

"Of course not. He played a magic flute."

"Technically, it wasn't quite a flute."

"Uh huh. But it sounded like mint. And chartreuse, neither of which, *technically,* is a sound."

"You're probably right."

"Oh God; objection withdrawn."

"Now who sounds like a lawyer?"

Perry points to three greenish starfish mashed together on a rock. He says, "Starfish orgy."

"Yeah, the whole apartment building is slutty. But you're only viewing King Aabee's story in one light. King Aabee was thrilled with his life."

"Thrilled?"

I say nothing and let my face mirror his confused incredulity, forcing him finally to speak.

He says, "He wasted his life."

I frown. "Wasted *how?*"

I skew my face as if I haven't understood the question.

"Seriously?" Perry says with a certain sharpness, and suddenly this feels real, this conflict. "Ten years among the Lost Kings burned his whole youth. He gets back with wrinkles and gray hairs and he's, like, spending his first year or two cleaning barns and fixing sewers? How many years did you say he spent in the sewers? Three or four? Then—"

I interrupt to say, "You're kidding, right? While living among the Lost Ones, Aabee earned a PhD at university. He met his wife during those ten years, a beautiful archaeologist. She required a man who understood giftedness in its many flavors."

"Oh, please. This morning you said he cleaned sewers and did crappy jobs. Didn't you say that he couldn't afford picture frames for his shitty apartment?"

"All true. Aabee was a graduate student when they met and fell in love down in the sewers. Remember my mentioning a luscious French woman? She researched ancient symbols in the lowest depths of our stone beginnings, and he shoveled away the waste of humanity, because this is what we do when we think our ancestors no longer serve; we shit all over them."

Perry stares at me with frozen irritation. A wave crashes against his knees, tickling him again, softening his anger and sweeping the unpleasant feeling back out to sea. It's just a story.

"Remember her cherry nipples? You didn't want me to elaborate over breakfast. I tried to bring it up again on the bridge."

"Yeah. Okay." His face and tone express reluctance.

I love the classic "You Wouldn't Let Me Elaborate" setup. Even if he demonstrated a higher tolerance for raunch, he would have eventually cried uncle; I had some extremely kinky stuff planned for Aabee and his wife.

After a brief standoff, I continue. "She heard the music and followed it to him. In her mind, his sewer cleaning was heroic; he loved history and wondering about ancient symbols as much as she. Yes, it's true, they never amassed many belongings in their early married years, but they often purchased irresponsible things, steamer passages to Egypt or plane tickets to Toulouse so they could spend Christmas with her family. They lived with all their love, and while it left them penniless, a golden trail of light swirled around them."

"Are you making up this part right now to contradict me?"

"I told you that King Aabee sometimes helped Lost Kings get found, right? Living as they did often attracted the attention of a lost king. She helped him stay *found*. There's a price to pay to live with all your love. King Aabee found the price tag acceptable."

Perry looks at me with suspicion.

He may realize we're not talking about King Aabee. Be careful, Vin.

"The two years helping King Diego?"

I consider my love for Pear and make my face gentle.

"King Aabee's wife loved Turkey; so much rich history. In Ankara, she published, the serious kind of published that makes your career. King Aabee and his family lived in the center of a thriving market city, so many different kings intermingling in such lovely languages. When he wasn't working on King Diego's behalf, Aabee and his two sons loved wandering through the tented street bazaars, feasting on autumn tubers and inhaling the misting blue incense."

"Wait. Now he has two sons?"

"Three. They got pregnant during the three-day party celebrating King Diego's release. But yes, when they arrived in Turkey they already had two sons, dark-skinned boys who held hands in public because in addition to being brothers, they were also good friends. When their father played music, they were not ashamed to dance. Those were some choice years for his family."

"And here?"

Perry's voice contains another new sadness, another surrender.

"*They lived here.* What other reward could you want? In California, King Aabee's older sons learned to surf, while the youngest trotted back and forth on the beach, anxiously admiring his brothers. Aabee's family met many oceanic kings and queens, those who forged special friendships with creatures in the deep. Don't even get me started on Liam, the Dolphin King."

Perry looks to the sun, radiating its California joy. We're on a secret beach, accessed through a cave of horrors, serving an important mission for King Bolinas. What could be finer?

"Aabee's family stayed here for six years, and then an extra five more, because Bolinas and Aabee became best friends. How would you like to spend eleven years with your best friend, giving second chances to homeless starfish?"

Perry turns from me and slowly wades back toward the shore. Not far away, he stops, bends down, and picks something up. He doesn't need me for approval. He walks into the surf, peering around until he finds a good home. I'm not sure if he forgives the starfish or asks the ocean to forgive, to wash away old memories and let the water sparkle again.

When he finishes, he stares into the rush of waves, unyielding in their pursuit of land.

After this weekend, I will remember Perry this way, in his rubber hip waders staring into the surf. The wind plasters a few wet locks across his forehead and blows the rest back. Well, rustles it. He's got a clump of wet sand stuck over his ear. Knee deep in the ocean, the Forgiver King's face reflects impending doom. He looks like one of those giant—

Forgive Billy.

What? No, a stray thought—

Forgive Billy.

No. *No.*

I'm going to think of something else now. I'm going to think of something else. Forgive a child-molesting—*tiredofthoseratsyet—*motherfucker?

That random thought didn't mean anything. Thursday, I thought about how someone should invent rip-off Velcro underwear for men. That wasn't a message from the kings; not everything is a message from them.

Perry waves me over to join him. Good. Good. Slosh over there, Vin.

I'll have to think about this later, I mean, there's nothing to think about, really. Just a random thought, synapses firing. Is this why I've been thinking about Billy all weekend? To forgive him? No. I'll confirm it's random, but later. I just.... I need to focus up. Don't be a moron, Vin, there's no time to get into this on a King Weekend.

But for the record, kings?

No fucking way.

FOURTEEN

MAKING our way back through the tidal pools, we discover Perry's first throwback riding a shallow wave a few yards down from its original location, a hardcore purple surfer with braised and callused skin. That makes seven starfish, as we finish our patrol in this smaller cove, if we count Perry's first starfish twice. We also find three dead ones, their skeletons beached further in dry sand. Perry picks one up to keep as a souvenir. Collecting souvenirs is a good sign; he's in.

Forgive Billy, huh?

Get softer, Vin. Maybe tonight I will find some time to think this through. But honestly, I don't envision much forgiveness happening, kings. Sorry, but he and his buddies were rapists.

I can't get into this now.

Focus on watching Perry. Watch him. Read him.

His face grows pensive, a word I prefer, but you can't toss it out there often; it rarely fits. But Perry's pensive. Oooh. *Perry's pensive, Perry's pensive.* His face says he's struggling to say something, carefully arranging words so that they don't accidentally lead into a cave of horrors. He was definitely quieter as we recovered the last few starfish, and while we still enjoyed some goofy exchanges, I felt a slight distance. No denying that.

I suspect there's a certain topic he'd like to discuss, but yesterday on the pier he made me promise to never bring it up. Of course, that may not be it. Maybe he's just tired; today is a long day. Or maybe I'm the one who is tired and misreading him. Could be anything.

We stare into the water.

He says, "I'm sorry that I said King Aabee is a tool. He sounds like he's doing okay."

I move in close to him and put my arms around his lower back, pulling our hips together and bringing our faces close. He breathes in the scent of me and locks his fingers around my neck. Forgiveness can be oh so sexy.

"King Aabee is doing great. So are you. You're amazing, Perry."

He blushes. "I like the story. You're a bit of an asshole, but I'm glad I came."

I shrug. "Fair enough."

Perry's lips taste warm, sunbaked, with a hint of salt. Kissing Perry is now a tangible manifestation of everything we've endured together: our first kiss in ski masks, our Hammock sex on Alcatraz, our shower kiss after my being a dick about the cake, our wonderful closeness on the Golden Gate Bridge. Every kiss now sparks and reminds us both that for this weekend, we are in love.

I break the embrace and point toward the rocky end of the beach.

Speaking almost right into his mouth, I say, "What's that?"

"Where?"

I point to a specific rock cluster.

We peer in that direction for a few seconds, but nothing appears out of the ordinary.

I say, "Low wave a minute ago. I saw something—"

He says, "Yeah, I just saw it. Something curved—a rope. There's a rope."

I say, "Let's check it out."

Perry follows my lead, genuinely interested. Examining tidal pools restored a certain inquisitiveness. Who knows what you might find in a secret cove?

He says, "Wait, you saw this while we were kissing? You were *looking around the beach* while we were making out?"

I dart away, jogging toward the rock. Over my shoulder, I say, "I'm an asshole, remember?"

Of course, I am splashed from behind.

Sure enough, tied around the base of a fat rock, we find a thick braided rope, double-tied, as well as knotted through a small opening between two other rocks. The rope floats into a large, secluded tidal pool, hidden from the ocean by three stone walls; the pool is pounded sideways by the ocean once in a while, but it's mostly protected. We're not particularly deep, a little over our knees.

Bound in fat leather straps and bungee cords, a blue and white cooler thrashes vehemently, protesting its shackles.

Perry sputters surprised beginnings, but he sees my face and he stops.

"Of course," he says.

We both chuckle, because, well, just because.

I say, "There's a hunting knife in the backpack. I'll go grab it."

"Why didn't you get it before we ran over here?"

"Why would I grab my hunting knife to go explore this rock unless I already knew of a cooler? That doesn't make sense, Peary-y-y."

"But you *did* know a cooler was here."

"No, I found it the same time you did."

"Vin, that's just fucked up. I can't even imagine what goes on in your head."

"I like surprises. Even when I'm the surprise planner."

"Ridiculous. If I had the whole week on vacation to do nothing and —"

"Pear, thoughts about the word ridiculous? Before you answer, think of the *c* as a *k* and a hyphen after the *i*. Even though I don't love *k*, I can't deny the word sounds better with a k. Say it like this, ri-*dikuluous*."

"I can't tell if you're a Ritalin junkie or if you use those stupid word things to end conversations."

"I could talk for ten minutes about the word *cooler*. You'll find my theory on double-o words quite fascinating. *Overlooked overlook, overlooked overlook.*"

Perry puts his hands on his hips and says, "It's effective because you sound like a psycho. And if I'm right about using that to stop conversations, you'll stay quiet right now or I'll ask more questions about how you planned this weekend."

Well, he's not wrong.

In conspicuous silence, I head over to the backpack and extract my hunting knife. I am so fucking hungry.

When I return, Perry remains silent with a big grin, challenging me to either give him the last word or engage in a conversation I don't want to have yet: Magician Tricks Revealed. His silence proves my mastery over him, while my silence simultaneously proves his mastery over me. He's complying in all ways now, no resistance, but that doesn't mean he's not winking at the joke and letting me know he can play at this too.

Man, I love this guy.

I use my hands to indicate where I think we should cut, and he argues back, pointing elsewhere. I guess we're going to cut the rope and rescue the cooler without any conversation at all, which is tricky but hilarious, both of us pointing at things to make our meaning known and refusing to speak. We splash each other to punctuate our points or interrupt the activity. We make snarky, quiet laughter when we catch each other's eyes.

A few minutes later, we float the cooler to shore between us, hauling wet, frayed rope over our shoulders. This lends credibility to a shipwreck scenario. We lumber to dry sand and plop down in our squishy, cold waders.

We shake our wet hair at each other. I'm at a distinct disadvantage as I mostly have bristles, but zooming my hand over my head, I launch ocean droplets right at his face. As we remove the leather straps, Perry's eyes shine because, honestly, this is pretty fun.

He says, "Is there a pirate king?"

"Please. There's a whole armada of pirate kings."

Once we master the leather straps and peer inside the cooler, we discover several bags of half-melted ice, Tupperware packed carefully with fresh papayas and pineapple chunks. At last, pineapple! Another Tupperware contains fresh mozzarella, tomatoes, and a baggie with flavored garlic oil and fresh basil. The tomatoes and mozzarella are beat to mostly liquid. Crap. I thought I packed those carefully enough. Water bottles, cranberry juice, and few Summit Pale Ale beers. Swiss cheese slices are triple-bagged as are the maraschino cherries.

I pull a plastic bottle from the bottom and extend it to him.

"Why, lookie here, it's King Vodka."

Perry reaches for the bottle and accepts it carefully, gently almost. Despite his earlier enthusiasm, he doesn't seem particularly glad to recognize his favorite booze and keeps his attention on the bottle as if studying the label.

I think long ago, Perry's heart made unwelcome room for sadness, and then believing that it could handle no more, slammed itself shut, preventing joy's free roam. What's the point of joy, if only followed by sorrow? Perry knows how to have fun; I've seen him with his friends. But I wonder how deep he lets joy flow, if he surrenders to the undertow.

I shouldn't read too much into how he takes the vodka bottle from my hand; it's too subtle. But I can't help what I notice, what I think I see. Who cares if my theory is right? I was wrong about him wanting to talk about his dad. Knowing the exact reason doesn't matter, because the truth on his face doesn't need a backstory, it's just truth. In this moment, sweet sadness pours out of him.

He hasn't noticed the bottom of the cooler. I better point it out.

"What's that at the bottom?"

He reaches in and pulls out a triple-baggied index card. He scoffs and begins unsealing each one. "Paranoid much?"

I say, "Wow, whoever triple-baggied that note totally planned ahead. Clever, clever person."

"Paranoid *freak*."

"I'd say whoever was here—he or she—was well prepared. I wonder what the note says."

He shoots me a casual dismissal, then reads the index card. A moment later he hands it over for me to study my own handwriting.

HELLO GENTLEMEN,
I CAME BACK TO VISIT A FAVORITE SPOT YESTERDAY.
PLEASE ENJOY THESE REFRESHMENTS.
KING AABEE

"Yesterday?" I say, gasping. "What an amazing coincidence."

Without another word, we unpack a few essentials from my backpack: a beach blanket, blue china plates, more of those yummy rosemary crackers, pistachios, and crystal tumblers. As we establish our meager picnic and Perry mixes his cranberry vodka juice, I'm delighted to witness a sturdier glow from him. He's exuding exuberance, the double *e* checkpoint achieved at last. Perry survived on prison land and now the ocean. If he makes it through the night in the sky, he's home free.

Before he dives in, he offers me my pick of the buffet. His smile beams, his eagerness so genuine that suddenly I feel terrible. I have to be an asshole again. Forgive me, Perry, for how badly I'm going to screw with you.

He says, "This king stuff is cool. Thank you for the snacks."

"I cannot take credit for King Aabee's generosity; he was clearly here first."

"Well, he has good snacking taste with the exception of the liquid bag."

"I bet he *intended* us to enjoy a caprese salad, but apparently it got beat up worse than anyone could have anticipated. Even a powerful king such as Aabee could not have anticipated how wild and rough the ocean would beat the crap out of tomatoes. And mozzarella."

In a doubtful voice he says, "You're giving King Aabee too much credit. Who couldn't figure out the ocean would pulverize tomatoes? Amateur move."

"I'm sure *King Aabee* tried a number of techniques over the years, and believed he had solved—"

Perry says louder, "When *I* pack ocean coolers, I always bag things four or five times."

"Now who's an asshole?"

He grins and mashes some pineapple and papaya into his vodka cranberry drink. I offer him a maraschino cherry, but he refuses. It's fun to have opportunities to say the word *maraschino*. It rolls off the tongue like a juicy, roly-poly cherry.

Mar-a-*schino*. I love that zip at the end.

Perry says, "To King Aabee."

I toast with my beer. "And maraschino cherries."

After we savor the moment, he asks, "How do you know about this place?"

"I've been coming to the overlooked overlook for years. I've been known to come out of the forests at night long after everything around here is closed, and of course, I'm always hungry. I sometimes leave a cooler."

"Tide?"

"Doesn't go that high. I sleep right over there."

"You don't sleep in the cave?"

"Water fills it to the waist. Honestly, the cave is terrifying during high tide. I almost died in there once."

We trade more stories about our lives, little things, TV shows and food we both enjoy. He likes lemon grass soup; I like lemon grass soup. He likes spicy fish sauce in his curry, and me too. Neither of us think *Will & Grace* will last long on network TV, but we both concede that the show already entered its second season, so what do we know? Our exchange is the getting-to-know-you stuff one might chat about at an art gallery opening with a stranger.

Snack break ends with us making out, me on top of him, and after some hot necking in kinky rubber waders, we wander the small, sandy area, holding hands, me occasionally rubbing his cock and then guiding him deeper into the surf. He laughs when I try to dunk him, and after two unsuccessful attempts, he pushes me back and we chase each other, kicking water and yelling.

I knew the waders wouldn't work that well. But I figured Perry needed help surrendering and they provide some measure of insurance to his investor brain: running in the surf is reasonable when dressed appropriately.

You've got to seduce the brain throughout a King Weekend, appease it, and occasionally confound it. The brain is so commanding, confident that every thought has always been right, is right, will be right, that tweaking a man's heart has no chance of success if the brain isn't distracted.

I have no doubt Perry's brain remains befuddled by King Bolinas's pointless mission, King Aabee's sewer cleaning, and small mysteries such as how I knew he liked Diet Coke in the morning. But it's too late. On the Golden Gate Bridge, Perry's heart finally agreed to the melody while his brain continued to analyze each note individually. Now his brain must sit back for the symphony to reach its inevitable crescendo.

During our water fights, I yell out, "Ever get sucked off in the ocean?"

"No," he shrieks, and to avoid my giant splash he races away down the shoreline, but the water in his waders throws him off balance until he splats face-first into two feet of water and soft sand.

The investment banker rises, laughing hard as water planes over his face. A clump of sand perches on his head like a lopsided hat. He peels off his soaked sweatshirt, tossing it toward the shore.

I cup my hands to my mouth and shout, *"Anyone want a blow job? Anyone? Line up over here for blow jobs."*

I find Perry incredibly sexy right now, soaked and leering as he crosses the distance toward me. He's not traditionally sexy because the tie-dye shirt and his water stumblings make him seem completely stoned more than anything. I love the water dripping off his chin, his sheepish grin, and I picture him in a perfectly white shirt, starched, and a shiny red tie. Maybe a gold tie clip holding it against his tummy. Oh man, I love bankers.

"What if I can't stay hard in the ocean?" he asks, unzipping his jeans and pulling them down as much as the waders will allow. Seems like a silly question when I observe his semi-hard dick bobbing happily over the edge of his zipper.

Perry looks down. "The water's cold."

"Leave that to me," I say, tugging his cock. "I'll take charge of cocksucking and you be in charge of getting blown, okay?"

"You're the boss."

He didn't even bother to scan the beach before whipping out his cock for semipublic sex. Good man, Perry. Let go of the world's compass.

I pull him by his dick, leading him to deeper water. We need to reach thigh-deep water for this experience.

Knee-deep, I say, "Plant your feet."

He does it, shaking his head and spraying me with droplets.

I engulf his cock in one motion, and he instinctively grips my head. I've been sexually taunting him since last night, not permitting him to come during our last two sexual encounters. His cock's not underwater so I don't have to force the water out of my mouth, and he's hard despite his worry, so a couple of deep strokes and he's already twitchy. Soon after, a wave splashes over my head, and I hear Perry yelp.

I burst straight up, splashing everywhere, a soaked and hairy nymph exploding from Neptune's depths.

"Hey," I say as casually as I can manage, wiping my face. "What's up?"

"Not much," he says, face registering happy impatience. "I'm getting my cock sucked in the ocean and that wave almost knocked me over."

"No kidding," I say, shivering a moment but not willing to break our casual tone. "How is the blow job?"

Damn, it's cold.

"Interrupted," he says. "Get back down there, man."

"Let's move you to a safer place," I suggest, grabbing his cock and leading him away.

I know where I'm taking him, a flat rock where Perry can lean back if pushed harder by a wave, a rock with no starfish to accidentally dislodge. He even has a footrest for his right leg, a stubbier black boulder devoid of high-schooler mussels. It's further out, more blue than clear, deep enough that a big wave could hit above our waists.

"Perfect," Perry says when I lean him against the rock. Seconds later he says, "Gah! Cold! Bad touch!"

"Who, me?"

He laughs and says, "You're good touch."

We laugh, and his fat cock points straight out at me.

I drop to my knees and start again. Now that his dick is almost underwater, I use the first few strokes to force the saltwater out of my mouth and he squirms while I recreate suction. I maintain this suck job easily by pushing water out my nose as I inhale his cock. He grabs the back of my head as I tug him closer. It doesn't take nearly as long as he expected to get right back to the brink. But I'm orgasm surfing: waiting for a good wave before throwing him over the edge. Right as he gets closer once again, I burst topside, wiping my face and taking big gulps of air.

"Hey, what's up?"

"Oh, man," he says. "You're killing me. I can't believe I'm getting blown in the Pacific."

"Yeah, it's a good ocean for blow jobs."

I descend and suck his cock for a while longer, bringing him closer and closer, his own cresting waves of pleasure threatening to topple him at any moment. I ease off and squeeze his balls, cold, hard nuggets, ready to explode. Sucking again, I play him until he wriggles like a fish, thrashing around with one hand on my shoulder and when he gasps, I bet he doesn't understand how we can pause right there, right on the edge.

I rise from the water yet one more time and let everything drip down my face. "Did you hear something?"

"Whaaa? Cmaaaawn," Perry says, slurring the words. "I was *so fucking close.*"

"I thought I could hear music."

"Fuck music," Perry says and looks around. "I get to come, right?"

"Strange," I say and make a great effort to scan the beach, "I heard starfish singing—tiny, thin voices, almost impossible to hear a single one. But in unison, I could hear this mighty chorus singing the song of the ocean, of her great love for all her children."

Perry says, "King Aabee's flute? Is that what you heard?"

"Maybe. Wouldn't be the first time King Aabee's music lingered."

"I'll keep my ears open, but in the meantime, king man, you wanna go periscope down?"

He jacks his thumb toward his bobbing cock, and I laugh because he's damn sexy when he lets himself go.

I suck.

Not long after, my whole body senses a bigger wave coming, so with a few deep tugs from my throat, I coax him over the edge, as it crashes over us. This isn't a rock-smashing wave, but we're far enough out that a bigger wave splashing right up to your chest probably creates a full-body orgasm, a smashing from the inside out, and as Perry shoots his load into my throat, through muffled water I hear him scream at the ocean.

The ocean screams back.

FIFTEEN

AFTER returning to land, I announce that it's time for the next adventure. We pack up our picnic gear, and I encourage Perry to rinse off as much sand as possible before we head back to the van.

"No fancy hotels in our immediate future?"

"You're gonna smell like ocean for the rest of the night. Sorry."

"God, Vin. All this camping and roughing it crap. Are you sure you're a homo?"

"You tell me," I say, carefully packing the glass tumblers. "Was that blow job gay enough for you?"

"Yeah, that was pretty great. I don't always come from that alone."

Perry strips off the waders and then peels off his jeans. A moment later he's running naked into the surf.

He turns around and gives me a victory stance.

I drop my packing chores and strip off my waders as fast as I can. There's a hot investment banker running naked in the surf, and I don't want to miss out. I dash to the beach, and Perry welcomes me by kicking water in my face.

Soon enough, Mr. Quackers greets us loudly, happy to catch us up on everything that happened to him during our absence. Sounds quite eventful. I hand Perry a water bottle and ask him to refill Mr. Quackers's water canister.

He says, "What exactly do ducks eat, anyway? Besides lettuce."

"Grass. Insects. They love snails, I found out."

Perry grunts.

While hunting under the tarps with both hands, I turn my head and watch his reaction. I stick out my tongue and bite it, as if lost in concentration. I laid out everything sequentially so I can find whatever's needed; that's no problem. I want to see his reaction to the mystery tarps.

Not much I can read. He's mildly curious but not impatient and not asking questions. He's not irritated or amused. Okay, that's fine, I guess. I took his temperature a number of times on the beach. Really, Vin, what else do you want? You just finished sucking him off in the surf. That ought to tell you enough for now.

My hands emerge from under the mystery tarps with a plastic box containing duck food. "Give him more of these pellets and some shredded lettuce. Fresh out of snails, unfortunately."

Perry says, "Yes, how unfortunate we don't get to watch a baby duck gum a snail to death."

Thick towels and baby wipes emerge from the magic tarps, and after some quick changes and rubbing our heads, we're as dry as can be expected, so we kiss again, to signify the conclusion of our beach adventure. I massage his cock through his next pair of jeans, and he does mine.

He says, "You haven't come yet."

"Not yet."

Perry doesn't bother to follow up, perhaps realizing some caves lead nowhere.

I store the cooler, wrap the soggy shipwreck ropes and wet clothes in one of the tarps, revealing nothing remains under that one. After I decline his offer to assist, Perry watches me until I'm almost done and then moves to open the passenger door.

I say, "Why don't you hold our little duck friend? Get settled in the front seat and I'll bring him to you."

"Can we do that? Take him out of the cage?"

"Sure. His owners told me he likes being held."

"Awesome."

Good. Glad he's on board. I want Perry to bond with our little friend, to feel his soft and vulnerable body.

I liberate Mr. Quackers and wrap him loosely in an unused bath towel. His head surfaces amid the deep blue folds, and he peers around anxiously.

I whisper, "Sorry, pal, no snails."

By the time I reach Perry, he's already buckled in, and he has arranged his brown bomber jacket in his lap as a nest of sorts. I watch Perry enjoy the pleasurable discomfort of not quite knowing how to hold and protect a living creature this way, and we discuss various duck-holding strategies until Perry feels confident Mr. Quackers has settled. We both agree that the van windows must stay mostly up, so as to avoid tempting our front seat guest. Once the three of us are situated, I pull out on the highway, heading back the way we came.

"What if he poops on me?"

"Then I guess you'll have duck poop on you."

Perry says, "Do I at least get a T-shirt that says 'I spent a weekend with Vin Vanbly and all I got was this lousy duck poop'? Speaking of which, I didn't get my Alcatraz T-shirt yesterday. I thought you were gonna buy me a souvenir? Why do I always have to buy the souvenirs?"

"Oh, so we're complaining now? Let's discuss Mr. Quackers's name. How unoriginal is that?"

"I thought he was stolen property. That doesn't exactly inspire creativity. Does he already have a name?"

"Doug."

Perry says, "Seriously? Mr. Quackers is way better." He peers more carefully at my face and says, "Are you lying about his name being Doug?"

"Yes."

He snorts. "Of course."

As we retrace our van's journey from earlier this afternoon, Perry talks about the bank, his favorite coworker, and he asks me a question or two about life in Minnesota. This leads to conversation about different places we've lived, and Perry shares that he loves it here, this golden state, but he does miss the desert.

He stares out the window at the never-ending parade of leafy greenery.

"My mom used to say that we're desert people. My dad grew up in Ohio, and while he loved Tucson, he hated not having a lawn. He actually bought a used lawn mower, and once or twice a year, he'd wheel it around the rocks and cacti in the backyard, just pretending. Mom would watch from the kitchen, laughing, and he'd wave whenever he caught her eye."

I nod and chuckle at this.

"He showed me how to start it, but I've never actually used a lawn mower."

This story was no accident; he's giving me an opening. Perry continues to fuss with Mr. Quackers and keep an eye on the beauty speeding by, which I interpret as a slight reluctance to make eye contact.

This is good.

"Pear, have you ever been down to Santa Cruz? I've been a few times, but I still don't know the area well."

"Just a winery tour with an old boyfriend. We spent a day."

"Chuck?"

"Yes."

"I think I'm jealous of Chuck."

We chat and love each other as the sun slips further west. 5:05 p.m. Good, we're exactly on track. Well, within an hour. We are exhausted explorers, men and a duck who have had one hell of a day, and it's starting to show. We're getting goofy.

"Who wants pasta in Sausalito?"

"*We do*," Perry shouts, raising the duck in his arms and trying to get Mr. Quackers to lift up his left wing.

Mr. Quackers will have none of it and asserts himself angrily until Perry quits fussing. We both have to listen to a quacking lecture on why you should not fuck with the duck.

I say, "Do you think Mr. Quackers is using the f-word on us?"

Perry says, "Sure. I would. He's probably calling you an asshole."

A few miles later at a strategic spot overlooking Sausalito, I say, "Can you hear that clinking in the engine?"

He turns his head and says, "No. Well, maybe something."

"This is one of the professional hazards of being a garage mechanic. I can never rent a car. Something always sounds wrong. Gimme a second to check this out."

Nestled comfortably into the foothills of Mount Tamalpais, Sausalito provides spectacular views in every direction. From where we are, near the topmost street looking straight down, your gaze flies straight to the cobalt bay and the sleek-sheeted sailboats wobbling about this ocean niche.

The van checks out fine, I explain, just a bit noisier than I prefer, and we zigzag to the bottom of town where I look up and enjoy the pleasant recognition. Hundreds of cheerful white homes recline into the steep hillsides, waiting expectantly for a fireworks spectacle. Sausalito reminds me of the people who show up first. Sure I'm irritated they got the best seats, but I have to concede that they wanted it more, this gorgeous life beyond the Golden Gate.

All along the main drag, art galleries and pricey seafood restaurants brag their wares with false modesty, attracting tourists eager to pay for a California experience. The shops specialize in expensive, eclectic clothes, upscale knickknacks, and a few crystal pendant shops. Perhaps Sausalito is the beach town's upscale cousin.

"Are we here to buy some paintings of dolphins?" Perry says, "Maybe something tasteful for The Dolphin King. That is, if we can find anything tasteful."

I flip on my turn signal to head over to a parallel street, Caledonia, the real main street where locals shop and hang out. I park us near the center of town, and Perry gingerly carries Mr. Quackers back into his cage. We have brainstormed several possible renames, including Perry's favorite suggestion, Darwin, after a former college chemistry TA, a doomed crush. But Mr. Quackers sticks. Sometimes a name simply reveals itself and there's no point in fighting it.

I guide us to my favorite Italian café in Sausalito, and we seat ourselves at a mosaic table near the front windows where we can watch the late afternoon street traffic. Perry looks pleased with the selection of this restaurant and happily excuses himself to wash up. Out the enormous front windows, I stare at the slow-moving cars. A girl on a bike confidently navigates sluggish pedestrians, and I find myself jealous of her because she lives here; she's headed home. We could have selected outdoor seating to better study the Sausalitians, but I selfishly want to inhale the combination of spice, meat, and sweet emanating from the kitchen. Whenever I eat here, smell and taste merge; each inhale feels like both.

While I await his return, I reacquaint myself.

At this early dinner hour, Anna Marie's café is half-empty. By 8:00 p.m. tonight, the restaurant will be packed to capacity with hungry locals and tourists who happily discovered this spot. The tables are close together, requiring a most intimate relationship between patrons and staff, and often inviting cross talk between diners. Despite the tight fit, a large piano commands the front corner, right behind me, always inviting great mystery as to how it once arrived. I could ask, but I prefer to speculate. The peach-rose walls match the small flames on every table, tea lights protected by beveled glass. The simple, blank walls reinforce the simple, good cheer, which modestly suggests you seek elsewhere for more nuanced ambiance. This, of course, creates the perfect ambiance.

Could I forgive Billy?

Maybe.

Maybe, Billy, but don't crowd me. I'll give it some thought later tonight. I find it challenging to nurse deep resentments in the presence of someone I love, and today, I'm in love. Who am I kidding? I will love Perry for a lot longer than this single weekend.

Could I forgive, though? Would I?

Forgiveness is a puzzle that's easy and hard, requiring both focused intention and abject surrender, obvious in its execution and yet often a big surprise. To do it, you just forgive. I like the phrase "just forgive," as if forgiveness is a twenty-dollar bill you reluctantly slapped into some homeless person's hand and were done with it. It's never that easy; on the next corner another hand comes out, another affront from the same source, requiring more forgiveness, then another hand, another demand, more, more, more—until the only way you can walk free is with your pockets completely empty of resentment. There is no such thing as "just forgive." There is only forgiveness.

Perry's father did nothing requiring forgiveness.

True.

But people underestimate how a father's death impacts a young boy. They don't understand what it means when the man you assumed would teach you everything suddenly doesn't exist. He doesn't die exclusively that one time when everyone wore black and cried. He dies every birthday. He dies at school award presentations when he's not beaming amid the proud parents, and when that horny teenager has no one to avoid for awkward discussions of wet dreams. His father dies every time Perry says, "Don't worry, that happened back when I was a kid. I'm over it."

Oooh—those people are getting the tiramisu. I hate being here and not having tiramisu. It's like a food crime. Maybe I could buy some and leave it—no. Stop right there. Don't make this about you. Focus on Perry.

I loved that he told me that story about the lawn mower. He's ready.

Perry's not back, so I cross the three feet to the flyers and announcements taped to the glass door. Next Saturday's fundraiser benefits someone named Randy, no last name needed, raising money to pay for hospital bills after his accident. A half sheet with scribbled handwriting promises Li'l Shirley will sing jazz later tonight with her husband accompanying on the piano. This isn't advertising; it's simply an announcement because everyone knows Li'l Shirley and her nameless husband. A kid's unpracticed lettering promises a reward for a returned skateboard and promises "no questions asked," underlining the last part as proof of his sincerity. There's a '93 Buick Skylark for sale. Hate those. Piece of crap.

I turn to catch Perry headed back from the restroom.

Wow, he looks sexy.

His hair isn't long enough to get tangled or disheveled, but it's stiff and sideways, a Saturday morning feel to this late Saturday afternoon. His top two buttons remain unbuttoned on his hunter-green shirt, revealing his golden-brown skin. At this moment, he could easily pass as a surfer himself. This morning at St. Anne's, we looked ragged and rough. He still looks that way, dark circles under his eyes, but it works now, as if he didn't quite inhabit his vagrancy this morning and now he does. When he spies me at the door, his face lights up, a blazing fire in his countenance, the reward for a day well spent, played hard.

We meet back at the table.

He says, "Check out the walls, it's never exactly the same color twice."

I say, "Looks like tangerine skin."

"I can see it. I think it's redder than a tangerine, though, rosier. The bathroom is cool too. It's Roman themed, with real marble," he says, and pauses. "But you know that."

"Yeah, I usually eat here before I head north to go deer hunting."

"You hunt deer?"

"Sure."

"You go out there and shoot deer? *You.*"

"I don't shoot them; I chase them. I mean, it's mostly a lot of sitting and watching, letting them get close. That's what I was doing last weekend. A few years ago, I followed these five deer for about a mile. They saw me, and they let me follow. I only hunt deer in protected forests, so I don't get shot. Plus, I couldn't kill a deer. Blood."

"Are you a vegetarian?"

"You saw me eat bacon this morning."

He laughs. "That was not meat."

"Well, maybe I don't mind a little blood in service to a good hamburger. I always feel like I shouldn't eat meat, but I love steak and ahi tuna. And chicken pot pie. And pork loin. Turkey, too. Oh, and ham, flavored with garlic or cloves… and bacon."

He says, "That pretty much covers it."

"I don't think I could eat venison, though. I'd keep thinking that maybe I chased this one through some forest."

He smiles in a new way, bashfully almost. It's not a sexy smile, it's not flirty, it's the "I like you" smile you offer when you're sure it's going to be returned. I wonder why that particular smile.

Oh.

We're on a first date; this is our first public appearance. We've spent a lot of time together wrapped in our private cocoon for two. Well, Golden Gate was public, sure, but we were duck thieves back then, hiding out amidst an entire world of vacationers. This is our first meal in public. Besides breakfast, I guess. But I don't think that counted for Perry.

I answer a few more deer-hunting questions, and he asks which state parks I frequent, though I don't think any of my answers satisfy the one question he can't quite fathom: why?

I say, "Hey, not trying to change the subject, but I'd like us to share an entrée."

Perry nods. "Fine. You order."

He points out a stationery store across the street, something in their display window he wants me to see. Maybe Perry doesn't recognize the full impact of letting me order for us; he trusts me completely.

I suggest, "If you like bacon, their carbonara is delicious."

"Perfect."

"It's a big plate. You won't go hungry. How about you order a wine to go with it. I'll drink anything."

After we order our single entrée, two forks, I ask his permission to get something from the van, and Perry readily agrees. I want him to trust that when I say I'm off to the van to retrieve something, I will return.

I REAPPEAR moments later with a black thermal box, appropriate for delivering pizzas but much fancier.

I can see disappointment in his face as he asks, "Are we getting dinner to go?"

"We're eating here. This is for something later."

"Are we doing a favor for another king?"

"You're probably right."

"I thought we retired that phrase."

"You're probably right."

He dips his fork into the melted candle wax and makes a motion to flip it at me, but he doesn't follow through.

When our server returns with our pinot noir, I ask her if she would please deliver this pouch to Anna Marie. Perry watches, and his eyes gleam. The next surprise.

Minutes later, Anna Marie bursts from the kitchen and makes her way to her dinner guests, stopping to chat with friends along the way. I've been here on nights when she makes the rounds, then stops almost midsentence as some invisible egg timer vibrates in her brain and she races back to the kitchen. She's got the visiting thing down.

When I rise to meet her, she says, "Vin."

We kiss on the cheek.

"This is the special man, eh?" she says, nodding at him.

"He is a special man. Perry, my friend, Anna Marie. This is her lovely restaurant."

Perry beams during our introductions.

"I'm heating your stones, Vin, to keep the pouch warm. I like this pouch."

"A friend in the restaurant business recommended it."

"Restaurant friends other than me? Perry, do you know this other restaurant friend?"

"Me? Nothing. He tells me nothing."

She says, "Ha. Good. I was ready to be hurt if you knew everything. He stays quiet about himself, this Vin. I have an aunt who moved to Minnesota. She said the people are reserved. I told her to find him up in the phone book, but there is no Vincent Vanbly."

I say, "I will happily give you my phone number, Anna Marie."

She ignores me. "Is he shy with you?"

Perry says, "I wouldn't call it shy. More like intentionally cryptic."

I do not love where this conversation is headed. Kill this.

I say, "Oh, c'mon. Ask me anything."

Anna Marie says, "What's your real name?"

I say, "Anything but that."

The three of us laugh, and I make jokes to cover my fluster, but I'll reveal my name if they both push me. It's not magic. I just don't like the name that belongs to him, the one before Vin Vanbly. No big deal, I guess. But saying a name aloud sometimes draws that person near. Like Billy.

Perry changes the topic, and I shoot him a thin, grateful smile. Even though I have been a dick all weekend, we're still adventurers together and he has my back; he has faith in Bolinas. Anna Marie leaves us and chats her way back toward the kitchen until suddenly she bolts, her internal egg timer driving her speed.

As she disappears, Perry says, "How long have you known her?"

"I fixed her car once a few years ago. She's a vacation friend."

He looks at me expectantly.

"We talked for a few hours and ate leftover mussels on the curb. And her chicken marsala is—"

He says, "I love my dad, you know."

Here we go.

I look into his face. "Okay."

Calmly, Vin. Be casual.

He says, "While it's definitely sad and I wish he didn't die, I always do something special on his birthday, and I'm definitely keeping four of his paintings. The three in the art gallery aren't the only ones I own."

I return his steady gaze and say, "Okay."

I wonder how long before this moment is considered a lingering silence. Nine seconds? Fifteen? I love the awkward pauses that underline the truth of a moment, an invisible red arrow blinking in and out of existence. He brought up this topic. Let him run with it.

Wait, how could an invisible arrow be red? Duh.

"I don't want you to think I'm a bad person because I sold his paintings," Perry says, pausing to breathe. "I want to buy a condo. I'll never afford anything here otherwise. He'd want me to have a home of my own."

"I'm sure he would. Personally, I think you're crazy to try to get a mortgage in San Francisco, but hey, if I had to sell a few paintings to live that dream, I'd do it."

He frowns and says, "Is this that thing where you agree to make me shut up? Or are you serious?"

"Perry, you loved your father. I'm not judging you for selling the paintings. I don't think you're a bad son. But doesn't the earthquake factor freak you out? At least a little?"

Perry shifts in his chair. His irritated stare mixes with uncertainty.

He says, "Earthquakes."

I say, "I don't get it. Living on a fault line that you *know* is active, I mean, not like two hundred years ago but just recently—"

Perry says, "How much did you know about my father before you came in to the art gallery on Tuesday?"

Good. He's tweaked.

"Last Friday before I headed north, I saw a flyer for the Tuesday night opening and figured I'd show up. I do like surrealism; I've read a few books. One book covered artists' relationship to form and convention, particularly math and physics. There was a whole chapter describing the Golden Curve. Your dad got some paragraphs. You should check it out; the whole Golden Curve thing is fascinating. Kind of like all the people who are into pi. The number, not blueberry. I like people interested in weird laws of physics, patterns in nature, and the underlying mechanics of the universe, as I consider myself to be a mechanic of the universe. However, I would still have to say that I am more interested in blueberry pie than the other kind."

"What book?"

"I don't remember the exact title, but I can find it at home. I'll mail it. It had the words 'convention and form' in the title, but half the books I read have the words 'convention and form' in the title, so, you know."

He says, "That would be great. Or maybe just copy those pages."

"I'll mail it. I have too many books anyway."

"Thanks."

He doesn't appear grateful or happy with the direction of this conversation.

Perry doesn't know why he's suddenly tense, and I'm sure doesn't recognize how his face muscles tightened while he discussed his lack of father issues. He's not furious. He's just irked. *Irked* could be a happy-go-lucky word if it didn't have that *k* stuck up its ass, right in the middle of everything.

He sips his wine and studies me.

Be blank, Vin.

The problem isn't that Perry doesn't love his father. Of course he does. However, mixed in with that love lives a strong resentment, a formidable and long-dragged grudge.

He says, "One of my best childhood memories is my father and me carving pumpkins for Halloween. I was eight. Mom said I was too young to use the big knife. But Dad stood behind me and we cut the eyeholes together. He had his arms around me. I felt safe."

We are silent.

We stare.

I say, "What shape were they?"

"What shape were what?"

"The eyeholes."

"I dunno, triangle, I suppose. Why?"

"Your face said you expected me to ask you a question, so I did."

"That's it?" Perry's voice quivers. "That's all you're going to ask about my dad?"

"What should I ask?"

Perry clamps his mouth shut and unclenches immediately. He says, "Never mind."

I'll get him more riled up. I say, "Listen to this. One time when I ate here, sitting over there at that table, these two guys were clearly on a first date, but I wouldn't say they—"

"No. I'm sorry to interrupt, Vin, but wait a minute. Aren't you going to ask *anything* about him? You can, you know, ask anything. I'll answer honestly, I promise."

I keep my face blank and say, "Okay. Cancer?"

"Yes. Stomach cancer."

There's a long pause.

"I'm sorry, Perry, I don't have any other questions."

"How did you know about the cancer?"

"Well, he died young, and it wasn't a sudden death since he had time to paint. Cancer seemed like a good guess."

We are silent for a moment, and Perry sips his wine with deliberation.

"I could ask more questions about him if you want me to."

This exasperates Perry further.

I say, "I admit I'm curious about him as an artist. That book I read showed a black and white painting of his I liked. I don't remember the title—"

His tone is sharp as he says, "I don't own that one. A relative has it."

I nod.

Silence.

A relative? Conspicuously vague.

He says, "I thought this whole weekend was about, you know, trying to fix this father thing. You said a dying king painted those paintings, and then your note said, 'remember the king'."

I keep my face blank and say, "I was trying to get your attention."

He studies me.

"Wow," Perry says with a grimace. "Boy, I figured you all wrong. I thought you were going to be Mr. Sneaky Psychologist and secretly dig out all kinds of information about my father, so I wouldn't catch it. Here I am, offering to answer anything."

I incline my shoulders slightly. "We can talk about him if you want; I'm not averse. I don't have any questions, though."

"I love my dad," he says again, simpler and stronger. "I don't talk about him much because I don't have a lot of great memories of the end. But I feel sad."

"Okay," I say, my gaze as soft as his is hard.

At this delicate moment I must give him little reaction; I have to monitor my expressions carefully for the next ten or fifteen minutes while he's chewing this latest development. I'm in dangerous territory, where a subtle twitch or an overly nonchalant demeanor will convey a clue, a hint that he's absolutely and completely correct. The whole weekend is about his father.

When Richard Mangin's coffin descended into the earth, the child version of Perry wept, "I love you! I hate you!" The curse came true as curses do: a dragon arose. After this great abandonment, I imagine Perry often found a reason to walk away from just about everyone at the slightest provocation. Better he leaves them before they leave him.

Perry advertises this lifelong pain more than he knows. We all broadcast our most private miseries in unconscious displays, large and small gestures. Sometimes strangers see it more easily than best friends.

But Perry doesn't need more blah blah with a therapist. He needs to get off his ass and fucking forgive.

In a sharp voice, he says, "Why did you pretend to steal a duck?"

"Are you sure that's the tone you want to use?"

Perry scowls, but immediately after, his gaze softens. In the last few hours, he's been coming around to loving this strange weekend, abusive host and all.

As he takes a deep breath, I imagine his brain fires a rapid communication to his heart: that Perry is not angry, that this irritation is the wrong response. It's what the brain does in all of us when communicating with the heart, explains why the heart is wrong to feel what it feels. So, move on. If the brain could dictate a memo, I'm sure the last line would conclude, "Because I said so."

His face melts further as he stares at me, unflinching.

This is good, very good.

I'm delighted Perry is so mercurial in his emotions right now—angry, trusting, happy, and suddenly tense. I tweaked him all weekend toward emotional and physical exhaustion, and we're only a few hours away from the big showdown. His heart now runs on fumes, weary from loving, withdrawing, embracing, resisting, and then loving even deeper. I'm guessing his heart is currently penning a memo of its own, something like, "Dear Brain, fuck off. I've got enough going on without your bullshit."

Perry says, "I'm sorry. I just—I had these expectations. That you were trying to be my therapist or something."

"No problem."

I probably shouldn't mention that I read psychology textbooks at night to make me sleepy. That particular detail may not provide any comfort.

I stroke the side of his face with my thumb, and he doesn't flinch with this public display of affection. "You and I had a long day. Not a lot of sleep. If I were you, I'd ask the same questions right now."

His eyes well up with tears because he really is exhausted. Our King Weekend didn't start yesterday on Pier 33. It began the minute he picked up my written invitation on Tuesday night.

Perry says in a halting voice, "If I may ask, why pretend to steal a duck today?"

While I'd prefer he not ask this right now, I'm ready with the truth.

"I wanted you to trust me. At the Golden Gate Bridge, your heart trusted me, despite plenty of left-brain proof that I am a criminal and a complete asshole."

Perry laughs, and he wipes away a tear.

"Oh, man," he says and wipes the other eye. "I have been racking my brain all afternoon to figure out how that damn duck relates to my father."

Show nothing.

You're absolutely right, Perry. *Remember the ducks.*

I say, "You needed to learn that you could trust your heart even after your brain disagreed. You passed your kingship test. In case you didn't notice, you just wiped away a tear. You can cry again."

This makes him pop out a few more tears.

I say, "Next up, we enjoy dinner, an ocean sunset, and spend our last night together. Tomorrow morning, you greet the dawn as a king and I reveal your king name."

Perry's expression changes slightly, relief or triumph, some subtle shade of purple swirling with his fatigued smile.

"I passed?"

I raise my pinot noir. "To ducknapping."

"Duck*ling*napping," he adds, clinking my glass to his with a soft and satisfying ping. "I should have known that was the big test. It was pretty horrible."

"True, true. You know, Perry, if you say the word 'ping' just so, the word sounds like the real-world sound."

Perry lifts his glass. "To King Aabee."

I raise my glass and respond. "To King Aabee."

He says, "And to people with fucked-up word issues."

"Who exactly are we toasting, *dude*?"

He says, "Piiiiiiiiiiiiiiing."

We lean across the table to kiss, and his thick lower lip tastes like red wine.

Moments later, our carbonara appears with a flourish. Definitely more than the standard serving. The heat swirling from this platter is a comic book moment, wavy steam lines rising between us and the two of us smacking our lips, leering bacon grins across the table. Perry insists we take a moment to smell it deeper as he prods it with his fork, commenting on its rich appearance.

He says, "Smell this bacon, all sizzling and succulent."

"I thought you didn't like bacon?"

Perry folds his hands together and says, "Oh, I love *bacon*. I just haven't had any today. Put your fork down. Let me smell this for a moment. It's incredible. How long has she been here?"

"C'mon, man. It's not art. Lemme eat."

Perry consents, and we dig in.

We attack from the middle, forks intertwining, playfully sparring for delicately drenched squiggles. The carbonara reveals bacon's finest hour: tender, juicy chunks dotting the egg-noodle landscape, the savory tang overwhelming any balanced sense of smell. Anna Marie's carbonara boasts a delicate, rich cream, not too goopy, not too thick. I am wrong. It is art.

Three bites later, Perry asserts that this tastes better than any other carbonara he's ever experienced, and when I don't seem to agree vehemently enough, he adds, "I'm completely serious," several more times.

We chomp away for a few moments, mostly not talking, concentrating on savoring every bite of this late California day. Daylight shifts as we eat, the sun no longer boasting its dominance. It's still high enough in the sky that I'm not worried about time; even if we leave as late as 6:45 p.m., we have almost two-and-a-half hours of remaining light. City dwellers may get only two more hours, but he and I will perch on top of a mountain, stealing more sunlight than is fair.

Anna Marie returns to make sure that everything agrees with us. Perry is effusive in his praise.

She says, "Wait until you taste the bruschetta. I made it myself because it's for you, Vin."

After she's gone, Perry says, "Bruschetta."

"More amazing than the carbonara."

Our college-age server brings us more wine and announces, "On the house."

After she leaves, Perry says, "Seriously, Vin, what happened with Anna Marie."

I raise my glass. "To Found Queens."

"To Found Queens," Perry says, raising his glass and then pausing before sipping. "Is there a tribe of Found Queens?"

"Absolutely. But she didn't get the full weekend, just a few hours after the restaurant closed while I fixed her car. She was going through a rough divorce. I had to keep clanking under the engine a full hour and a half after I had finished fixing it because I wasn't finished with her. Honestly, I'm not sure it's as effective without the ocean cocksucking."

He lifts his glass again. "To ocean cocksucking."

"To ocean cocksucking."

He laughs as he sets his glass down. "Fine. It does sound like a 'ping'."

"Plus, she and I never stole a duck together."

Perry laughs. "I helped steal a duck today."

I raise my glass. "To stolen ducks."

He says, "Piiiiing!"

With the fashionable dinner hours drawing near, the restaurant grows more crowded. After the transfer of the bulging bruschetta pouch into our custody, Perry hugs Anna Marie enthusiastically, as do I, and we navigate the additional patrons with a series of *Sorry*s and *Excuse me*s.

As we pass the last table, Perry speaks to two women studying menus. "Have you tried the carbonara?"

I think if he examined his heart, he'd know the truth: it's not over. No man earns his kingship that easily.

Night is coming for you, Perry Mangin. And me. At the top of Mount Tam, I'll have to deal with Billy. Night is coming for me as well.

SIXTEEN

WE REACH the van in comfortable silence.

Perry is happy to see Mr. Quackers, and the duck rides first class again. Perry builds him a nest with his jacket, and the duck responds by turning around a few times in Perry's lap. Despite a few little reluctant quacks, our feathered friend seems comfortable enough to go exploring: he charges up Perry's left coat sleeve. Of course, he's trapped seconds later, and we both chortle as we try to extract our friend from the twitching leather tunnel.

"Hey, I'm quick gonna recheck that engine belt."

"Is it serious?" he says. "Is it okay to drive?"

"Definitely. Aesthetics is all. In case you couldn't tell, I'm a little controlling about details."

Perry says, "You? I hadn't noticed."

I leave Perry and Mr. Quackers for a moment or two alone. I tinker with a few things, mostly for show. Eventually, I slam the hood shut and return to him grumbling.

"That wasn't smart," I say.

"What's wrong?"

"I don't have any tools, so I shouldn't have been tinkering. I messed with a piston…"

I see the look on his face.

"… which, in conclusion, I zigged left when I should have zagged right."

"You shouldn't assume that investment bankers don't know about cars."

"The third cam is bent, which causes—"

"Fine, I know nothing about cars. Okay to drive?"

"Totally okay to drive. May clack a little louder, though."

As predicted, the van does clatter with more regularity as we leave the curb and head out of Sausalito. Since I'm obviously not worried about it, neither is he.

We drive through neighboring towns, full, content. Perry points out landmarks to Mr. Quackers occasionally, little bits of California geography. Once in a while Perry comments on our carbonara, and each time he does, I rub my belly in fond remembrance. Perry babbles like a man exhausted, and though it's early enough that the sun remains over treetops, bedtime doesn't seem far away.

He says, "We're not going jogging, are we? I don't think I could right now."

"Do I look like I jog?"

Mt. Tamalpais is the highest peak in the California Coast Ranges, those intimidating mountains outside San Francisco. The van creeps up the green and twisting roller coaster roads, ascending, ascending, always ascending, the slight engine clack the only distraction and even that is not much of a distraction. Actually, it fits. I am pleased by the idea of a roller coaster car clacking up the chain.

"Hey, doesn't this belt sound like a roller coaster clacking as you inch up the first big hill?"

"Sure, I guess. Hadn't really noticed it."

Which is why I brought it up.

Something changes in Perry, because the one forbidden topic, his father, turned out to be nothing. He speaks freely about anything, initial conversations pursued deeper, such as details of his career choice and how I like being a mechanic. We talk about fear, the experience of feeling fear, and he does not shrink from the topic. He asked me if foster care sucked, and I said mostly, but I admit I met some nice people along the way who thought they could actually help. And who knows? They probably did.

As we climb higher, he tells me a soft insight acquired this afternoon about his ex-boyfriend Chuck, and we share small victories we've enjoyed with each other. We speculate on what various bridge friends are doing right now, NICHOLAS and Tired Mom and the teenager who said, "Say sleaze." Perry asks for a point or two of clarification on why the Alcatraz guards don't want to know my real name. No secrets remain between us anymore, so I tell him the truth. We don't need answers to our questions, but we both want to celebrate moments from our short time together. Of course, I steer us from the big topics. We're not really chatting about anything I wouldn't want revealed.

Despite Perry's lifted ban, I notice that he still doesn't bring up his dad. Once or twice this weekend, he has shared a "My mom once said…" story, but that's it. He no longer edits intentionally; this is Perry being Perry. I bet he edits his father out of most conversations naturally, not remembering the time when his father meant everything.

And if I learned anything over dinner, it's that once upon a time, Perry's father did mean everything; he was Perry's whole world. Rage flashed briefly in Perry's eyes as he told the pumpkin-carving story. That event alone contains an ocean of Perry's love but remains hostage to a kid's fury. The world stole his father, and the world is not forgiven. Grief dragons grow up too, no longer visible in childish pouting and bad behavior, instead adopting a respectable gray suit and always lingering nearby, influencing conversations in subtle, discouraging ways. When Perry sees this gray-suited grief, he barely recognizes that part of himself; it's just another bank customer making his regular withdrawal.

Higher and higher, steeper and steeper we soar.

A few breathtaking views along our route slow our progress as we pull over to be dumbfounded. The ocean, the northern hills laden with late-day mist, and insanely ancient redwoods four feet away bombard our shared sense of awe. I never can accept their trunks, how wide those trees can be, how impossibly strong. It's *alive*. How can that fucking tree be eight hundred years old?

A duck in captivity might observe the forest out our windows and decide, "I could live here." For that reason, we return Mr. Quackers to his cage, and this allows us to open the windows, breathe the moist, primeval scent. We smell the big world, get ourselves drunk on crisp autumn air, each breath crunching like October apples.

The roller coaster keeps clacking higher, steeper, and then higher and steeper.

"There," Perry says, the word solemn, as he points to the miniaturized San Francisco when it at last comes into view, a tiny little Lego Land surrounded by lush green in almost every direction. Except where we see lush blue.

It feels wrong that downtown San Francisco can now be obscured by my thumb. Did we really pick up Mr. Quackers down there? Geographically, we're not that many miles from the city, but most of those miles are straight up. Onward we drive, a few miles higher, then a few more. Switchback driving through tight mountain passes with no guardrails and no shoulder causes us to grow silent. Whether the silence is inspired by reverence or unvoiced terror, we do not discuss. For me, it's both. Two cars meeting at this height must navigate each other very, very carefully. Almost makes me regret renting a van.

Jesus, this is high.

Our final destination, Mount Tam's east peak parking lot, contains a dozen cars. Watching the sunset from this mighty peak is yet another well-kept public secret. When we arrive, we emerge and stretch out the tension because though the experience was unbelievably stunning, I also felt faint, mountain disaster lurching around every steep curve.

"I hope there's an oxygen tank under one of those tarps," Perry says, trying to laugh out his nervousness.

"Can you imagine if we actually encountered another van coming the opposite way?"

"Did you see those bikers zooming downhill? Could you ever do that?"

We make more mountaintop observations, walking through our fear in parking lot circles.

We are not alone.

Last minute hikers return from somewhere green, and other hikers depart for somewhere else. I spot several couples getting snuggly as they prepare for the quarter-mile summit hike. Boy, are they in for a surprise: that last quarter mile isn't romantic as much as scream inducing and sweaty. A man in sunglasses grips the steering wheel of his car as if steeling his nerves to drive back down. He nods.

God, I miss— This is not the time for that. Focus up, moron.

A nearby family rejoices together, obviously freshly off the summit. The parents barely notice their kids, running crazy through the grass. They're too busy congratulating each other on keeping the children alive.

Alive.

The world is alive here. Reality shimmers. Every tree fascinates; the small grassy park glows uniquely green, as if we have only discovered this new invention utilizing both blue and yellow and we are virgins to the experience. Green dazzles, and we agree to be dazzlees.

The energy from the rocks and spirit from sun-dappled trees feels tangible, not just a heartfelt bumper sticker seen in Lower Haight. We're touching it. We're so close to something sacred, the earth containing this raw piece of creation alters us. The crisp-apple air is conspirator to this invisible secret, shocking each breath with something magic. There's a reason shamans live on mountaintops.

To the right of the parking lot, a picnic area provides a respite for those not eager to immediately climb the summit trail. We spy a few long wooden tables and a building devoted to bathrooms, an outdoor drinking fountain, and a few scattered signs forbidding fire. The view from this height makes me whimper, both in raw joy and aching vulnerability. I love California, I do. But this shit freaks me out. I'll take a flat state any day, thanks.

"Perry, if you don't feel like pissing your pants when we reach the top, you may want to take advantage; we won't be coming back down tonight."

He puts his hands on his hips. "Why are you so prejudiced against hotels? There can't be a campsite up there."

"No, but there are a few spots where we can lay out our sleeping bag and make space for Mr. Quackers."

He scoffs. "Sadly, this is an improvement over chasing a man with a gun," he says over his shoulder as he leaves me. "I suppose I should be grateful for that,"

Perry disappears into the bathroom.

Good. I could use a moment or two without him to confirm some props.

PERRY looks astonished when I fling back the last tarp to gather what's underneath. Not because the contents are all that unique—just a backpack—but the tarps represent Vin's Mighty Van of Secrets. Now there's nothing left to hide; everything is out in the open.

Perry's surprised face barely registers, so quickly comes his cool reply, "What a surprise, another backpack. I hope you kept the receipts. You must have spent a fortune at a sporting goods store this week. Seriously, it makes me nervous about your finances, Vin."

I grab the sleeping bag. "You haven't met the King of Bargains. Plus, think of how much we're saving on hotels."

I ask Perry to pack what's left of our duck food and grab an extra water bottle. I attach the latest backpack to the sleeping bag frame and drag out the heated pouch of the most exquisite bruschetta I have known. Sometimes beautiful food that comes lovingly into my world makes me cry. I'm such a wuss that way. *Wuss* is a good word too. I like that word, a deflating balloon. Wuuuuuuuuusssssssssssss.

Vigor vs. *wuss*.

Huh.

"Duck is locked and loaded, Commander," Perry says.

"Let's cover the cage. We'll need to cover our friend tonight if we want to sleep."

"Sleep," Perry says wistfully. "The sunset will be beautiful, I'm sure, but if I weren't completely exhausted, I would talk you into going back to the hotel. That bathroom had four different scented soaps. One of them was blueberry."

"Did you take them when you left?"

He says, "The soaps? I should have."

I say, "I love hotel soaps. For some reason, I always believe those little soaps will bring me luck. So far, they have only brought me soap. The word *soap* sounds slippery, and it slips right out of your mouth. Sssooooooooap."

Perry says, "Sssooooooooooooooooap."

We begin our final quarter mile.

Unlike most California park trails, the east peak hike isn't easy. The trail starts out perfectly fine: we traipse over two-hundred feet on solid railroad ties and enjoy a metal bar railing. The railing provides some illusory protection against the incredible distance a person would fall. You comfort yourself with how easy this seems, how safe.

Soon we reach a crossroads. A sign warns the path to our right is CLOSED - DO NOT ACCESS, and a metal gate actually blocks this access, symbolically at least. People skirt the gate all the time. At this moment, nobody flaunts that directive. I kept us in the parking lot long enough that we began the final ascent without company. That route is a shorter path to the top, a little steeper, but for the surefooted, easier. I don't want this to be easy for Perry.

We press forward.

Almost right after the CLOSED sign, the wide wooden path and metal railing end abruptly, which means going forward it's nobody's responsibility but yours not to plunge to your death. Perhaps you'd only fall thirty feet and crush your spine against a giant boulder. But the brain can't help but calculate the damage from falling all the way to sea level.

A dirt trail leads us, narrower than the wooden railroad ties, and rock stubs poke out, like enormous potatoes forcing themselves up, demanding harvest. The half-buried rocks are easy enough to navigate for a while, until suddenly they're bigger and closer together. A few feet ahead, they're bigger, and they are strong enough to form a union. Suddenly you're climbing over instead of stepping around, remembering fondly that comforting safety rail.

I say, "Whenever I'm here, I feel I'm hiking through a life-sized diorama about how gravel grows into giant mountain boulders. And everyone knows what mountain boulders grow up to be."

Perry stops eyeing his next strategic climbing move and says, "What's that?"

"Mountains. Duh."

He looks nervous.

"Vin, can we make it up here with all this stuff?"

"Yes, Pear, believe in me."

With a smile he says, "I do."

It's a good thing we already like each other, because as expected, our sweaty exertion is not so sexy. Perry's trying hard to keep the duck cage level, his hair plastered against his head, dripping profusely. I'm precariously balancing the weight of the pack frame against my back and the warm bruschetta pouch before me, which means I have to stop every other boulder and wheeze and plan my next footsteps.

I need to lose some weight.

I offer a couple of tricks on moving slowly, how to center the body while straddling two rocks, strategies for carrying a bulky object gracefully.

Between raspy gasps for air, he says, "How can you do this? You bring ducks up here all the time?"

Between my own raspy gasps for air, I say, "Coolers."

We crawl the next two hundred feet over what appears to be an avalanche of house-crushing rocks that got confused and tumbled in the wrong direction.

I say, "Something to drink, Sir? Peanuts? Pretzels?"

Perry grunts in appreciation.

"That's it? A grunt? I was proud of that joke."

Perry grunts.

We are passed by a couple in their sixties, then a small family, everyone startled by how much baggage we drag with us. We exchange "High enough for ya?" type comments, and Perry waves them by with good cheer. He had to carry the duck to the summit. And he doesn't seem to mind, actually. Instead of the faux-crime turning into the last straw, the duck now represents his ability to trust again, his adventurousness.

We take a moment to catch our breath.

"Ginger peach soap," Perry says. "We could be soaking in ginger peach goodness right now, Vin."

"Were you lying on Tuesday night when you said that you liked to camp and go hiking?"

"It's not lying. It's flirting. I was *flirting*."

"Serves you right. Of course, I was fishing, trying to manipulate you into saying you liked camping, so perhaps that was unfair."

"If I had more breath, I'd call you an asshole right now."

"Please," I say somberly. "Not in front of the duck."

Moments later, facing north, we face a staggering vista and Perry wants his picture taken. He stands on an enormous boulder, and his backdrop is an uncountable number of avocado-green, humpbacked hills. Staring at these hills already blanketed in soft mist, a person might believe that the land got jealous of the ocean's whale population and created these hills in loving imitation.

Like a magician, Perry slowly draws the black curtain from Mr. Quackers's cage.

"Check it out," he says to our mutual friend. "Someday you could fly up here if you wanted to."

Mr. Quackers belts out a steady stream of exuberant sentences, saluting the world, announcing that he belongs, that he has always belonged.

"You're traumatizing Mr. Quackers, Perry. He's going to need therapy."

"Great," Perry says. "We can share a therapist. There's probably a Vin Vanbly support group we can join."

I set my burdens on a nearby boulder and free our camera from the backpack. People climbing by stop to watch. They were curious about us moments ago but now stare openly.

"Ready?"

"Absolutely," Perry says, smiling hard.

I start laughing because he's contagious. "What's wrong with you?"

Perry laughs hard and it takes a moment for him to stop long enough to say, "I'm holding a duck you convinced me was the victim of a showbiz kidnapping."

A few photos will develop blurry either because I laughed hard while snapping the shot or Perry doubled over exactly as I clicked the button. We manage a few photos where Perry is only beaming, splitting at the seams. Of course, we are not shy about asking someone to take our photograph together; Perry is all over that.

After one of our photographers shakes her head at our maniacally quacking friend, Perry informs her, "It's the Tourist King's birthday today."

We boulder-crawl our way around the summit area, Perry occasionally splashing water or food pellets around Mr. Quackers' quarters. No trail exists for up here, just enormous rocks, the ones that always seem to crush cartoon coyotes.

A brown ranger station dares to straddle the tallest tip of the east peak, selfishly hogging the best view, but because the building is draped in Tibetan prayer flags, we forgive. The engineering and architectural skill necessary to create this sturdy little house atop mountain boulders rivals the Golden Gate Bridge's masterful achievement. Definitely worth photographing the foundation just to figure out how they built the damn thing. Once again, I can't help but think, *Engineers. Got it.*

Perry says, "What do you suppose is in there? Weather equipment?"

I say, "Yeah, some. A bunch of reporting instruments. Two board games and some communication stuff. It's mostly just floor space."

"You've been in there?"

"Yeah, I spent the night in there twice."

"Up there? *In* there?"

"Yeah, but it's not really worth the effort. It's ridiculously hard to get a cooler up there."

Perry turns away to stare.

At this moment, hundreds of green miles and hundreds of blue miles are visible in every direction, and it's perfectly apparent why our planet is portrayed in those two colors. I always forget how stunning our planet is from this height, the curve of the earth visible at last, and how you suddenly feel like Superman commanding this unique view of creation.

The sun seems fascinated to get closer to this paradise landscape, and keeps dropping half inch by half inch in the west. Tenderly he flies to his lover, the Ocean, who twists in delight with his imminent arrival. "Patience, my love," the Sun whispers in long golden rays. "Soon I am yours."

As expected, the east peak boasts a happy gathering of tourists like us. Or locals. There's no need for that distinction, no snobbery here. It's a crime not to love the world and each other at this altitude, a crime almost as terrible as spilling red wine in an art gallery.

Everyone greets us, because, well, we have a duck. Duckling.

Perry answers all questions in good humor, sometimes answering truthfully, sometimes teasing that we represent a local zoo on a field trip.

We don't trade names like at the Golden Gate Bridge. Perhaps because it's offensive amid this level of intense beauty to think *my name matters*. We are worshippers here, and only She matters, the Queen who carries us all.

Everyone wants a photograph of the man with his duck at the top of the world, and Perry grins for each photo, proudly displaying his adopted son. Two frowning couples won't come near us; we scare them. It's not entirely fair to blame Mr. Quackers. As soon as he becomes a mountaintop celebrity, out comes the fragrant bruschetta, still dripping warm olive oil. Luckily, Anna Marie packed plenty of napkins. That pouch thing works really well.

When people ask, I describe how to find Anna Marie's restaurant, and after devouring their share, an older couple write down the restaurant name. They live in San Francisco but never go to Sausalito. "Too touristy," they explain.

When invited to partake, a German family of six discuss amongst themselves. The father expresses suspicion in his native tongue until I take a big bite to show him my willingness. I probably didn't have to eat one to convince them, but I love her bruschetta, so I am happy to prove my devotion. The oldest of his children, a woman in her twenties, speaks patiently to her father. I do not speak German, but I'm fairly confident she's explaining how American murderers would never draw such attention to themselves. *They have a duck, father.* That's what it sounds like to me.

"Parents," she says, and hands him a piece.

He insists on a first bite before letting any of his over-eager children taste it.

I like him.

Our friendship finally negotiated, the Germans love the bruschetta and become eager conversationalists through their adult daughter. German Dad observes how uptight American parents are at this height, and we watch his kids leap from boulder to boulder, eating Italian bread and quacking happily in their native tongue. Duck love is recognizable in any language.

As we shake hands to part, Perry says, "We're delighted to meet you guys. You're beautiful."

German Mom says, "Thank you."

Among our small crowd of twenty or twenty-five, most come to investigate. Those who chomp away on Anna Marie's bruschetta wave the remaining strangers to meet us. Some return for seconds. I have to apologize several times for running out. Once everyone who wants a photo of Perry and his duck has one, we are free of party obligations.

I nod around the area. "Look for a spot to lay our sleeping bag."

We find a suitable patch of dirt, smaller than the Hammock, braced on either side by rock, but enough ground to lay flat. Less than one-hundred feet away, this dirt area becomes the alternate path, the one we avoided. I don't want us exploring that path any further.

Perry sets the cage on solid ground and joins our tourist friends in gaping at everything. The sun and ocean draw closer to an actual kiss. Last photographs are snapped as our party guests depart. We will have the actual sunset entirely to ourselves, because nobody dares stay as light disappears.

I point toward a spot nearby, six feet away with more room. "How about over there? Break from the wind?"

A flat bit of earth offers an ocean view and stony shelter from the east and south. Plenty of space to sit together, cuddle together, and watch the day slowly end over the Pacific Ocean.

Perry believes I have spontaneously selected a suitable spot in this unfriendly campground. But we have to sleep right here. Otherwise, all my work yesterday was a huge waste of time.

Perry fusses with Mr. Quackers's cage so he's not facing any strong wind.

It's hard not to hear the stories of the trees, the low keening of these mountain rocks; everything sings at this height. The wind stings us, explaining in sharp, brittle words the stories of the earth and her tricky relationship with ocean. We're tiny ukulele players sitting up here, staring at the Hawaii-themed birthday cake all our own. We're so close to upside down, more sky than anything else visible, that if one of us were to stumble over a rock, there's no telling whether we would fall down or up.

It could go either way.

We stay silent for a big part of this time, cuddling together in awe. The sun makes actual contact with the ocean at last, thrusting deep its hard disc, prompting the last new friends to bid us farewell.

Perry soaks up each goodbye.

German Dad shakes my hand, and he puzzles over our refusal to depart. *Seriously*, he says with his eyes. I nod to him, and he gets it, that this is part of the plan. He stares at me a moment and then ushers his family away.

We wave back and forth until they have disappeared from sight.

Perry makes a joke or two about the hotel again, and each time he does so, I kiss the side of his head. He takes my hint and chooses silence as the sun's hard curve begins to disappear.

He says, "I wish you'd saved some bruschetta."

"Who do you think you're dealing with?" I say, making sure my voice sounds hurt as I reach for the pouch. "We're talking about *food*, Perry. I still have regrets about not getting a hot dog on the ferry."

He says, "My God, was that just yesterday?"

I pass him the second to last piece, and he munches away, licking olive oil off his thumb. From the backpack, I grab two organic grapefruit juices, a delicious local brand so tart and sweet it's hard not to drink the entire bottle in one gulp.

He says, "Aren't you going to have the last piece?"

"No, it's for you, if you're still hungry later."

"Go ahead. I'm good. I only wanted one more taste."

"But later."

Perry stares at me with soft eyes. Maybe he can't quite figure out how a guy built like me could turn down amazingly delicious food, and sometimes I can't fathom it either. But I love him.

We pass a few more moments together in silence, sitting shoulder to shoulder. I would prefer to just stare at the fire-truck-red sky and guess how it will merge with the indigo pressing downward, but these last minutes of sunlight are crucial.

"We better get ready for night."

I roll out our sleeping bag while Perry drops the black cloth on Mr. Quackers's cage. Mr. Q expresses dissatisfaction at this instant nightfall, but children always resent their parents' later bedtime. I pull free our Mexican throw rug and flashlight from the bulky backpack and fuss it over our laps as we snuggle on our private boulder couch.

A mere hint of sun remains above the horizon. Maybe the sun departed a few seconds ago, and these last rays are a mirage. Perry snuggles against me, head on my shoulder. His body purrs.

With our remaining juice, we toast. We had a day.

It's time to bring Perry to the summit.

"Perry, I love you."

He tenses against me. Not much, an involuntary spasm.

"Don't say it back. I'm not looking for that. But when my heart feels this open, I must say it out loud or disrespect the power which brought you to my life."

Perry relaxes during this, even deeper. He wants this too.

"Saying I love you does not mean we have to date, nor is it an obligation to send each other Christmas cards every year, with our annual one-line joke about Mr. Quackers. This is what it means to me. Right now, if I could choose to be in a five-star hotel with blueberry soap, I would change nothing; I would choose right here with you."

I say, "Forced to choose between you or onion rings with melted cheddar cheese and jalapeño peppers, I choose you. When I think about the men whom I have loved, you are on that list. Your name is written inside me now."

Perry trembles as his last wall crumbles down.

I say, "You might be tempted to say 'I love you' because I said it or you're slipping into my moment. If you want to say it, wait for an hour to pass and speak when your heart can no longer stand its silence. And if you don't say it, that is equally cool. Even kings cannot make rules about saying 'I love you'. The only rule is doing what's right for you."

"Okay," Perry says. "I can't believe you picked me over onion rings. I'm touched."

"Really thick-sliced jalapeno peppers and scalding hot cheese." I pause. "Tough decision, but then I remembered I loved you."

And while this humor ruins our moment, it actually doesn't ruin anything. In fact, we're sealing this moment, a maraschino cherry on top, remembering today as one of the surprisingly good ones. What could be more delightful than to wake up with Nut Rolls on Alcatraz and end with a mountain sunset in the company of a duck?

I kiss his lips and speak into his parted mouth. "I love you."

We're quiet for a few more moments as a bruised navy blue begins to dominate our formerly golden-red sky. We gaze in silence as twilight makes itself comfortable. Stars poke out, prairie dogs checking who else is coming out to play.

Time passes.

Perry breaks our silence and says, "Two years ago, I had about five dates with this guy, nice guy, and then on the fifth date he said, 'I love you'. Our connection was okay and growing, I guess, but it wasn't love and he knew it. I think he was lonely."

He gets quiet for a moment.

"Coming from you, Vin, I believe it. I don't understand why, but I believe you. I barely know anything about you, which is—"

We kiss with bruschetta breath. Mr. Quackers mutters, eavesdropping from his bedroom. Everything we could ever need is within our grasp.

"I don't know if I can say it back," Perry says. "I have only said 'I love you' to two guys in my life. The first time, I was seventeen. The other time was Chuck, someone I really loved. Those words aren't always easy for me to say. I don't want to say it without being sure I mean it."

"I didn't tell you so that you'd repeat it back. I said it because my heart commanded me to open my damn mouth."

Perry nods and permits me to fold my arm around him, pull him into me.

"All my love, Perry."

Without seeing him exactly, I feel him shake, and I'm sure he cries a few tears.

His brain has quit fighting these spontaneous and seemingly random attempts to cry. The brain pleads exhaustion, never getting a break from its leadership. Perry's heart is so ready to pound out commands right now, so ready. There's just one more grief dragon blocking the way.

I rub his shoulder, fuss with the blanket around him and say, "Sleep if you want to."

Perry squeezes me. As tired as he is, I'm sure he won't sleep. Not intentionally at least. He won't want to miss a moment of this. It's cold with no trees to block the wind at the top of the world, but we are cozy and happy together. We'll stay like this for a few hours as the night sky comes alive.

Perry is on top of the mountain.

We have a duck and a sleeping bag.

King Aabee is with his family.

We're ready now, kings. We're ready.

Let it begin.

The Forgiver King is ready to come home.

SEVENTEEN

THE moon triumphs high in the sky, the initial, bashful appearance easily overcome. She now sashays with easy confidence as she ascends Mt. Tam's summit, so unlike our scrabbling, sweaty ascent hours ago. Tonight, I must name her Li'l Shirley in honor of the entertainment happening right now at Anna Marie's. The world looks awfully bright all around us until you notice the enormous boulder shadows everywhere and realize that the moon's protective glow has some serious limitations. Navigating this terrain at night could lead to surprising, serious injury. Li'l Shirley, you minx.

According to her, it's almost midnight. My estimations are never an exact science, but years of sleeping under the night sky gives me confidence that I'm within thirty minutes. I could calculate it within ten minutes if I was back home, but I'm always a little off when on vacation.

I clear my throat and wait a few seconds, because I don't want to scare Perry out of whatever breezes through his soul right now.

I click on the flashlight, shine it on the cage. "You need to hold Mr. Quackers for the next part of the story."

"I don't think I can fit inside, Vin."

I sigh the "what I have to put up with" sigh.

I keep the light steady while he retrieves our water fowl for this bedtime story. Mr. Quackers is none too pleased, though we were generous with the lettuce leaf an hour ago. This latest intrusion is definitely not cool with him, and he expresses his discontent. It's colder than earlier, so I decide we need the sleeping bag.

Soon the three of us settle in together, arranging ourselves like nested Russian dolls: the unzipped sleeping bag wraps around both of us, I lean back against our flat rock, arms wrapped around Perry. Perry creates a nest from the Mexican throw blanket, which now holds our duck. We require a few minutes of fidgeting, but once comfortably established, we stare silently at the visible stars far outside the range of Li'l Shirley's brilliant glow.

Mr. Quackers lives up to his name and belts out a loud one. His head darts in each direction, and he seems shocked by the magnitude of the sound, so he remains quiet and alert in Perry's protective hands. At some point today, Perry discovered that strumming his thumbs along the duckling's back calms our friend. Or maybe the soft repetition calms Perry. As I watch over his shoulder, Perry performs this massage almost unconsciously.

Yesterday on Pier 33, had I explained how we'd spend the second night with a duck on the east peak of Mount Tam, I do not think Perry would have stayed. I believe I would have watched him stride away vigorously.

Fuck me, it's like a mosquito bite this weekend.

Focus up, moron. It's time.

I say, "The Lost Kings were angry. They had a grievance."

"What a surprise."

He pulls more of the blanket into his lap, fussing, his hands acting as cage bars. Mr. Quackers seems pleased with this arrangement as he tucks his head toward an underdeveloped wing.

"They were furious that the Found Kings never sent a representative to live amongst them for ten years, as they once had been promised."

Perry is completely relaxed right now; he has fully surrendered.

"What about King Aabee?"

"Exactly. But they forgot. They bemoaned how their request had been summarily dismissed, which they claimed was typical of the Found Kings."

He says, "Fuck 'em. They're dicks."

I wait for an extra moment before responding.

"What would you risk to find a lost king? And what if he doesn't remember you?"

Perry says nothing.

I hoped for a flinch, some further tell, but there's nothing to read. That's okay, I still think we're good to go.

I would love for this to happen during the midnight hour. When I snuck a peek at my pocket watch, I discovered I was off by twenty minutes. It's only 11:30. This is good. How often does a duck transform a man into a king on a mountaintop at midnight? It would be cool, like a fairy tale, and I'm a sucker for happy endings.

"The Lost Kings demanded a Found King be sent to them."

"Another ten years?" Perry says, sounding worried.

"No. To be put to death."

After he lets himself hear the words, his entire body jerks. "No. Don't say it."

"I will go. Send me!"

"No," Perry says, sitting forward, sounding surprised and anguished, similar to when he mentioned his mom on the Golden Gate Bridge. As I pull him back into my arms, his body tenses, quickening his return from the previous hours of well-earned peace and great, goopy love.

"Vin, c'mon."

I remain silent.

He turns awkwardly in my arms, faces me enough for me to see his alarmed expression. "It's your story. You don't have to do this."

"Your face right now," I say, stroking his cheek with my hand, "is exactly how many of the Found Kings reacted. They said, 'No, King Aabee. Not this time. Not you. You left us once, great leader of our people, and we almost could not bear it. Please do not leave us again.'"

The duck chafes in Perry's protective grip, as his fingers have unconsciously drawn closer together. His profile expresses grim resolve until he hears the soft duck complaints and relents, allowing Mr. Quackers a little more room.

"You know he volunteers, Perry. It's not really a suggestion."

"This is bullshit. Send that one king who, no, wait—send the Bear Walker king. I don't give a crap about him."

"King Aabee argued that he was the best qualified king to go."

I pull Perry back into my Russian nesting doll position; I want him to feel safe.

Reluctantly, Perry turns around to face the world.

"This older and wiser King Aabee claimed that having spent ten years amongst them, he knew the Lost Ones better than they knew themselves. They might see him and remember his face. Plus, working on King Diego's case for two years in Turkey polished King Aabee's negotiating skills; he excelled at logic arguments. When logic failed, all his investment banker skills allowed him to barter in the heart's gold."

Crap, crap, crap.

I wanted Perry soft and gooey, not thinking of his career. Was that a mistake to add in investment bankers? I knew it could kick me in the ass. But I don't see an impact; his body didn't respond. Maybe I didn't fuck up.

"It's gotta be him?"

"I cannot change King Aabee's true story, not even for a man I care about deeply. To do so would disrespect Aabee's courage."

Perry leans back against my chest. "Whatever."

Okay, breathe easier. No damage done. Crap, that could have undone hours' worth of work. Age regression works best when you forget your day job. Tread carefully now that we're here, Vin; this is the precipice.

Our sky is unstoppable, the stars giving the moon wide berth, huddling under the black cloak which wraps everything. The stars wink at Perry, telling him to trust. Li'l Shirley watches with a biased expression; she knows this tune. From isolated spots in the hills, faraway lights blink on and off as if a few tiny stars crashed to earth and forgot to burn out during their descent.

"All of Aabee's work with the ocean's homeless population grew his patience and compassion. If ever a Found King were perfectly suited to reach the Lost Ones, it was he. Only he could remind them that he had kept his word.

"Plus, his beautiful French wife reminded everyone that he knew the sewer system better than any king, lost or found. He could always escape if things got dangerous."

Perry says, "What was her name?"

"Llewellyn."

He says quietly, "Queen Llewellyn."

After a few seconds of silence, he adds, "Does he take his cocksucking flute?"

"It only sounded like cocksucking to some of the gay kings, but yeah, King Aabee wielded that subtle advantage. Because everyone experienced his music in so many different ways, it seemed likely that someone he met during his ten years among them would recognize the music and vouch for him."

I kiss the back of his neck.

Believe in the Strange Musician, Pear. You're going to need his help tonight.

"The night before King Aabee's departure, the kingdom celebrated, this party a more somber affair. All the kings lit tapered candles that burned blue flames. In fact, miles and miles of hillsides were covered with families and friends holding up the candles, walls of solid blue. And while they knew the futility of arguing with his decision, they nevertheless tried. 'Let me go in your place,' begged an elderly king who worked at the Department of Motor Vehicles. 'My time in this world is short anyway.' King Bolinas argued that he himself should go instead of his best friend. 'Your three sons, my friend. Think of your *sons*.'"

Perry stiffens.

"The night was not all gloom, Perry. King Detlof whipped out his chessboard again, and everyone laughed, remembering the failed attempt to stop a much younger King Aabee. Gatherers buzzed about how well that particular risk had turned out. Some former Lost Kings stepped out and told their stories encountering the Strange Musician, how Aabee had found them, sent them home. Some kings read poems inspired by the first time they heard Aabee's flute."

"Technically, it's not a flute."

I nudge him and continue.

"King Aabee's youngest son, Myrrh, gave a rousing speech, championing his father's bravery and cunning abilities, and during his passionate words, all present realized that among them walked a king braver than Aabee, the one currently addressing them. Throughout most of the celebration, the three brothers held hands."

Perry's body does not respond, but I think that's enough pounding the father and sons button.

"Queen Llewellyn thanked their friends, their beloved families, and announced that her husband wished to play a tune, a coming home song. Everyone on the blue-dotted hillsides grew silent. When clear grace emerged from the tip of his flute-like instrument, everyone thrilled to touch the power in such small, living things. Every Found King and every Found Queen allowed the song into their heart, and for the first time ever, everyone heard the exact same tune, for their one true king loved them through this soft goodbye and gave his promise to return. The song intertwined sorrow with strands of purple hope, because King Aabee had always kept his word."

We rock together in silence, listening for the echo of King Aabee's flute. There's no need to hurry the story along, not even to make this happen near midnight. That's just a nice piece of drama. Tonight, I serve the Found Kings and Perry, not my own foolish whims.

After a few more minutes, it's time.

"You have to scooch up, Perry. I have to get something from the van."

"*What?*"

"I gotta go."

I kiss the back of his head and start extricating myself.

He barks out a laugh and says, "You're kidding."

"I have to grab something for the next adventure. I couldn't quite bring it out until night, and plus you'd see it if I brought it with our other supplies."

I stand up, shaking out my legs.

"You're not serious. You're not *serious*, right?"

Perry scoots back to the rock with as little disturbance to the duck as possible. I fold the sleeping bag around Perry, creating a soft, warm cocoon. Perry's silence suggests he's processing this latest turn. He saw the tarps revealed; could there be anything else left? Nope. Nothing.

He says, "It's too dangerous. You could die."

"I'll take the flashlight."

"This is… this is crazy. You're serious? How long will you be gone? Wait, why are you taking the bruschetta pouch?"

"We don't need it anymore. I'll put the last piece in a plastic baggie for you."

Perry considers this as I pull out and wrap the last piece from Anna Marie.

"You're taking the backpack?"

"Yeah. I'm putting the pouch in there so my arms are free."

"Leave it. Grab this stuff in the morning."

"I have plans for us in the morning requiring us to travel light."

"Vin, c'mon. I don't think you should go."

"Now's good. Don't worry so much."

My tone shifts from affectionate lover to something slightly different.

I take out some essentials for him: toilet paper, aspirin, and two large bottles of water. I toss the plastic bag of duck food onto the earth casually, as if it means nothing to me. Three days ago, if the jaded investment banker watched this unfold in a movie, he'd throw popcorn into his mouth and say, "Anyone can see what's coming."

But Perry loves me. Even if the words are stuck in his throat, I can feel it. He loves me.

"Is there a second flashlight?"

"Nope. I think I need it more than you do. Don't you agree?"

I am impatient to begin.

"Yeah, all right. Hurry back, okay. I don't like it up here alone."

"Sure."

He says, "What about mountain lions?"

"Not up here. Too many human smells. But to make sure, yesterday afternoon I brought two gallons of human piss and splashed it in a wide radius around where we are right now. The scent alone ought to scare any nightlife away for a week."

Perry says, "You did not."

"Do you doubt me?"

"No," he says; his face gets serious. "Clearly, you're a guy who thinks about these things. I'm just…. Where did you get two gallons of urine? This is truly the most disgusting and thoughtful thing I've ever heard. I might vomit when you tell me, but I'm dying to know."

I ignore him while fastening the pack to my back and swinging the light toward the ranger station. The funny thing is that in this moment, he doesn't doubt me. He doubts himself. A full day of emotional hurdles guaranteed that I may be an asshole, but I am trustworthy.

"Vin, seriously? The piss?"

Oddly, Perry's face is innocent as he asks this. Staring at him, I see both the investment banker with dark circles under his eyes, and the surprise of a nine-year-old kid, his age when his father died. I have tried very hard to imagine what his tenth birthday felt like.

I stop him with my hand, as if sick and tired of all these interruptions. "Some of the piss is mine; I've been drinking lots of water since I got to San Francisco last weekend. I use it for my camp perimeter in the woods. But most of the piss came from a sex club. Wednesday night is their water sports night and they let me collect it from a bathtub. When I told guys that you and I would have sex inside a perimeter of piss, some of them found that hot and pissed right into the jug."

He twists away and chuckles. "Oh yeah. Definitely going to vomit."

My adventurous friend's confidence returns. Everybody put on your ski masks.

I say, "Wednesday night at Suck Buddies. Yellow hankie night."

Perry scoffs and says, "This is completely—I am completely horrified. What's worse is that you already had a container of piss in your rental van."

"If it makes you feel better, I don't do casual sex, only King Weekend sex, so nothing happened at the bathhouse other than me saying 'Thanks for your piss.'"

He says, "You are unbelievable."

Perry forgives.

"I'm worried about you, Vin. Seriously, this seems too dangerous. You have to go right now, huh? And you've done this before?"

"I'll be careful."

My tone is stiff.

"Yell or something when you get to the van. Honk the horn so I know you're safe."

"Sure."

He knows I'm lying, even if he doesn't know it. Perry seems confused by my mood shift, but I have swapped roles and tones all weekend, from king story mode to playful lover to demanding boss, so perhaps this is the next part of the adventure.

Better get him focused on worrying.

"I know what I'm doing. Enjoy the night sky. Don't spend the time worrying. "

"Yeah, okay. Hurry, but not too much. Are you sure about this?"

"Don't worry."

"You're *completely* sure about this."

"Yeah, I've climbed this mountain at night."

Despite being a flat-state man, I'm quite good at boulder-crawling. Mountains are like grandparents: out of respect, you must visit. And to never get trapped up here, you gotta boulder-crawl pretty regularly. I never had grandparents, but if I did, I would visit them. Well, unless they were super racist. Then I'd just write letters.

Perry smiles uneasily from the sleeping bag fort and his fingers stroke the duck's back. Mr. Quackers peers about the moonlit boulder park, perhaps plotting his own escape. He remains silent and watchful for now.

I take a step up and over the rock near us and get four or five more steps away when he calls out to me.

"Hey, wait. When you get back, do we get the next chapter of King Aabee or do we have sex?"

Perfect. I didn't have to bring it up.

I splash light on the next boulders and climb a few more feet away. He's already far enough away that we must raise our voices. I shine the light away so he can't see my face and he hears only the coldness in my voice.

"Not much to tell. They killed him."

In the moonlight, I see Perry's entire shadow jerk. I climb a boulder, now another. I'm already twenty feet away.

Mr. Quackers barks.

"Wait. What do you mean '*They killed him*'?"

I turn off the flashlight. I don't need the prop; I just didn't want him to have it.

Make it icy. I say, "The Lost Ones murdered King Aabee. See you later."

I disappear, swallowed in shadows.

"*Vin!*"

It's good that I didn't use the Terminator line. I think that was tighter without a movie reference.

I drop the flashlight over my shoulder into the pack. I crouch toward the rocks and lean forward, feeling my next precarious steps with my knees and entire length of my arms. Standard crawl down this side of the mountain until I'm back on the dirt trail. No hazardous conditions, which is good. But I can't hurt myself and leave us both vulnerable on a mountaintop.

I hear Perry yell, "*Vin!*"

Ignore him.

Leading with my hands and feeling each rock with my knees, I scurry across the boulders as fast as I dare, creeping in silence, a rat in the moonlight.

What is he thinking? What does he feel?

Who knows?

Perry is truly alone.

EIGHTEEN

ROUGHLY thirty-five minutes later, he hears it: our van roars to life.

He jerks his head to the right, toward the moon-drenched rocks and dark shadows, scrambling to his knees, then standing to verify the sound. I'm sure he recognizes this as our van, because I took great effort to point out the clacking sound. I want to make sure he has no doubt, none whatsoever, that I am driving away.

Tires screech across the parking lot, as if I cannot *stand* to waste another minute here. But the van slows as soon as it reaches the narrow road, beginning its dangerous descent down the mountain. The acoustics are undeniable, unable to be faked with a boom box or some clever imitation.

I left.

He searches for taillights on the narrow mountain trail. Sure enough, blazing red eyes, unblinking in their terrible judgment, retreat between tree trunks, sinking further and further away. Because he's holding a duck, his first responsibility is to this fragile life, so there's nothing he can do. I know a few who might take this out on the duck, but Perry is not one of those men.

Billy would be that man.

No. Later.

The faraway light from hillside homes can do nothing. No one can help him now. The ocean's roar muffles into a faraway knocking, an almost unconscious heartbeat. Perry staggers around his mountain prison, duck in his hands. He has been left behind again by someone who promised, "I love you."

Boy, that was some kick-ass screeching out of the parking lot. I'll have to compliment him on that tomorrow afternoon. I thought Perry's eyes would explode.

Perry's mouth hangs open, his eyes stunned wide. He's been here before. Leave it to a nine-year-old's broken heart to crawl into the cupboard under the kitchen sink to meet his gloom. Perry's heart forgot to come out and play a different game. I happen to enjoy hide and seek, especially helping the other kid get found.

And I can't believe how much expression I can see in his face.

These night vision goggles are much better than my ones at home. I thought I knew about all the latest models, but these are fantastic. I have to make a note to research new surveillance equipment. I need some little handheld computer, an electronic gadget I can use to write notes to myself, book titles, and things like "out of eggs." I need to invent that. With a tiny little mouse attached so you could navigate right in your palm. Wouldn't that be adorable?

Focus up, moron.

Perry might be tempted to race down the mountain chasing our van, pointless and death-invoking as that may be, except for the duck. He can't drag that cage over mountain boulders with no flashlight. I have gambled that he unconsciously prides himself on being the exact opposite of his father in this regard; he would never desert a helpless young life to the mercies of our uncaring world. Perry is *nothing* like a man who would do that. And if he is tempted, Perry will experience the grief of his father. Because the *Siren Song* imagery explodes in celebration, Perry may not recognize his father's deep mourning painted into every stroke. He may not have realized the agony his father felt knowing he would not see his son become a man. But Perry will taste that grief tonight, whether he opts to flee or decides to stay. I understand Lost Kings.

Perry leans against our boulder, completely still. He turns his head sharply a few times because he can't actually believe that this has happened.

"*Shit.*"

It almost doesn't matter if he figures out this latest trick; it may not matter one bit. I have wagered everything that the sheer gut punch reaction, this latest abuse during a weekend of exhausting emotions, must now rip through Perry in such a visceral way—the agony so core to his identity—that if his screaming brain logic argues this as another of my deceptions, it probably changes nothing in his heart: Perry trusted love and then got ditched.

Again.

He sits for a while, in his giant kitchen cupboard atop Mount Tam. But watching his legs twitch, unable to keep still, I can guess that pent-up feelings grow inside him. Soon he returns Mr. Quackers to his cage. I catch a few angry quacks from where I'm hiding.

Perry paces. He looks toward the darkness, hoping to see headlights returning. But he will see none.

"*No*," he yells at one point, loud enough for me to hear.

To the rock I'm hiding behind, I whisper, "Yes."

Help us, kings. Go to Perry now that he has been once again deserted by love. Please come, King Aabee, and bring an old friend.

"You will come back," he says again, louder, perhaps realizing there's no need for him to be quiet.

He waits.

Nothing.

His investment banker brain must gloat right now. All sorts of miserable messages broadcast, all under the similar theme: too bad you didn't listen to me, your brain, because I calculated that something horrible like this would happen. Not this awful, of course. I told you not to believe the invitation from the art gallery stranger. You were an idiot to trust—

He yells, "*No.*"

He throws the heavy black cover on the duck cage haphazardly, as if he blames this tiny creature.

Mr. Quackers protests, an irritated little "*Hey.*"

Perry stops and looks at the black box. He opens the cage door again and calls the little creature into his hands, perhaps to apologize for creating instant darkness. Perhaps he needs to hold something soft for comfort. It's hard to read his shadowed face.

Something happens: his shoulders hunch over, jerking a few times. Instead of comforting Perry, I think this squirming creature provoked the opposite, perhaps unlocking something forgotten, grief and rage for the soft and vulnerable creatures in this world, discarded by people they love. Maybe Perry, for the first time, wonders about the duck's parents.

The sound starts as a groan. The groan becomes a sharp intake of breath, and Perry stumbles back to our boulder, leans back, inching downward, each half-inch descent accompanied by a bigger sob. By the time he squats on the earth, his mouth stretches wide open. Mr. Quackers wriggles hard, but in silence.

The low moan which emerges next is a death moan, a surrender to that which cannot be denied. I would pay money to never hear that sound again, the starter pistol to despair.

Perry really did love me, and I really did leave him.

Nobody told Perry that he would never quite trust men because buried deep lay a secret fear that they were somehow in collusion with his absent father, and wouldn't everyone laugh heartily when Perry fell for it again. He doesn't know this ache binds all boys who have lost fathers, gay and straight. Girls too, of course. We all want our dads to come back. Even those kids who lived through shitty fathers long for the good versions of those men, the ones who will love us and show us the way.

Help me, Dad. This life is harder than I thought it would be.

Perry weeps.

Seeing his despair ignites it in me. I cry for Perry and his lost father, I cry for my own lack of parents. I cry for all of us who thought adults could be trusted, only to experience disappointment again and again. I cry because those who had good fathers do not understand the void for those of us who did not.

I have no doubt that I remain unheard; I have mastered the art of crying without sound.

I will never feel exactly what Perry feels. I can never fully know him in that way. Hell, I never even met my father, I don't think. But to make it safe for him to touch this aching part of his life, this bleeding wound that defined his entire existence, someone must say, "I will go. Send me!" Sometimes you have to work the sewers.

To grieve alone is hard. To grieve with someone who meets you under that green-thistled tree is shared grief, a different hard. The deepest compassion I know is the most gnarled tree in the desert. It is also the only one with shade.

Perry cries, and somehow during this time, he manages to get the duck back in the cage. He covers it lovingly this time, still crying, and then carefully stands. He wipes his face on his arms.

"I'm not going to freak out," he announces to no one. "I don't care, you son of a bitch."

King Perry awakens.

"You *fucking* asshole," Perry says louder, his voice still unsteady and raw. "I'm not leaving."

Perry chokes out a sob and cries again for a while. He sits, he stands. He walks. Pacing angrily does not seem to stop the flow of his tears.

"I have faith in Bolinas, you *dick*."

Saying this aloud makes Perry crumple to his knees, because when you stand up to a bully, even if you lose, a tiny piece of your own untouched power sparks alive. For reasons I have never understood, believing in yourself sometimes hurts as much as being abandoned.

I wipe my eyes and scold myself to come back, be present. I'm not here to break down; I'm here to protect the one true king. If he trips or if he attempts to prepare Mr. Quackers for travel, I fall back on Plan B: flute music. Plan C is to appear. But Plan A seems to be working, so I remain invisible. I urge myself to remember the ugly names, the ones they used to call me. It works; my heart grows harder, hard enough to let go, let him carry tonight's grief alone.

"Fuck you, Vin. I believed in your stupid kings and your—"

He cries again and covers his face. Maybe he remembered that King Aabee died suddenly and unjustly, away from his wife and sons. Maybe it's something else. Who knows? It's agony to have no idea exactly what he feels, but if I stood at his side and asked him to explain everything happening, would he? Could he? Can anyone articulate the language of the heart?

He stops soon enough, sputters down and stares all around him, the rocks, the sky, the navy cotton ocean all rumpled in the corner.

Perry stares at the night, and Li'l Shirley winks his way. She's in on the joke. The stars snap their fingers as they did last night when we raced around Alcatraz, while we made love. Hear it, Perry. Hear the song of the Strange Musician. A thousand muffled stars chittering and snapping, the echo of crunching ocean, the wind's "eeeeees" stinging your ears, the thick trees below, wrestling their own breezes. The sky, the earth, and the ocean live in sound; everything sings.

King Aabee has come at last.

When he speaks again, I cannot hear the words. He talks to his stone, like I talked to mine. Maybe we can use them as communication devices. I'm tempted to speak into my rock, "Can you hear me, Perry?" A moment later he turns in my direction, and I hear his subdued ranting once again.

"… much. *Please*, like I couldn't figure *that* out. The stupid blue castle, the hillsides of blue flames, constant references to forgiveness. Well, fuck that. As if saying 'I forgive you' makes me—"

He cries again, another heart-wrenching series of staccato sounds. He wipes his face and peers into the duck cage to make sure Mr. Quackers listens from his darkened room.

He puts his hands on his hips.

"I forgive you, Vin," he says, trying to sound sarcastic, but like earlier today, the words come out all wrong: half-sincere, half-surprised.

He stops and wipes his eyes. He cries for a moment. A smaller huff comes out of his chest, another letting go. He says, "I forgive you."

I think the words startle him. Maybe not the words, but the tone. He has a look about him, unguarded and open, but also devastated. Something is wrong, or something is right, an unbalanced expression that makes my heart beat faster.

"I forgive you," Perry says, in an empty voice. "Even though you abandoned me."

His head snaps up; arms zing out straight, like in the alley when the birthday cake smashed against the pavement. He staggers and drops to his hands and knees, falls hard, coughing, gasping for air, and making cawing sounds into the dirt. It's terrifying to convulse that way, the hard juncture of puking, hiccupping, and crying, the body unsure how to process an overwhelming emotion, so it tries everything at once.

He cough-barfs this way for what seems like five minutes, though it must certainly be less time than that, and I watch with great attention, legs coiled for action until everything stops. Still on his knees and his upper body pressed low to the ground, I witness his shoulders heave, decreasing convulsions. The words are wet and soft at first, a gentle repetition of a phrase repeated louder as a groan until finally I understand his repeated mantra: "Oh Dad, Oh Dad, Oh Dad, Oh Dad...."

We all telegraph the message to somebody: *Don't leave me. I would be lost without you, searching for love but finding only fog. Please don't go.* Then, that person leaves. Death, the end of a relationship, or just unreturned phone calls, leaving is leaving.

Perry cries harder, the deeper well opened at last. While I am sure he cried plenty for his father prior to this night, I wonder if those tears came from the place where he now finds himself, moans of an ancient oak door, slowly creaking open.

King Perry crawls out from under the sink cabinet.

I watch him with longing, having learned long ago that my instinct to go comfort him in this moment will not serve. These tears need to be shed, wept into the earth where there is no hope of consolation. Sometimes a man has to cry alone.

I have no idea how long we stay this way; checking my pocket watch would be blasphemous, as if something like this could be, should be, timed. Who cares? We've got a few more hours before the sky shifts toward light. But after another long period, Perry gets to his feet, and I feel my own heart swell in wild anticipation, because the way that Perry stands, it's different.

He surveys his world.

Am I crazy to think he stands differently? Maybe. But I don't think so. He's not a victim anymore: that part of life is over. He is no longer a prisoner of a mountaintop; no, he is a man *standing* on a mountaintop. It's a very different experience.

He looks like hell, his face raw, staggering to each direction in turn, peering into the night. While pointing north, the words are muffled, but I hear him say, "I forgive you both, you bastards."

When he turns back my way, I see fresh tears streaming downward.

This triumphant moment probably does not feel all that triumphant to him, but instead a new submission, recognition that sometimes your heart just gets broken. That's just how it goes.

Something makes him cry again, hard for a moment, and then he stops. He puts a hand against the stone and stares at the ocean for a while, the watery castle painted a sparkling, glittering black except where Li'l Shirley gives a kiss, and only there, a transcendent blue. He opens a water bottle and drinks half of it at once, learning against the rock and taking more swigs every few minutes.

Perry gathers our Mexican throw blanket around his shoulders and torso, climbs a nearby boulder, and settles in. He's not facing me, so I only see the side of his head as he stares into the ocean and sky.

LESS than a half hour passes before his body jerks hard, as if pelted by a small rock.

I tense up and scan the area quickly to see if he heard something I have not. I see nothing. Nothing over there. I turn a full 360 degrees, preparing myself to move quickly. Anything? Nothing over there. I've got an air horn at the ready that will fuck over any creature with ears. I grip my bowie knife tighter, unsheathed and ready for action, though I hope I do not have to use it. I hate violence.

"No," he says, and he wipes his face again. "No, no, no."

Perry slides off his rock and begins looking around, searching for something.

Duck!

I'm happy that the Mill Valley couple helped me test out this hiding spot. As soon as I saw them wandering around here, I could tell he was military. He scanned the landscape the way men who have been in wars sometimes do. I was doubly pleased his girlfriend was named Amanda, because I had been thinking of that name earlier in the week. She was sweet, though I doubt they would have been so helpful if they had seen my two gallons of piss.

"*You're still here.*" Perry's voice rings out sharp and loud.

He laughs. "I can feel you, Vin. I know you're still here."

He laughs harder, because while he believes it in his head now, he also *knows* it. And knowing a thing that is impossible to know, well, nothing is more exciting.

It's like recognizing the cellist is actually the painter's son, or seeing a Tired Mom stand proud and believing you know why. It's like an Alcatraz guard offering a beer to a Human Ghost because he knows an impossible truth: *I'm not alone tonight.* That's possibly the biggest thrill of all, recognizing not-aloneness. When this occurs, the brain looks to the heart with newfound appreciation, saying, "I thought I was the only one who could figure stuff out."

"You're still here," Perry roars, full of joy. "You crazy fucker, you never left. Just like my dad."

Perry stops and puts his hands over his eyes.

He is silent for a moment.

"It worked," Perry cries, his voice trembling. "*It totally fucking worked.* It's not about him dying anymore, it's about me. I don't even know what you did to me, but it worked!"

I do not answer.

"*It worked, Vin.*"

Perry laughs more, stopping to wipe his face on his sleeve.

He says, "I wasn't sure if you heard that the first time, so I thought I'd repeat it. I bet I don't have to shout, do I? You're not far. Of course you're not far."

He switches directions every other sentence. He repeats himself a few times, but I can easily piece together what he's saying as long as his back isn't to me. I should snap a twig—nah. Bad idea. He might try to come over here.

He says, "You know how I know you're still here? The birthday cake."

He waits for a reply but receives none.

"I was sitting there just now, thinking about how she was another person you screwed over, and maybe I could find her. Then I realized my name, P-R-Y, fit right in the middle of her last name. Then I thought about how twice, *twice* you emphasized the spelling of her name, worried you spelled it wrong in the frosting, and then that stupid thing with her middle initial. You tricked me into memorizing her name."

"I knew you dropped that cake on purpose, *you fucking Ghost*," Perry calls out, and he laughs again. "There is no Marie N. Grypn. She's an anagram."

He waits.

Perry says loudly, "At one point on Tuesday, you asked a question about my best childhood birthday present. You asked the weirdest questions of anyone I'd ever met, Vin. Swear to God, I was half-repulsed by you the first time we met. But you were already drilling me for information, trying to find out my age when he died."

He laughs hard for a moment and then catches himself. His face winces and gets soft, this time without him fighting it every step of the way.

"You were right; I was nine. My tenth birthday sucked. Because of the medical bills, I didn't get any good presents, but worse was how much of a brat—"

He turns to face the exact opposite way.

Crap. Now I'm going to have to ask him to repeat that part tomorrow. C'mon, Perry, look around. Nobody could hide over there. *It's a mountain cliff.*

He finally turns my way.

"… cruise ship, didn't I? But we never went. We couldn't afford it."

He pauses and then says, "Sometimes there is no other cake."

Perry stops and sits on the ground for a while, his head in his hands. The wind still lashes him regularly, but he stays this way for a long time. Every now and then he scratches his ankle or wipes his sleeve across his face. I finally get to see him when at last he raises his head to watch the moon. How can a person look tan under moonlight?

For his entertainment, Li'l Shirley dances a few solid inches across the sky. Beyond her reach, the Big and Little Dippers ascend, a father and son team who have managed to never abandon each other. A few million years in our universe's future, they will, as all fathers and sons must. But not tonight. Shirley's nameless husband tickles the ocean, his personal baby grand, each sparkling reflection a recently plunked key. This ebony musician plays the ocean's great medley, a never-ending tribute to the life glowing within.

Perry stands, walks around to shake out his legs, checks on Mr. Quackers. He stretches his arms, pulling one then the other, leaning against the rock and pushing as if preparing for jogging. He looks at the sky.

"More than half the night is gone, Vin. I don't know about you, but I am fucking exhausted."

He stares at the sky in every direction before he speaks again.

"I feel amazing. I want to stay awake and experience this, I do, but I also feel like I got run over by a truck. I—

"*Thank you, Vin Vanbly,*" Perry screams at the top of his lungs.

Silence.

"Fine, be that way. I can honest-to-God feel you, Vin. Is this king energy? Is that what this is?"

When he gets no reply, he shakes his head and says, "God, you can be irritating."

After a moment, Perry says again, "I'm exhausted."

He does sound exhausted. But exhausted is good sometimes, with an *x* like a pillow so that the whole word can lie down. You can trust an *x* to keep you safe. It's not as dramatic as *g* or *q* or regal as capital *R*. But it's a surprisingly strong letter.

"Mr. Quackers turned in a while ago. I'm going to bed too, if you don't object. And I know," he stops speaking for a moment, but then says, "I know you're going to watch over me, Vin. You wouldn't let down a king brother, I know that now. Especially not the Forgiver King."

This prompts him to choke up, and he rubs the palms of his hands into his eye sockets. After a moment, he chuckles and wipes his face again.

"I love the king name. You don't even know the half of it, why it's so perfect. But it hurts a bit, actually. Good hurt. None of my friends are going to believe this. What happened to me? I feel—"

Perry looks around in every direction, perhaps waiting for me to emerge, but I don't think so. I suspect he's drinking in the rocks, the sky, the ocean reflecting faraway moonlight. He zips the sleeping bag back together, restoring its original purpose. He checks on Mr. Quackers. He drinks more bottled water and sits on the bag.

"I sure hope that somehow I wake up right before dawn because honestly, I totally want to see the sunrise, *dude*. But I'm worried about oversleeping because I'm really, really tired right now."

He pauses and looks around the hills, waiting for a reply. He cups his hands to his mouth. *"Yes, I sure hope something wakes me up for this king dawn. If I'm presumptuous right now, forgive me. See? I'm already workin' the word, you damn bear."*

Perry strips off his pants. Right when they're at his ankles, he stands up straight and looks around again. He grins and kicks them off. He unbuttons his shirt and slides the hunter green over his left shoulder, slowly rotating and caressing the bare skin, gyrating his ass in every direction. Gyrating? Is that the right word?

Who cares—it's sexy as fuck.

He pulls up the heavy undershirt over his pecs, his flat stomach exposed. He rubs his hands up and down his solid chest in lazy circles, as if showering for me. He peels the sexy blue briefs down an inch or two, so the top of his pubic thatch is visible, and he stops, hooking his thumbs over the waistband and pulling them a sconch lower so I see the base of his fat dick right at the top. Of course, he has to turn in each direction as he pretends to shower, unsure of my exact location.

My cock is getting hard.

He yells, *"Sure would be fun to have sex right now."*

He knows I can hear him at normal volume, but this louder tone is more hilarious.

"I'm so horny I will have sex with anyone who can hear my voice. Anyone? I'm right here."

He slips the underwear lower, and his fat dick bobs out. It's not a porn star cock, but it's his and I love him, so the sight of it makes blood rush to my face. He's such a great kisser, and I loved sucking him off in Alcatraz. My Alcatraz King!

He stops.

"But Vin, seriously, whatever you want. This is your show. However you want this to go down is cool with me."

He nods, apparently satisfied. He lifts up the shirttail on his final slow circle, dancing to a slow groove only he hears. The two globes of his gym butt jiggle as he sways from side to side. Damn. That ass. He is definitely fucking with me, knowing I'm not coming for him tonight.

He says, "I do believe I'll have that last piece of bruschetta now."

While snickering over his great joke and my apparent inability to do anything about it, he moves to the plastic baggie, looks around, and pretends to inhale big smells coming from inside. He attempts to pull out the last piece and jerks his hand away, shaking it off.

"It's still hot," he says. "Wow, can you believe that? Almost burned my hand."

Fucker.

He chomps a big bite for my benefit, resuming his sexy, slow dance in all directions, licking his fingers and shaking his ass. With his free hand, he pulls off the remaining shirt.

"So delicious, but I don't know if I can finish it. I may throw the rest in the dirt."

I can't believe he's taunting me with food. And sex. Boy, the next few hours will make me crazy, my cock hard and waiting for him to wake up. God, I love him.

Perry immediately forgets his threat and finishes the bruschetta with deliciousness-inspired groans. After making a big show of sucking each fingertip, Perry crawls into the sleeping bag, fussing the blanket into his pillow and wrapping part of it around his exposed arm. During tonight's mountaintop drama, I bet we both forgot how fucking cold the wind is at this height. Of course, I've got my ski mask and black gloves, so I'm okay.

After only a moment, he struggles out again, standing naked in a small patch of dirt and calling to the woods with his hands by his mouth.

"Also, I'm interested to know who you hired to follow us here and drive away our van. That's pretty damn sick. I was waiting for the next big trick, but you still nailed me."

Satisfied with this salutation goodnight, he returns to the sleeping bag, snuggling himself deeper.

After a few minutes he calls out, "Oh man, my cock is so hard right now."

I guffaw into my hands, muffling any sound.

"Is there a Back Massage King?" he yells without leaving the sleeping bag. "Please tell me he's among the Found Kings because *I broke my fucking lungs* crying so hard a while ago."

Perry knows I'm laughing behind a rock.

"Back Rub King? You out there, buddy?"

He's quiet for about two minutes.

"I know you're wearing a ski mask."

He makes a few more of these quips, but they get quieter, and more time lapses in between. Perry dozes and then sits up. He rubs his eye and says in a loud tenor, "I love you, Vin Vanbly."

Perry lowers himself, and he does not move. I believe he's asleep almost immediately.

Li'l Shirley, the wriggling ocean, and a baby duck are the sole witnesses to our nightlife. Perry has left us, perhaps already in a reunion long overdue, near the river Styx, where sad memories melt into something greater, a richer river of love.

Nineteen

NOW that Perry is found, I feel my entire body relax. I love this night, the early morning hours. Everyone gathers, all the kings from every land, in eager anticipation to welcome back the newest brother. This inky night feels rich with royal secrets and wispy love, preparations for the feast of homecoming. I feel honored to be able to escort a king through the eastern gates, back to the Found Ones.

Perry made it through so many slippery spots along the weekend when he might have said, "No more." But he never quit, even when he quit, because his heart simultaneously urged a deeper message, subtler and more desperate, tired of its strange captivity. I think he stayed because the biggest forgiveness needed wasn't for his father. I don't think Perry had forgiven himself for feeling so devastated, for letting one man's departure hurt so damn much.

Okay.

Okay, kings, you win.

I'll give Billy a few minutes' consideration.

I'm sorry. I'm trying to be open here.

You tired of—

Quit running that line. Let it go, let it go.

Billy had a hard life, I'm sure. I can picture the weary wrinkles down his face, like faded rings on a long-dead tree trunk. His uneven crop of angular whiskers, his dirty gray hair. I can still remember his gray eyes that wouldn't ever look at you directly, blue-gray really, just like mine. I know how this goes: someone abused him, so he's an innocent victim turned into the bad guy himself, trapped by destiny, so he and his poker buddies rape kids. Maybe his poker buddies were the rapists and his job was to supply the kids. Maybe he only did it for money or something.

The accidental rapist.

No. He *raped*; they *raped*! That verb doesn't get any softening adjectives. Fuck that.

Wait, I can do this, I can forgive.

Forgiveness? *I was chewed on by rats.* That's, like, God-hates-you biblical punishment. Except it happened every third Wednesday and nobody cared. Billy was sheepish Thursday and Friday, so maybe he felt bad. Maybe it was okay—

OK. OK.

Uh oh. Not OK, not okay to think of him. I knew this would happen if I thought about Billy, I knew it would definitely not be OK. Took me long enough to drive his name out of my head. But I have to believe he's probably okay, okay out there somewhere, Other Kid.

I told him it was okay, that you get used to them biting you, not that you enjoy it, but I had a theory that the poker men wouldn't like it, that maybe fucking a twelve-year-old covered in bloody rat bites might not feel victorious. I had just learned that word.

I wanted to win, to be victorious.

OK, OK, OK.

I didn't know Other Kid wouldn't be able to handle the rats.

I tried to tell him Billy and the poker men were waiting, just waiting up there. Billy knew all the good hiding places in the house and yard, and her next door house too. The one place he would not venture was the basement; he hated the rats. *Other Kids.* I tried to tell him that there were Other Kids; though I covered my ears, I heard them screaming. I argued, I pulled on his arm and tried to keep him down with me, but he fought and pushed me down the remaining stairs. Other Kid couldn't handle the rats.

It's my fault he got raped.

And that is why, Billy, despite doomed destiny's pushing you to arrange group rape on poker night, I will not forgive you, you sick, motherfucking asshole. I was *twelve* when you made me an accomplice to gang rape.

Enough.

My hands are shaking, and I don't need to see rats to feel their vibration, to relive those prying teeth against my skull. My fingers seek out my bite scars to feel if this was real, did this really happen to me? Did I really lie there on that basement floor and let them chew on me? My middle fingers touch the soft crinkled flesh, my own Keith Haring imprint from the 1980s. I yank my hand away.

It's disgusting.

I am disgusted touching myself. What kind of freak lies there and lets rats bite him?

Breathe, Vin. *Breathe.*

I can't forgive you, Billy. Other Kid won't let me.

And so, I remain a Lost King.

The Forgiver King sleeps forty feet away, golden sparks of power radiating from him, zipping around his body even while unconscious. I can see it. All the love we have shared this weekend and yet, I still cannot forgive. How messed up is that?

I can walk a king through the eastern gates. We can have a big party, and we love each other with all our love for the whole weekend. But I never get to stay. I couldn't possibly date Perry or make a life with him; I'm too fucked up. He will always be a better person than me.

My Lost King name is the Human Ghost.

Quit it, Vin. This isn't helping.

It doesn't help to get all worked up. *Breathe.* It's not that bad being a lost king. I got to rescue starfish today, and I finally realized a dream of mine, to take the right man to Alcatraz. Plus, that ocean blow job was hot. I am a lucky man: I got to love Perry Mangin this weekend. My heart is full of him. I will love every minute with him tomorrow, trying not to focus on how sad I will feel after we part, miserable that I am not good enough to be his true love.

I won't forgive Billy, not yet. Maybe not ever. I don't know. I'll keep trying every now and then, I guess. I suppose it helps to get this stuff stirred up, because I wept for a while tonight. I've never been one to enjoy a dark night of the soul, where a man is destroyed and replaced by another man, better or worse than the one who fell to his knees. But who does love it, necessary as it may be?

Get out of this funk.

Look at Perry.

I stare at the strong, graceful man sleeping not far away.

Think of Perry.

Perry won't ever say, "That night on the mountain was one of the best nights of my life." He may love this night eventually. Hell, as early as tomorrow he may love this night. But he'll never claim it as one of his best nights. Too raw.

I learned a beautiful new king story, several in fact, woven into the fabric of The Lost and Founds. I got to visit King Aabee, whom I love. And hey, maybe I'm a better man now than the one who wept earlier. Maybe I'm a better man for loving Perry. It's not over for me: even a lost king can find faith in Bolinas. He is the Forgiver King, after all.

But I think downtime is over.

Stretch out your arms, you moron, your legs too, and limber up. Get back focused on the man slumbering within view.

Thank you, kings, for letting me visit your side this weekend, to inhale the azure sky, to stand amazed in the green grass and see how much love is around me. I'll try to let a little more in. I'm not coming home, I guess, not today. I don't mean to complain. Today will be a pretty good day. Later, there's going to be french toast and cherry crepes.

Okay, fine. I *was* complaining. I'm tired of being the Human Ghost. I want someone to see me.

But enough bitching; this pity party is over.

Before I set up for sunrise, I'll go check out the other side of the perimeter for traces of nightlife, but I'm sure I will find nothing. That piss was potent. I wonder if those two guys I introduced on Wednesday hooked up.

I advance toward him in silence, boulder crawling until I am a few feet above him. Not too close, of course, but I lean forward so I might see his expression.

His face is relaxed, yet retains a certain intensity, intention perhaps, as if he's looking down a long hallway but his eyelids happen to be closed. Those sharp planes of his handsome face are so crisp I want to run my finger over his jawline. It's not hard to imagine the Forgiver King inhabiting his fortress, the veiny stones glowing brighter as the master draws near. He strolls through wide castle hallways, his hand occasionally stroking the walls and blessing those who gasp in surprise.

I place an alarm clock six feet away and begin my perimeter tour.

The scene is set.

Less than two hours from now, the sun rises.

In the meantime, the Forgiver King wanders his ocean-blue castle, helping lost tourists, listening to their woes.

TWENTY

GOLDEN GATE, Golden Gate, it's an early morning date.

I remember my Golden Gate years, obsessing over the bridge's letters and relation to the structure's actual shape, its grace and gusto, guilded gyrations, and all the explorations into the letter *g* that even I can muster. And boy, can I spend a lot of time with that sultry, squiggly little bitch. Oh yeah, *g*, you're the middle of an orgasm, gushing and goofy. You're giggly and girly, but you're gentlemanly too, a fedora-wearing letter when need be. With your guttural ja-ja, you're gentle and genuine, unassuming soft touch. Legs uncrossed and recrossed right before us, so we get those sexy goose bumps. Show me those curves, *g*.

Okay.

I am punchy. I'm punchy now.

This, Vin, is why we value sleep in the land of the sane. Sleep revs down the crazy that might knock someone over if they saw me full strength. Snap out of it. But I can't help it. I love Sunday morning when I no longer have to be a dick. He's a delicate pear, graceful planes, soft but strong and surprisingly juicy. I loved a pear. Plus, I'll sleep like the dead for the next few weeks, my reward for service to the realm. There's that to look forward to.

When the alarm clock shrieks its horrible clang, Perry wakes yelling, *"Damn it, Vin."*

The sound is distorted almost instantly as Perry knocks it across a rocky surface.

I hear him scrambling to the alarm clock, one of those cheap gold ones that creates a deafening jangle of unpleasant screeching, and is therefore, by definition, the most wildly fucked-up way to awaken. The new Castro Walgreens: $7.99. Seriously, who buys those?

Thankfully, he finally hits the right button, and the metal hammering ceases.

Wow, that really echoes.

Light streaks through the sky making last minute preparations for The Big Entrance. It's possible to believe the house lights are coming down, gradually descending, except for the small shifts incrementally dragging in the new day.

I imagine he crawls back to the sleeping bag and then checks on the duck. I would. On top of the duck's cage, he will find a purple-wrapped package with a purple ribbon and bow, addressed to King Perry the Forgiver. Inside, his king shirt. I figured he'd make the connection last night; I worked it awfully hard. I just like to cross the *t*'s. It's the least you can do for a friendly ol' *t*.

Ah, I hear paper shredding.

He laughs a short laugh, a '*g*' laugh, a guffaw. Guffaw! Guffaw!

I bet the gold spangles are sparkling off his face. Gold, gold, gold, goldgold. Goldgold. Quit it with the *g* thing, Vin. Keep it together.

Gold spangles are perfect if you do drag or crave glittery attention. Perry may not fit either category, but somehow this shirt suits him, the dazzling gold lamé called out his name. Always lots of king shirt options in the City of Fog. The real challenge was not including a matching feather boa. He's gay; he'll accessorize on his own.

I do not know what he does the next few minutes, waiting for dawn. It's quiet over in Perry's camp. I tried to time the alarm with the expected sunrise, but it's tough because the Farmer's Almanac doesn't give you the time estimate for mountaintops. But he won't have to wait more than ten minutes.

After a few peeks around my latest hiding spot, I spy our sun, as expected, peeking back, a slim curve over the horizon, already a buttery yellow, but tragedy has struck, as vandals have doused him in gasoline and thrown down a match.

It pokes up higher.

My brain can't even comprehend its size, but with the actual horizon so many hundreds of miles away and our favorite star blasting yellow flames over the earth's curve, I can only—wow.

Wow.

The scorched butter color becomes a body sensation, but unfortunately the sensation isn't warmth. Daylight means a certain unclenching of my muscles as a new vulnerability ripples over my skin, reminding me the night was hard, but it's over. I am spent and chilly, shaking, exhausted, and yet free to roam the world again. The captain has turned off the seatbelt sign.

The orange disc rises another inch. Ah, orange now in addition to scorched yellow. I peek my head up, curious to see how yellow becomes gold, gold becomes orange, and watch hazy red streaks of light, like reluctant lighting dragged behind this thing, this star out in space.

Star, star, star, star—

I forgot to play Star Game last night, I was so happy watching Perry, thinking about him. Well, that and thinking about Billy. I gave it a shot, kings. I really did try.

I guess that Perry also digs this morning, perhaps seeing something out of the ordinary, because while the sun blesses the faraway hills, I hear someone nearby, could be anyone, I suppose, yell, "*I am King Perry The Forgiver.*"

I feel wonderfully bleary right now, sleepy and happy.

Last night, misery. Today, french toast.

The sun is not quite a quarter over the horizon.

He says, "I love you, Dad."

I imagine that all the kings who scream and cheer during a dawn celebration get quiet as a father reunites with his son.

He yells other affirmations that mean nothing to me, but obviously something for him. I don't know everything about this guy; we just met Tuesday. A lifetime shaped him, sculpted him, some of those events are stodgy recliners scattered around his heart. Right now, at dawn, it sounds like he rearranges the furniture instead of tripping over it. He's making room.

I shouldn't have axed that part about the dragging your beat-up furniture to the curb and having it carted away to Castle Forgiveness. I liked that. But I worried about laying it on too thick, prompting Perry to ask direct questions. Malcolm likes to remind me that subtlety is not my forte.

Tomorrow, when I call him to tell him I found another king, I bet the first thing he says is, "What did you make him steal?" My brother knows me too well.

I try to muscle around some of those couches every now and then; I've left a few resentments out on the curb. Who knows, maybe I moved something a foot or two last night.

Enough randomness; focus up, man. It's showtime.

Suddenly, another alarm clock jangles the morning air. It's the same irritating sound as his Walgreens clock. What are the odds?

Perry barks out a short laugh.

I turn off the alarm. *"Grab the duck. Take off the cover and pick up the cage."*

He says, "Okay. Gimme a sec."

A moment later, I hear him say, *"Ready."*

I gotta do this quick.

I peer over my back support and turn on the alarm before tossing it down to the rocky earth, careful not to disturb any other props. I probably damaged the clock face, but for $7.99, who cares? Plus, fourteen other gold alarm clocks tick away patiently inside the circle of rocks Perry is about to discover.

I drop my head as I hear him draw closer because I cannot risk him seeing me at this critical juncture; I may not have the luxury of watching Perry the moment he finds this rock corral. On the other hand, I'm fairly sure the slender crack I peer through will keep me hidden.

I'll risk it. I peer through the crack and watch.

Perry steps over a smaller rock on the opposite side of this misshapen circle. The first time I saw this formation, I remember thinking, *My, what great teeth you have, grandmother.* This space of barren earth is not wide, only eight feet across.

He's half-naked and scruffy; the dark circles under his eye are purple and softer. Hair is all fucked up. But those details do not describe his true appearance. His eyes glow oceanic blue, the power of the Forgiveness Castle right there. The shimmery gold shirt throws sexy sparkles to his brown face, adding little magic twitches to his fat, griefy smile. His face welcomes joy, which always renders the plainest of us radiant.

He frown-smiles, his smile frowns, some combination of both, glancing around the collection of knickknacks I assembled, and then I see him melt into sad understanding, his gaze zigzagging, reading everything again: a half dozen pumpkins near golden alarm clocks, their shining curves gleaming in the newly-awakened sun. Two tree branches stuck in the earth boast long crimson ribbons rippling the sky at various heights every time the wind blows, which is pretty constant up here. White angel wings from a costume shop crouch against a nearby rock, interspersed with silver plumber's rods, looking much like prison bars.

On the right side, a polished, shiny cello reclines, as if the instrument recently awoke and needs this rock to steady its morning movements. The support rock is suitable for sitting, in this barren outcropping. Call it a throne.

And he's holding a duck.

I hope he remembers my first comment to him was about the V of ducks in his father's painting. I'm truly a lucky duck that they were ducks because I had no fucking clue how to get a goose up here. I struggled enough planning a faux ducknapping. I love the silent x, my co-conspirator in so many faux crimes.

Faux, faux. *Faux, faux.* I really should learn French.

Perry sets down the duck's cage.

He speaks quietly to Mr. Quackers, who crabs unhappily about the early morning antics. He's right to complain; that braying alarm clock is horrible. Perry moves to the clock and silences it. The echo hurts my ears. I only see parts of him, but I can tell he's walking to the pumpkins. I'm so glad he told me the pumpkin-carving story. That was fun, to carve out triangle eyes. My knife sits near the pumpkins.

"I am the Golden Curve," he says with sadness.

That's my cue to retreat. I turn away and sit on the earth, my back to the rock. This is not about him and me; it's about him. His dad too, but mostly him.

Looking through his back windows, I never saw a cello case inside his apartment. Of course, I could only see in the living room and kitchen.

I hear strings tickled and tightened; he found the tuner and rosin.

I don't know much about the cello, just what I researched while Perry worked and I had the day for errands. I'm no music expert, but I did buy some good stuff from Tower Records. Safe to say, I'm not qualified to interview people for orchestra, but I'm ready to recognize something awful.

Note to self: I have to remember to go to Coit Tower and get my boom box and supplies out of the underground stairwell. We didn't need that location after all. No, wait. I'm sure I put it on my post-weekend checklist. Dammit, I need that electronic gadget I was thinking about last night, with the cute little mouse.

More light creeps into our day. Half over the horizon now? Not quite. The world is still not awake, and I can't look for a while yet.

"Here it is, Dad."

The first note stretches out, long arms unfurling and morphing into gorgeous ebony, the molasses texture you might find on a darker-skinned black man as you rub your goatee along his smooth thigh. That sensation.

My eyes open wider. Any sluggishness disappears.

Clearly, I was wrong.

This sound flourishes too rich for an amateur, too strong and loving, long bow strokes that end in silvery fingers. A few clunker notes appear every now and then, not wrong notes exactly, but I'm guessing forgotten knowledge races back to his fingers. These notes are steep turns, like the physical roads that brought us here. I decide this is a redwood song, regal and yet gentle, approachable. I recall yesterday's ascent, the heart-lurching vistas as we inched higher and higher toward the east peak, the fresh smell of ancient decay, the soft-patterned leaves dragging their shade across our sunny faces as Mr. Quackers wobbled around in back, chatty and glad for a break from us.

Perry's nimble notes flow over the hillside, running together, long purple streaks, intertwining loosely. Sound flows much further than it should because we're so high. His stage drowns these spectacular colors, beautiful black and silver notes slipping through the boulder cracks, energetic earthworms squirming in delight. Certain notes leap higher than others, sprout wings, and race each other to the bottom of Mt. Tam, where they must burst unheard, uncelebrated. The rocks sway, as sometimes they do when no one is looking.

Well, not unheard; we're not alone. Soon, they will gather to meet him.

The sky is lighter, gold asserting its right to stay.

Perry's notes climb higher, chasing the sun. I swear he pours out all his love because at last he found a way to communicate with his father, a way for them to chat about life and its sorrows, and what makes a man.

All hail The Forgiver King.

This weekend won't cure his life. Anyone who reaches the age of thirty-four acquires a few chinks in the armor; he will carry those all his days. But his kingship will bless those struggles, and the ones yet to come, because he wept alone on a mountaintop, used up all of his love, only to find it replenished from a source he did not expect. He will have his father's help now in facing life's problems, a necessity he mistook for a forgotten luxury.

Suddenly, it's my turn to know a thing that is somehow true: the world is forgiven for taking Perry's father.

The siren song lives.

In Greek mythology, the siren song heralds doom, and I get it; I do. "You will go mad," we Lost Kings warn each other. "Cover your ears. It will kill you to live with all your love." Despite that dire interpretation, the Found Ones know the true purpose of a siren song, and sing it, thank God. Or Goddess. I guess I'm not sure on that point, either.

Perry's song zings down the neighboring hillsides in all directions, greater confidence tumbling further into the valleys. The music streaks naked, strong and solid, masculine in its tenor, and I'm guessing years of investment banker decisions pay off, because his brain must calculate the best returns on split-seconds decisions.

When the heart serves the brain during a musical performance of this caliber, the technical proficiency is impressive. But when the brain serves the heart, surrenders its dominance, the technical proficiency isn't impressive at all; it's breathtaking, forcing you to turn your head.

Which I do.

His whole body moves in concert, arms jerking in seemingly random directions, yet they snap back to center with synchronicity, sometimes in slow motion, sometimes swiftly, and the gold sparkles ripple across him, blinding me temporarily, almost like staring at sunlight on the ocean.

He yells forgiveness and love to several people without breaking the tune, and I smile because he has friends and he is loved. But when I hear the words, "I forgive you, Cecilia," the words are thick with hurt. The cello chokes out low, painful notes, and even stutters at one point, as grief overtakes him. Whoever she is, Cecilia is a couch in his heart.

But then he's back into the song, slow skating in thick, luscious curves, making more room. Solid oak notes tether earth to sky with stunning richness everywhere, ocean and heaven fall victim to the sun's dazzling array of diamond-tipped beams.

Lowering myself back against the rock, I let myself collapse.

I put my head in my arms and cry for Zhong and Jian, for the hardships they face at home, for children whose parents will die this year. I cry for men I have met who were damaged by life, and those who were damaged by me when I was who I used to be.

I cry because of the way the world breathes sometimes, a strong man playing his love on a mountaintop, a song of joy and grief. Perry won't forget his grief, and why would he? The Castle Forgiveness is looking to expand, and grief makes such beautiful blue stone.

Now that the Forgiver King is enthroned, perhaps I will feel less intimidated wandering those cavernous blue hallways. Maybe I will find my own secret entrance while pressing against the polished rock. And perhaps one day I can be forgiven, because Perry's cello sounds like seals spelunking in the ocean, the slippery sounds swimming once more into absolute joy.

The Forgiver King's music will call us home.

Find us, King Perry.

We need you.

TWENTY-ONE

AFTER three resplendent melodies, definitely resplendent, Perry stops. The sun is officially up, not high in the sky but balancing precariously above the destroyed horizon, the hour at which sun worshippers pop out of bed with a satisfaction I do not understand. Generally, I prefer the beauty of 10:00 or 10:30 a.m. But hey, King Weekend.

It's still dark over there. Freaky, to see daylight right here and yet night still chasing its tail over the faraway foothills.

I peer through the crack to see him stand, facing California in the new light. His initial audience numbers in the tens of thousands, even if they didn't quite pay full ticket prices, nestled comfortably in their overpriced homes. He plays for the growing trees, bewildered campers, and the early risers. Those still sleeping in Sausalito and Mill Valley remain unaware of why their dreams just grew softer.

He definitely earned one adoring fan in Mr. Quackers; exuberant quacking chased the cello's music. If you were forty miles away and listening to this ethereal concert seeming to rise from the earth itself, you might ask, "Is it my imagination, or is that music powered by a duck?"

I spy on Perry as he struts around the rock pile, taking deep bows before his invisible fans. His arms stretch skyward in a giant *V*, the bow in his right hand seeming to show the sun which direction it should travel.

I poke my head up high above my hiding rock. He sees me and grins.

The duck quacks.

I wipe my eyes dry. Truly an amazing concert.

"Hey, what's up?"

"Hey, not much," Perry says, laughing. "I'm on a mountaintop at dawn and I just finished a cello recital."

"You play the cello?"

Wow. He's shining.

"Almost majored in it, in college."

"That's cool. What changed your mind?"

Perry's face studies mine. "I decided I hated it."

I nod. I bet he killed his love for the cello the same way cancer killed his father: slowly.

"That and I got tired of being poor."

"Sure. Gotta eat."

"Aaaaand now, I'm wearing a king shirt that showed up mysteriously during the night, gift-wrapped in a purple box."

"No kidding."

"Yeah, I found it a while ago."

"Huh."

"Vin, check this out: I'm part of a green desert with pumpkins and alarm clocks and wings. Something my Dad painted."

"How about that?"

In a growling voice he says, *"How about you quit fucking around and come down here?"*

"Sure. If it's okay to come into your painting."

He smiles, but I can see him studying me. "I grant you safe passage."

From my tear-stained face, perhaps his heart gossips a little truth right into his brain. My tears make us equal somehow; I did not expose his deep grief while I took notes on a clipboard. Like recognizes like, which means we have something really shitty in common. And it's true: I would have loved to have had a dad. I would have liked that very much.

I unsnap my jeans, kick off my shoes, and navigate to a smaller rock for me to climb over, stripping completely naked by the time I step into *Siren Song*.

He puts his arms straight out and says, "King Perry the Forgiver welcomes you."

I bow. "Your majesty."

"Oh, please. We don't have to talk that way, do we?"

As he closes the five feet separating us, his big grin disappears. I reach for his hand, and he offers it, tears already streaming down his face. It's too bad he can't see me while I kiss the underside of his thumb, but his eyes clamp shut and his face shakes. He leans in and cries against my chest.

I hold him, rocking him.

He says, "I don't know why I'm crying anymore. I'm all broken. I swear I can't stop."

"Is it awful?"

"No." He pulls away and wipes his face. "Unsettling, though. I feel drunk."

"This may overwhelm you at first," I say and kiss his neck, "but you'll grow into it. You have to let king energy pour out of you, like yesterday on the bridge, or when we played in the ocean. I'll give you a full debriefing on the way back to San Francisco. Short version, though, is that you should plan to get a few massages this week, drink lots of water. Take it easy. I set up a four o'clock appointment with my massage guy out here. It's paid for, but you don't have to show up. Totally optional. But he's really good."

"Okay," he says.

Perry sniffs heavily, and his head rests on my shoulder. We rock more, growing calm together.

His hand reaches between my legs and cups my balls.

Wow, that's nice. Warm.

It's a nippy morning to cuddle naked on a mountaintop, but one must define cold differently in California than other parts of the world. East coast cold is unbearable. Midwest cold is worse but bearable somehow. Here in Northern California, you bitch about the cold because the weather so often approaches perfect, the chilliness is like a fly in the soup. Plus, cold means shrinkage.

He says, "I could channel it into other parts of life, huh? Like sex?"

"That's a distinct possibly."

I pull his head back and kiss his Adam's apple, a wet, lingering kiss.

He moans, and his cock starts to harden against me.

"By the way, what happened to you last night?" Perry says, pulling back.

I smile and say, "I notice you've still got your hand around my nuts. Symbolically, pretty hilarious."

Perry twists his mouth. "Last night, I could *swear* you said you were coming back. I could also *swear* I heard our van take off. You should have been here, Vin, because before I fell asleep, I was offering my body to just *anybody*."

"Damn," I say, grinding our cocks against one another. "Sounds like I missed out."

He says, "I assume you had to run an errand for a king."

"Well actually," I say with dramatic hesitation while stroking his cock, "it's your fault."

Perry says, "Of course."

"You don't seem surprised."

He says, "I should have assumed I pissed you off because you were the *ideal* weekend boyfriend, Vin."

"Oh no, you didn't piss me off. But right at sunset, we talked about onion rings with cheese and sliced jalapenos. So when I got to the parking lot, I started thinking: here I am, standing next to a van, and I know a place with good onion rings. I figured you would *want* me to get some. I mean, last night before you fell asleep, you said that you *loved* me. So, if you *loved* me, you'd want me to get onion rings with melted cheese, right?"

He laughs. "You heard that, huh?"

We kiss more fiercely because we're damn happy to see each other again.

"I think *jalapeno* sounds like a bunch of letters piling into a beat-up old word to go get tacos."

Perry leans in and says, "Only to you."

Fuck, does it feel good to kiss a Found King. Whoever dates him next is in for a surprise.

We break and breathe heavily against each other for a moment or two.

I nudge my knee between his legs and say, "Ready for cello sex?"

"Absolutely. Let's do it."

But our resolution takes a backseat to more kissing, more of my massaging his neck.

"You gonna come this time?" he asks during our next break. "I don't think you've shot your load all weekend."

I nod at my hard-pointing cock, a thick strand of precum drooling toward the earth below. "I believe I've blue-balled it long enough."

"Agreed."

He eyes my dick eagerly and strokes it a few times in appreciation. "You've got a great dick, Vin."

"Why, thank you," I say, dipping my head in deference and nodding toward the cello. "Why don't you grab that and turn around."

He says, "May I assume there are condoms and lube under a rock somewhere near here?"

"You may. That one."

He bends over to the nearby rock I pointed out. I can't believe I didn't get to eat his ass all weekend. It's so damn perfect.

"How many rocks in the United States have your condoms and lube under them?"

"Not many. I try to pick up after myself."

"So how many?"

"Just the U.S., right?"

"Sure."

"Under ten."

"*Ten?*"

"I like to travel."

He hands me the same condom brand from last night and kisses me while I struggle to rip it open.

"We're really going to do this while I play the cello, huh?" Perry says, turning to wiggle his succulent ass. I love that he's playing with me.

"We don't have to."

"No, I'm game. I had a boyfriend in college once who wanted to try it but we broke up before we got around to it. Trombone majors are the kinkiest fuckers," he says in a playful tone.

"Turn around. If this goes well, I predict a new kink in your sex life."

We kiss for a few minutes, front to back, while I stroke his slight treasure trail dipping down the underside of his stomach, and he leans back into me. My cock rubs his butt, the crack, and I feel no resistance in him now, not a jot. Our bodies sway slightly in this protected little enclave of rocks, so we're not feeling the wind, merely the briskness of morning cold air. Each breath still tastes like crunchy autumn apples.

We discuss the cello sex and decide immediately that the only way this will work is with him sitting, cello between his legs and his ass hanging over his throne, giving me access.

"You lean forward, there. That's it."

He leans back, despite my instructions and we kiss, his head on my shoulder. The kiss feels odd, a goodbye kiss perhaps, acknowledging that today brings the last chapter of our weekend together.

He doesn't have to suck me this morning for me to get hard; my condom-covered dick won't stay soft in his presence.

I love him.

When we break from our latest and possibly best kiss, I ask in a puzzled voice, "Now, where did I leave off with King Aabee?"

He says, "His death, you dickwad. I can't believe you killed him."

"I didn't kill him," I say, bending him forward and leaning over him to rub my goatee on his shoulder. I encourage my cock to slip back and forth along his ass crack, teasing him, seeing how much further I can relax him. "The Lost Kings killed him."

Perry moans.

He pulls the bow across the cello strings, and what crawls out is low and ominous, a wet screech dragging along the earth. He continues a few other low strokes, thunder and despair, sometimes matching my rocking motions, sometimes striking out on their own, a morbid roll call of the lost as we search for a position that will work. Our practice strokes require fine tuning as I figure out how to angle myself so that I can fuck him without knocking over the cello. He continues to play during our warm-up activities, including my caressing more lube right over, ah, there. Sometimes he switches to a high pitch, brittle and steely strings, another flavor of lost.

This music intoxicates both of us, and I drag my teeth over his neck while he strokes out the Lost Kings melody. I believe he invents this heartbreaking tune spontaneously. King energy inspires new life into existence.

I clear my throat and try speaking at a few different levels, a sound check so he hears me and we can both hear this music. Soon we discover that with my mouth right inside his ear, he can play louder than expected.

My cock is slick in his ass crack, and we are also old friends; he remembers me from Friday. As I wedge my dick inside, the music pauses only briefly and then flares into something rich and juicy.

Oh God, he's so warm.

"A month after King Aabee's death, a Russian king named Ivan lost his mother to the ravages of age. She died in peace, he at her bedside holding her hand. Ivan missed her terribly, because she loved his flaws before he could bear the weight of them."

Perry slides the melody into something graceful and feminine, long and swooping, a sound that swivels through the instrument.

I push inside him with slow strokes and my balls confirm that this isn't going to be a power fuck. Nope. The climax of this tune is long overdue. The heat of his butt around my dick is so beautiful, so perfect, I feel like it's another flavor of him saying, "I love you." I hear chords of growing intensity vibrate within each note, an extra urgency. Perry may not last long either.

"This Russian king begged her to come back and let him know that she found his infant sister, two other brothers, his father, and several others important to their family. His misery gripped him hard because he missed them all so eagerly, and he especially wanted to know his mother still smiled upon him."

A smoky Russian flavor emerges as well, a thick maple sound, which musically, impresses the hell out of me.

"Then one day, Ivan was whistling and eating an apple when—"

I bark out a laugh because honest to God, it does sound like an apple.

"—when he was approached by King Charles the Diamond, a friend who worried about his mourning."

Perry skips into a Renaissance-y kind of thing, which is oddly perfect.

"Charles said, 'You look—' Actually, wait... wait. Perry, scratch that."

Perry continues playing some elongated notes, waiting for me in musical limbo.

"King Charles the Diamond rode up to the Russian king on his bicycle, quite vigorously. You remember, *The Vicar with Vigor*, my show for the BBC? You got any—?"

Perry strokes his cello as if he's jacking it; his fingers skate with commanding authority across the taut strings.

Fuck, yeah.

I fuck Perry harder, because Perry is vigorous, the music brags vigorously, and I feel powerful having sex with a vigorous man. Wow, those notes are strong. I punch his ass with the strength of my cock, pushing him upward, and he pushes down. *Fuck.*

We attempt kissing over his right shoulder, lips bouncing off one another while I try to distract his tune by tweaking his nipples. But he's a pro, and the cello continues slicing out thick, rich, gingerbread notes. I grab his balls with one hand and press my other forearm into his upper chest, push him back into my mouth. I don't understand why some think the top is "the man" during fucking, when most of the time, the bottom must demonstrate more strength, endures a greater physical challenge, and he bears it all for sheer, glorious pleasure. What could be more manly?

Finally, we break and we both huff a few appreciative laughs.

"Thank you, Perry, you scratched an itch I've had since Friday afternoon. Anyway, King Charles the Diamond said, 'Ivan, you look great today.'"

"Holy crap," Perry says. "How can you just... I can't... breathe."

It's true. He's huffing, and I'm ready to keep fucking the story forward.

"Practice, I guess. Anyway, King Ivan offered Charles a thick slice of apple and said, 'Yes. Thank you. I feel much better. I had a good talk with Mother last night.' 'Your mother?' said Charles. 'How exactly did that happen?'"

I must whisper this next line into Perry's ear. "Ivan explained, 'King Aabee arranged it.'"

The music skips into something brighter, confidence underlying the tenor of this new song. He trusts he's headed in the right direction. Perry pushes back to me and clenches his ass muscles, and I in turn thrust harder. I reach around to grab his cock and find it stiff and rubbing against the back of the polished wood.

I lean in and grip him tighter.

Perry moans in harmony with the cello.

"'Aabee?' asked King Charles with surprise. 'Are you sure?' Ivan was completely sure. After all, he heard Aabee's flute."

"Technically," Perry says, "it wasn't... exactly... a flute...."

This makes me laugh hard, and then Perry laughs, and while he laughs, the cello jerks and the strings bounce under his bow. My cock falls out, but it's okay, because I hold a man I love, and he holds me and a cello, which he also loves.

Oh good lord, I'm in a three-way with a cello. Well, we're fucking inside a surrealist scene painted roughly twenty-five years ago, so it's probably de rigueur.

Do not start with *de rigueur*.

I push my cock back inside, and we're instantly back in our rhythm. All three of us.

"King Aabee's visit was confirmed two weeks later, by an older king, one in his eighties who missed his autistic son, many years deceased. He missed the smell of his son, the way his son rocked back and forth on the balls of his feet, and those elusive half hours of perfect coherency, which used to nourish this old father for months at a time."

Perry's cello warbles out some silver notes, heavy with age and grief-won wisdom.

"The aged king showed up for work at the DMV with homemade blueberry tarts, giving them freely to all who came in to pay fines. The tarts celebrated an unexpected visit. 'King Aabee arranged it,' the old father told everyone, excitement in his voice. 'I got to see my son.'"

The music booms with grace, strong old notes, regal and Victorian.

"You must understand. The Found Kings had frequently wondered if they could somehow access the great love from the next life to help recover Lost Kings. Many times, they discussed the possibility amongst themselves, making plans with dying men who promised to send a sign once they crossed over. But no king could figure out how to return from Death's realm."

My grip around his cock shifts gears, tightens. I make sure to graze his fat cock head with my index finger, the delicate spot where the pink knob touches the shaft. He moans and pushes back; I fuck him deeper and faster. Keep it together and keep your voice even, Vin.

Getting close.

"Everyone came to understand, after more sightings and the reports of strange music whenever such a visitation occurred, that King Aabee had found a way."

Perry saws off a triumphant note.

"When that Russian mother pleaded with Death to let her see her son, Death said, 'None but I am qualified to serve as your guide. And I cannot leave.' King Aabee turned to Death and said, 'I guess I could go.'"

Perry barks out a laugh, but the bow does not falter as it slides across the strings. "You *asshole*. Tell it right."

"Boy, you're snippy without your morning caffeine. But you are correct, King Aabee actually said, 'I will go. Send me!' Death replied, 'You are not permitted.' But this made Aabee laugh. Death did not understand Aabee's distinctive style of volunteering."

The cello laughs. The music gets my cock harder, more engorged, more ready. The notes shimmer around us, and if I close my eyes, I might hang on longer. Luckily, I have years of experience telling stories while fucking my brains out. He's right; this is definitely a fetish. I suppose I'll have to confess that over breakfast.

"Death offered King Aabee a deal."

I change my voice, making it raspier. "'If you play your flute-like instrument for me, I will grant you passage.' King Aabee smiled and said, 'Death, I will play my songs for your entertainment whenever you wish, you only need ask. But I shall play when I return, because you must learn your place, my friend. You do not command kings, even as the gatekeeper to this special realm. I am King Aabee. I am needed and I will go.'"

Perry laughs.

"Back when he was alive, none of the Found Kings could stop Aabee. You laughed at the chess game, but King Detlof was a powerful man. King Aabee lived with all his love, and after he died, he kept it. Next, Aabee visited his three sons, and they stopped their mourning, loving each other once again as they had when their father was alive."

Perry's notes waver for that last part, and he cries out but channels this feeling into the music, rich and mournful. That counts as a hit: Perry has a sister named Cecilia. He has not mentioned her this weekend, but over pasta, he made a vague reference to another family member, plus it's all right there in the music: he misses her, he has always missed her.

"Of course, Aabee became the king you called when you wanted to visit a deceased loved one. You invited him and then waited for the strange music, be it crickets chirping, mint, Barry Manilow, or yes, sometimes the color chartreuse."

"Manilow?" he gasps. "Was that a request?"

I fuck him harder and harder, my fist works him faster. The music sings happier, lighter. A climax is not far off for any of us. I hurry the words to match our pace.

"Soon, more found passage from Death's realm and some required no guide. Loving kings and wise queens found ways to communicate with the living, according to their skills and gifts. They just needed someone to go first."

I swear Perry's doing a Copacabana riff, but the notes run slurry, squirting into each other in tiny little bursts.

Crescendo.

I loosen my grip on his cock, which throws off his balance, allowing me to punch his ass from behind in a slightly new angle. I graze his balls and find them pulled up tight, embracing the inevitable. I feel his sweat all over me, my sweat leaping to him, my voice fucking his ear with tight little strokes, invisible tensions we create in each other.

"The Found Kings gifted Aabee a second king name, because while he was, and always would be, the Strange Musician, he came swiftly when men wished... ugh... to speak to their deceased fathers, bec... because after all, he had three sons of... his own."

Perry's music squeals erratically because he can't keep this up, this pace, this deep fucking and long strokes with his arm.

"His new king name... had a certain poetry... about it. King Aabee... the... Father King. Which made sense, because the Somali word for father—"

Cumming.

"—is pronounced *Aaaaaabeeeeeeeeeeee.*"

Perry screams and I scream and the cello screams.

Of the three of us, the cello screams loudest, its elongated moan stretching far into the surrounding morning as it goes on, and on, and on. I keep pounding my cock into Perry's ass, yelling and shooting, all of me spurting into him and all of him welcoming me deeper. His arm jerks heavily, but the cello barely reflects this, his brain compensates somehow, delighted to be invited to our concert. The brain's not such a bad guy. He just needs to step aside sometimes.

A series of shorter musical bursts tell me that Perry shot his juice as well. That and now I feel warm liquid dripping down my clenched fist, and glancing down, I see a bunch spilled against the back of the cello.

Breathe.

Gamba let me know that this wasn't the first time he'd rented a musical instrument for sexual role play. He emphasized "bring it back clean" but otherwise seemed cool with it. Good shop.

Breathe.

I sweat over Perry's back, my cock falls out of him, and he groans in relief. Holy fuck. All my concentration remains fixated on keeping us upright, holding him against me, as we feel each other's ragged breaths.

Through my hands on his pecs, I feel our heartbeats, drumming brothers.

He staggers away, sideways, and lays down the jizz-splattered cello.

He stands again and lurches at me drunkenly. Though neither of us has the air capacity, we lock in a mouth-sucking kiss as he shows me all his breathless love, wrapping himself around me.

We gasp as we pull apart. I really should lose some weight.

I say, "You... call him... anytime."

Perry tugs my hand to join him on the ground. The earth is cold, but there are little patches of tickly green under us, softening the hard rock and dirt. We lie in silence and soak up the morning. The voyeur sun now peeks over our private rock circle, and the wind also expresses its curiosity, racing over us, touching every exposed, naked plane. Mr. Quackers paces back and forth, silent as soon as the cello grew silent.

"Oh man," Perry says at last. "I love King Aabee."

Perry knows when it's time to get up; the song lives inside him now. After we stretch and peer at the blue sky in every direction, Perry announces his intention to play a song about kings. Still early at this point: maybe 6:45? 7:00? Hard to tell. Perry picks up the cello and sits once again, perhaps a little gingerly. I dance to keep warm, shake off the dirt stuck to my ass, and watch my flab bounce around. I decide that Mr. Quackers deserves a morning stroll.

He jumps out of my hands immediately, determined to free verse along with Perry's latest tune. He quacks louder as he ditches me, lurching erratically through the maze of shining alarm clocks, seeking freedom from this bigger cage of rock. Over and over, I lunge and miss him because every time Mr. Quackers escapes my clutches, his scuttling makes Perry laugh, and when he laughs, the notes soar.

I think I am in heaven.

TWENTY-TWO

"HI, NAKED guys."

The two female hikers seem comfortable with our nudity. Not really bothering to hide my cock, I nod toward them, holding our duck.

Perry stops and nods in their direction. "Hey there, early hikers."

"You guys the ones who laid out the big buffet on the picnic tables down there?"

Perry says, "I bet we are. Vin?"

I say, "I hope you tried the cherry crepes."

"Yes, thank you. Good lobster bake," says the dark-haired woman.

Her friend adds, "The cherry crepes were delicious."

This is one of those California moments, and these two women now have their own dose of surrealism to share with their friends: the mostly naked, mountaintop cello player and his even more naked, duck-holding friend. Everyone here grooves on those stories, where the line between locals and tourists blur, and for a moment we're all Californians because we share the same love.

"A man wearing a sparkly purple shirt served us breakfast. He said he made the crepes himself."

Perry laughs at me, eyes full of joyful demand.

Toward them, I say, "That's Liam, the Dolphin King."

The raven-haired woman says, "Yeah, he said. Very beautiful music by the way. Just so you know, more people are down there, about ten or twelve. Probably hiking up here soon."

"Thank you. We'll get dressed."

They wave and move away.

Perry didn't bother to notice his own nudity. Or he didn't care. Yup, Perry got kinged.

"He's real?" Perry says, leaning across the cello. "The Dolphin King is *real*?"

I feel my face blush red. "I like to vacation in San Francisco."

Perry announces his intention to play a jaunty little "Let's-Go-Have-Lobster-Bake" song, and I dance to the deep belly laugh from his cello. Mr. Quackers gets a last-dance reprieve while I dress and go retrieve Perry's campsite and my abandoned backpack.

By the time I return from my second trip, Perry has dressed himself in his jeans but not the warmer shirts. He remains in his short-sleeved king shirt, gold spangles shimmering. Or spangling, I guess.

The duck runs straight to Perry.

Before putting our friend in his cage, Perry holds him up to eye level and says softly, "King Quackers."

WITH my hands free, our descent is easier, handing the uncovered duck cage back and forth over difficult rock passages. Later, we'll make trips to gather all the props, but right now the goal is breakfast. Even King Quackers seems more relaxed this morning, as if he found his sea legs during our uneven mountain descent. Perry insists on carrying the cage whenever we're not sharing the load.

Twenty minutes later, as we cross the wooden planks at the beginning of the summit trail, Perry says, "I can't wait to meet this guy, Liam."

"He's gone by now."

Perry bumps me with his shoulder. "Damn. I wanted to compare notes."

"What is with you guys wanting to meet each other?" I say, growling. "Besides, our weekend isn't over until noon, *pardner*."

He pushes me again and says, "Pardner."

I must admit, I'm glad Liam left. I never dreamed all the men I kinged would seek each other out, choose to be in each other's lives. It's getting a little weird.

As we continue to stroll toward the picnic area, he grins at the gathering. Two crisp, white tablecloths anchor the feast. Sunlight gleams off silver-domed pans, their contents warmed by Sterno, boasting a banquet for three or four dozen diners. This works out well, because already I can see roughly a dozen people grazing off blue china plates, piled high with lobster bake, rosemary-hickory sausages, and goopy-frosted cinnamon rolls as big as my head. There should also be minty halibut filets, french toast, scrambled eggs, fresh fruit, three different juices, and two potato dishes, one tailored to my preference for cheesy potatoes, a lovely inside joke from the Dolphin King, a man whom I once loved with all my love. God, I miss Liam.

Oh, and cherry crepes.

And a huge birthday cake, Hawaiian themed, which reads HAPPY 10TH BIRTHDAY, PERRY MANGIN. Sometimes you get a second chance at a shitty birthday.

I love saying the word *cake*. Cake. Cake!

The diners turn to greet us, because the only thing odder than a full service buffet in the woods is a golden man carrying a caged duck down a mountain trail.

"King Liam is a chef. He gave me the pouch thing with the rocks."

Perry nods because it seems perfectly reasonable right now to share breakfast off white linen with Sunday morning strangers. They greet us with happy suspicion, wondering aloud if we are connected to the woodsy appearance of orange-flavored french toast.

Good lord, I am fucking hungry. Jesus.

A man says, "Are you the cellist?"

Perry nods. "Yes. I am."

As the small gathering parts to make room for us, murmuring appreciation for the musical interlude, Perry sees the cake and stops. He sets down the duck king and squeezes my hand.

"Happy belated *birth-day*," I sing into his ear.

While our fellow hikers express their appreciation for the food and the music, some are uncomfortable now, not sure what to make of Perry's steady tears while he accepts their gratitude.

"Heard it a while ago...."

"We were meditating on the roof of our RV...."

Perry wipes his face repeatedly, and keeps saying, "Thank you."

"Are you King Aabee?" says a gray-haired woman wearing a sturdy pack.

Perry's jaw drops, and I worry about his heart, so I point to a folded card on the table which announces, ENJOY THIS COMPLIMENTARY BREAKFAST. WE APOLOGIZE IF WE DISTURBED YOUR PEACE THIS MORNING WITH OUR SUNRISE CONCERT.—KING AABEE

"No, that's not me," Perry says, shaking her hand. "I know him, though."

I thought about writing "one-time-only concert," but honestly, who knows? Perry may play here again next weekend. Or five times a year. I've met enough Found Kings now to know that Perry's life will change. He is no longer a passive ripple; now he's a duck in the ocean, creating his own wake. Gotta watch out for ducks. What other creature thrives on land, sea, and sky?

Hands shaking, he takes a Diet Coke from the silver ice bucket and scours the parking lot for a moment, his gaze resting on a white van. With a nod, he asks me if that's ours, and with a nod, I confirm. He looks to the sky, and I can see him fighting more tears. It's a lot to take in.

A man eating sausage congratulates Perry, explaining that he and his wife, new parents, spent the night awake with a fussy, colicky baby. They don't live far away. While preparing to drive to Mill Valley for a well-deserved breakfast, they decided to follow the music instead.

"This is awesome," the man says, haggard for lack of sleep. "I mean, if you want to wake the neighborhood with music and these fat cinnamon rolls, go right ahead. We'll be up."

We laugh, all of us, our happy knot of foresteers. I think that's a word. Or it should be. Those who find instant kinship with others who love to smell the earth. We can't ever bond for extended periods because we all long to experience the forest alone or in couples. But we can do breakfast. As Perry cuts his birthday cake, another few people wander over. More cars pull into the lot; it's a perfect morning for a hike. I keep hoping for one set of guests, specifically. If they don't come, it's fine, I guess.

Two more groupings approach from the parking lot, children outrunning admonishments from shy parents, until Perry waves them all closer.

"You guys were the shit," says the haggard father. "That gorgeous music ended a very fucked-up night. Sorry about the swearing. I'm blathering."

Perry laughs. "Not a problem. Where's your kid?"

"Get this," the man says. "She fell asleep on the way here. She's sleeping in the SUV over there."

His wife had excused herself a moment ago, and we glance that way to see her peering into the backseat, forty feet away. He nibbles off her plate.

Perry says, "You're a good father."

The haggard father blushes and starts talking about the lobster bake.

Perry puts his hand on the man's shoulder and says, softer, "A good father."

The man smiles bashfully.

Two more people head toward us from the parking lot, hesitating hikers, wait—*yes.*

I touch Perry's elbow and nod in their direction.

Perry cries out when he sees them. He jogs over.

"PLEASE JOIN US," my note from the Golden Gate Bridge begged. "MT. TAM BREAKFAST PARTY, EAST PEAK PARKING LOT. START TIME ROUGHLY 7:30AM? PLEASE, PLEASE COME."

I misgauged the time because I didn't realize Perry would be so accomplished a cellist. That was quite a concert. But they're late anyway, so it worked out. We'll have to ask them if they went out to a gay club last night as they threatened to do.

I watch Perry raise the inside of Zhong's hand to his lips. Then he does the same to Jian.

Really, it's the best way to recognize a man's kingship.

AN HOUR or more later, after the last cherry crepe is devoured and no more puffy cinnamon rolls can be found, Zhong, Jian, and every other foresteer depart to hike somewhere beautiful. Perry and I take the shortcut trail up toward his concert circle of stones.

He says, "How the hell did you get the cello up here in the dark?"

"I didn't. At dinner, when I walked out to our van, I met Liam who had parked around the corner. He had the cello with him. He had moved everything else up yesterday afternoon, probably while we were at the beach, stashed under a tarp that said 'property of California Parks'. When you and I arrived at the parking lot last night, Liam gave me a nod from his car to let me know everything was set. While you were in the bathroom, we confirmed a few last-minute details, but we didn't really need to. I had already showed him how to fix that engine clicking sound, so he could drive back this morning with the food."

"I saw you pocket the rental van keys."

"I made a spare set."

"I thought it was illegal to make a copy of rental keys."

I grin at him. "Illegal and dangerous."

"So, you made the car belt louder on purpose."

"I asked you twice if the sound bothered you because I needed you absolutely sure that it was our van squealing out of the parking lot and not some random car."

Perry laughs and says, "Man, you schemer. You should work in finance. And by the way, this trail is a lot easier than the one we came up last night."

"That's why we took the other one. But this one is steeper, so be careful. It's closed off for a reason."

When we reach the *Siren Song* circle, he says, "I dunno, Vin. I'm a king. Does a king really do heavy lifting? Shouldn't you be my bitch boy now?"

I chuckle and say, "Remember the part where the kings keep their day jobs? Grab a pumpkin, princess, and a few alarm clocks. If I happen to kick your ass on the way back to the van, your majesty, keep in mind I'm giving you another chance to forgive."

This strikes Perry a funny way. Well, perhaps not funny exactly, because his face shifts into something different and he comes to me, wrapping his whole body around me, holding me tight. Maybe he's afraid I might disappear from the mountain, for real this time.

"Thank you," he whispers into me, and the words are mangled.

After a minute, he shifts his body and I go rigid as he kisses me gently, very gently, on my rat bite scars. *He forgot.*

Perry pulls back, and he lets me see his eyes, filled with a depth I cannot fathom. I might call it pity, but it's not that, not with the love pouring from him, it's too rich. *Too rich.* He leans in, and I tense as he slowly kisses my hairline again.

He didn't forget. He knows exactly what he's doing.

I feel Perry's grip on the back of my head, and he guides my skull to his, temples pressed together, skin to skin, blood pounding against blood.

We stay this way until our heartbeats slow down.

Twenty-Three

ON THE drive down the mountain, the banquet dishes clatter with good cheer, packed amid alarm clocks and pumpkins, tarps, and a bulky cello case. He insists on cuddling King Quackers in his lap.

Perry wants explanations.

Personally, I don't think he should bother, explanations being mostly logistics, entirely unromantic. But we're in a goofy space where everything is asked and answered as we love back and forth. We're in our final hour together, grooving on our own Charlie Brown wall, philosophizing about life, our elbows not even getting sore.

"The duck came from a website called Craigslist. You ever? No? Well, it's a giant swap meet. Mostly it's people selling and buying computer parts, but there's more. Massages. Find a contractor job as a graphic artist. Buy a VCR. And apparently, you can rent a duck. I can't believe that actually worked. The farmers who responded to my ad couldn't believe someone would *want* to rent a duckling for the weekend."

"I bet it's a scam. How much did you pay for this website?"

"It's free."

"It's a scam."

"No, it's real. Craigslist started last year right here in San Francisco. Read the damn business section of the newspaper, local boy."

"I assume this is an AOL thing, right? Hey, how did you know foods I liked? How'd you know about the Diet Coke? Or that I like cherry crepes."

322 | EDMOND MANNING

Before I can reply, Perry says, "Hey, you mentioned cherry crepes Friday night in King Aabee's story."

"Golly, that's *right*."

Perry laughs. "Seriously, how did you know that stuff?"

I knew this question would come, but I remain uneasy about the explanation. "Tuesday night, after you came back for my invitation, I followed you home. For the next few days, I watched your breakfast, your morning commute, and your evenings. I followed you through Safeway twice. I studied who you avoided on the street, and I ran some experiments."

Perry shakes his head, amazed but not angry. Good; that's a relief. Our conversation now slides into that easy California rhythm on these green and twisting roads.

"We passed each other twice on Market and you didn't notice me in my hooded sweatshirt. Of course, I wore sunglasses both times. I paid a homeless guy to shoulder bump you to see how you responded. I also paid $50 to a businessy-looking woman to offer you a cheese sandwich."

"That happened Thursday," Perry says, surprised. "That was you?"

He is quiet for a moment.

He says, "Why a cheese sandwich?"

"I figured you for one of those foodies into cheeses, and if so, you'd ask her 'what type of cheese?' That would have influenced our menus and a few snacks. Also, I was testing how to make you uncomfortable, and it turns out you had some personal space issues."

"I will forever be suspicious of strangers offering me cheese sandwiches. What type of cheese was it, by the way?"

"Ha. I knew it."

"I'm just asking."

"Smoked gouda. The woman also shared your suspicion of cheese sandwiches, so I ended up eating it myself. Deeee-licious."

Perry huffs. "Where were the exotic cheeses all weekend?"

"You never answered her. Oh, you'll like this: Friday morning you and I commuted on the same Muni car for two stops with our backs pressed together; I played that way too fucking close. I hopped out at Van Ness and got back in the same car through the doors at the other end."

"Unbelievable," he says; his voice is full of soft affection.

"We drank champagne on Alcatraz and ate bruschetta on Mount Tam. I'll take unbelievable."

Perry's smiles widens, and he says, "Me too."

Our duck quacks louder right at that second.

Perry quacks his own laugh and says, "I swear, I didn't make him do that."

I'm sure we both want to believe that King Quackers understood every word, so we spend a few minutes teasing him, asking him questions and waiting for his reply.

"See, Vin? He wanted cheese too."

"Next time, take the damn sandwich."

Our chuckling leads to pleased silence, gliding through the golden, emerald canopy around us, hearing accolades from the cheering redwoods, our private victory parade.

We did it.

We survived the long night.

AT LAST, he says, "I'm going to Australia. My sister lives in Perth. We were really close at one point. We still talk on the phone regularly, but we haven't spent a Christmas together in five years and we always say it's because she lives so far away. I'm calling her this afternoon to set up a trip."

He is quiet and looks out the window.

Perhaps Perry and his sister secretly blamed each other for making their dad go away. Irrational? Sure. But kid decisions are often unconscious and very often brutal. Maybe it's not blame, but rather fear that drove them apart: if this father who I loved so much could leave me, couldn't you?

He says, "Celie and Mom begged me to play at my dad's funeral. They pleaded with me, but I wouldn't do it."

He puts his hand on the passenger window glass.

I get it.

While his mom and sister did their best to love and grieve, Perry did his best too. But the one person who might have shown him how a man feels grief, and how he lets his grief show, had excused himself from the table. Well, that's my interpretation.

He says, "The cancer completely devoured him. In his last two weeks, he was this destroyed person with gray skin, no longer my dad. One of his eyes wouldn't open. I hated being in the room with him, but Mom made me play Bach for him every day, something he loved. Before he got that bad, I would sit by his side and hold his hand for hours, like, hours and hours, hoping it might do something magic, like in a movie. But he only got worse."

Perry stops speaking.

He says, "I played his favorite Bach this morning, but I don't think I'll ever play it again."

I say, "Really? That's too bad. If your dad liked it, you could play it as your invitation whenever you wanted him to visit."

Perry's eyes open in surprise, hurt again, the good hurt where your heart gets softer when you thought it could not endure any more. He says nothing but stares out the front windshield for a moment.

He says, "Celie had a daughter almost nine months ago. Kimberly. Twice I canceled vacations because emergency bank stuff came up. *Twice.* My niece is almost a toddler, and I've never smelled her head. I don't even know if Kimberly smells like a Mangin."

We're quiet for a moment. I watch the leafy green tunnel open before us and I grin wide, occasionally shooting sly looks to the passenger seat.

"You know," he says, "when I said I wanted to smell—"

"Fucking weirdo."

Perry offers his fingers to the duck's gentle nipping and says, "Daddy Vin doesn't recognize a setup, King Quackers."

I chortle through the windshield.

Perry makes throat scoffing noises and says, "You wanna talk weird? Stalked me for days to see which vodka I drink."

"Oh, please. You walked like a bear in a homeless shelter."

Perry laughs. "You rented a duck from the World Wide Web. Now that is fucked up."

"Actually, I think the Craigslist website could catch on. A couple years ago, I had to find a rabbit for this Detroit gang banger, and pet stores aren't really into rentals. Luckily, he wanted to keep it."

"Really? I've been thinking about keeping King Quackers. I never thought about a pet duck, but my place isn't big enough for a dog. If it's all the same to you, I'll return him to his farm or whatever and check it out. If I don't like his home, he's coming with me. Also, if they're going to eat him, no way."

"What about the snails?"

"I may have to work up to snails. If they don't want to sell him, you might actually read about an honest-to-God ducknapping in tomorrow's papers."

I say, "Better take your ski mask."

Perry chuckles and then is quiet for a moment.

"How often does this happen?" Perry asks, facing his side window. "The Detroit guy, the Dolphin King, and me."

They usually want to know this. Was I special? Were we truly in love? Or did you simply get off on flipping my heart? These are vulnerable questions to ask, because a Found King will hear the truth even if it stings and still forgive.

I say, "Twice a year, maybe, but there's no quota. Depends on timing, the guy, where the conversation goes, etc. I rarely get the right combination of spark and mutual attraction that suggests, 'King him.' Even with a great connection, there's no guarantee he wants it bad enough to accept the invitation. One year I didn't king anyone and two different years, four men. I was ready to spend the weekend alone if you didn't show on Friday. But I hoped you would, because I really, really liked you and I wanted you to let me love you."

Perry says nothing, but he puts his hand on my shoulder to let me know he's okay with this answer. He mattered; this meant something to me too.

He says, "You're kind of a slut, Vin."

Our promising morning blossoms into a perfect California day as we coast down these emerald twisting roads, through this green and shimmery serpent, a writhing Chinese dragon. We snake through its mythological belly until at last we emerge from the dragon's mouth, the Friendship Tunnel beyond Sausalito. For a split second, the tunnel's circular mouth perfectly frames the mighty Golden Gate Bridge: white froth crashes against the orange girders and the cobalt blue fills most of the view, sparkles appearing and disappearing like glittering snowflakes.

We get quiet and hold hands.

It's a good day to be a king, lost or found.

Twenty-Four

SAN FRANCISCO closes in around us again, wedding-cake mansions, corner grocers displaying wooden boxes heaped with fresh lemons and limes, and the inescapable car exhaust pulling us back from our fantasy landscape. We're getting closer.

"Should I drop you off at home?"

Perry says, "Castro, please. I want to get to that gallery right away and try to buy back *Siren Song*."

"Wow, you're in a shopping frenzy today. First a duck, now this."

"That damn painting sat wrapped in basement storage for eleven years," he says, "dragged from apartment to apartment. I moved four times in the first two years I was in San Francisco. I can't believe I'm going to buy it back."

"How much would you pay for it?"

"Anything," he says.

Perry looks surprised to hear the word emerge so vehemently.

"The Castro it is."

"And you?"

I indicate the clattering serving pans behind us. "Returning stuff to Liam. Polish the back of the cello before I take that back."

He laughs. "It's not particularly high-quality wood, and pretty heavily varnished, so I don't think you have much to worry about."

"Good to know. Your duck handling means I'll have time to stop and get my favorite San Francisco ham sandwich with cheese baked in, so thank you for that. Then, the airport. I'm on a late flight back to

Minnesota. I'm going to snore so damn loud on that plane, everyone around me will be super irritated."

He makes a fake gasp. "You, irritating? Is that even possible?"

We chuckle as we enter Lower Haight on Divisadero.

Perry says, "You're really leaving, aren't you?"

"Yeah."

A moment later, he says, "For a while, I thought you lied about being a tourist. I thought you lived here."

"Some days I still think I'd like to, but I'm a Minnesotan now. I have a certain responsibility to my state. Who knew that people cared about their state that way? I like it. Before I forget, I'm taking one alarm clock as a souvenir of our time together, but if you want thirteen others...."

"Thanks," Perry says dryly. "I'd prefer the painting."

My tone is appropriately apologetic. "Sorry about the bidding war thing. I was trying to get your attention."

"Don't worry about it. I photographed it plenty before the gallery show, so I don't have to own it. Plus, I have more of Dad's paintings at home. Plus, I'm trying not to get my hopes up."

Perry's smile lets me know I am forgiven.

Soon after that, two blocks beyond the giant rainbow flag at Market and Castro, I flip the hazard lights. It's almost noon. The sidewalks teem with gay brunchers, chatting about last night's adventures and plotting how to spend a golden California afternoon. I can only double park here for a minute or two, and honestly, forty minutes would not be enough time to say goodbye. It's hard to find words, to strum the soul, to let out what is almost always ineffable.

King Quackers peers about now that we stopped moving. He's eager to see what's up.

Perry's voice quivers as he says, "Do I ever get to... talk to you...."

I caress his face.

"I already left my contact information for you in your backyard. Under the third round paving stone. I taped another copy to the backside of your drainpipe in case condensation under the stones smeared the ink."

"Oh my God," Perry says, laughing, wiping his eyes.

"I had to stick around for a few hours to make sure you stayed in bed. You'll find roughly eleven or twelve notes with my contact information hidden in that shared backyard space. Phone, email. My AOL website. Say hello sometime."

Perry's face is pleased as he says, "Freak."

"I got bored watching you after 10:30 p.m. You're an *investment banker*, for God's sakes."

Right in the moment he's smiling widest, I take his right palm and guide it to my lips. I kiss the underside of his thumb.

His smile disappears and Perry's face transforms to a grief-stricken ten-year-old boy. Yes, he's about to get abandoned once again, yet his face transitions into a softer sadness almost instantly. Maybe the river of grief runs different, less bitter than it once was. Perhaps now his father's love gurgles down this brook where it was always meant to be. When I finish, he mirrors my goodbye, kissing the underside of my thumb.

Never a required salutation, but lovely when executed with heartfelt intention.

The Forgiver King gets out of the van.

Our duck king gets reintroduced to his luxurious cage, and he immediately races to dunk his head. We load up two backpacks with wet clothes, acquired knickknacks from the weekend, including two rolls of film, a dried up starfish, and a ski mask. And his snow globe of San Francisco, of course. He relents, requesting an annoying alarm clock. I get him the paperwork on King Quackers and ask him to rip up my deposit check if they're satisfied with the duck's general well-being.

We look into each other's eyes. Careful, Vin, the weekend is not over.

"Goodbye, Perry Mangin."

"Goodbye, Vin Vanbly."

Perry and I shake hands, and he lets go reluctantly because something remains unsaid. He looks at me with surprise, as if he can't believe I'm leaving without listening to what he desperately wants to say. But he offers no words.

I wait.

He says nothing.

I return to my side of the van and pull myself into the driver's seat. Snap on the seatbelt. Perry moves to the sidewalk, sets down the duck cage, the knapsacks, and stares at me through the passenger window. People point at the duck, and I catch some admiring glances in Perry's direction. A few people chuckle at the sequined shirt under his bomber jacket and at what I'm sure looks like me dropping off last night's trick.

His eyes are wild, but the words won't come. Sometimes, even words with the letter *x* fall short.

I nod to him and prepare to turn into traffic, flipping my blinker. Cars behind me wait impatiently, so I have to pull away. Perry looks as though he's going to scream until he finally does.

"*Vin!*"

I keep my foot steady on the brake and turn to the passenger window.

His hands reach high in the sky, clutching air and squeezing tight while his face contorts in a twisted, body-wrenching growl. He swings around, demanding space from the Castro walkers, and then attempts to destroy a nearby US postal box mauling it with his big, swaggering, bear claws.

"RRrrrrrrrrrrrrrrRRRRRRRRRRRRROOOOOOOOOOOOOOOOOOO AR."

As far as I can see, the mailbox has done nothing wrong.

Sunday brunchers have to sidestep the gold-spangled Perry and his baggage because he commands so much space, staggering around, slashing the air. Damn. He's good.

"Bitch, please," says a drag queen behind him, a Latino beauty with honey-colored skin and some killer titties. "That's no bear. *This* is a bear, you white-assed bitch."

She growls toward him with ragged, high-pitched movements that threaten to topple her tube top. Admittedly, her long fingernails could tear human flesh; she's got that on him. But Perry's no quitter and he redoubles his efforts toward her, squatting and advancing like a Sumo wrestler. She swears in bear-swear, calling him a bitch, and the entire thing is ri-dikulous.

I love seeing Found Kings and Queens, the ones whose love simply refused to shut down. Sometimes I wish I had been born one of those who go first, those blessed followers of King Aabee.

Castro pedestrians must navigate around in an irritated way, or stop and stare at the street theater. Two scruffy guys, ragged baseball caps laid out for spare change, scoot away from the spectacle. A blond twink with frosted tips skirts their fight with complete indifference and in a lilting tone says loudly, "Get a room."

King Quackers races back and forth in his cage, shouting, whether in a panic at finding himself surrounded by so many grizzlies, or perhaps doing his own bear imitation, I can't really tell.

I throw the van into park, hop out, run to the front, and mine for fish in the gutter. I outroar all of them when I spot a speckled, silver-back trout swim by, and I dive, snatching it with my teeth from this icy, mountain stream on Castro and 19th.

A car honks behind me, and I hear a man yell, *"Goddamn tourist."*

I thrash my head from side to side, chomping harder against the imaginary fish belly, the slippery creature flopping desperately for its very life.

Bear versus fish.

Totally surreal.

EPILOGUE

JASON looked up eagerly from inventory paperwork as the front chime signaled a customer entering but felt instant disappointment. It wasn't *him*. Jason lived with the *Siren Song* mystery for almost a full week and called Perry Mangin's number repeatedly over the weekend. Would it kill Perry to return a call or make an appearance? Instead, a derelict bumbled through the front door, overloaded with knapsacks and what appeared to be a caged duck.

With crisp strides, Jason clacked noisily across the polished wooden floor, and his voice took on an intentional frosty tone as he said, "No pets."

The derelict turned and smiled broadly; Jason experienced a thrill of shock.

"Oh my God," Jason said before he could stop himself, "what happened to you?"

Perry laughed and said, "I got kinged."

Jason found himself unable to speak. Beyond the features he had admired on Tuesday, nothing looked the same. Had Perry's eyes been blue on Tuesday? Jason hadn't noticed. Even the way that Perry stood was different.

"You may not remember me, but my name is Perry Mangin." Perry's smile melted into something more earnest, and his eyes grew wet. "You sold two of my dad's pieces on Tuesday night. I was actually hoping to contact the new owner and buy back *Siren Song*."

"Buy it back?" Jason said. "I don't understand."

As he re-explained, Jason studied Perry's facial expressions, trying to understand where Tuesday's aloofness had gone. Perhaps Perry had a twin brother, which would explain how someone else now inhabited this body. That was ridiculous. Of course this was Perry, but how?

Jason came to himself, frowned, and said, "Wait, didn't you get *any* of the messages? I left you, like, two Friday and two yesterday. One this morning."

"I was camping all weekend. Haven't been home yet," Perry said, grinning. "I know I look like hell."

Jason blushed, realizing his scrutiny had not gone unnoticed. He turned and crossed to the desk. "Sir, you can't buy it back."

Perry followed him and said, "I'll pay anything. Just let me ask. I know the purchaser demanded anonymity, but you could contact them…."

While he pleaded, Jason retrieved the paperwork from his special pile and presented it to Perry. He waited until Perry had glanced through the documents before he said, "You can't buy it because you already own it."

Perry held the cashier's check for double the asking price and the bill of sale, which listed his own name as the seller and the new owner.

Jason said, "Everyone on Tuesday said Mr. Vanbly practically instigated the bidding war. Why would he do that if he intended to buy it and give it to you? We've been discussing it all week, but it doesn't make any sense. And why did he forbid us from telling you who purchased it until Friday evening?"

Perry's hands trembled as he confirmed the details.

"I'm sorry if I'm being nosy," Jason said, trying hard to sound demure. "I know it's not my business. But we've been talking about it all week. Mr. Vanbly left another note, this one couriered over with the full payment Friday at 6:00. I called you as soon as it arrived."

Perry studied the second envelope addressed to "THE PAINTER'S SON," running his index finger over the three words.

Jason watched impatiently as Perry slowly opened it, read it, and then turned to face *Siren Song*, still hanging in its original placement. Perry walked across the gallery to stand in front of it. The note fluttered to the floor as Perry sank to his knees, so Jason came around the desk and picked it up, eager to read the mystery revealed.

KING PERRY,

ENJOY THIS GIFT. THIS ARTIST'S CREATIONS HAVE ALWAYS BEEN A PERSONAL FAVORITE OF MINE.

DAWN WAS SPECTACULAR THIS MORNING, DIDN'T YOU THINK?

INVITE ME ANYTIME, AND I WILL BRING KING RICHARD MANGIN, THE LIVING PAINTER.

ALL MY LOVE,

KING AABEE

*A specialized M/M romance line
from Dreamspinner Press*

Bittersweet Dreams, stories of M/M romance with nontraditional endings. It's an unfortunate truth: love doesn't always conquer all. Regardless of its strength, sometimes fate intervenes, tragedy strikes, or forces conspire against it. These stories of romance do not offer a traditional happy ending, but the strong and enduring love will still touch your heart and maybe move you to tears.

http://www.dreamspinnerpress.com

E DMOND M ANNING has always been fascinated by fiction: how ordinary words could be sculpted into heartfelt emotions, how heartfelt emotions could leave an imprint inside you stronger than the real world. Mr. Manning never felt worthy to seek publication until recently, when he accidentally stumbled into his own writer's voice that fit perfectly, like his favorite skull-print, fuzzy jammies. He finally realized that he didn't have to write like Charles Dickens or Armistead Maupin, two author heroes, and that perhaps his own fiction was juuuuuuust right, because it was his true voice, so he looked around the scrappy word kingdom that he created for himself and shouted, "I'M HOME!" He is now a writer.

In addition to fiction, Edmond enjoys writing nonfiction on his blog, http://www.edmondmanning.com. When not writing, he can be found either picking raspberries in the back yard or eating panang curry in an overstuffed chair upstairs, reading comic books.

Feel free to contact him at remembertheking@comcast.net.

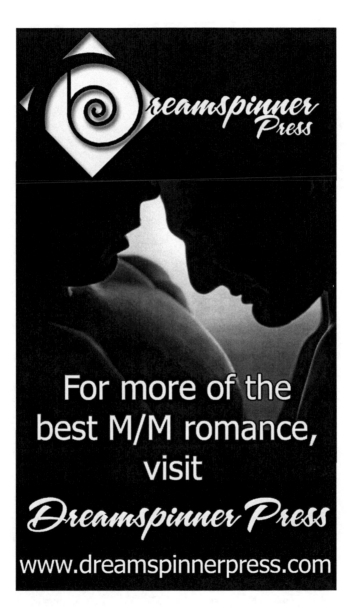